A Forgotten Place

ALSO BY CHARLES TODD

THE IAN RUTLEDGE MYSTERIES

THE BESS CRAWFORD MYSTERIES

OTHER FICTION

A Forgotten Place

A Bess Crawford Mystery

CHARLES TODD

wm WILLIAM MORROW *An Imprint of* HarperCollins*Publishers*

A FORGOTTEN PLACE. Copyright © 2018 by Charles Todd. All rights reserved. Printed in the United States of America. No part of this book may be used or reproduced in any manner whatsoever without written permission except in the case of brief quotations embodied in critical articles and reviews. For information, address Harper-Collins Publishers, 195 Broadway, New York, NY 10007.

HarperCollins books may be purchased for educational, business, or sales promotional use. For information, please email the Special Markets Department at SPsales@harpercollins.com.

FIRST EDITION

Library of Congress Cataloging-in-Publication Data has been applied for.

ISBN 978-0-06-267882-9

18 19 20 21 22   LSC   10 9 8 7 6 5 4 3 2 1

This year we all lost furry friends, once-forgotten kitties
who made life joyful for those who took them in and
found how much love they had to give.
CHARLIE turned out to be a girl, but she didn't mind
being Charlie.
SUZIE, who left no doubt in anyone's mind that she was a she.
CU TEE, a tuxedo kitty whose purr could be heard all over
the room.

And then there were those kitties who preferred to be in the wild,
but who came to dinner and let you know how grateful they were.
GROUCHO and ROSIE, who have no known grave,
but left paw prints on the heart all the same.

And there were four little ones who didn't make it.
Two who had names and two who left us before they could
be named, but were loved too.
TINY BASH, Ziggy's feisty black kitten.
MING, the sweet little Siamese, who joined her smaller sister
all too soon.

Finally, for VERDI, wherever you may be . . .

AND for Chelsea Marie: Congratulations on your graduation,
and best wishes for a bright, bright future.

A Forgotten Place

CHAPTER 1

December 1918

THE WAR HAD ended, but not the suffering.

While the war raged, the wounded had been desperate to rejoin their companies, to fight beside men they'd had to leave behind. We'd had to be on guard against the tricks they used to prove they were up to returning to the Front. They were remarkably clever at it. Those who'd been given their Blighty ticket were often too ill to think beyond whether they would live through the night. But I knew from experience that once they began to recover, their thoughts flew back to France, to the fighting, where they felt they ought to be. That need often helped them heal. Now, with peace, there were no comrades to return to.

For others—like the patients I worked with—their war had finished in quite a different sense.

I spent December in a base hospital in France, tending to the wounded who hadn't yet been ticketed for England. Many of them had been brought in during the last ten days of the war. Serious wounds that we now had time to deal with here. Most were amputees, fighting infection as well as the loss of a limb. There were gas cases too, burns, and more than a few damaged faces.

As Christmas approached, a good many of the patients in the wards had lost even the incentive to recover. Too often they feared being a burden on their families, to be pitied by wives and sweethearts, to be told that the position they'd held before the war, whether as a tenant farmer or a bank manager, had already been taken by someone else. Someone whole. There were no shaving mirrors for those with burns or damaged jaws, but they already knew how terrifyingly hideous they were—they only had to look at the man in the next bed. And the amputees told us over and over again that they would rather be dead than live without a limb.

No conquering heroes, these men. No victory parades for them. Our patients were the ultimate reality of war. And a suicide watch was maintained twenty-four hours of the day.

Sadly there were other men just like them in hospitals spread across northern France and in clinics in England.

Many were still in pain, often requiring more surgery and not fit to travel. I dealt mainly with the amputees, whose stumps ached in the night or who felt a phantom limb—the lost leg or arm or foot, which itched and burned and throbbed. They were often desperate to find relief. The doctors could explain it away as damaged nerves that hadn't yet realized the limb was gone. These struggled to read signals that no longer existed, remembering what had once been there. For the men experiencing such symptoms, it was bad enough that the limb was lost. The fact that it still tormented them was unbearable.

This was the detritus that war left behind, those who would have no place in the nation they had fought to protect.

I did my best to cheer them up, and I held their hands when they wept over letters from home. Well-meant letters, to be sure, but only serving to point up that families were already seeing their loved ones differently. One in particular had begun, *We are trying to do something about the stairs so that you can have your old room again, but we don't quite know where to start. Perhaps you can ask the other men in your ward how their families are coping. And the rector has promised to call often to keep your spirits up.*

I came to know the Welsh patients particularly well, for they had enlisted out of the collieries in the valleys, and they already knew all too well that they couldn't go down into the pit again, that the heavy work they'd done at the coal face before the war was physically beyond them now. Most of them had only rudimentary education. They'd followed their fathers and brothers into the pit as soon as they could, to bring in more income. Their worried families, asking how they were to live with no prospects of work, lowered the men's spirits even more. I spent a good many of my hours on duty trying to find a way to cheer them. But after a while even I could see that cheerfulness was beyond men who had lost hope.

Two of them had been the sole support of their mothers and sisters, after a pit disaster had taken their fathers and brothers. Their pensions wouldn't go far. Their Army pay, sent home every month, had barely been enough.

My first night in the ward, we had nearly lost Private Evans, a tall, slim man with dark hair and darker eyes, whose left leg and right arm had become so infected that they had had to be taken off. He'd needed several more surgeries after that, and had of course been given morphine for the pain. Apparently he'd managed somehow to hoard a little, enough to take all at once after the last bed check by the night nurse. He nearly managed to kill himself.

The patient in the bed next to him, a burly Sergeant from Chester who had lost a foot, noticed something was amiss, and shouted for Sister Grayson. She had come running, discovered what Private Evans had done, and sounded the alarm in time. We gave him an emetic, then pumped his stomach, working over him until nearly four in the morning before Dr. Herbert pronounced him out of the woods. But I saw his eyes as he lay exhausted in his bed, and I knew he would try again. There was a burning determination in their depths.

He was one of a number of patients who had come in together. They'd fought side by side until the first of November, eleven days before the Armistice, and during one advance, a concealed machine-gun nest set up to protect the German retreat had caught them in the open and taken out two entire companies. Most of the men had been killed outright or had died on the way to the aid station or the base hospital. These men were all that was left. One Captain and eight other ranks.

Captain Williams was worrying. His leg had been badly lacerated, and when gangrene set in in his foot, Dr. Childress, the surgeon, had had to take the leg to the knee. The Captain had fought all the way to the operating theatre, shouting and demanding that they carry him back to his bed.

"I'll be damned if the Germans will have my leg as well," he'd exclaimed as he was tied down on the table.

"You'll die without the surgery. A slow, painful death," the surgeon told him.

"I don't care. I'll take my leg to the grave with me."

I'd witnessed this battle, and I'd helped hold the ether mask over his face.

He hadn't forgiven me for that. Nor Dr. Childress. When he'd returned to the ward after spending several days in Recovery, he lay in his bed with his eyes tight shut and refused to eat or speak or let anyone touch the stump.

It was Matron who told him he was setting a poor example for his men, for they needed him rather badly as they dealt with their own feelings about their lost limbs. He took that to heart, but it did little to change his own attitude toward the staff.

With Christmas barely two weeks away, the general mood of the hospital was bleak. The wards showed no interest in making decorations for the tree that one of the orderlies had brought in from a nearby wood. It wasn't the traditional evergreen, just a small bare-limbed tree. Matron ordered it put up in the large room where men could sit during the day and learn how to cope with their injuries. But no one was in a festive mood, and it stood there for three days without any attempt to do anything with it. And so Matron asked the staff to take charge.

Easier said than done. One of the orderlies made a star for the top, cutting it out of flattened tins from the kitchen dustbin. Another had collected cartridge casings, to help the wards pass the time by making things from them. But there had been little interest in that either, and we used them like candles, with bits of boxes cut out and painted with whitewash to put around the bottoms like a cuff to hide the wire that bound the casings to the branches. By this time, more and more of our ambulatory and wheeled-chair patients found excuses to come to the room to follow our progress, although they made no effort to contribute. One of the ambulance drivers brought us small glass medicine bottles from Rouen, which we tied to the tree. Another brought us paper from Calais, which we fashioned into chains to loop around the branches. And then one of the patients from Scotland, who had lost both legs, used firewood to carve a rough and ready manger scene to put on the sheet we had draped around the base of the tree to simulate snow. An amputee from Cheshire made cards for the staff, which he passed around for patients to sign and hang on the tree. A doctor who had taken leave in Paris brought us chestnuts to string.

Although it was rather a funny little tree, Matron was quite pleased with our efforts and commended us, but we hadn't done it for her.

The chaplain had arranged a special Christmas Eve service, and one of the orderlies volunteered the information that he could play carols on a piano, and one appeared—God knew from where—and was brought in to stand next to the tree. It was sadly out of tune but the orderly did what he could to improve it.

I went to one of the Welsh patients, Corporal Jones, and asked if he and the others of his company might sing for us during the service. Welsh choirs were famous for the extraordinary way they blended their voices, and I hoped this might make a difference in their spirits if they took part.

To my disappointment, the suggestion was met with a shake of the head.

"What's there to sing about?" the Corporal asked. "Anyway, Evans is our best tenor, and I don't see anyone persuading him to sing."

Private Evans had been withdrawn since his attempt at suicide, and kept his face turned to the wall. He wasn't the only one who had tried to end his suffering. One of the burn cases had stolen a scalpel and cut his wrists.

"Perhaps it's what he needs most, a chance to think about someone other than himself."

"Oh, yes? And how would you be knowing that?"

I took a deep breath. I felt like shaking the man, because this was our first Christmas after the war, and we couldn't let it go without marking it somehow. It would be wrong not to try. But I said only, "Why don't you at least speak to the others and see how they feel about it. Surely before the war you sang in Chapel at Christmas services? It might remind them why they fought for King and Country."

"We don't need reminders, Sister. We live with them every day when we see our missing limbs."

"At least try, won't you? Look around you at these wards. If you could give these men a little joy, would it be so difficult a thing to do?"

"For you I will ask," he said. "But I wouldn't raise my hopes too high if I were you."

Later that afternoon when I saw him at tea, he told me the answer was still no.

Refusing to accept defeat, once I'd finished with my other patients, I went to find Captain Williams. He was sitting by a window in the officers' ward.

As I came down the aisle, his back was to me, and it wasn't until I paused by the foot of his bed that he turned slightly, so that I saw his profile. He was an attractive man when he wasn't scowling, and just now there was a sadness in his expression as he said, "I've done my exercises, Tomkins."

"It isn't Tomkins," I said, and he moved in his chair so that he could see me.

"Still."

"Actually, I've come to ask if you will help me persuade your men to sing for us on Christmas Eve."

I had watched him deal with his own men after Matron's talk with him, at times quietly reasoning with them, and at others barking orders as if on parade. His was still the voice of Authority, and they respected it.

He wanted no part of singing and said so bluntly.

I said, "Don't tell me you're the one Welshman who wasn't born with a pleasing voice?"

He glared at me. And then he drew a breath and answered.

"What the he— what in God's name is there to sing about, Sister?

Look at your patients. The lot of them have already given everything but their lives for their country. They want only to be left in peace where no one will stare at them, where no one pities them. After all, peace is the meaning of the Season, is it not?"

An educated man, for his speech was very English, but when he was feeling strongly about something, it sometimes slipped into that rhythmic pattern of his birth.

"Is it so wrong to want to bring us all a little comfort? The war is over, yes, but none of us will be spending this Christmas at home. Perhaps you've been out of Wales so long that you don't remember what it felt like to sing?"

He was angry now, and bitter. "I left Wales when they did. To fight for *England*." He nearly spat the last word, as if he hated England and all she stood for.

I raised my eyebrows as if in surprise. "Well, then, Captain, I expect I shall just have to make other arrangements for the evening."

"Do that," he told me curtly.

And so I went to speak to Private Williams—no relation to the Captain, just as neither of the men called Jones were connected. This Williams had also been a miner in the valley. I had been told he was a tenor, and I hoped to convince him to sing a solo at the midnight service.

He didn't want to sing either. "And I told Corporal Jones as much."

I said, letting my disappointment show, "I had thought it might cheer Captain Williams. He's been having a difficult time of it."

"Has he now?" Private Williams asked, actually listening to me.

"We had to clean out another pocket of infection in that leg. It's getting him down, I think." True enough, but this was something many of the men in this hospital had gone through more than once.

"He was all right this morning."

"Do you think he wants you to see how he feels? He's still your officer, it's his duty to care for you all and see to it that your spirits are kept up. How many times has his face been the first you see by your bed as you come out of the ether? How many times has he held your head as you were sick from it? And told you to buck up and face it like a man when you want to pity yourselves? Who is it who does these things for him?"

I don't think it had occurred to him that Captain Williams was suffering too. He hid it well when his men were around. "It's not my place to tell Captain what to do," he answered me slowly.

"Then don't. Tell him you all wish to sing, and beg him to join you. I can't believe he'll refuse."

In the end, somehow, we had four tenors, three baritones—including the Captain's—and two bass voices. Even Private Evans refused to be left behind. And the music—without accompaniment—soared around us, filling the room with its power. From where I sat, I could see the faces of the audience, for a moment transfixed by something outside themselves. I felt like weeping in gratitude.

We carried the decorated tree to the wards afterward for those too ill to come to the service. The chaplain, Father Johnson, read from Luke and led us in prayer. And Matron surprised the men with a tot of rum in place of the traditional Christmas sherry.

Not very much like a Christmas any of us remembered from before the war, but it was better than we'd hoped for the spirits in our wards. Better still than a Christmas any of the men had enjoyed in the trenches these last four years.

After the wards were asleep, the Sisters gathered in Matron's quarters for a small glass of sherry and her gratitude for all our efforts.

I thought surely Captain Williams was going to be difficult the next day, especially since I'd more or less tricked him into joining the choir. I encountered him in the passage leading to the dining room.

"A happy Christmas," I said, smiling as I was about to pass him. "I hear there is a fine goose for dinner."

"There is," he said, and paused. "I've been a curmudgeon. I'm sorry."

Surprised, I replied, "It hasn't been the happiest of times for many of you."

"No. It's one thing to find courage on the battlefield. We're brave because we don't want others to know we're afraid. But what we fear most is letting the side down." He gestured to his missing leg. "This takes a very different kind of courage. I watched the faces of the men listening to us last night. They've lost their way. So have I. I was ashamed of what I'd said to you."

It wasn't a confession that he found it easy to make. Least of all to me, I thought. But I said only, "It was a gift you and your men gave us. We were grateful."

"I'd like to make amends," he answered. "I can read to the other patients. Write letters for them. Whatever they need. It will spare you and the other Sisters. I saw something else—how tired you are."

I wasn't sure just what had touched him last night or shifted his mood. The music? Whatever it was, I was glad to see it. We had learned, dealing with the wounded, that the state of a man's mind could make the difference between life and death, often in the face of the doctors giving up hope that they could save him. It was true of amputees too.

"Thank you, Captain. That's very thoughtful of you."

When I said something to Matron later, she smiled. "I don't know if it was only the singing. He doesn't receive any letters, our Captain. But one came in the last post from his sister-in-law. It raised his spirits no end. Apparently he and his brother were close."

I knew that Matron kept an eye on the letters men received, and sometimes read them first when she had reason to think they would distress men already struggling to address their future.

"He's never spoken of his family. I didn't know he had a brother."

"And nor did I. I debated whether to give it to him, but in the end decided I had no right to withhold it. And a very good thing I did." Matron smiled. "I must say, the Captain was the most cheerful I've ever seen him."

My parents came to the base hospital for New Year's. I wasn't sure just how my father had managed it, but I was so pleased to see them. There was only time for a meal at a small restaurant that my father had found. The food was barely edible, but we didn't care. It was enough to enjoy each other's company.

Afterward, while my mother had tea with Matron, the Colonel Sahib toured the hospital. I watched from a distance. He had a way with men, speaking to each one with a personal warmth that made them sit up a little straighter in their beds and smile. High-ranking officers had visited hospitals often during the war, but since the Armistice, they had come infrequently.

When he had finished the tour and rejoined my mother in Matron's tiny sitting room, I came to say good-bye and walk with them to the official motorcar that stood waiting by the door.

Matron was just behind me as the motorcar drove away. "Your parents care deeply for you, Sister. They would never say so, but I have a feeling they would be happy to see you at home again, now the war has ended."

"I'm still needed, Matron."

"Yes. We must not fail these men." And then she turned and went inside.

I stood there in the cold wind and watched the tiny red rear light disappear in the early dusk of January, feeling a sudden loneliness.

But I was on duty at four, and went to relieve Sister Grant in the burn ward.

I hadn't told the patients that the Colonel Sahib, as we called him, was my father. It was best if they believed that he had come out of concern for them. Which was true enough.

Captain Williams was the only man to put two and two together. He said the next day, when I saw him at breakfast, "He's a fine man, your father. I wish there had been more like him at HQ. The war might have been conducted differently. And I see where you get your strength and determination."

I took it as a compliment, not a reference to my persistence over the Welsh choir.

Ten days later, many of our patients were sent to England as the Medical Corps found accommodation for them in various clinics around the country. The Welsh patients had somehow arranged to be sent to the same clinic. I was fairly certain that Matron had had a hand in that, because they had not only served together but also been wounded on that same frightful morning. What surprised me was the news that Captain Williams had managed to be sent to the same clinic, although he was an officer and it was for other ranks.

When I commented on that, he said, surprising me by grinning, "I've got accustomed to telling that lot what to do and how to behave." Then, the grin fading, he said, "They're worried, Sister. Private Morris has already asked me what he's to do when they're released to go home. There's no work for them in the mines. They don't have the education I was given, and so they aren't prepared for any other work. Now that we're returning to England, it preys on their minds. I'm concerned about them."

"I've noticed," I said. "Private Jones in particular is not doing well." He had lost both feet, and he'd become increasingly moody. When the other men had been given crutches, he was confined to a wheeled chair. "And there's Private Evans as well. I can't believe he's resigned to his lot. I've asked the orderlies to watch him on the crossing. It would be all too easy to fall overboard."

It wasn't done, discussing one patient with another, but I thought the Captain already knew who was at greatest risk. As he'd learned to manage his crutches, he'd spent a good bit of time in the wards with his men. I knew that was not a sign that he himself was comfortable with the loss of his leg, only an indication of the responsibility he felt for his men.

Perhaps because he could return to his position in the mine office, he felt he owed it to them to see them through what lay ahead.

"I wanted to be a schoolmaster," he'd said one day as I was changing his bandages. "I had a gift for mathematics, and that was why I was sent off to school. It was expected that I'd come back and work in the office. When I asked if I could teach instead, I was told to be grateful for the opportunity I was given."

"That must have been a disappointment."

"It was. I was saving as much of my pay as I could, to go back to school, and then the war came along. I expect this"—he pointed to his leg—"will put paid to any hope of teaching."

"You never know," I said, encouraging. "Stranger things have happened. You won't be the only schoolmaster on crutches, surely."

We readied the patients being sent back to England, and in mid-January, we said good-bye to them.

Captain Williams said, as he was being loaded into the first ambulance, "I shall miss your meddling, Sister Crawford."

I smiled. "You'll find that most Sisters are rather good at getting their own way."

He nodded. "It's a good thing you weren't your father's son instead of his daughter. You'd be running the Army by now. I'd give much to see you in the same room as General Haig."

"It would probably have meant the end of my career as an officer," I retorted, and wished him well before turning to settle the next patient being brought forward.

We watched them out of sight, my fellow nurses and I, then went back to the wards to prepare for patients being sent to us from a smaller base hospital that had now been closed.

The winter roads were crowded with refugees trying to return to whatever was left of their homes, and sometimes we found ourselves helping a child with the croup or a man with blisters on his feet from walking in shoes that didn't fit. We found the man a pair of Army boots from a patient who had died from pneumonia that same week, and sent him on his way. Pneumonia was our enemy as the rains began. And then I was sent back to England with another convoy, as additional space was found in clinics there, and my ambulance drove through a cold rain all the way to Calais.

The facial wounds were going to a clinic in Sussex where some attempt at reconstruction was being made, but a Sister who had been there told me privately that it was mostly a leather shield that kept the wound from shocking people. The burn cases were going for special surgical repairs of ears or nose, and something to help smooth out the tight, bunched scars. Amputees were destined for clinics where they would be kept until their stumps were healed. One Yorkshire man told me he was going to whittle himself a wooden leg, "like pirates wore."

I wanted to weep for all of them.

The orderlies kept a suicide watch on board the ship as men grew more and more anxious the closer we came to Dover. A few sat in the lee of the deck, to watch for the white cliffs to loom out of the sheets of rain.

One said to me as he spun his cigarette over the rail, "I never thought I'd see England again. I expected to die out there."

He'd been a solicitor in his life before the war. Although he'd lost an arm, he could go on being a solicitor. What worried him was his wife's reaction to his wound.

She had been told about it. But that was quite different from seeing it.

But there she was, on the docks at Dover, waiting for him, and I could see the relief in his eyes as she watched him come awkwardly toward her. He would remain in a clinic for several weeks, but she had come all the way from Hereford to see him as soon as possible.

Most of the wounded dreaded pity above all. Pity in the eyes of their loved ones and in the faces of people on the street.

We'd run out of the rain halfway to London, but it was a cold, dreary evening all the same. It was after midnight when at last I was free to enjoy the four days' leave I had coming to me. Not enough time to go to Somerset, but my mother had written that she and my father would be driving up to London to meet me.

I walked out of the station with my kit in my hands, and there was no one waiting for me.

Surprised—and more than a little worried—I looked around for a cab that I could take to Mrs. Hennessey's. I'd kept my flat there for just such short leaves, and over the four years of the war, it had become a second home. And in a way I'd come to enjoy my independence. I was no longer the young girl I'd been in 1914, looking forward to tennis and parties and weekends in the country. Many of my prewar friends were already married. Or in some cases already widowed. I was still finding nursing satisfying—if sometimes heartbreaking. While men needed care, I was unwilling to resign from the Queen Alexandra's.

I was just about to hail a passing cab when I heard someone call my name. I turned and saw Simon Brandon walking briskly toward me.

"Hallo," I said, smiling. "I didn't expect to see you this evening. Mother mentioned that you were in Scotland."

"My train got in earlier. There was a telegram waiting for me asking me to meet you. Your mother has taken a chill and won't be coming after all. Your father is in Paris, some conference or other. He thought he'd be finished with all that now, but he was right more times than the generals in France, and the Army is getting around to recognizing that." He took my kit from me, smiling down at me. "How are you?"

"Tired. We left the hospital last evening, in order to reach the *Sea Maid* before the tide turned. And when we put into Dover, the trains hadn't arrived from London. I think I'm sleepwalking."

He laughed. "You'll be in your bed soon enough. I stopped in at Mrs. Hennessey's to let her know you were coming in. That's why I was late. She's expecting you. Have you had any dinner?"

"A bowl of soup in Dover. One of the ship's officers brought it to me. But I don't think I could stay awake through a meal, even one at Buckingham Palace."

"My motorcar is just over there. Mrs. Hennessey will have tea and hot water bottles waiting."

"It sounds heavenly," I answered.

Mrs. Hennessey lived up to his promises, and even allowed Simon to carry my kit up to my room.

"There's no one in at the moment," she said, rather spoiling the effect of this unexpected relaxation of her rule that no man could go up the stairs unless he was carrying luggage for one of her ladies, as she called us, and escorted by her. Even the Colonel Sahib was forbidden, which always amused him. Still, he was a very attractive man, and she guarded our reputations like a dragon.

Simon came back, stayed for a cup of tea, and then was gone, promising to see me in the morning.

Mrs. Hennessey, delighted as always to have me back in London, said as she followed me up the stairs, "You have fresh sheets and towels, and there's already a hot water bottle in your bed, and hot water in the pitcher on the washstand. Is there anything else you'd like, my dear?"

"That's more than enough," I reassured her. "Any word from Mary or Diana, or Lady Elspeth?" They had been my flatmates throughout the war, although we seldom were on leave at the same time.

"Lady Elspeth is visiting Peter's family at the moment. Mary was here a fortnight ago, then returned to France. And Diana is still on her honeymoon in Cornwall, although I can't think how that could be very pleasant in January."

She had had a lovely wedding, and I'd begged leave to be one of her bridesmaids. Her gown was absolutely stunning—Diana had always had wonderful taste in clothes—and the groom, whom I'd known for some years, was extraordinarily handsome in his uniform. His fellow officers lined the short path from the church door to his motorcar, swords raised above their heads as the two of them ran laughing through a hail of flower petals specially ordered from the Isles of Scilly. How so many of his officers had managed to get leave for the wedding was still a mystery.

Mrs. Hennessey had been there as well, wearing a dark blue dress with a matching coat and hat, flushed pink with happiness for one of her young ladies.

When she had gone back downstairs, I put out my light and lay there in my comfortable bed, my feet warmed by the hot water bottles and my sheets smelling of lavender, wondering how my charges from the convoy were faring in their new surroundings. It would be a different homecoming from the one they had expected when they enlisted.

Four days later Simon drove me down to Gloucestershire to my new assignment. A telegram had arrived while I was in London ordering me to report to duty at a clinic there for amputees. I had wanted to return to France, and I went at once to QAIMNS head-quarters to request a French assignment, but I was told that I was needed in England just now.

One didn't argue.

CHAPTER 2

February 1919

AND SO I arrived in the middle of a wretched downpour at a large country house that had been converted into a clinic. I said good-bye to Simon, who was on his way to Somerset, and gave him all sorts of messages for my mother.

Watching him drive away was hard. I'd have liked to go to Somerset too.

Matron was pleased to see me, and she assigned one of the staff Sisters to show me to my room and acquaint me with the wards and my duties.

Sister Baker said as she led me up the grand staircase, "I'm glad you've come. I served with Mary, you know, near Ypres. Any news of her?"

I passed on what Mrs. Hennessey had told me. "I'd been looking forward to going back to France myself."

"So was I," she said, turning down a passage on the second floor. "But they closed my base hospital, and I was posted here. And we're *needed*, you know. I can't really complain."

There were other ranks here, some of them undergoing more

surgeries to clean out infection or to improve their stumps. Some were able to manage with crutches, and others were still in invalid chairs. A few were due to be released soon.

Sister Baker was giving me an overview of the patients, their regiments, and their wounds. "And there are quite a few Welsh patients as well. Their commanding officer is here too. I don't know how he managed it—he should be in Dorset, at the clinic there. But I'm glad to have him. He keeps them in line."

"Don't tell me—not Captain Williams and his men?"

Surprised, she said, "Yes. Do you know them?"

"They were in the base hospital where I was posted in December. How are they faring?"

She frowned. "I'm worried about several of them in particular."

"Oh, dear. Private Evans?"

"Sadly, yes. They keep to themselves, the Welsh. I think because they know they'll be released soon. Matron says we shouldn't try to change that. They'll need each other when they go home."

"I understand. They probably don't have much in common with the English patients anyway. They're from the mines. It's a different world."

"I expect it is."

My room had once belonged to servants, I thought, up here under the eaves of the house. I shared it with Sister Baker, and she sat on her bed as I unpacked, telling me about the staff and what to expect from them.

An hour later, when we went back downstairs, tea was being brought in to the patients. Those who were able to get around gathered in what had been the billiard room of the house, and I had an opportunity to meet them.

They were eager for news about what was happening in Paris, and I told them what I could as the orderlies brought in their tea.

Captain Williams sat in a corner of the room. His dark hair had been cut, but there were still circles beneath his dark eyes.

His face brightened as I came into the room, and when I reached him, he said, "You're back. For my sins."

"Yes, indeed, Captain. They told me in France that you still needed to be sorted out."

He laughed, but it faded as he said, "We'll be leaving here soon. I'm told they're sending us home. That won't be easy."

I remembered suddenly that he hadn't received letters from anyone when he was in the base hospital, except for one shortly before Christmas. That must mean he had no idea how his family felt about the loss of his leg.

Now I wondered.

As if he had read my thoughts, he said, "The men haven't had any visitors. It's a long way from Wales. Most of their families don't have the money to travel this far."

And then several of the other Welshmen came up to speak to me, and I was told that they'd be singing that evening.

"How nice," I said, meaning it. "I look forward to it."

But this time the songs were from their other lives, folk songs and hymns and one or two songs from the war. There was a sadness in their voices now. When they'd finished, I went up to thank them. Sister Baker was talking to Captain Williams, and I realized that she found him attractive. It was there in her face and her posture.

He didn't show the same interest in her, which was just as well. Matron saw everything.

When we went up to bed, I asked Sister Baker if they sang often.

She grinned. "I think they were showing off for you tonight. But we encourage them to sing. And the other patients sometimes join in, if they've had any musical training. Most of the time, though, they just listen." She finished brushing her hair. "Heaven knows we need distractions to take their minds off their wounds. Sister Melvin reads to them, one of the orderlies plays cards with some of them, and there's a room here where they can learn a new trade, one that doesn't need both arms or legs."

"What sort of trades?"

"Sedentary ones. Shoemaker, tobacconist, and the like. The problem comes with finding people who will hire these men. They see themselves as useless. I go to bed at night tired from the emotional effort of cheering them up."

The next morning my schedule was posted along with that of the rest of the staff.

In the afternoon, I found Captain Williams sitting in the conservatory, looking out at the first snowfall. It wasn't destined to last, but it was quite pretty coming down.

"A penny for your thoughts," I said lightly.

"They aren't worth a farthing. I was remembering. In the valley, the few times we've seen snow it turned black almost as soon as it touched the ground. And in France it was a misery."

It was an opening, and I took it.

"Do you have a family waiting for you at home?" I asked.

"A sister. She isn't much for writing. She's busy with young children. At least, they were young when I left the valley. I won't recognize them now. The eldest must be eight or nine."

If she hadn't written since his wounding, he had no idea how he would be received when he returned.

"No brothers?"

"One. Tom. He went missing at Passchendaele."

He didn't mention his sister-in-law, and I wondered if she'd written since that Christmas letter.

He changed the subject, making it clear he didn't want to talk about them. Instead, he went back to studying the snowfall and said, "Will you do something for me?"

"Yes, if I can."

"Could you see to it that all of us are released at the same time? It will be best for morale."

"I'll speak to Matron. I see that Private Jones isn't here any longer. Has he already been released?"

"Private Jones managed to kill himself." His voice was harsh, as if he disapproved. But I realized he was trying to conceal his own shock and grief.

"I didn't know," I said, appalled. "I'm so sorry. It must have been very difficult for the rest of you." Why hadn't Sister Baker told me?

"There was a letter from the girl he was to marry. She broke off their engagement. There was some mention of her parents needing her to care for them, but Jones took it to mean she couldn't face his wounds. He went up to the third floor and managed to get a window open. And threw himself out. The fall didn't kill him straightaway. He died of his injuries two days later." His voice was bitter. "It's for the best, I keep telling myself that."

"I'm so sorry," I said again, remembering the man I'd known in France.

"I wrote to his family. I think they were relieved, in a way. And I asked about Sarah. She'd married someone else. Two days after her letter to him."

"That's awful!" I replied.

"That's why I want to be there, to ease their homecoming. If I can."

I wondered if his concern for his men, as he considered them, was a way of avoiding thinking about his own return to the life he'd left behind.

He was talking now about Private Morris, who had lost his right arm. It was difficult to find a trade he could learn, and his depression was deepening.

"I feel guilty that my old position in the mine office is waiting for me. I don't know how some of them will manage. Morris is married, with children. He's desperate."

"Surely the owners of the mines ought to be able to find work for these men."

He laughed sourly. "These men will be extra mouths to feed. It will take a toll on their families." He looked away again. The snow was finally stopping, a few flakes still floating lazily down from the gray sky. "I don't know what to do."

"I don't know what you can do," I said quietly.

"That's what haunts me."

Was this the teacher he'd wanted to be speaking? Or the officer? Most likely both. Whole villages had enlisted together all over Britain, fought—and died—together. Wiping out a company meant wiping out most of the young men in a single village, or even a street in the larger towns. The published lists of the dead, missing, and wounded often read like a memorial service.

And of course we had lost men from the Colonel Sahib's regiment. In India and other postings, and during the war. I'd known so many of them, danced with them at balls, played tennis with them, been table partners at dinners. I'd tended more than a few of them myself, when they were brought to my aid station or the base hospitals. My mother had visited many recent widows in her role as the Colonel's Lady, because she had been a part of their lives in happier times. We were a family, and so I understood what the Captain was feeling.

"I don't know if Matron can do anything about that," I told him, "but you might let her know that you are worried."

"What can she do? We're speaking of the valleys. Her views hold no weight there."

Three days later, Private Evans managed to throw himself down the stairs, all fourteen steps, in the wheeled chair that was his only means of getting about. There was an orderly assigned to push it, but Private Evans had left his pipe in his room, and while the orderly was fetching it, he managed with one foot and one hand to make it as far as the head of the stairs, and fall.

I heard the racket as the chair bounced and ricocheted off the walls, and raced for the steps. I came through the door nearest the stairs just as the chair brushed past me as it slid toward the outer door. Private Evans rolled down the last step and lay still. I got to him first, with Matron at my heels. He was bleeding from his mouth and ears and nose, but what struck me first was the odd angle of his head. As Matron knelt beside me on the hard marble floor, she gently lifted my fingers from his pulse and placed her own there.

"He's dead," she said quietly. "I think his neck is broken."

All I could think of was that look of determination in the poor man's eyes in France, when we'd all but pulled him back from the dead after he'd taken an overdose of morphine. It had taken him weeks to find a way to try a second time. And he'd made sure he'd succeed.

The orderly, his face drained of color, was thudding down the stairs, the Private's pipe still gripped in his hand.

"My God," he said over and over again, then came to a halt six steps away from the body.

Others had hurried to the scene, among them Captain Williams. When he saw that it was one of his own men, he stopped, such an expression of sadness in his eyes that I turned away.

He maneuvered his crutches around the chair, one of its wheels still spinning slowly, and looked at Matron. She shook her head.

"How did this happen?" he demanded harshly. "What was he doing so near the stairs? Why wasn't anyone with him?"

A lift had been installed in the house in 1910 when the owner had had a stroke and was confined to a wheeled chair.

I thought at first the Captain was going to try to kneel by the body. Instead, he saw the orderly and started toward him. I sprang to my feet and stepped between the two men as the orderly retreated.

"Damn you!" he said through clenched teeth.

"Honest to God, Captain, we was by the lift, and he remembered his pipe—"

Captain Williams cut him short. "Didn't you think, you idiot, that it might be a trick?"

"No, sir, he sometimes forgot it—"

The frustration of having lost a leg, of being on crutches and unable to reach the frightened orderly made the Captain swing one of his crutches hard against the newel post, and Matron said sharply, "That will do, Captain," in a voice that stopped him in his tracks. She turned to several of the other orderlies who had come running. "Willis, Strong, will you carry Private Evans to surgery, please."

They came forward, lifting the body gently, and started for the surgery wing. It was then that I had a moment to notice the others who had come to the hall, three of them from the Private's own company. Their expressions were as grim as the Captain's, and they started after the orderlies, with Captain Williams by right moving ahead of them.

Matron started to object, then thought better of it. Turning to the other onlookers, she said briskly, "A tragedy for all of us. I think it best that we carry on with our duties now. But I will confer with the chaplain, and there will be a service for Private Evans later today. That will be the appropriate time to express our sense of loss and sympathy."

As people began to move away, still showing signs of their shock, she turned to the hapless orderly, standing as if rooted to the step.

"Please come to my office, Manners. We will speak there, not here in public."

To me, she added, "See to the other Welsh patients, if you please, Sister. They will need our every care."

It was her way of telling me to keep a watch over them. I went down the passage to the surgical wing, and reached there as Willis and Strong were coming away.

"Where are the others?" I asked.

"They wanted a minute of privacy, Sister. I thought it best," Willis said.

"Yes, thank you." I walked into the room. The orderlies had laid out the body of Private Evans on the table, and covered all but his face with a sheet. One of them had also cleaned the blood from his face and brushed back his hair.

As I stepped forward, the Welshmen turned as one to stare at me, as if I had come from the moon.

I said, "Matron asked me to give you time alone with Private Evans. I wonder if you could tell me more about him. I have only known him as a patient. I would like to know the man."

It was clear that Captain Williams resented my presence here, and my request.

Then Private Lloyd said, "I worked alongside him in the pit. He was a good man with a pick. Sure and easy. A good soldier as well." His Welsh accent was musical, with a lilt to it. That made his words more poignant.

Private Williams said, "He has a mother and a sister in the valley. Who's to tell them about this?" There was anger in his voice. "Who will look after them now?"

Private Morris said, "He didn't like the dark. Much of the year we never see the sun. We're down in the pits before it comes up, and we walk home after it's set."

"What will they do with the body?" Corporal Jones asked. "Will they send him home to be buried?"

Although I had seen markers near the woods to the west of the house, and some stones, I didn't know what the policy was here. For all I knew, the stones were in a private cemetery belonging to the family who had once lived here.

"I will ask Matron," I said quietly.

"They won't let us go back with him, will they?" Private Jones asked, but Private Lloyd didn't wait for my answer.

"I don't want to go back." His voice was low and savage. "Not like this. He had the right of it, didn't he? To end it before his family ever saw what was left of him?"

Captain Williams spoke for the first time. "I'll have none of that."

Private Lloyd shuffled his feet, as if embarrassed to have put into words what all of them must have been thinking.

"I can't look at him any longer," one of the others said, and turned his crutches toward the door, moving as fast as he could. When he got there, he slammed it with his fist and walked out. The others slowly followed, all except for Captain Williams.

"He was a good man," he said quietly. "He shouldn't have died like this, not after the trenches. *Bloody damned Hun!*"

I wasn't meant to hear that. I had gone to the door to catch the others up. Captain Williams brushed past me and went out into the passage. I went back and gently lifted the sheet over Private Evans's face. I hadn't known him well, but he'd been polite, done whatever was asked of him, and never wrote letters to anyone, not that I was aware of. Soft-spoken, not very well educated, but a reader of books.

It was the only epitaph I could offer, then I said simply, "Poor man."

The chaplain was just coming into the room as I reached the door. "Was it suicide? That's being whispered about. Or an accident?"

"I didn't see what happened," I replied. "But I should think it was an accident. He couldn't manage the chair very well."

"That's true," the chaplain agreed. "Thank you, Sister." And he moved on to the body. I saw him lift the sheet.

"I think he might have been Chapel," I said.

The chaplain looked over his shoulder and smiled sadly. "It doesn't matter. In death we are all God's children, never mind the door through which we enter His presence."

I left him there and hurried after Private Evans's comrades. Catching them up I said, "Will you come to Matron's private sitting room? She isn't there, but I can ask that tea be brought. It's quieter. You'll have a little privacy."

Corporal Jones cast a glance at his Captain. "Thank you, Sister. If you don't mind."

They followed me to what had once been a morning room, still quite pretty with floral wallpaper. The white morning glories against a blue background was appropriate, I thought, for men who were mourning a comrade. There was a small desk and several comfortable chairs as well as more around the tea table set by the windows. I left them there and went to ask for tea to be brought in.

I didn't stay with them after I'd poured their tea. I knew they resented my presence but were too polite to say so, and the quiet room was what they all desperately needed.

As I closed the door behind me, I heard Captain Williams say to his men, "We have got through worse together. We'll get through this."

It wasn't until two days later, after the service for Private Evans, that I found Captain Williams waiting for me in the library.

The chaplain and one of the other Sisters had accompanied the Private's body to Wales and the valley where he had been born and brought up. The family had wanted him to come home, and I thought they would probably mourn the man they remembered marching off to war, not the man in the coffin. The chaplain had taken it upon himself to read the letters from the dead man's mother and sister, to give him some insight into what they knew and what they felt.

"They never mentioned his wounds in their letters," he told me afterward. "I don't know if they were being kind. Or blind. It might have helped him if they'd at least acknowledged the fact that he was an amputee."

And I'd agreed with him.

The Captain looked up as I came into the room to find a book one of the patients was asking for. I smiled at him, but he didn't return it.

"Any word from the chaplain?"

"No. I expect he'll wait until he's returned to tell us how it went. Evans won't be the last of us to die by his own hand," the Captain went on slowly. "Tea and kind words won't wipe away the sight of his body lying there. I don't think any of us have got it out of our minds. Those of us who are left haven't found his courage yet—or Private Jones's—but we will."

We were alone in the library, but I crossed the room so that my words wouldn't carry to patients on the other side of the thin partitions that had turned this home into a clinic.

"You should be ashamed of yourself, Captain. These men look up to you, and they desperately need your support and your encouragement. Stop feeling sorry for yourself and try to help them find the courage to go on, not to die. Be the leader they believe you are. If you haven't forgotten how."

And I walked out of the library before he could answer me. Only after I'd closed the door did I remember I'd gone there for a book. I stood there, hearing my words in my ears, feeling I'd overstepped my bounds and said far more than I should to a man who was all too aware that he was little better off than the dead man, except that he had lost a leg, and not an arm as well. I turned, intending to go back and apologize to Captain Williams. But when I took a deep breath and opened the door, his chair was empty. He'd left the room by the other door.

It's hard to apologize long after the damage is done, and Captain Williams avoided me after our encounter, making it all the harder to say anything to him when we were in the presence of others.

I waited for Matron to send for me to tell me I'd forgot myself and upset a patient, but she never mentioned anything about it. I assumed the Captain had kept the matter to himself. I had done the same.

But I heard from several Sisters that he had tried to help his men deal with their grief. How he'd dealt with his own was another matter, and I spoke to Matron about it.

Her response had been kind—but I thought she'd misjudged the Captain.

"I see no signs of unusual distress, Sister. Perhaps you've worried yourself into believing it's there. Still, I'm grateful that you've come to me."

Before I left her office, I broached the subject of the release of the Welsh patients.

"Do you think it might be possible to release all of them on the same day? I think it might be for the best."

She looked at her chart. "I don't see why not. Yes, a very good idea. Meanwhile, I'll make certain that they're all ready to go at the same time. I'm worried about Private Owen. That arm isn't doing as well as it should be. And the doctors aren't eager to clean it again."

We talked about several other patients, ones from Surrey and Northumberland and Shropshire, before I was dismissed.

Soon enough we said good-bye to the Welsh wounded and

wished them well. They smiled and thanked us for our care, and set off down the drive with those smiles firmly in place. The rest of the staff went back indoors out of the cold wind, but I stayed where I was, watching the coach as far as the bend in the drive. As it negotiated that, the windows came into view again, and I saw that the smiles had vanished and the men staring back at the house looked pale and uncertain.

I went on about my duties, which now included tending two cases of pneumonia. Neither man seemed to have the will to fight, although we did what we could medically. We managed to save Sergeant Meadows, but we lost Private Whittle. His parents came from the town of Gloucester to claim his body, and we held a small service for him, which seemed to comfort them.

By the end of the week we'd received another twenty patients from France. We were hard-pressed to find beds for all of them, putting three in the small room that had been a library. We needed more staff, but Matron's requests seemed to fall on deaf ears. We were working twelve hours a day, and there were several serious infections that required more surgery.

A letter came for Private Meadows from the girl he was to marry, and it lifted his spirits no end when I read it to him.

I don't care, Priscilla had written, *how serious your wound is. You get well and come home to me. I'm the one who will walk down the aisle in St. Mary's, you need only be waiting for me at the altar. And I shall be very angry with you if you disappoint me. I have waited four long worrying years for this war to end, and I will not be truly happy until you arrive on the train and I can see for myself that you are safe at last. It's you I fell in love with, not your leg, and don't you forget it.*

From that moment onward, I watched him improve almost by the hour. I wished I could write Priscilla and tell her that she had done more than the doctors in France and in England had managed to do.

Truth was, she'd raised my spirits as well.

Half a dozen new patients were brought up from the railway station, but there were two experienced Sisters with them, and three more orderlies.

Matron, who had had the responsibility for finding enough hours in the day for all that needed to be done, began to look a little more rested. Still, it seemed that as soon as we released a patient—or lost one—two more appeared in his place. New cases of pneumonia, two suicides, patients whose limbs turned gangrenous, infections that wouldn't heal kept us busy day and night. When I did have a few quiet minutes, I found myself wondering how the Welsh patients had fared. Not that I expected them to write, but we knew how a few other cases had ended, and I was afraid that they were vulnerable to the same choices.

One afternoon I was just finishing a late lunch before going upstairs to see to some ironing when the post arrived, and Sister Anthony, one of the new staff, brought me a letter.

"Not the usual postmark from Somerset or London," she said, smiling. "This one's from Wales. Don't tell you have a beau there?" She hadn't been posted here until after the Welsh patients had been released.

Taking the letter she was holding out, I looked at it. Captain Williams had written.

"No such luck," I said, smiling in return. "I should think it's a note from a former patient, thanking us for our care." We sometimes did hear from the fortunate ones.

"Oh, better luck next post," she told me, laughing.

I took the letter upstairs to read, and was very glad I had.

It was brief and to the point.

Captain Williams must have been in dire need of someone to talk to, to write so frankly. It was worrying that I was that person, not someone in his family or his valley.

Sister Crawford,

We have lost Private Morris to suicide. That's not what the doctor has called it, of course, and I am grateful for the sake of Morris's family. But he left a message for me that I burned as soon as I read it. In it he asked my forgiveness. I have told no one. What worries me now is that the others were too quiet at the funeral, and I have a feeling that they're taking his death to heart and finding the thought of ending their own lives more and more palatable. I'm at my wits' end, and I am writing to ask your help in bringing them to their senses. I have no right to ask this of you, but if someone doesn't do something, we'll all be gone by the spring.

It was a shocking message. Their wounds had done what the Germans never could—broken their spirits. I was suddenly very angry. We'd asked so much from these men. And with the war at an end, when we no longer needed soldiers, we tossed them aside like broken chairs.

I went at once to Matron and showed her the letter.

She read it over, then said with sadness, "I am so sorry to hear about Private Morris. But I'd feared for him, you know. He was in a depressed state when he was with us, and nothing seemed to help then. As for the others?" She shook her head. "We can work miracles here, sometimes, Sister Crawford, but we can't go home with our patients and work more miracles there. Our duty must stop at the door. We do our very best, then we wish them well when they leave, and we pray that they will prosper."

It was what we had been called on to do all through the war. Heal men as quickly as we could, and send them back to the Front as soon as we could. Some of us had tried to find ways around that, when the need was there.

"But surely there's something to be done. Some way to give them hope?"

"I can't very well write to the mine owners and tell them their duty," she replied, resignation in her voice. "My sister in London tells me that there is little work open to many of the soldiers coming home. She saw three begging on the street just last week. She sent one to hospital with a very bad chest, but there was nothing she could do about the others. She collected money from friends and took it to them, but it's only a temporary solution. Neither she nor anyone else can take on responsibility for all of them."

I hadn't been in London, not to walk about on the streets, since the war ended. I hadn't known.

"You're from an Army family, aren't you?" she asked after a moment. "I can imagine how difficult this must be for you. Sadly, it's beyond our ability to help."

It was dismissal.

Captain Williams's letter had taken over a week to reach me, and I wrote to him that same evening, offering what advice I could, knowing even as I sealed the envelope that it wouldn't be enough. But no reply came, although I watched each day for our own post to arrive.

It was useless to apply to Matron again. She'd already made it plain enough that she had no way to help a former patient. And so I wrote to my mother, asking if the Colonel Sahib was in London. He could speak to the Army. But he was in Paris again. I was glad I hadn't told my mother why I was trying to reach him, for it would only have worried her.

I wrote again to Wales, praying that *this* letter would reach the Captain.

Days later my letter came back marked RETURN TO SENDER.

I told myself it could be explained away. The Captain had taken rooms of his own, rather than continue to live with his sister. But surely the valley's postmaster would know that? Unless of course the Captain hadn't thought to inform him. But then why write to me, if he hadn't hoped for a response?

I didn't want to consider the only other possibility, that something had happened to him. And what about the others? Were they lost too?

It was clear enough that the only way to know for certain was to travel to Wales myself. But to ask for leave when we were so short-handed was impossible. And in the back of my mind was the fear that it was already too late, that these men I'd known since the base hospital in France were dead.

Twice in my dreams I heard their voices singing as they had at Christmas, but when I tried to find out which room they were in, I kept getting lost. I'd wake up, and then it was hard to get to sleep again.

Matron stopped me in the passage one morning, looking at me intently. I knew what she must be seeing. My mirror had shown me the dark smudges under my eyes. Worry had put them there, but she interpreted them as fatigue. "Sister Crawford, you haven't had leave since you arrived. Why don't you take a few days? Ten, perhaps. At the moment we can manage without you for a bit, and it will do you good to go home to Somerset and rest."

She meant well. But Somerset wasn't going to help me or Captain Williams or his men. Now I could finally go to Wales.

I knew those men, I'd treated them, and I hated losing them to despair.

"Perhaps a leave is just the thing, Matron," I said quietly, so as not to arouse any suspicions. "But are you sure that you can do without me?"

"We're expecting three more Sisters any day now. Their base hospital in France is reducing staff. I'd asked for four the last time, and we only got two. London is about to rectify that. They're experienced, and I shan't have to worry about training them. I hear we'll also be getting in more patients. A small clinic in Kent is about to close its doors and we'll be taking their amputees. We've also been asked to do more training in the use of crutches, and there's some talk about artificial limbs." She smiled. "You are so conscientious, Sister Crawford, and I appreciate that. Now go and pack your kit. And come back again restored."

"Thank you, Matron. I'll do my best."

I turned my patients over to Sister MacNeil, and went upstairs to pack.

CHAPTER 3

ONE OF THE kitchen staff was going into the village below the clinic for Evensong that evening, and it was arranged for me to go in with her, to take the 5:20 train to London. I'd explained to Matron that I had taken a flat in the city at the start of my training and I could spend what remained of the night there before taking the next train home. She considered that a very good plan, and wished me well.

I went to the wards to speak to my patients, cheering them up as best I could, and promising to come back before they were discharged. And then I was waiting at the door when Nan came round in the dog cart she kept to do errands for Cook. The horse was fresh and eager for a run, and so we arrived at the station well before time. I sat by the stove in the tiny waiting room, warming my toes and chatting with the stationmaster until the whistle warned us that the train was coming.

I arrived in London in the middle of the night but at the station found a cab to take me to Mrs. Hennessey's. The stationmaster there escorted me out to the street, telling me about his son and the Sister who had treated him after Ypres, and how grateful he and his wife were that Andrew's wounds had healed.

I thanked him for his kindness, and gave the cabbie Mrs. Hennessey's direction. She must have been soundly asleep, for she didn't come out to greet me when I let myself in with my key, taking the stairs as quietly as I could and crawling in between cold sheets in a colder room.

The next morning I startled her when I tapped at her door to ask for a cup of tea and a pitcher of hot water. She pulled me into her kitchen, fed me, and let me use her own room—warmed by a fire on the hearth—to bathe and change. She took it for granted that I was on my way to Somerset.

By eleven o'clock I was on the next train to Cardiff. From my neighbor in the first-class compartment, I learned that I could hire a driver to take me to my destination. "The mine owners often use them. Very reliable," he assured me.

And so it was that early the next morning I found myself leaving my hotel in the bustling port city with a driver who had little to say but who knew the roads well enough to make reasonably good time.

We arrived in the valley a little after four o'clock in the afternoon. On the heights as we climbed into the hills, the snow had been pristine white, sparkling in the pale light of the sun as it dodged in and out of clouds. As we'd descended on the track leading to the village, I looked up at the mountaintop across the way. It was oddly shaped, lumpy and unnatural. When I asked, my driver told me that the lumps were where the tip from the mine, the refuse of operations, was piled out of the way.

"It's ugly, as a rule," he explained. "The snow does its best to hide that."

As we made our way down the valley, the snow was already blackened by coal dust. The houses were too, and even the faces of a handful of miners I saw coming down the road toward the pit head. Older men, mostly. The younger ones had gone to war and had never come back.

"The house number again, Sister?" my driver asked, turning down a muddy street to our left.

"Number one hundred ten."

"It will be just down there." He pointed toward another narrow street that led up from the river.

I looked at the row of houses ahead. No better nor worse than others on the street we'd just come up. The terraces were plain, and in need of paint or new steps at the door or missing slates from the roof. A church was just beyond, rectangular and plain as well, without even a steeple, just the narrow housing for a small bell at the peak of the roof. A chapel, not a church, I reminded myself. These were Chapel folk.

My driver pulled up in front of a door. It had been a pale green once, but was grimy now, and one of the lace curtains at the front window had a long tear in it. With a sinking heart, I prepared to get down. It didn't look welcoming.

"Wait for me," I said. "I shan't be staying the night with these people. Is there a hotel or an inn—some other place you could take me to?" For the house didn't look large enough to have a guest room, and I hadn't seen any other accommodation as we came through the village.

"Not really, Sister."

It was dusk now in the valley, for the sun had disappeared over the heights above us. Toward the west the sky was still bright, and on the ridgeline the tips were pink, the snow catching reflections from the clouds. Lamps were lit in number 110, and in the other homes along the street. Across the river, houses clung to the shelf of flat land along it or climbed up the lower edges of the hillside, picked out by the glow from their windows.

I went up the three shallow steps to the door and knocked.

A woman came to answer it. Thin, in a dark dress that was faded around the neckline and across the shoulders, and a stained once-white apron, she stared at me with tired eyes. "Sister?"

Behind her I could hear young children quarreling. She glanced over her shoulder as a man's voice shouted to them to be quiet, then she turned back to me, waiting.

"I'm Sister Crawford," I said. "I'm here to see Captain Williams."

"Are you now?" she said, looking behind me to where my driver leaned against the wing of the motorcar, smoking a cigarette. "Well, you're too late. He isn't here."

I could feel my heart turn over. I couldn't bear to ask if her brother was in the churchyard. But it was what I'd dreaded since his letter had come. And tried to ignore.

"Not here?" I looked at the number painted next to the door, desperately telling myself that I must somehow have got the wrong street. For that matter, even the wrong village. My driver had sworn he knew this valley, but how could I be sure? "I'm sorry," I said then. "I was sure this was the address given in the Captain's letter."

A baby began to cry, and she glanced over her shoulder again. She said to me, "How did you think I could do anything for him here? With that lot to look after as well?"

"I wrote—" I began, and then stopped.

"I burned them. The letters. What else was I to do? He's not here," she said again, as if I were hard of hearing. "I told you."

"Yes, all right," I answered, falling back on Matron's voice of authority to conceal my despair at failing the Captain. "I understand that. What about the others? His men?"

"In the churchyard. What did you expect? That's the only reason he was willing to leave."

"What do you mean, *leave*?" I held my breath, waiting for her answer.

"He went to stay with our brother's widow somewhere below Swansea. On the sea. She's taken him in."

The sister-in-law, who had written to him just before Christmas . . .

"Where is that?" I asked. "How can I reach him?"

"There's your driver. Ask him. I'm needed."

And she shut the door in my face before I could say anything more.

Angry with her, I debated knocking again, then gave it up. I went back to the motorcar.

"The patient I'd come to see is living somewhere below Swansea. How far away is that?"

"Out on the peninsula? Is that what you mean? That's a goodly distance, Sister," he answered me in the pleasant rhythmic speech patterns of the Welsh. "Surely you'll not be wanting to go there? It's the back of nowhere."

"We can talk about that later," I said, still taking in what the Captain's sister had said. "But first I must find a tea shop." It was the best place to ask for the information I needed. She might have been wrong about the other men—but I'd only had the one address. I didn't know where to find them.

"I don't know of a tea shop here."

"I thought I saw a general store just over the river. Where we turned off the main road to cross to here. Surely they're still open at this hour?"

When we pulled up in front of the dingy building, I got down. "While I'm here, I'll find something for our dinner. Or would you prefer to find your own?"

Grunting, he got out and followed me inside. "Like as not, they don't speak English," he said gloomily.

But to my dismay, the shelves in the store offered little of inter-est. Staples, but nothing more. And the prices were exorbitant. It dawned on me that the people in this valley couldn't afford things that I'd have taken for granted in Somerset.

I settled for a loaf of bread, a tin of beans, and a few slices of cheese. My driver shook his head, but I'd served in France where one learned quickly not to be too fussy about one's food. The woman behind the counter looked at my coins as if surprised to be paid in currency.

I had put it off as long as I could, afraid of what I'd hear. Still, if Captain Williams's sister wouldn't speak to me, and this woman couldn't help, I'd find the local Constable or even the nearest clergyman. I wasn't going to leave until I'd learned what had become of my other patients.

While she was laboriously counting out my change, I asked about Corporal Jones, using his name instead of his rank.

Her frown deepened. Without looking up, she said, "Llewelyn Jones? He fell down the mine shaft. A week ago, it was, just as the rain was turning to snow. They say his crutches slipped and he lost his balance."

Horrified, I stared at her. "It was an accident?" I found that hard to believe.

The woman shrugged. "There were witnesses. He'd come to wait for his father, and he got too close to the mouth."

I was almost afraid to go on. "Owen Lloyd?"

"He's in Cardiff hospital. Pneumonia. I've not heard since they took him away. Josh Williams is at home with his wife and mother. If you're interested." She studied me. "You must be the Sister they spoke of. At the clinic."

"Yes, they were my patients. All of them. I'm so sorry. I'd hoped for better news."

"What did you expect to hear?" she asked harshly. "They marched away on their own two feet, and you send them back half men."

"Blame the war, if you like. The doctors and Sisters did what they could."

"You saved them," she said bitterly. "Aye, but for what sort of life? It would have been better if they had died there and then. With dignity. As heroes, giving their lives for King and Country."

"You can't mean that!"

"Can't I? Owen is my cousin. Doctor said he's lost the will to fight the pneumonia. I remember Owen as a big man, the best face man there was. He's lost three stone, and I watched him cry when he thought no one was looking. Not happy tears, mind you, for God bringing him home safe. Tears of despair. There's none left now but the Captain, Josh, and Owen. And we'll be burying Owen soon enough."

She handed me my purchases and turned away, as if I'd been personally responsible for the valley's lost men.

"Why is Josh Williams different?" I asked. "Why is he safe at home with his wife and mother? Did they help him more than you and the others helped his comrades?"

She didn't turn around. "You haven't met his mother. She will hold on to him and fight the Devil for him if she has to. Whether he likes it or not."

I carried my purchases back to the motorcar, and hoped there was enough tea in my thermos from lunch to finish my meal.

Sitting there in my seat, I tried to come to terms with the fact that those wonderful voices were stilled. That men who had lived through the hell of battle and amputation had been lost to peace. I debated calling on Private Williams, to find out more about each of the men. But I wasn't sure I'd be welcomed there, any more than Owen's cousin had welcomed me. I felt like crying for the lost Welsh soldiers. And I understood now the Captain's despair at saving any of his men, once they were home. *Too late, too late . . .* The words seemed to chase themselves through my head and my heart.

44

"I can't drive all night," my driver was saying, setting his own small sack at his feet.

"We can stop whenever you find a place suitable to spend the night," I told him firmly. "I don't relish sleeping on the road any more than you do."

My last words were lost in a dreadful roar, seeming to come from everywhere at once as the echoes picked it up and tossed it back and forth across the valley. I flinched from habit, accustomed to shells coming far too close. But this wasn't artillery.

People were coming to their doors, out of the mine office down the road, all of them looking up.

I followed their gaze, in time to see a dark shadow moving fast down the face of the mountain just above me.

Part of the tip, weighted with the recent snow, had broken free and was sliding down the mountain. There were three cottages directly in its path, their windows a bright patch in the darkness. Someone had the presence of mind to race to the heavy iron bell on a tall post by the mine office and ring it wildly.

Still watching those three cottages, I saw their occupants flinging their doors open and starting to flee. But they couldn't outrun what was coming. It seemed to be moving with massive slowness, but I could tell that was deceptive. People along the street where I was standing were already starting to run, some of them with shovels, toward the disaster unfolding.

I turned to the driver. "Quickly. We can help bring the injured down."

He stammered, "But my motorcar—" And then he was behind the wheel, and we were reversing in the midst of that throng of people, turning to climb toward the oncoming monster.

My face pressed to the glass of my window, I watched helplessly as first one and then another of the cottages were crushed by the onslaught, praying that this wouldn't shake the rest of the tip loose and send it cascading down the mountain as well.

"Why do they pile the tip there? Surely it's just a disaster waiting to happen. I don't understand," I said as we drove toward the slope. I could see the rest of it high above, lying there like a sleeping giant, just waiting.

"Where else can it go?" he asked, threading his way through the rescuers racing up the mountain.

The third cottage was caving in now, the roof buckling and swaying before collapsing. I saw two older people swept away, then a child.

"*Hurry,*" I urged my driver, even though I knew there was very little I could do.

He slowed as several men with shovels flagged us down. We hastily lowered our windows, and they clung to the running boards as we picked up speed again. Two more flung themselves onto the wings.

The slide was slowing, having spent itself finally, but I thought again how awful it would have been if that slide were wider, heavier, loosened by rain or melting snow, and not stopping until it reached the river's edge, sweeping away everything—and everybody—in its path. A swath of death and destruction.

We reached the edge of the slide, although it was still creeping a little, as if refusing to give up.

The men who had jumped on board our motorcar were already off and running toward where they had seen the child vanish, digging frantically in the heavy sludge. One cried out as he found an arm, and his companions came to help him, dragging a little girl of about eight out into the frigid air. A woman, panting for breath, rushed past me, blankets in her arms, and went to wrap the child. I was already out of the motorcar too, following her.

The men hurried on to where the older couple had been, leaving the woman and me to minister to the child. She was limp and barely breathing, and I was suddenly afraid that we'd lose her, for she was frail. Her family had come up behind us, her mother crying her name in such a terrified voice that the child stirred a little, and her mother pushed us aside, pulling the little girl into her arms, rocking her back and forth. I realized she was singing to her, a lullaby or possibly even a hymn. I was trying to discover whether she was hurt badly or just shocked and bruised, but the mother refused to let her go. And then the child began to cry, and I realized how tense I myself was, waiting for sure signs of life.

The men shouted something, and I saw that they had found the older couple.

I rose, on my way to them, when a graying man with a black bag, who looked like a doctor, came running up and, with a glance at the little girl, hurried on to the next victims.

I turned back to the child, gently touching the mother on the shoulder. "She may be hurt. Please let me see."

There were two older children beside us now, shock in their faces, tears leaving dirty runnels on their cheeks. The boy brushed his away fiercely, as if trying to be brave.

The mother finally let me examine the little girl. I thought she might have broken an arm, but when I ran my hands over it, I saw that it was scraped and bruised, and mercifully not broken. There were other scrapes and bruises on her face and legs, but somehow she had been spared. She stared up at me with large dark eyes as I worked, and I spoke to her in a soft voice, telling her she was a fine, brave girl, and her mother would take her home soon.

But there was no home.

Other women were there now, speaking to the children and the mother as I wrapped the blanket more closely about the little girl and let her mother hold her again. Several of them began collecting the little family, nodding to me before carrying them off to a house on one of the streets below. For a moment I watched them go, the mother clutching the child, as if fearful she still might lose her.

I was glad to see they would be safe, and turned my attention to the older couple. They had been pulled out of the slide and carried a little distance away. Someone had covered them with blankets. But I saw the doctor look up at the men who had dug them out, shaking his head.

Stopping halfway there, I felt like crying myself.

I saw the doctor gesture to the slide and the men shake their heads, and I realized he must have asked if there were any other victims.

From somewhere came a mewing sound, and I turned to look for it. And there was a gray kitten, half buried in the slag where the child had been.

I hurried back to it, hardly able to see it as darkness came down, but following the sound, I pulled it free.

The little girl must have gone back for it, and have been carrying it, her body protecting it. Now it was shaking with fright, staring up at me with wide green eyes. Its claws, like little needles, were digging into my coat, and I held it tight.

Someone came up to me and said, "That's the child's kitten. She'll be glad it's safe." I turned to the man who was holding out his hands to take it, and I disengaged its claws before gently passing it to him. He put it inside his coat, and with a nod, turned to walk down the hill.

I hadn't realized that a great many more people had come up the hill. They were quiet, for there was nothing to be done, simply staring at the place where three families had lived. The cottages and everything in them had vanished, but I thought they had slowed the slide just enough that it had stopped much sooner than it might have done. Turning, I saw a young couple standing by the bodies, the woman shaking with sobs and the man offering what comfort he could. The motorcar's headlamps lit the pitiful scene with a bright and garish light now, and I turned back toward it.

Men had appeared, to carry the dead back down to the village, stretchers in their hands, and those who had come to help, standing in clusters, were talking among themselves.

One of the men who had clung to the motorcar going up nodded to me as he passed, and I smiled in acknowledgment. And then the doctor was coming up to me. "Sister?"

"Yes. Sister Crawford."

"I saw you were with the child. How is she? I'm just going down there now."

I told him what I had seen. "I think she needs warm milk and her mother. And her kitten," I added, remembering. "Then the scrapes need to be cleaned. That left arm will be badly bruised. I thought at first it might be broken."

"I'll have a look. With children it's often difficult to be sure there's a break until the swelling begins. Thank you for attending to her."

"I was glad I could help."

He was about to turn away, then paused. "You wouldn't be the Sister those men from the clinic spoke of, by any chance?"

"Yes, I've come to see how they were getting on. Captain Williams had been worried."

"He had good reason to be." He drew in a breath. "I just heard that Owen Jones succumbed to his pneumonia. I was afraid we might lose him."

"I'm so sorry," I said, and meant it.

"I'm concerned about Williams as well. He's gone to stay with his sister-in-law. His sister simply wasn't able to cope, not with young children and an ill cousin. And the position Hugh had held at the mine was given to someone else while he was away fighting. Did you know? That was surely a blow."

"I didn't know." I looked around, but no one was close enough to overhear, the villagers politely giving the doctor and the nurse space to confer privately. "The man who fell down the shaft. Was that an accident?"

"Everyone swore it was, but I have my doubts. I kept them to myself. Are you staying in the village tonight, Sister?"

"I wanted to find a way to help those men," I said, uncertain what he was asking me. "Only it's too late."

"Sadly. I hope you'll look in on the Captain. But I expect that's well out of your way. Where he's gone to live with his sister-in-law. The circumstances might be even worse there. I have no way of knowing. She's a widow herself." He shook his head. "I did what I could for those men. It wasn't enough."

"I don't know where Captain Williams is. His sister wasn't forthcoming."

"I expect she wasn't." He drew a crumpled sheet of paper from his pocket and in the glow of my driver's headlamps, he scribbled something on it. "It would be a kindness if you could see your way to going there. Now I must look in on that child. Good night, Sister. Thank you."

And he walked on to his carriage, putting out a hand to touch the horse's neck as he reached it.

My driver was standing there, shifting from one foot to the other. "Sister?"

I hadn't noticed how cold it was. Now, with the shock and the worry fading, I was aware of cold feet, cold hands, and a cold nose.

"There's nothing more we can do here," I said with a sigh as he opened the door for me to climb into my seat. I'd debated searching for the churchyard, but in the dark I'd stand little enough chance of finding the graves I wanted to see. "Let's be on our way."

"Surely you're not going on? Late as it is?"

"But of course I am. And I have a new address here." I handed it to him, and he peered at it in the glow of the headlamps, then shook his head.

"My firm doesn't do business in Swansea," he said. "You'll have to find another firm to take you to this village."

But something in his voice belied what he was telling me. As if he himself didn't want to go there. I was too tired to pursue it. Once back in Cardiff, I could take a train to Swansea and find the best way of going on from there.

It was cold in the motorcar, and the tiny heater didn't offer much in the way of warmth in the rear seat as we climbed the hill and set out on our way. I tucked the blanket I'd brought from Mrs. Hennessey's more closely about my skirts, to keep my feet and legs warm, and wished for another to drape over my shoulders. Yes, I'd known it was winter, I'd known there would be mountains. But I hadn't expected to have to face a night on the road. Coming out of Cardiff, where I'd taken the train from London, this journey had seemed to be imminently possible.

It had turned out very differently from expectations.

Resigned to being uncomfortable, I sat back and munched on cheese and bread as we climbed back to the heights and set off back toward the city. And tried to hold the ghosts at bay.

We stopped for the night in a village inn where the rooms were pleasant and breakfast was lovely. Reaching Cardiff in time to take the noon train to Swansea, I found another firm that could provide a driver to carry me the rest of the way, as there was no rail service to the address on the scrap of paper the doctor had given me.

The owner assured me there would be no difficulty in reaching my destination.

We were soon out of the city and into the wild windswept open spaces of a peninsula jutting out into the sea. I looked at a sign that read—in English—THE MUMBLES.

"And what is The Mumbles?" I asked, watching the sign pass us.

In his heavily Welsh-accented English, the driver explained that it was an area on the north coast of this peninsula. "We're turning to the south instead. Still, there's Loughor Estuary on the same coast. It's where the people of Penclawdd drive their horse carts out into the sea at dawn to collect cockles. My sister married a Penclawdd man."

I knew what cockles were. Shellfish. I'd heard Welsh patients talk about eating them.

The Mumbles was the only name on the signpost that I could make out. I had an ear for languages—according to my governess—which must have helped me learn several Indian dialects quite easily. Or perhaps it was the fact that I had been a child and heard them all around me, soaking them up like a little sponge. Urdu from the grooms and the man who kept our gate. Hindi from the women of the household, including my ayah. I'd also learned French without too much trouble, even picked up a smattering of German. But Welsh defeated me, as did the pronunciation of those clusters of consonants and vowels.

I said something to that effect to the driver.

"Not to fear, Miss," he told me. "South Gower area is English." And then he settled to his driving, trying to make his way around the worst of the ruts that we were bumping over, ignoring me.

It was already afternoon. I'd managed a cup of tea at the railway station before hiring the motorcar, but as I watched civilization thin out behind us and the road become more wild and desolate ahead of us, I was beginning to wonder if I should have waited until tomorrow before setting out into the peninsula. The first village we encountered had a tiny stone church in the Norman style, but was hardly more than a hamlet. No tea shop, no inn, just a scattering of farm cottages.

And then the road branched again, this time into a track that looked as if it had seen more cattle or sheep than vehicles.

As we bounced into the turn, shaking madly and slowing considerably, I had to be practical. I could find accommodations in Swansea. What would I find at the end of this road?

"The firm's owner told me it wasn't far to where I'm going. How much longer?"

"Another hour?" As he fought the wheel, Mr. Morgan added, "Two? The rains have been bad out here."

"There's no better road?"

"It's the only one."

Resigned, I settled back as best I could, bracing myself against the jolting and sending up a silent prayer that the tires held.

Still, after the blackened hills and valleys of the pits, then the railway lines and industry and cluttered ports in Swansea, I could see the beauty out here. Windswept, what trees there were telling me its direction, only farms and pasturage for cattle, it reminded me of South Devon, only not as soft and manicured and friendly. *South Devon in the days of the Normans?* I wondered. A far cry from the usual chapel architecture.

The sun was just going down over the sea as we came at last in sight of a long, blunt headland that appeared to be another mile farther down from where the motorcar was now pulling up.

There was the usual church. And lights were appearing in the few scattered houses, the only signs of life out here, save for the humped white bodies of a small herd of sheep in a pasture beyond.

"This is where you wanted to go?" my driver asked, staring around.

"I—yes. Well, at least I think it is," I said doubtfully.

To my right, the land dropped away precipitously, a single rutted lane that ran down past a winter-bare hedge to where more houses were scattered across a green Down rising sharply above the sea. From here, I couldn't tell where water and land met. But there must have been a strand at the foot of the Down. I could hear the sea on the wind, and smell it too.

"Which house, Miss?" my driver was asking.

Ahead of me was a long, low cottage on the crest of the high cliff, and far down to my left were the white buildings of what appeared to be a coast guard station put up during the war. It was too dark to see what lay beyond that, but I could tell there were no more villages in that direction. It was pitch-black, not a single light.

Just behind me was the only good-sized house out here in the wilderness, but there were no lamps lit when we came by, and it appeared to be closed up. Empty.

The driver came around to open my door, and I stepped down.

The wind whipped at my skirts as I stood there, undecided. Surely the valley doctor had given me the wrong address, and I'd come all this way for nothing.

This must be a glorious sight in the spring or summer, I thought, but what was I to do *now*? There was no sign of an inn, not even a shop where I might inquire.

The driver got back behind the wheel, waiting for me to decide what to do. I wished for Simon, suddenly. I wouldn't feel quite so alone if he were here to help me knock on doors.

Go? Or stay?

Stay where? I asked myself.

And a craven little voice in my head suggested that I get back in the motorcar and return to Swansea and civilization. A hot bath, a good dinner, and a hot water bottle in my bed. Even if it was nearly dawn by the time we got there, I added, thinking of the drive back.

But I was my great-grandmother's great-granddaughter, and a nursing Sister to boot.

I said briskly, "Sound your horn. Someone must be about."

For a moment I thought he might refuse, then he reached out for it.

It seemed lost in the ceaseless roar of the wind, a pathetic man-made noise in the teeth of Mother Nature's force.

Nothing happened. And then a man came to the door of the long, low cottage to the right of us and peered out.

I hailed him, and he disappeared for a moment, returning with a coat he was shrugging into, a knit cap on his head.

"Trouble with the motorcar?" he called as he came across the open ground toward us, taking in my uniform.

"No, I've come to look for a—a former patient. I was told by his sister that I might find him here. Captain Williams." I'd almost said a friend but thought that it might seem far too familiar, to explain my presence at this end of the world.

I could just see, in the light of the headlamps, that he was frowning.

"What do you want *him* for?" he asked suspiciously.

I'd noticed one thing, coming into Wales: that people said what was on their minds, where the English often circled around it in a polite, noninvolved sort of way. This might be English-settled countryside, but this man was Welsh blunt.

"I came to Wales to look in on a few of my former patients. Captain Williams is the last on my list."

"They didn't come looking for Booker's son, after he was sent home," he said, a bitterness in his voice. "Lungs rotted out by gas."

"The war is over," I replied. "We can spare the staff now."

He nodded.

Just then I saw a woman coming up the lane that ran down to the houses below. She was walking briskly, two large dogs trotting at her heels. Then she saw the motorcar, a Sister hanging on to her cap for dear life, and the man from the cottage standing ten feet away, staring unhelpfully.

"Hallo. Can I help you?" she called.

A friendly voice. But at the same time, a wary one.

"My name is Sister Crawford. I've come from Gloucestershire to find Captain Williams."

"Have you now?" she said, stopping in her tracks. "And what would you be wanting him for?"

Exasperated, I said, "He wrote to say he needed help. Well, I am the help that has been sent to find him." Not quite the truth, but close enough for strangers, since I had no idea what was wrong here. "Has he gone back to the valleys?" I asked then, suddenly considering the fact that he might not be here after all.

"The valleys? Have you been there?"

"I have."

"Oh," she said, and I thought she was frowning, but her dark windblown hair covered her face. She'd pulled off the scarf she was holding to let the wind take it, not expecting to find a crowd of people at the top of the walk. A crowd by the standards of this desolate corner of Wales.

She took a deep breath. "Well, you'd better come in, then." And with the hand holding the scarf she gestured toward the house behind me.

All this time the man I'd first spoken to had listened to our exchange with undisguised interest. But before I could thank him, he turned on his heel and went back where he'd come from, pointedly slamming the door.

I said to my driver, "Will you follow me there, please?"

He gave me some argument, but I told him, "I don't intend to be stranded here. You'll wait until I see what transpires there in the house."

As I'd paid him only half of his fee, the other half to be handed over at my destination, he had no choice but to wait.

I hurried to catch up with the woman striding briskly toward the house. It was more the size of a bungalow, but by local standards, it was large, with two stories.

The dogs bounded ahead of her, scratching at the door. A lamp was lit by the window, just before she opened the door, and I heard voices as she stepped inside. And then a man's silhouette was outlined against the brightness of the lamplight, and a familiar voice called, "Sister Crawford?"

There was astonishment in his voice.

I was beginning to feel as if I'd come on a fool's errand.

"Yes, indeed, Captain. You are a hard man to find," I said brightly.

"Come in," he said, moving back, and I saw the crutches then. "It's good to see you."

He was being polite. There was no relief, no warmth in the invitation.

I hesitated, then took a deep breath and went up the path to the door. Stepping into the narrow entry, I said, "I received your letter. And I understood why you wrote it. I've visited the valley, and I came on here to make certain you were all right. Your sister wasn't very forthcoming." And then, watching the woman's face in the shadows behind him, I added, "Matron will be glad to hear you're all right."

A spark of amusement appeared in his dark eyes, vanishing almost as quickly as it had come.

The woman said, "I'll put the kettle on. Do ask your driver if he'd like a cup."

I thought perhaps it was a way of saying ". . . before you go." But she didn't add it. It seemed that she was waiting to see what the Captain wanted to happen.

He swung around on his crutches and led the way into a front room, obviously the parlor. He found the lamp, lit it, and said, "You must be tired after such a long journey."

As the lamplight brightened, I could see that he looked better, stronger—and yet there were dark circles beneath his eyes, as if he wasn't sleeping well.

"I didn't intend to intrude, Captain. I am merely carrying out orders." Again not quite the truth, but I thought it might save face for both of us if I left shortly, duty done.

"I'm sorry about that letter," he said after a moment. "Any news of Josh or Owen?" But there was no curiosity in the question. Just dread.

I told him, and he winced at my answer.

"I didn't want to leave. But I didn't have much choice. There was nowhere to go. And the others were dead."

It was a painful answer, cutting into his pride.

"I understand," I said quietly. "I'm sorry to be the bearer of such news."

He shook his head. "My sister isn't much of a letter writer. I am grateful for your news, bad as it is."

I gestured around the room. The furnishings were of an older generation, dark wood and darker upholstery. The round table by the windows had a marble top, and there were framed photographs and other treasures taking pride of place on it.

"You seem well settled here. You look stronger too. As if the sea air agrees with you." But I remembered that the house had been dark before the woman came home. Not a good sign, surely. People who were depressed preferred the dark . . .

"Sister Crawford. Bess—" he began and broke off.

I waited.

He glanced toward the door of the room, then dropped his voice. "You mustn't stay," he said softly. "It isn't safe."

CHAPTER 4

I STARED AT him.

"What do you mean, it isn't safe?" I asked, keeping my voice as low as his.

But before he could answer me, we could hear footsteps in the passage, and the woman came in with a tray. And only two cups.

I smiled, and thanked her.

This was my first clear look at her. She was nearly my height and close to my age, with dark hair (now confined in a knot at the back of her head) and dark eyes. Her face was heart shaped and very pretty. I wondered if the danger the Captain had mentioned had to do with gossip about an attractive widow and her brother-in-law.

As if he'd suddenly remembered his manners, he said, belatedly, "I'm so sorry. It was the sho— the surprise of a visitor. Sister Craw-ford, this is my brother's widow, Rachel Williams. Rachel, I don't think any of us would have survived as long as we did without the Sisters. And this one in particular. I've told you about her."

She acknowledged the introduction, then said, "I'll just call your driver. And take him into the kitchen, so that you can talk."

"That's very kind of you," I said, smiling. "On both counts. We won't be long."

She nodded, but I'd seen the way she looked at Captain Williams.

And I knew she was not happy to see me here. She was in love with him, and he had no idea.

Patients fell in love with their nurses all the time. And out of love just as quickly when they were released from our care either to return home or to go back to their sector. It was a part of healing. It wasn't done to speak of their exploits, but flirting with the Sisters made them feel like men again. We didn't encourage it, but we understood, and as a rule we took no umbrage from their teasing.

But I'd seen no indication whatsoever that the Captain had imagined himself in love with me or any of the other Sisters treating him. The loss of his leg and his worry for his men, not romance, had kept his mind occupied.

Of course, Rachel wasn't to know that. A Sister appearing at the edge of night was surely trouble . . .

She closed the door when she left the room, and I heard her calling to my driver. He came in and followed her down the passage, thanking her for her thoughtfulness.

I said, "Captain?" And waiting for an answer, I got up and poured two cups of tea, handing him his, then sitting down again with my own cup.

It was heavenly, warm and comforting. For there was no fire in this room, and I was beginning to feel the chill.

He took a deep breath and looked away, toward the table with photographs on it.

"Some days ago a body washed up on the strand just below us here. I don't know if you saw when you came, but well below us there's a crescent-shaped bay where the tide runs in. Quite striking, with sand instead of stones along the strand."

"It was too dark, but I could hear the sea."

"Yes. I've not grown used to that sound. To tell the truth." He turned back, busying himself with his cup, and I could see the courage it was taking to go on. "The body was in the uniform of the Welsh Fusiliers. It was difficult to know what had killed the soldier. Drowning, a fall from a cliff or even a passing ship. There were no visible wounds. And no identification."

"How sad," I said as he stopped again.

In for a penny, in for a pound. He'd told me that much, he knew he had to tell me the rest of it.

"I don't know where or how. But a rumor began to make the rounds that this was my brother, Tom. He'd been reported missing two years ago, his body never found. Nor was he reported as a prisoner. Just—missing. Presumed dead, in the end."

How many men at the Front had been blown to bits, with nothing to show what had happened to them? They were one of the tragedies of the war, the missing.

"Could you identify the body? *Was* it your brother?"

"God no, it wasn't Tom at all. But that didn't stop the rumors. Or the suspicion that he'd come home at last, and I'd killed him. For Rachel."

"Who would start such a rumor?" I asked, astonished. "And *why*?"

He shook his head. "God knows. Rachel swears it's for the property. This house and the farm and the sheep she runs. They belonged to her parents, and her brother, Matthew, was to inherit. She and Tom had lived in Swansea after they were married. But when Tom was reported missing, she came home again, unable to live in the house where they'd been so happy. Her brother was killed soon after Tom was lost, and that killed her parents. Literally. Her mother simply died, and two months later, her father followed. The house was hers. There had been some talk of selling up, because she found it hard to manage alone, but then I arrived, and with someone to help her, Rachel decided to keep the farm." He hesitated. "I don't know the real reason. Whether she was glad—or felt I needed a home." It had cost him to add that last. Pity went against the grain in this man.

"I've only just met her," I said, "but she doesn't appear to treat you as someone to be pitied."

"No." But he didn't sound convinced. "I do what I can."

"How does rumor claim you killed him? This dead man?"

"If you walk on from here, down toward the empty coast guard buildings, there's a sharp drop just where you can look down at the bay. Even a cripple could push someone over, if the victim wasn't expecting to be attacked." His voice was bitter. "It was said he reached the house after dark. Much as you've done, but on foot. And we rid ourselves of him before anyone else knew he'd come home." Setting his cup aside, he kept his face down so that I couldn't read it.

"And your neighbors are ready to believe such nonsense? It doesn't speak well for them. Or the village. Were you and your brother close?" I asked, trying to divert him from his embarrassment.

"Very. He was two years younger. With my help he'd escaped the mines too, finding work with one of the shipping companies in Cardiff. That's how he met Rachel. She was visiting friends there. They were married just six months before war was declared, and before he enlisted, they moved to Swansea so that she would be nearer to her parents." He shook his head. "It would have been for the best if he'd survived and I'd been the one who went missing."

"It wasn't your right to choose who lived and who died," I said firmly, unwilling to let him pity himself. "The question at the moment is, who might wish to hurt you or even Rachel? You must have some suspicions?"

"Don't you think I've asked myself that a hundred times? Rachel knows these people down here at the back of beyond. She tells me they know her well too, and still they gossip. That tells me it's because I've come. The people out here don't take to strangers. I came to help, and instead I've brought her trouble. It was the last thing I wished to do."

"Why did you choose to come here?" I'd seen the house in the valley, and his sister. But I wanted to hear what he had to say.

"I've told you. I had nowhere else to go."

"That's all very well and good. But surely you didn't simply drop a letter into the post, telling her which train you intended to take from Cardiff."

He grinned suddenly. "I think that's why you were so good for us at the clinic, Sister Crawford. You refused to tolerate nonsense." The grin vanished. "I'd kept in touch with her after Tom died. I was in France, there was nothing I could do, but at the very least I could try to help her make decisions. When her parents died, she told me how hard it was to manage by herself. And I offered whatever advice I could, what I thought Tom might advise. Rachel wrote to me before Christmas, telling me that now the war was over, she must either hire someone to help or sell up by spring. When I saw it was impossible to stay with my sister any longer, I told her that and asked if I could help in any way until she could find someone. Rachel answered by next post. She told me I could at least listen to her arguments against selling." There was a sudden glint of pride in his eyes. "I've managed to do more than that. The dog minds the sheep better than I could ever hope to do. And Rachel's training a second one. I know damn— almost nothing about sheep. I watched my mother knit, and that's about it. But I can tell the dogs what Rachel wants. They do the rest."

"Then she's right. There's your reason for the rumors. Someone hoped to buy Rachel out, and you've put paid to that possibility."

"Yes, it explains the rumors," he said impatiently, "but not the fact that others—who have no interest in the property—find it so easy to believe them."

"Has anyone made an actual offer for the property?"

"Not to my knowledge. I've come to the conclusion that whoever he is, he was expecting her to be desperate to sell by spring, and he could pick it up cheaply."

"Who did she turn to for advice before you arrived?"

"No one in particular, as far as I know. Rachel has always been rather independent."

Not jealousy, then. But I could hardly ask him that.

"*Are* you in serious danger of being taken up on charges of murder?" I put down my cup and looked directly at him.

"I don't know. That's what worries me, Sister—Bess. The people out here are entirely different from everyone in the valley. They see matters differently. Rachel tells me they wouldn't call in the police, but I'm not as sure about that as she is. It's almost as if they want to drive me out. To my face they're distant, but not actually unfriendly. I sometimes wonder if it would all go away if I just left."

"And you didn't recognize the body on the beach? It wasn't someone from the village?"

"No. Both Rachel and I also saw the body. It wasn't anyone either of us knew. But the problem is, we'd lie about that, wouldn't we? We'd deny that it was Tom. He wasn't a frequent visitor out here—he was working, and Rachel usually came to see her parents on her own. But they were married here, and surely the local people would have known it wasn't Tom. Couldn't have been."

"What did the police have to say? Or the Army? Surely if it was one of theirs, they'd know he was missing."

"Apparently not. The rector told us that inquiries had been made. But neither the police nor the Army came out to have a look at the body."

I didn't want to say the words aloud. That the dead man was someone like Hugh and the other Welsh soldiers, someone who had been released from a clinic and was no longer the concern of the Army. But surely the *police* would have looked into a suicide?

As if he'd read my thoughts, Hugh added, "He wasn't an amputee. For all I know, he fell off a passing ship or went over one of the cliffs out here."

I was beginning to agree with the Captain, that the local people must not care for strangers. Alive or dead. I was about to ask who had claimed the body when Rachel tapped at the door, then stepped into the room.

"It's rather late," she said, looking from the Captain to me, "and there's still the long drive in the dark back to Swansea. Perhaps I ought to ask Mr. Griffith across the way if he could put up Mr. Morgan. He's the only one with a spare room. But we have a guest room, Bess. We'd be happy to have you stay with us."

I couldn't tell if she was sincere in her offer or hoping I'd protest and be on my way.

The Captain smiled at her. "That's very kind, Rachel. Bess, will you stay? I can't promise a London dinner, but Rachel has made a fine stew."

He hadn't asked permission to call me by my Christian name, but I didn't say anything about that.

"I don't wish to impose. I came to see if you were well, and if your wound had healed properly."

Rachel smiled. "We so seldom have guests this time of year. It will be a treat. And if there's anything you need to borrow, I'm sure we'll manage."

I thought about that long drive in the dark over the ruts and uneven places in the road, and finally said, "If my driver is agreeable . . ."

"I've asked him. He's tired, he said, and is willing if you are."

"My valise is in the motorcar. I wasn't sure how long it would be before I found you."

Before the Captain could volunteer, she said, "I'll ask him to bring it in when I go across to speak to Mr. Griffith." She hesitated. "May I call you Bess too? It seems so formal to use Sister Crawford when there are only the three of us."

"Yes, please do." I could hardly say no, but I wondered why she was so willing to be friendly.

"Then it's settled. Hugh, will you keep Bess company while I see Mr. Griffith?"

I thought he was as uncertain as I was about her willingness for me to stay. Then I realized she might want to watch us together . . .

"I'm willing to pay for his lodging," I told her. "If that will make a difference to Mr. Griffith."

"Is there anything that I can do to help?" Hugh asked.

"No. It will only take a moment." She closed the door, and I heard her leave.

"We've had no guests. Not since I've been here. But she keeps the extra room ready." He looked toward the windows, rattling now in the wind. "Her parents sometimes took in paying guests in the summer. That was after Rachel and her brother had left, of course. Not many holidaymakers come this far, and they don't seem to stay long. There's no place to shop or bathe. Rachel has talked of opening an inn, to make the farm more viable. If I stay on. She believes that there might be an upsurge in the holiday trade." There was doubt in his voice.

I wondered if she had suggested the inn as a way to keep him here.

It was settled. Mr. Griffith asked rather a steep price for taking in Mr. Morgan. Reading between the lines, so to speak, I got the distinct feeling that he wanted no part of a guest, but because he had a spare room, he couldn't very easily get out of it under the circumstances. According to Rachel, he'd been put out when I agreed to the sum without arguing.

"It will do him good," she said, smiling. "He lives alone, and he's got so set in his ways that everyone has noticed. He probably won't sleep a wink for fear Mr. Morgan might abscond with the silver. On the other hand, Mr. Morgan might cheer him up a bit."

I had my doubts. My driver had been polite enough on the drive out from Swansea, but he was hardly gregarious. If anything, he was more likely to persuade Mr. Griffith that in the future, loneliness was preferable to a guest, whatever the sum offered.

Still, I smiled with her, but when I looked at Hugh, his expression was grim. I wondered if Mr. Griffith had believed those rumors, and Hugh wanted no part of being in debt to him.

After a very filling dinner of lamb stew in a thick crust and steamed dried apples, I said good night to my hosts and Mr. Morgan, pleading fatigue. But what I really wanted to do was to write a letter to Simon that could be posted for me in Swansea. It had been a quiet meal, for we hardly knew each other and could only make general conversation. I thought my driver was glad to escape, for he bade everyone a good night too, and left at the same time.

It was a comfortable room, the "guest room," small but cozy under the eaves. What in many houses of this size would be the Nursery. The two larger bedrooms were next to each other, and I wondered if that had fed the rumors. It was still not considered proper for a single man and a single woman to live together in the same house, brother and sister-in-law or not. But the war had changed many things, and this was one of them: the need for people to depend on someone other than their families, which had been so common in the past. There were usually aunts and uncles and cousins about to turn to in emergencies. Now women like Rachel had to make do.

Chintz curtains were hung at the small window, matching the chintz on the chair, and besides the narrow bed there was a tall chest with drawers. A curtain pulled across an alcove served as the wardrobe, and I hung my coat there. On the floor was a pretty rag rug of the type that one often saw in country cottages.

There was no large table at which to write my letter, but I had paper and a pen with me. The truth was, I hadn't told my parents that I was taking leave to travel into Wales. I'd expected to be back in England sooner rather than later, and then I could spend at least a few days in Somerset. The problem was, I'd had no idea just when that would be. Now I knew. I'd reach Swansea tomorrow and might even be lucky enough to find a late train to Cardiff, and then from Cardiff to Bristol. Simon or my mother could meet me there and drive me home. If I had the letter ready to post as soon as I got in to Swansea, it would arrive in Somerset in good time.

No need to worry anyone with any mention of a desolate coastline or of bodies washed up in the little bay or a man rumored to be a murderer sleeping next door to my room.

After thinking about it for a good ten minutes, I finally settled on a rather vague message.

Simon,

I've taken a brief leave from the clinic to look in on a patient who has had a very difficult time after several of the men from his village felt that suicide was more bearable than losing a limb. He was their commanding officer, and he had done his best to give them hope, to no avail. He is at present living with his widowed sister-in-law in the village out on the peninsula south of Swansea. Quite a different world, Wales, but it is very beautiful out here. Now my task is finished, my patient seems quite settled in here, and I shall be arriving in Bristol in two days' time, on my way home for a bit. It would be lovely if you or my mother could meet me in Bristol. I'll send a word as soon as I know

which train and when it will arrive. If neither of you is there, I'll
find my own way to the house, never fear.

Satisfied that there was nothing in the letter to worry anyone
at home, I signed it and found an envelope for it—during the war
I made certain I always had stationery so that I could stay in touch
with my family and friends. Then I realized that I had no stamp
with me.

Well, that was hardly a problem: I could find one in Swansea.

I sealed the letter, tucked it in my handbag for the morning, then
prepared for bed.

I *was* tired. The journey to the valley and then out here had been
long and difficult. The loss of hope in men I'd known, men I'd done
my best to help heal, cheering their victories and commiserating
with their defeats—and there had been too many of those as they'd
learned to cope with their wounds—had dampened my spirits more
than I was willing to admit. The war was over. The dying wasn't.

I opened the curtain as soon as I'd blown out my lamp and
looked out at the night. I could just see where the land ended, the
darkness of the sea beyond melting into the night sky so that it was
impossible to tell how broad the bay might be or how high we were.

I could see something moving out there, to my left. As my eyes
adjusted to the ambient light, I realized that a dozen or so sheep
were penned closer to the house, and I wondered if they were ewes
about to give birth. Most were just white lumps where they had lain
down in the shelter of the pen wall, while a few moved about, as if
restless. I could just make out to my right the end of the cottage
across the way, and the gleam of starlight on the metal of Mr. Morgan's motorcar.

Finally turning away, I climbed into bed. Rachel had thoughtfully given me a small hot water bottle to cut the chill, since there

was no hearth in my room, and I stretched my toes gratefully toward the warmth at the foot of my bed.

It wasn't long before I slept. I woke up with a start about an hour later from a dream that the pit tip was sliding down toward me and, try as I would, I couldn't run fast enough to get clear of the inexorable horror that was on my heels. Quite literally. For I could even hear it.

And then I realized that Captain Williams was coming slowly up the stairs, his crutches making a low thumping sound. I heard Rachel say from the foot of the stairs, "Sleep well, Hugh."

A dog gave a soft, excited bark, and the outer door opened and closed as she took the two of them out for the last time.

The male was a working dog, and he'd taken his place on a pallet set out for him in the kitchen while we ate our meal. The female, with more white on her face and throat, was younger and a little more excitable, but even she had settled after a word from Rachel.

The Captain's door opened and shut, and ten minutes later, Rachel came back with the dogs, walked them through to the kitchen, and shortly afterward came briskly up the stairs in her turn, closing her own door.

The house fell silent but for the sound of the wind rising outside, and I soon drifted into sleep once more, this time without dreams.

Early the next morning I awoke to the sound of rain lashing at the window, but clouds had obscured the dawn, and it was still so dark outside that I couldn't judge the hour. I reached for my little watch, lying on the tiny table by my bed, and was startled to see that it was nearly seven. In the room next to mine, I could hear the Captain humming, presumably as he shaved. It brought back memories of the Welsh patients singing at Christmastide.

I stretched one more time, then got up, washed my face, and

brushed my hair before putting on a fresh uniform. It was wrinkled but clean.

When I came downstairs, Rachel already had the cooker heating nicely, and the kettle was on the way to a boil.

"I'm so sorry," I said, greeting her. "I'm usually awake well before this."

She smiled at me over her shoulder. "I wouldn't know what to do if you offered to help. I'm so used to doing everything for myself." She glanced at the windows as a particularly hard burst of rain beat against the glass. "Not a very pleasant day for travel. The roads will be impossible."

"Mr. Morgan is not a great one for conversation, but he's a good driver. We'll manage." We'd had to raise our voices a little over the sound of the rain. I could see it blowing sideways before the wind, sheet after sheet sweeping across the headland. "Is such weather common out here?" I asked.

"Yes, there isn't anything but water between us and the Bristol Channel. The storms sweep across, gathering strength, then break over us. Still, it helps us stay mild enough to farm and keep animals. Cattle are still driven from here into Swansea. The old drover roads in Wales were famous. They even drove goats and geese. And they made them special shoes to wear, to protect their feet. I saw a pair on display once." She bent down and took a pan of bacon out of the oven.

That explained the state of the road yesterday. More hooves than wheels must pass over it regularly.

"Where do you go from here?" she went on, setting the pan where it would stay warm. "Are there more names on your list of patients?"

"Sadly, no. But it means I'll be able to spend a few days at home before returning to the clinic."

"Hugh tells me that only one of the men who went back to the valley is still alive. It's upset him rather badly."

"I'm sure it has. I didn't want to give him such news, but he asked. Is he any stronger since he came here, do you think?"

I needed to know. And I was asking about his mental attitude as much as about his physical well-being.

"I think so. Perhaps it's my imagination, but the air here seems to have given him a better appetite. And he feels the need to be useful, which is a good thing in my view." She frowned. "His sister wanted him to keep to the house and mind the children. I know she had her hands full, but I think she also resented the fact that Tom and Hugh escaped the pits. Her cousin has been ill, and that's worrying for her as well. During the war, Hugh had his pay sent to her, and Tom did what he could. But it's never enough, is it? Not with small children. Still . . ."

She let her voice trail off as she finished slicing the bread. I thought she might be feeling a little guilty that she was benefiting from her sister-in-law's loss. I also wondered how much Rachel had had in common with her valley husband's family. In outlook, in language, in heritage, so very different. I'd noticed that she hadn't used the sister's name, she hadn't said, *Poor Ahnhaireid*. Or *Mary*.

Changing the subject, she said, "Hugh's taken the dogs out to have a look at the ewes. They're clever at finding shelter in all kinds of weather, but this is near to lambing time for some of them. And so we keep those close in." She paused on her way to the pantry. "I worry about him, I'll be honest. That wind is fierce, I don't see how he stays on his feet. But I can't tell him that, can I? He insists on doing whatever he can to help me, and he manages his crutches well enough. I mustn't say anything, it would be wrong. But the ground is uneven, and it's so easy to fall. I'm convinced he has, a time or two. I see the signs on the back or shoulders of his coat, and I turn a blind eye."

"He needs to test the limits of his ability for himself," I agreed as she brought back a bowl of brown eggs. "Otherwise, he'll feel useless. And hopeless."

"All the same, it's hard to watch him struggle." She began to set the table. "Was he close to those men back in the valley? He doesn't talk about them at all, and this too I'm afraid to ask him. When he wrote to me about coming, I had the strongest feeling that he was close to sinking into a depression. And of course his sister never writes. Which means I can't ask her anything."

"Yes, they were very close. He'd known them before the war, and he'd got most of them through the war. He took their deaths hard. I'm glad he isn't back there, to be honest." I told her what I'd learned. "Sadly we can heal wounds but not spirits. There was so little work waiting there for men who had lost limbs. They couldn't go back into the pit. And pity is the last thing they wanted. Or charity."

She turned to look out at the rain. There was a kitchen garden just beyond the windows, and I could see wide puddles standing here and there. "I wasn't offering either pity or charity when I asked Hugh to come. I truly needed all the help I could find. But this is such an out-of-the-way part of Wales, men don't come here looking for work. I love it, of course. Many people wouldn't. For Hugh, I think it's as far from the valleys as he can get."

She went again to the pantry to fill the little pitcher with milk for our tea, then said, "I thought that being away from daily reminders of those men would be enough." She hesitated, then went on. "But there have been rumors. Did he tell you? They've troubled both of us."

"I can't understand how they got started."

"Nor do I. That man on the strand was not Tom. I'm as certain of that as any wife could ever be. But if Hugh or I had killed him, we'd be sure to say that, wouldn't we? And there was no identification to prove who he was. Poor man. No one ever claimed the body." She looked up at me, wanting to read in my face that I believed her.

I wondered if the man had chosen the sea as a cleaner death than leaving his body for his family to find.

"There were no—wounds on the body?"

"He'd been in the water. And the fish . . ." Shaking her head, she said, "It was rather ugly. But Tom was taller, like Hugh, and this man was more compact. Even that was hard to judge. Still, looking at him, I didn't feel anything, not even a doubt."

I'd seen drowned bodies. The water took so much away that had once been familiar.

"Who could dislike you enough to cause so much trouble?" I asked. "For it must be you. The Captain hasn't been here long enough to make enemies, has he?" I couldn't really believe that being a stranger could make Hugh a target of animosity.

She took a deep breath, her hands dropping the eggs into a pan of cold water, but her mind on her problems, not our breakfast.

"There's a neighbor—well, he lives out on the Down. That's beyond the cottage where Mr. Morgan stayed the night. Those houses are part of the village too. His wife died in the influenza epidemic last year. She'd been in poor health, and she wasn't able to put up much of a fight. At Christmas this year—before Hugh arrived— Barry Dunhill suggested it might be easier for both of us if we married. He could help me with the sheep and I could keep house for him and his daughter. I liked his wife and the little girl, Anna. But I've never really thought of him as a husband. He's nothing like Tom, I don't know that I could have come to care for him even if we'd tried. And so I just said it was too soon to think about the future. He wasn't very happy when Hugh came. Still, I hardly think he'd start such rumors. It's not as if he and I had been close."

In other parts of England, it would have taken longer for Rachel to feel she could confide in someone who must seem to be a perfect stranger to her. But who else could she discuss Hugh with, out here? Or the rumors? Or even Anna's father?

And yet, talking to me seemed to be a relief. As if it had all been pent up too long.

"How old is Mr. Dunhill's daughter?"

"She's twelve. Just the age where she needs her mother most. I can understand why he thought we might marry, for Anna's sake. And she knows me, it wouldn't have been like bringing a stranger into the family." She smiled wryly. "I had love once. I know what love feels like."

She turned to put the eggs onto the stove as the kettle boiled.

I heard the outer door open just then, banging against the entry wall, and then two very wet dogs came bounding into the kitchen.

Rachel smiled. "They always know when I'm cooking eggs."

The door had been slammed shut against the wind, and after a moment I heard the thump of crutches as Hugh came down the passage. He was carrying a dripping coat and hat, and I took them to drape over the backs of two chairs. "All's well," he told her, then greeted me. There was a wariness in his face as he turned toward me.

I thought he might be feeling a little embarrassed about my coming, although in truth he'd more or less sent for me. But by the time I'd reached him, his circumstances *had* changed . . .

Rachel said, "Did you tell Mr. Morgan to come straight over? The tea is steeping, and the eggs are nearly done. I've only to toast the bread."

He was silent. She looked up at him, waiting for his answer, the bread knife in her hands, poised over a dish of butter.

"He's not there," the Captain said slowly, his eyes on her face.

"Not there?" I asked, rising from where I'd gone to sit out of the way.

"He left in the night. Griffith didn't hear him go, but when he looked out this morning, he noticed that the motorcar wasn't there. He went back to the room where Morgan had slept, and it appeared that he'd left in some haste."

"But I hadn't paid him the rest of his fee for bringing me here. And there was also what he'd earn, taking me back to Swansea." I stood there, stunned.

How *was* I to get back to Swansea, much less Cardiff and Bristol?

There was silence in the small kitchen, except for the sound of one of the dogs lapping water from its bowl.

Into the silence, I asked, "Is there anyone else out here on the headland who could drive me to Swansea?"

"No." The Captain was still looking at Rachel. "There's no one with a motorcar. And the horse carts aren't up to such a journey. We're isolated out here."

"Then what am I to do?"

"I don't know," he said, turning to me. "Of course you can stay here. As long as you like. That's not a problem."

"That's very kind," I answered, "but I'm expected back at the clinic. And I'd hoped to spend a few days with my parents before that. Surely someone must go out for supplies? Or there's a van that brings things to sell?"

It was Rachel who answered. "We make do as much as we can. And then we send for supplies." She turned to lift the eggs off the stove. "The tea will be cold, if we don't sit down. And the eggs are ready."

"I can't understand why Mr. Morgan would simply drive away and leave me here," I said, still striving to comprehend why I had been abandoned like this. "It makes no sense."

"He might have been worried about the storm," Rachel said doubtfully, putting the eggs in a dish and setting it on the table.

"He had only to come across the road and knock at the door. The dogs would have heard him, even if we hadn't, and started to bark."

"You didn't give him the impression that you might wish to stay?" the Captain asked.

"Of course I didn't. You were here in the kitchen when we said good night, and Rachel told him that she would make breakfast for the two of us."

"That's true," Hugh said, setting his crutches aside and sitting down. "I agree, something's wrong."

I poured a cup of tea, then passed it to him and filled two more for Rachel and myself. "If he was suddenly taken ill, he could have asked me to drive him to Swansea. Coming down, I remember telling him that I could drive." Of course he might not have believed it . . .

A thought struck me. "Did either of you mention those rumors about Tom?" I couldn't imagine that they would bring it up. But I had to ask. Mr. Morgan hadn't struck me as a man who could be frightened off by gossip, but then I'd only known him for the better part of a day. Still, if he *had* been concerned, he could have refused to stay the night.

"It was the last thing on my mind," Rachel said, for she had given him his tea in the kitchen. "It's not the sort of thing I'd dream of telling a stranger."

But Hugh had told me, last night. Had it been necessary? I tried to remember how that conversation between us in the parlor had gone. *It isn't safe . . .*

"What about Mr. Griffith? Would he do such a thing? He hadn't wanted to take Mr. Morgan in." That still didn't explain my driver leaving in the middle of the night rather than marching straight back across the road and telling us he wasn't staying here after all. "What else did Mr. Griffith tell you?"

"That was all of it. He seemed to be upset about Morgan's departure as well. He kept saying, 'I don't know what could have got into the man.' I expect he was afraid you'd ask him to return the money you'd paid him."

"If he frightened Mr. Morgan away on purpose, I really ought to do just that," I replied in exasperation.

But what if Mr. Morgan *had* come to the door looking for me? And because of the wind, no one had heard him? I looked at the waiting dogs. *They* would have heard him, even if we hadn't.

Hugh understood my uncertainty. He said, "Griffith is an odd sort. But I've never heard anything against him. He keeps to himself and doesn't appear to have much in common with the other villagers."

"His wife was a Morton, the cottage belonged to her family," Rachel added. "They were very close. I expect that's why he stayed in the cottage after she died."

We ate our breakfast in silence, while the dogs shared the extra eggs that would have been served to my driver, wagging their tails all the while. I know, because I could feel them sweeping back and forth across the rungs of my chair.

Finishing my tea and the last bit of my toast, I said, "You've been so kind, but I can't stay until someone happens along who would be willing to carry me to Swansea. Or even to another village, where I might find someone else to take me the rest of the way. How *do* you send for supplies?"

"Someone takes a list to one of the villages above us, and it's passed on to the next village as soon as may be. Then a van brings it out from Bishopton." Rachel smiled. "In my parents' day, there was a peddler who appeared from time to time, carrying whatever he thought he might sell out here. Flour, sugar, nails, seeds for the garden. Vegetables and potatoes and bacon. Tins. Packets of tea. I bought ribbons from him once, and Mama bought embroidery threads. A pair of gray horses with large yellow teeth pulled his caravan, and they would nip if we got too close."

I looked at the window, where the rain was still coming down in sheets. I couldn't very well ask Hugh or Rachel to go anywhere in such weather—or try to go anywhere myself.

"Is there a post box here in the village?" I could send a letter to the firm where I'd hired Mr. Morgan, asking them to send another driver for me.

"I'm afraid not," she said apologetically. "When there's post for us, someone brings it down from the next village but one. And if we have a letter, it waits until there's someone to post it for us."

I was beginning to realize just how isolated this village was. Such a far cry from my home in Somerset, where we took the post and shops and carriages for granted—where traveling twenty-five miles was nothing.

"Then I'll write to the firm in Swansea, and ask them for another driver. We can post it at the next opportunity." I remembered. "Except that I don't have any stamps with me."

"Rachel must have stamps," the Captain said. "I'm so sorry. Bess."

I smiled. "You couldn't possibly know that Mr. Morgan was going to desert me. But it does look as if I'll be staying with you for a few more days."

"I'll be glad of the company," Rachel said, making an effort for my sake, which was very kind of her. "You can tell me about the new fashions in London."

She'd changed the subject, hoping to relieve my worry, and I tried to act as if being stranded on a rain-swept headland was a commonplace thing. As we cleared away, we talked about London, and all the while in the back of my mind was that letter I'd written to Simon. I'd intended to mail it in Swansea before I took the next train to Cardiff. It was still here, in my kit. And no one in Somerset knew I'd left the clinic . . .

I tried to tell myself it was just as well I hadn't posted it. I wouldn't have been on that train into Bristol. Either Simon or my mother or both would have been there, on the platform, waiting. When I didn't appear, they'd meet the next train, thinking I might have missed the earlier one. Then they would begin to worry.

At least they'd have had a starting point for the cavalry, although even the cavalry would still have a hard time finding me. I smiled to myself at the image of the Army scouring Wales for me, the Colonel Sahib directing the operation.

The smile vanished as the thought underscored just how isolated we were out here. The cavalry would have to find the right valley, and then the house of Captain Williams's sister. Would Matron think to tell them about the Welsh soldiers? She believed I was on my way to Somerset. And from the clinic I'd taken the train to London, not Wales. Mrs. Hennessey had no idea where I'd gone when I left her house. She too probably believed I was on my way to Somerset.

My mood was as bleak as the morning outside the kitchen windows.

When we'd finished with the washing up, Hugh and Rachel went out again to look at the sheep. The rain hadn't let up, coming down with almost tropical force, reminding me of the monsoons in India.

I went to the parlor, where I'd been taken last night, and tried to look out. Through the curtains of rain, I could just see the Down where Anna and her father lived. The bay was out of sight, but even so it was obvious how the land dropped off just beyond the Griffith cottage across the road. To my far right was the village church, stonework dark with rain, and that odd square tower on the west front, looking as if it hadn't quite been finished enough even to call a tower. Beyond were other cottages, whose roof lines I could just make out. There wasn't a soul in sight, everyone keeping in and dry.

I considered going across to Mr. Griffith's cottage to see if I could find out anything more about Mr. Morgan's departure in the middle of the night. But he probably wouldn't come to the door, for fear I was there to ask for my money.

And so began what was going to be a very long day.

CHAPTER 5

RACHEL AND HUGH had been gone for nearly three-quarters of an hour when there came a loud knock at the door.

I'd been sitting in the kitchen, staring out at the storm, wondering how long it might last and what I could do about my circumstances as soon as it moved on. My first thought was that Rachel had come back with a lamb that was in trouble from the weather and couldn't manage the door.

And so I hurried down the passage to open it for her.

But it wasn't Rachel on the doorstep. It was a man I'd not seen before.

"There's a small boat in trouble off the—" He broke off as he realized that I wasn't Rachel.

"So it's true," he said, frowning. "They told me there was a Sister come to Rachel's house."

"I was in charge of Captain Williams's care after he was wounded," I replied coolly. "I'm afraid Mrs. Williams and the Captain have gone to look for her sheep."

I opened the door wider, expecting him to step inside out of the cold wind, but he stayed where he was, wet to the skin, his hair plastered to his scalp.

Gesturing over his shoulder, he said, "There's a small boat in trouble off the bay. We can't get out to her, but I've come to borrow the Captain's field glasses, to see how many are aboard."

"I have no way of knowing where he keeps them. But I'll have a look."

I glanced in the parlor, but there was no sign of the field glasses. Turning, I went upstairs to the Captain's room. It was very old-fashioned, and I thought it must have belonged to Rachel's parents. The wallpaper was a pale blue with white and darker blue morning glory vines, and the coverlet on the brass-framed bed was the same darker shade, while the curtains at the windows and the chintz covering the chair were white trimmed in the darker shade. There was a framed photograph on the wall, but I made a point of not looking closely at it.

I spotted the field glasses on the windowsill, caught them up, and hurried back down the stairs to the man waiting there. The damp chill from outside had spread into the entry, and rain was puddling on the floor just over the threshold.

"Thank you," he said, and then hesitated. "Did you know the Captain's brother? Thomas?"

"I'm afraid not," I said.

"A pity," he answered, and was gone, head down against the rain. I got the door shut, and went into the kitchen to find something to wipe up the puddle the man had left.

His question lingered in the air, and I wondered why—with an emergency on the doorstep, so to speak—he'd asked about Thomas. It indicated how pervasive the rumors were. Did he think I might know something? Or did he wonder if I'd come all this way to find out what had become of Tom Williams?

Ten minutes later, the kitchen door opened, and Rachel came in, dripping madly. "It's terrible out there," she said, "but the ewes are huddled in the shelter of the stone wall around the pen. They look rather wretched, but they're all right." She began to remove her wet things.

"That's good news, indeed," I said, handing her a dry towel. "But before you take off your Wellingtons, you had a visitor just now. He came to borrow the Captain's field glasses. There's a small boat in trouble in the bay."

She stared at me. "Oh, dear God. There's no hope of reaching it in this storm. It would be unsafe to try even if we had a lifeboat." She hesitated, looking out the window just beside her, as if judging the wisdom of going out again to see for herself. And then she began to button up her coat and put the heavy man's rain gear back on her head. "I expect I ought to go have a look. The last time a body came ashore, they blamed us for it. Have you seen Hugh?"

"No, I expect he's still out."

She nodded and was gone. I went up the stairs again, but from my window I couldn't see the bay, much less a boat in trouble out there.

Finally, I caught up my own coat, and my woolen hat in place of my QAIMNS cap, and went out myself.

After I'd crossed the road, head down against the wind, and walked on to where the hedge marked the path to the Down and the bay beyond, I stopped short at the sight before me, in spite of the wind almost taking my breath away as I turned into it.

The bay curved in, a long crescent of seething water just now, covering the strand and clawing greedily for the land itself. I could see the waves breaking high in the air, and then beyond them, to one side of the wide mouth of the bay, a boat caught in the currents there, some pushing it in, others sucking it out, as if deciding the fate of the little craft, spinning it back and forth like a game of shuttlecock. It had a single mast, but the sail hung from it too battered to be of any use. I couldn't tell if the craft was empty or if there was someone on board.

Half a dozen men and women had collected near where the waves were crashing in, and one of them was trying to use the Captain's field glasses. But the boat wouldn't stay still long enough for the man to focus on it well, for I saw him try several times.

The others were shouting at him over the racket the incoming waves were making—I could hear the sound of voices in spite of the wind, but not a word of what they were saying.

Half a dozen more people were hurrying from the scattered cottages out there. Rachel had said these were still part of the village, but they looked forlorn and vulnerable on the high Down.

And then I glimpsed Rachel coming out from the edge of the embankment where the track to the other houses and to the strand ran on to the sea. She was hurrying too, head down, anxious. I watched as she reached the cluster of people, and wasn't surprised to see them ignore her.

Behind me I heard someone swear, and turning quickly I saw the Captain had come quietly up beside me, the dripping dogs at his heel.

"She should have stayed away," he said. "She thinks they'll forget the past soon, but they're not the sort to let it go. Small-minded and insular." I knew what he was saying, having had some little experience with small-village narrow-mindedness.

"Shall I go down, to keep her company?" I asked. "And someone came to borrow your field glasses. I gave them to him. Was that all right?"

"No, it won't help matters if you go," he said wearily. "As for the glasses, I'd have done the same."

"Will the little boat make it into the bay?"

"His only hope is to beach himself on the strand, and worry later about damage to the boat," he answered, the wind whipping at his words. I could see he was having trouble with his crutches too, as this narrow space by the hedges tunneled the wind.

A cry went up from the watchers, and I turned quickly to see what was happening.

The mast must have snapped, for it was lying across the boat now, the sail dragging heavily in the water. Like a rudder—and in the worst possible place for one, broadside to the gunwales. The effect was to spin the craft slowly, like a child's toy top winding down.

And I still couldn't see if it was empty—or occupied.

But if there was someone on board, why wasn't he trying to do anything to save himself?

Was he hurt so badly that he couldn't help himself?

If so, he was surely going to drown.

I shivered.

We stood there watching for what seemed like hours, the little craft struggling to stay afloat. I was wet to the skin, and shaking in the cold wind, but I couldn't turn away.

And Hugh stood behind me, bracing himself on his crutches, breaking a little of the wind's force. Rachel was still below, and once or twice I saw her turn and look our way. But if she knew more than we did, there was no way she could let us know.

Finally, almost in slow motion, the boat capsized, having taken on too much water, and it spun around twice, briefly anchored by that dragging mast and sail before it began to break up from the battering it was taking.

I saw what I thought was a leg flung into the air, and almost at once, a head bobbing for a few seconds. Then man and boat went under. And didn't come up again.

Another cry had gone up from the watchers down by the water. The man with the field glasses strained forward, trying to see what had become of the drowning man. The hull reappeared, upside down, and then that too began to splinter and break apart.

The man with the glasses lowered them, then he looked over his shoulder, back toward the cottage next to where we were standing.

I couldn't tell if he was looking for us or toward the rear of the cottage.

I heard a man's voice near at hand shouting something, and I realized that someone had been posted by the cottage as a lookout. But he, like the rest of us, could offer no hope.

After a while many of the watchers began to trudge back to where they'd come from. A handful stayed on, in the event something could be done, there to raise the alarm. The man in the boat would eventually find his way to the strand—or be taken out to sea. There was nothing anyone could do to help.

Their faces as they turned away were drawn and tired, and they were silent.

I turned to start back to the house, and after a moment Hugh followed me and we made our way there with the dogs pacing in front of us. I tried not to notice the effort he was making, to keep going against the wind. Or his grim expression.

We left our wet coats in the kitchen to dry in the warmth from the cooker. I went up to change into dry clothes, then put the kettle on, to make tea.

Hugh was still not down, and I thought he must be sitting there in his room, where no one could watch him, giving in to his exhaustion.

By the time the kettle had reached a boil, Rachel came in, looking tired and dispirited.

"Did you see?" she asked, taking in the wet coats draped over chairs and adding her own to the jumble. For the table could seat eight easily in this large kitchen.

"Yes," I answered. "It was hopeless. And so very sad. He can't possibly survive."

"Is Hugh all right?" She drew his field glasses out from under her coat and set them on the table.

"Frustrated just as I was by the fact that there was nothing anyone could do."

She nodded, then said, "Thank you for making tea. I'll just change and be right down. But pour your own, if you like, don't wait. And there are biscuits on the shelf just there. A plate on the dresser there."

I began to set the biscuits on the plate, all the while replaying in my mind what I'd seen out there on the bay.

It hadn't occurred to me then. I'd been too drawn into the tragedy unfolding to think clearly. But now it seemed rather odd to me that the man in the boat had made no effort to signal the watchers, or even wave his arms in a desperate plea for help that had no way of reaching him. It was human nature to fight to live, although there was no rescue boat drawn up on the strand below the Down. Even if there had been a dozen boats, it would have been impossible to launch one. Even I, with so little experience of the sea, could understand that. The faces of the watchers as they turned away had been drawn and tired, and they had been silent. That moment when the boat went over had touched all of us, somehow.

So why hadn't its occupant at least tried to cry for help, or show that he was alive and in dire straits?

Because the man was already dead.

I felt cold, even there in the warmth of the kitchen.

They came for me, when the little boat had finally washed up on the shore, close enough that men could wade out and beach her on the strand. It was past three, and the light was going. The sun hadn't appeared all day, but the wind was dropping a little.

I pulled on my coat, and with Hugh behind me once more, I set out down that long twisting lane that eventually turned to cross the Down. There I continued on the path to the shore.

It was a long way for a man on crutches, and would be even

harder coming back, but I knew better than to suggest that Hugh stay above and wait.

When I got closer to the wreckage of the boat, I saw the man. I hadn't been told he'd been pulled from the sea as well. But then I could see that his right foot was tangled in the ropes from the sail. He had never gone far from the little boat . . .

I bent over the body, observing him as I would a patient brought into a forward aid station. He was in uniform. A Corporal. But his regimental insignia was missing. It was something that I, a soldier's daughter, would look for, because the regiment was itself a form of identification—where a man had served and often where he'd come from.

He was small in stature, with dark hair and a thin build.

And dead. Possibly had been, just as I'd expected, before the boat overturned. Rigor had passed, and the gash on his head, just behind the ear, had been washed clean by the sea. Still, it was ugly and deep. I couldn't tell if he'd fallen and struck his head on the gunwale or even the mast. That would explain why the little boat had sailed on erratically with no one at the helm, until it was caught by the storm and brought up here.

I was also thinking that the gash was where an attacker might have struck him from behind when the man going through his clothing said, "There's nothing in his pockets to tell us who he is. Poor soul."

Someone behind me said, "That's not a very seaworthy craft. Look at the state of the wood. And there's rot in the mast. See there?"

Another man was untangling the dead man's foot and dragging him higher up on the strand. "What are we to do with him?"

I reached for the dead man's hand, cold as the sea itself, to feel for a pulse. It was perfunctory, I knew I'd find no heartbeat.

A woman said, "He had no chance, with that cut on his head. A kinder way to die than drowning."

I straightened. "I'm sorry. There's no sign of life."

They nodded in silent agreement. But the formalities had been observed.

One of the men spoke. He was about forty, lean and strong, with a square jaw and high forehead. "Was it the sea, then, Sister?"

"I honestly can't say. A small boat in a storm, the mast swinging—losing one's footing? I don't know that anyone could be sure. He must have been alone in the boat. It really isn't large enough for two."

Hugh said, "A man doesn't go out in a boat without carrying some identification, so that his family can be notified if he's lost. And where's his insignia?"

But the others ignored him.

This wasn't a fishing community, but these men lived near the sea and understood it. The man who'd asked me if it was the sea clambered aboard the wreckage and looked around. "Nothing," he said at last. "Nothing to show where she's from, this boat." He nearly fell getting out again, and someone caught his arm to steady him. He nodded his thanks, then turned to stare at Hugh. "A man wearing a uniform and Army boots wouldn't put out to sea this time of year. He'd have proper gear. Makes no sense."

His voice, raised to carry over the wind, couldn't conceal the sinister threat in his words.

"This one did," I said shortly. "How he got to be in this boat and what happened to it tells me he knew nothing about the sea. With a storm of this magnitude coming in? It was madness."

There was silence around me.

"Surely this boat must have come from somewhere around here." I waited, scanning the grim faces forming a half circle around me. They stared back at me. "Someone should inform the police. They can ask around on the other side of the peninsula. I don't know the currents here, but it might have come from one of the villages there."

They didn't particularly care for the suggestion. I had the feeling that nothing of a criminal nature happened out here at the far end of the peninsula. And if it did, these men dealt with it. Without involving the police in Swansea, or whoever had jurisdiction over the village.

And another thought came unbidden: if the police came, perhaps I'd be able to beg a lift back to Swansea with them.

"We ought to pull the boat higher, where the tides can't reach it," I said, "and take the body to some shelter. There's no doctor close by?"

I'd already guessed as much—they'd summoned me, after all, a stranger. But there should be some more official examination.

"Not close by," the man who'd clambered over the wreckage informed me. "But where to put the body, if we take it up?"

That was a quandary—no police station, no doctor's surgery. They couldn't put the dead Corporal in the church.

"What about Ellen's cot?" one of the bystanders asked.

There was a short conversation among the men. I couldn't hear most of it. There was mention of a worm. And then they seemed to come to an agreement.

Then one man asked, "What will Ellen say?"

There was a prolonged silence.

"He'll be gone before ever she comes again," someone else replied.

"Who is Ellen?" I asked.

But no one answered me.

Someone produced a blanket. I thought a woman had brought it in the hope it might be needed. It was, but not in the way she'd intended. They laid him in it. Then four of the most stalwart men took a corner each while others pulled the boat higher.

Behind us the surf was still pounding in, and the wind whipped at my skirts as the pathetic cortege began to climb up toward the road.

I fell back to the tail of the line, out of their way. Hugh soon dropped back to join me. I was sure his shoulders must be aching from the crutches, but I said only, "It must be a beautiful little bay, when it's calm."

"It is. The first day I was here, Rachel took me to the overlook. You must see that too, before you go."

"When the police come."

He smiled grimly. "I expect they'll bury him in the churchyard, just as they did the last one."

"At least they can't blame his death on you. They can't claim that *this* man might be Tom as well."

"We'll see."

I wanted to ask him about the worm the men had mentioned. It was an odd term to use in regard to a dead body at this stage. But I could see he was having trouble with the increasingly noticeable incline.

I slowed my own pace, but he said sharply, "Keep going."

"I'm sorry," I retorted. "Nursing doesn't prepare one for Down-climbing."

He managed a laugh at that.

We had a long way to go.

By the time we reached the top, I was breathing hard, and out of the corner of my eye, I could see that Hugh was red-faced and haggard.

I stopped, turning to look back the way we'd come. It *was* quite a lovely view, even with the massed storm clouds and the waves crashing in. I couldn't quite decide what I was looking at, what body of water. It was hard to get a feeling for where the headlands were pointing, with barely any sunlight to help me find the points of the compass. Rachel had said there was nothing out there but the Bristol Channel. She would know. When my breathing was slower, I said, "I live in Somerset. Far from the sea. It's really incredible to watch, isn't it? You grew up in the valleys. Do you find it as amazing?"

"Yes." He was slowly catching his own breath.

"On a clear day, you must be able to see for miles."

The cortege had disappeared from view.

"I don't think I can keep up with them," I said doubtfully as I walked on, past the hedge and into the road. The cortege was at the head of a long downslope that seemed to disappear into the heavy clouds. "Going down is all right, I expect. Coming back will be beyond me."

"I don't think they want you to follow."

"Will they take care of him all right? Do I *need* to be there?" I was still concerned about the worms they'd spoken of.

"They'll see to him. I don't think you should worry."

In reality I thought I'd be able to follow them without much trouble. The incline was nothing like the lane up from the beach. But I knew that if I went, Hugh would insist on going too. Still—where were they heading?

"Well, then, I could use a cup of tea. I'm cold through and through."

We turned toward the house, and I could ask my question now. "I heard someone say something about worms. If the body is properly cared for, it's too soon for worms."

Hugh smothered a grin. "Actually it's an odd-shaped island off the tip of the peninsula just there." He thought about it for a moment. "I'm sure you'd describe it as a turtle with a raised head. My brother, Tom, went exploring out there once. It's tidal, you'll be cut off if you aren't careful. And there's a land bridge of sorts. Local families may call it The Worm, but it's actually the head and body of a great serpent or dragon to them. In the days of coastal raiders, centuries ago, this strange-looking creature frightened them off. When the storm moves out, you'll see it. Tom talked about it several times."

Then why mention it in regard to the poor man's body? I didn't care for the sound of that. Had someone suggested tossing him back into the sea? Where the tide would take him out again and he would no longer be the community's responsibility?

But I said nothing. I was the stranger, I must have misunderstood. Maybe Ellen's cot was near the worm. Worm.

After drying off, I came down to find Rachel and Hugh in a soft conversation. They looked up—almost guiltily, I thought—as I reached the door to the front room.

Rachel said quickly, "I've kept back our meal. You must be starving by now. Hugh was just telling me about the poor man on the boat."

"It was sad. But there was nothing to be done for him," I said.

"Do you—was it an accident? Or—or something else?" she asked as the two of us walked down the passage to the kitchen, leaving Hugh in his chair. I thought he must be too exhausted to eat, but he'd make the effort.

"I couldn't tell. It's best for the police to handle his death."

"I don't think they'll come. Not for a drowning. That's how they'll see it," she told me, taking food out of the warming cupboard and carrying it to the table.

"Is it that? Or the reluctance of the families out there to send for them?" I remembered suddenly that my driver had left in the middle of the night. A stranger . . .

There was no smuggling out here. And no whisky stills, like

those one might stumble across in out-of-the-way places in Scotland. What made these people out here so *clannish*?

I decided to ask Rachel outright.

She considered the question. "I don't think it's because they're doing anything wrong. People have lived on this peninsula for ages. There are places here where all sorts of ancient artifacts have been found, belonging to quite primitive people. Caves with bones dyed red. Bits of pottery, even a line drawn on a cave wall. My father had seen some of them. He must have been rather wild as a boy, because he'd seen the cromlechs and explored the caves. That was before he met my mother, at any rate. But as for the people here, I think it's just that they're used to the isolation and don't see it as important as you do, having grown up with modern conveniences like police and hospitals and lots of people around to help. They're used to making do."

I took the plates she handed me and set them round the table after spreading the cloth across it, then dealt with the utensils. "Your parents lived here. Your mother had her children here. Was there no doctor or midwife?"

"There was an older woman who came to help. Gwennie, her name was. My father went for her when the pains began. Mama managed just fine." It was said with a smile.

I smiled in return and let the matter drop. But I wondered how the children were educated and what the rector of that small church must think about all this. I hadn't seen him down by the strand. Or I should say, I didn't recognize him—most of the men were dressed alike in heavy work clothes against the weather. I wouldn't have seen a collar.

"Hugh was telling me about The Worm."

She laughed. "Our one claim to importance. Yes, it's a landmark, in this part of Wales. I think it's on the sea charts. My father told me that. Seabirds nest out there. Guillemots, razorbills, fulmars. Shags. The only time I ever saw my father really angry was when he thought my brother had gone out there to hunt for eggs. There's only a very short time when one can cross over the land bridge, and I'm sure he was terrified that Matthew had been cut off or even drowned. But Matthew was only exploring some of the prehistoric caves—nearly as dangerous, some of them, either because they're also tidal or very hard to reach."

Just as the meal was ready, Hugh came in, looking more rested now. I had a good appetite. The dishes were plentiful if simple, and Rachel knew how to make the most of what was available out here.

We talked about France and the war, and then in a lull in the conversation, I asked, "Who is Ellen?"

"Ellen Marshall. Her father was from Cardiff. Ellen grew up there, but she adored her grandfather, and she would come to stay in the summers. His cottage is still here. After his death, she stopped coming regularly. And since the war, she only comes when she can."

Hugh said, "There's a rumor the cottage is haunted. People usually avoid it."

Rachel shook her head. "I knew Ellen's grandfather. He was a lovely old man. He had the longest beard I'd ever seen, with a lot of black still in it. And thin black rims to his glasses. He must have been ninety, at the very least. My father said he'd been a wild one, in his youth. My own grandfather claimed he'd killed someone, but my father didn't believe that. Still, I can't imagine him coming back as a ghost."

"From what I've heard, he's not the ghost," Hugh put in. "Tom claimed it was the murdered man."

"You're a stranger here," she teased. "People think you're gullible. But there's said to be a real ghost at the old rectory. Only it's a coach that careers along the road that climbs the Down. People claim they can hear it on stormy nights. It had something to do with a ship-wreck, centuries ago."

Wreckers along this coast? As there had been—so it was said—in Cornwall?

"She ran aground in a terrible storm, and everyone on board drowned," Rachel went on. "People here never mention her. It's rather odd, to tell you the truth. But my mother always maintained that bringing in that many bodies, burying them in a common grave, had made people *want* to forget. There was no way to know who they were—they weren't English—or where they'd come from, who might mourn for them."

Hugh started to comment, then stopped.

Watching them, I thought how like a comfortable married couple they seemed to be. Companionable in their silences, and talking together as if they had known each other for a very long time. I didn't think they were aware of it.

We went up to bed early, and Rachel brought me a hot water bottle to put at my feet. And in spite of the howling wind, its probing fingers rattling the panes in my window and swooping around the corner of the house, I slept well.

I woke to a very different morning.

The sun came up in a great orange ball, sending shafts of golden light across the land. I could see the distant sea, a deep blue and much calmer than yesterday. And toward the land's end, I could see a humped green island.

It did look like a turtle from here.

I rose quietly, dressed, and crept down the stairs so as not to wake anyone. The dogs looked up as I went into the kitchen for my coat, left there to dry overnight, but didn't get up from their beds by the cooker.

I let myself out the front door and walked over the road to the hedge by the Griffith cottage. I stood there, looking over the green Down out toward the bay. It too was calm today, and if there hadn't been a battered boat with a broken mast pulled up beyond the tide's reach, I'd have been hard-pressed to believe the tragedy I'd watched unfold yesterday.

Cattle were everywhere, dotting the green hillside, taking advantage of the fairer weather. It was colder today, as it often is after a storm, but crisp, not that same penetrating damp. In the distance, I could see more cattle grazing as well. On this side of the hedge, there were fields for crops, long strips in an old system.

I returned to the road and walked on past the line of Mr. Griffith's cottage, part of it shuttered, as if he'd had a café or a shop there in better times. And then on toward the white bulk of the coast guard station farther down.

And then I saw it. The Worm. Rising out of the sea, as green as could be, the head jutting out into the water, and then the large body behind it, the tail snaking away into the land behind that. It really *did* look like a dragon from here, hunched, waiting, protecting the headland. Daring any raiders to come close enough. Superstitious people could easily believe it was real, dangerous even, and turn away.

To my right, I could look down into the width of the bay from a different vantage point, and I took in a breath of surprise and delight. From here, I could see the entire expanse of the sandy strand, crescent shaped. And the incoming sea, a deeper shade of blue farther out, became the loveliest light blue as it rolled into the shallows, then turned white and frothy as it reached the strand.

I thought, *It's like a woman's ball gown.* Her shoulders the pale sand, the lace draping them, and the blue gown falling away toward the deeper blue of the sea. Someone could paint this scene, and no one would believe that it was what the artist had actually seen. It was that unusual.

For several minutes I just stood there, admiring it, wishing I could share it with my mother. She had such a wonderful eye for color.

It was then that I noticed the women.

A dozen of them? Perhaps fifteen, all told. Several of them with children walking beside them.

They were almost at the waterline, staying out of the frothy wavelets washing in, but close enough that I saw one of the children almost caught out by the water unexpectedly changing course. I thought I heard the little boy's squeal of delight as his mother yanked him back in the nick of time, then bent over to scold him.

Watching them for a moment, I noticed something else. They weren't just strolling along the waterline as I'd first thought. There was a—a *method* in the way they worked, a pattern.

The only thing I could think of was a search of the shoreline for anything that had come from the little craft. Anything useful that could be salvaged? But flotsam wasn't hard to spot in such pretty water.

This was a closer inspection, almost as if they were searching for edible shellfish stranded in the shallows by the retreating storm.

Or for any identification from the dead man?

I had no idea how early they'd come out here to look. But even as I watched, unseen, from the high cliffs above, they began to walk back to their cottages. Breaking off their search one by one, although two or three lingered, staring after the others, as if wondering how successful they'd been before weaving along the waterline again.

And then the strand was empty, a few gulls taking possession almost at once.

I turned back toward The Worm, scanning the rough land beyond the abandoned coast guard station for Ellen's cottage, where the dead man had been taken. I wished for Hugh's field glasses, to bring in the area. I had just spotted the rough outline of a roof when I noticed movement there. Was that the cottage? It must be. There was no other sign of habitation that I could make out.

I thought wryly that Ellen might well have had an unpleasant surprise if she'd suddenly decided to come for a visit.

Before I'd finished the thought, I realized that there were several people coming out of the cottage. It looked too small for guests . . .

But those weren't guests. I understood as the straggle of people formed up into a square, with someone in front of them and someone behind.

I felt cold.

They were bringing the body of the dead man back up to where I was standing. They'd almost reached what might euphemistically be called a road. It was in reality hardly more than a rough, overgrown track running from Ellen's cottage past the coast guard station and all the way up to where the actual road began in front of Rachel's house.

It was only just a very little after dawn. No one was up and about except for the women who had been searching along the strand. But they had gone inside now. Yet the body was being moved. While everyone was still abed?

Had someone gone for the police after all?

All at once I had the feeling that I shouldn't be seen, not out here, watching. I don't know why, but the feeling was so strong I hurried back up the slight incline and got myself to Rachel's house before the group of men had looked in my direction and seen me standing there watching them.

I let myself in the door, slipped into the parlor, and stood waiting behind the lace curtains to see what was being done with the body.

Small as the Corporal was, he still must have been a burden. But the little group moved faster than I'd thought possible. Working against the rising sun, which was now spilling light across the land not in swaths but in a broad sweep, these men were hurrying as much as they could. Hoping to reach their destination before anyone else was up and about to see how their land had fared after the storm.

They came into view just as I was about to turn away. The fire hadn't been lit here in the parlor, and it was icy by the window. But there they were, scarves around their faces against the cold, but their breath steaming all the same, little puffs coming through the knitting.

Silent, except for their footsteps, they didn't stop to catch their breath. Instead they came on, moving at a good pace. The ground was a little more level here, and they were making better time. I watched them pass the house and disappear up the road.

Curious, I moved to the parlor's other window, this one on the side of the house, and watched as the men reached the church and the churchyard that surrounded it.

I couldn't see any sign of a policeman waiting. Where were they taking the Corporal's body? The church?

But they hurried through the gate into the churchyard, walked some twenty paces toward the far wall, and then, to my astonishment, they lowered their burden, blanket and all, into what I realized was an open grave, already prepared.

The men began to shovel earth in over the body as quickly as they could. When that was done, sod that had been taken up in strips was carefully laid into place over the freshly turned earth. And two men with shovels patted it down so that it would grow again.

Before my eyes, they had buried the Corporal. Without the police or even, as far as I could tell, clergy standing in their way.

As soon as it was done, the men walked briskly out of the

churchyard, then scattered. I didn't recognize any of them, but of course, bundled as they were against the cold, they could have been the men I'd dealt with yesterday when the body finally came ashore. And I wouldn't have known.

More than a little shocked—and disappointed too that there apparently would be no policeman to give me a lift to Swansea—I turned away from the window.

And nearly bumped into Hugh Williams.

I couldn't believe how quietly he must have come down those stairs and into the room, stopping behind me. I gulped, then smiled uncertainly.

How much had he seen?

I said, into the silence, "I expect there will be no policeman called in. But I don't understand *why*. There is a proper procedure in a death like the Corporal's. A doctor, the police, an effort to identify him, an inquest. It's the way things are *done*."

"Let it go, Bess," he said harshly. "I've learned. These people follow their own ways. They've had to, for a very long time. There's nothing you can do about it. To try would be—foolish."

I thought he had meant to say *dangerous*, but changed his mind at the last moment.

"Will they accuse you of murder this time?" I asked, knowing that it was not possible for him to have killed the Corporal. And yet, rumors had made the rounds once, and they could begin again. I found myself thinking that in a place guarded by a great green Worm, where strangers were buried without ceremony when no one was looking, anything might happen.

"I don't know," he answered, but under his breath, as if he truly didn't know.

CHAPTER 6

OVERHEAD, WE COULD hear Rachel moving about in her room.

Hugh glanced up at the ceiling, then looked at me. "Say nothing about this to her," he told me softly but firmly. And then he was moving toward the kitchen and leaving me standing there in the middle of the parlor.

I slipped quietly up the stairs and divested myself of coat and scarf and gloves, then made sufficient noise to announce that I was also up and dressing. Then I went on down to the kitchen, where Hugh had fed the embers in the cooker and already put the kettle on.

"Good morning," he said, turning to greet me.

"Good morning," I answered, as if this were the first time we'd met. I could hear Rachel coming down the stairs.

She wished us good morning in her turn, saying ruefully, "I don't know when I've slept so deeply. I expect it was because the storm had moved on and the house was quiet."

And so the day began.

I didn't feel comfortable asking about leaving. Not after what I'd just seen. I needed time to think. About this place. The people out here. Instead, I asked Rachel if there was anything I might do to help her, since it appeared that I was to be their guest for the foreseeable future, but she smiled and shook her head.

"I'm so used to getting done whatever it is I need to do. But I'm grateful for the offer of help," she said

I too was accustomed to being busy from early morning to late into the evening, and with time on my hands and nothing to do, I felt rather at loose ends as they prepared for their day.

I would have given much to go over to the churchyard and see what had been done to mark the Corporal's grave. But I had a feeling that it would be very unwise to show open interest in that grave.

Instead, once I was certain that Rachel and Hugh would be busy and away from the house for a time, I went up to Hugh's room and borrowed his field glasses, then went into Rachel's room—pretty and looking as if it had been hers before she was married—to see what I could from the vantage point of her window.

But neither hers nor Hugh's looked toward the churchyard. Only the parlor window.

Was that why these men had felt safe to dig that grave in the middle of the night, to be ready at first light for its occupant? They had decided what to do about the thorny problem of a corpse, and acted at once.

But what about the boat?

I was about to shut Rachel's door and return the field glasses to their place by Hugh's window when I noticed something on the shelf above the small table that held her lamp.

It was an odd piece to find in the middle of a Welsh peninsula. I went back to look at it, then decided I must be wrong.

I'd been in the palaces of Indian princes, I'd seen treasures that were beyond the dreams or even the imagination of ordinary people. Gemstones, pearls, gold, silver, in every conceivable combination.

What had caught my eye looked like a cabochon ruby set in a small but elegant silver cross lying on that shelf.

But when I took a quick second glance, I was sure it must be something from a fair, the sort of thing that looked pretty and sold well but had no real value.

Shutting Rachel's door, I hurried into Hugh's room to return the glasses, then went to my own for my coat and my woolen hat. By the time I had reached the bottom of the stairs I had buttoned my coat, and then I was out the door, slowing to walk sedately across the road and out to the hedge.

It had been there, on the high ground, away from the draw of the tide, when I'd gone out at first light. Now the little craft was a shadow of itself. The mast had been cut away, the sail as well, and the hull was being cut into what appeared to be firewood.

With no body, and soon enough, no boat, it was as if the entire incident had never happened.

Was this what had been done to the other body as well? The one that rumor had named Tom Williams, Rachel's missing husband?

I turned away, afraid to be caught gawking. If they were so eager to erase any sign of the previous day's disaster, those men would begin to wonder about me, if I wasn't careful. I didn't live here. With any luck, I'd soon leave.

And carry with me a tale of a wrecked boat and a dead man? Bringing the police and even perhaps the Army down on this hamlet above the sea? After all, I held the rank of an officer in the British Army. All the QAIMNS Sisters did. It gave us standing in the wards. And with it came a certain responsibility . . .

Would they actually try to stop me from leaving? I shuddered to think what lengths they might go to if I showed too much interest in things best forgotten.

I was just turning away when I noticed the man Griffith watching me from the window of his cottage. I really hadn't got a good look at him the night I'd arrived in the motorcar from Swansea. But I didn't recall seeing him there on the strand when I'd been asked to have a look at the dead Corporal.

I considered knocking at the door and questioning him about Mr. Morgan's abrupt departure, but before I could make a move in that direction, the face vanished. And I had a feeling that even if I did knock, he wouldn't answer.

Yet oddly enough, I could feel his eyes on me all the way to the door of Rachel's house. As if he moved from one window to the next, to make certain where I'd gone.

I stayed out of sight for the rest of the day. Rachel had said that she needed no help, but I could see for myself that she was barely able to keep house, prepare meals, do the washing and ironing—and still tend to her sheep. It was far more than one woman could physically manage. And so I looked in the kitchen cupboards, found what I needed, and set to work.

There was a large feather duster that made short work of the windows and the wooden furniture. I found an old rag from the kitchen cupboard to clean the smaller, more fragile treasures. On the mantelpiece were several bits of porcelain and china, two of the shepherdesses with chipped fingers, and a basket of Coalport flowers in perfect condition. On the table between the windows was a bell jar with what appeared to be wax wedding flowers preserved inside the glass carapace. Her mother's, I thought, judging from the style.

I paused for several minutes to look at the photographs in their ornate frames. Rachel's parents, standing by the house door, smiling at the camera. Her mother had a sweet face, but a firm jaw that Rachel had inherited. Her father was tall, with the look of a man who was thoughtful by nature, although his broad shoulders indicated physical strength as well.

And a young man in uniform. Her brother? The obligatory Army photograph, I thought. Another one, a Lieutenant standing by Rachel, his arm around her. I picked that one up for a closer inspection.

Tom was younger than his brother, with the same dark hair, but with a rounder face and a warm smile that was quite appealing. I could see why Rachel had fallen in love with Tom. Searching for a resemblance to the Captain, I finally decided Tom looked more like their sister. Hugh's face was longer, stronger.

That meant the young soldier must be Rachel's brother. He closely resembled the little boy with her in the next photograph. They were grinning, ankle deep in the surf in the bay, squinting up at the camera and into the sun. The boy had something in his hand, although I couldn't see what it was. A shell, I thought, scuffed up in the sand.

A much older photograph of an elderly couple, dressed for an occasion, stared back at me from the last frame. Rachel's grandparents? Unsmiling and yet somehow conveying happiness. Someone's birthday, perhaps? Or a wedding anniversary?

The carpet sweeper made short work of the carpet in the front room, and a broom and dustpan worked nearly as efficiently in the rest of the downstairs. I found a bucket and mopped the floor in the entry, where we'd tracked in rain during the storm. Then I climbed the stairs.

My room took me no more than ten minutes, and I debated whether or not I should clean the other two bedrooms.

It would give me something to do—and I felt the need to earn my keep. I wasn't sure Rachel and Hugh could afford to care for me and feed me for very long, although the servings had been generous. At least I could take on a little of the burden of upkeep.

But in the end, I didn't feel I could intrude on their privacy, and mopped the landing instead.

That done, I discovered vegetables in a bowl in the pantry, and set about preparing them and dressing them down with goose fat for roasting.

Hugh came in first, in a whirl of cold air, and he was aghast to see me with rolled-up sleeves, my hair swept up in a knot on the top of my head, and my cheeks flushed from working.

"Good God—Bess—you shouldn't be doing this."

I'd done far more—and far worse tasks—as a probationer in the hospital where I'd trained, but he wasn't to know that. I was the caring angel, the Sister who brought comfort and healing.

It was rather sweet, and I smiled. "Nonsense," I said bracingly. "I can't sit in the parlor and stare at the four walls all day. And I'm much better at these tasks than I would be working with the sheep."

"But you're a guest of the house."

"Even guests like to be useful. Rachel can't do everything. If I can lend a hand while I'm here, so much the better."

I could see he wasn't convinced. But when Rachel came in, she said, "Oh, how thoughtful, Bess! But you needn't have done so much. I can manage."

"Of course you can," I said lightly. "I just found time on my hands. And my instructors at the training hospital would have been horrified to see me idle. They felt that a probationer who didn't look around her to find what needed doing without being told was not fit to serve."

She had taken off her coat, put it on the rack, and gone to the sink to pump water to wash her hands. "I'd have been glad to train as a nurse. But Tom didn't want me to, and my parents worried about me going quite so far away." She shrugged. "Just as well. I was left with the house and land to see to, when they died." After a brief hesitation she added almost shyly, "What I really love is my weaving. Did you see?"

I hadn't. I'd been careful to stay in rooms that I had ready access to, and not to appear nosy.

Rachel turned and, next to the cooker, opened a door that led to a small room, possibly where the cook or scullery maid might have stayed, once upon a time.

"My mother was a weaver," she said, lighting the lamp on a small table by the door. "And she taught me."

It had been turned into a workroom, with a spinning wheel and a small loom. On a shelf to one side, I could see her finished work, neatly sorted by color.

"She knew how to make her own dyes. I've the recipes for them in a book there on the other shelf. There's been no time—" Rachel broke off. "Not that I'm complaining, of course."

I walked across the room and touched the folded items. The wool was soft, light, and the colors were those of the sea at dawn or as rain swept it, or as moonlight caught it. And here was a soft apricot of first light, a warm deep rose, a fresh green of early spring, a soft yellow of daffodils. Blending and mixing and sweeping together with an eye to what worked, so that the shawls and scarves and caps were breathtakingly beautiful.

I said as much. Rachel, blushing a little, ducked her head at the praise. "I've sold a few pieces to people who come to walk or fish or watch the seabirds. They seemed to like them."

And so they should have done. I only hoped that Rachel had been paid what these pieces were worth.

The little room was warm, cozy, even with the cold wind outside, tucked as it was behind the cook stove.

She blew out the lamp as I walked back into the kitchen. "I find it rests me, to work in here. But that's not often this time of year. In the late spring and the summer, even into the autumn, the sheep fend for themselves, and there is more opportunity."

Still, the garden they depended on to fill the root cellar would need tending in the warmer months, weeding and hoeing and watering. And there would be endless other tasks to be done, repairs to be made inside and out. I could see why Hugh's help had been a godsend. And the new dog, sleeping now next to the older one, was another support. But she must need still more help, a woman to tend the house, a man to help with the heavier work. Where they were to find such help, and how they were to pay for it, was another matter entirely.

The next day was Sunday, and Rachel came down dressed for morning services. "Would you care to come with us?" she asked. "I'm afraid Rector is a little long-winded. But it shouldn't be more than an hour and a quarter."

After what I'd witnessed yesterday, I thought it best not to attend the services. The less the local people saw of me, the less likely they'd be to consider me a threat.

"I'm still tired from yesterday. If you don't mind, I'd rather rest."

Rachel nodded. "I'm still tired as well. But I have to go. And so does Hugh. If we didn't, they'd think it was a guilty conscience and hound us even more. But if you stay, would you mind putting the roast into the oven in half an hour? It should be ready by the time we come home."

"Of course," I said. Hugh came in then, shaved and dressed in a dark suit of clothes, his empty trouser leg pinned up out of his way. I'd only seen him in uniform or his work clothes. He seemed different, somehow.

I could see how his education had put him outside the circle of those he'd lived among in the valley. As the old expression went, neither fish nor fowl or nor even good red herring. No longer fit for the coal face, and yet not really one of those who owned and ran the mines. Offered a clerical position because he was good with numbers, but having nothing in common with those he'd grown up with, nor those he now worked for. I began to understand why he and the others had looked at the war and the call to arms as a way out of that black land with its narrowness born of poverty and an employment that meant not seeing the sun from one season to the next.

Hugh had become an officer. Had he felt he finally belonged somewhere? Would he have stayed in the Army if he hadn't lost a limb, a career soldier?

For that matter, had he ever really known where he belonged? His education had opened some doors—and slammed others firmly shut. And at the end of the war, he surely understood where he must return.

It was such a different world from where I had grown up, in Somerset and India and Africa and other posts of Empire. I found myself wondering what my father would have to say about Hugh.

Rather a lot, possibly . . .

After breakfast, I watched them join the steady stream of people walking up to the church.

It had such a *sturdy* look, built by the Normans to last. Perhaps the Romans never made it this far, but Wales was full of castles, big ones that guarded river crossings and the tops of hills. I remembered that many of them had changed hands often. The Welsh being more warlike, and smart enough to let their enemies build superb fortifications before coming in to capture them and make them their own.

There was no real attempt to decorate the outside of the church. There might even have been hermits living in this part of Wales at one time. Perhaps that was why arches and architectural features hadn't caught on. They were out of step with the past.

In fact, the church had no windows to speak of . . .

No windows. Once inside, worshippers wouldn't be distracted by anything happening outside. Wind or weather or someone skipping the service and enjoying himself.

Or someone walking in the churchyard . . .

Through the front room window, I made certain that Griffith went to the service, and that there were no stragglers from the sloping Down above the strand.

And then I waited another half an hour, to be absolutely certain.

Finally, dressed in my coat, wearing my wool cap instead of my nurse's white cap, I slipped outside, walked slowly up what passed for the road, and stepped into the churchyard.

It didn't take me long to find that new grave. I was careful not to walk too close, where my boots might leave an imprint in the soft earth.

There was no marker. It might not exist as a grave.

And I found the other one, a little distance away, already beginning to heal enough that it was harder to pick out.

Two men who had come to grief here, washing up in the bay, and were given no resting place, no identification, not even a small cross to comfort their souls.

Surely the men and women who'd attended morning services today must know the bodies were there. Or had that been the reason for such a clandestine burial at first light? People might guess, but they hadn't been a party to what had been done.

Men cast upon the bosom of the Deep, as an old sea chantey called their end, hadn't found a safe haven even after they came ashore.

I wondered why.

I didn't linger there. I left the churchyard and hurried back to the hedge by the Griffith cottage.

Looking down on the calm blue bay, with its fringe of lacy froth, I saw that any sign of the Corporal's boat had disappeared too, except for a patch here and there of bruised grass where the dismantling had been done. But that would soon heal.

I walked on a little way down toward the abandoned coast guard station. I could just pick out Ellen's cottage. I was tempted to go on and explore in that direction, but I wasn't really certain that I should. The service might end before I'd made it back up that long slow incline. And right after the body had been removed and so hastily buried, it wouldn't be wise to be seen down there. I wasn't precisely sure what my curiosity would set in motion, but there was something distinctly sinister about bodies disappearing, and I had no intention of finding my own winding up in an unmarked grave.

Or of causing trouble for Rachel and Hugh . . .

Retracing my steps, I went to the pen where the ewes were confined, and they grazed quietly, uninterested in graves and morning services or even me watching them. They hadn't even bothered to sneeze when I approached.

I got myself inside before there was even a chance of the service ending early. It was one thing not to attend, but quite another to be wandering about on my own as if I was taking advantage of Sunday services to pry into village affairs when no one was looking.

Which of course I had been doing. But there was no need to advertise that . . .

It occurred to me as I shut the heavy front door behind me and listened to the silence of the house around me that I was already learning to fall in with the ways of this godforsaken corner of Wales. Whether I agreed with them or not.

I was just hanging up my coat and pulling off my cap when it struck me that we only had that man Griffith's word that my driver had left suddenly in the middle of the night.

I hadn't walked *all* the way around the church, had I? There might be another grave on the far side, his motorcar tucked away in some outbuilding on the Down, where I couldn't see it.

A cold that had nothing to do with the chill in the house swept over me.

Nonsense! If my driver went missing, someone would have come down from that Swansea garage by this time to find out what had become of their motorcar and their man. And taken me back with them.

Somehow that thought wasn't as comforting as it ought to have been . . .

Sunday dragged on. Sheep were no respecters of Sabbath quiet. As soon as the meal was finished, Rachel went out to have a look at the ewes while I cleared away and began to wash up.

Hugh stayed to help me, and after we'd finished with the teacups and saucers, I said, "Did you know? They've buried both bodies in the churchyard. I saw the graves. Will they put markers up, do you think? Or hope that those men are soon forgotten?"

He showed no surprise. Or even shock. "Leave it alone, Bess. It's different out here. There's no way to find out who he was. At least he's in the churchyard, not buried along the strand some-where."

It was my turn to be surprised. He saw it in my face, and said, "The appearance of another body has at least given the people here something else to think about than whether or not Rachel and I killed my brother. It lends weight to the fact that the first body might also be a stranger."

I could see why he felt so strongly about what had happened to the two dead men. But I still found it hard to accept that they were hastily buried, no service, no gravestones, as if they had never come ashore here.

They must have belonged to someone. A wife. Parents. Sisters and brothers. Families that would always wonder what had hap-pened to two men. Even if they no longer mattered to the Army, they had been wearing British uniforms when they died, and someone somewhere ought to care.

After a moment, I said, "This is a strange part of the world. But you seem at home here."

"My home is in the valley, Bess. But there's no place for me there. Not any longer. I can't work in the pits, and my sister has her hands full. I refuse to be a burden on her. And that's all I was. Rachel has taken me in. Out of the goodness of her heart—out of a need to have someone, even a man with one leg, to help her keep this house and her land—out of pity. God knows. But I'm grateful. I can't judge these people because they're her people, at least in some sense of the word. She had nowhere else to go either, when Tom was killed, except to this house. We're both refugees, in a way. And I—"

He broke off as the outer door opened and the dogs came racing down the passage and into the kitchen.

"All's well," Rachel said, coming into the kitchen after them. "I think it's getting colder. I hope not. One can't take ewes a cup of tea, can one, and ask them to carry on?"

She was smiling as she said it, pulling off her scarf and coat, then divesting herself of muddy boots before taking them out to the kitchen passage.

"The stove's still warm," I said. "Shall I put the kettle on for you?"

She shook her head. "I think I might work on the loom for a bit. It always soothes me. Even if it's Sunday. Do you mind, Bess?"

"Not if you don't mind if I bring out the board and the iron, and press my aprons."

"Hugh?" she asked.

But he said, "I've work of my own to do."

"A wicked lot we are," Rachel said. Then with a shrug she added, "There isn't much else to do out here, except work. I think that's what I miss most. At least in a town there were places to walk, gardens—even the cinema or stopping in a shop for tea and a bun."

"I should think some enterprising soul might consider that this village needed a tea shop."

"There was one for a while. Mr. Griffith and his wife opened up part of their cottage as a tearoom. She looked after the kitchen while he served. It never quite caught on, and so they closed it. She died early in 1914. When the war began, he talked about opening it up again for the men at the coast guard station, but nothing ever came of it. Then word came that his son was dead. You can see why he shut himself away."

"His son died in the war?"

She was putting on slippers before going in to work at the loom.

"He was one of the first to enlist—didn't wait for any of the other young men out here. We were surprised. He was always such a quiet lad, never any trouble. I couldn't picture him as a soldier. But they say the quiet ones have hidden strengths. Still waters, and all that."

And so began our afternoon, the three of us finding something to do that kept our hands busy, giving us no time to think. I was beginning to see that it might be for the best, not thinking.

Because before very long I would be due back at the clinic.

And what would Matron have to say, if I didn't return?

CHAPTER 7

THE WIND PICKED up after midnight, rattling my window-panes.

I was still awake. I would have given much to go down and make myself a cup of tea, but I didn't want to disturb Rachel or Hugh. My hot water bottle was only lukewarm, in spite of being wrapped in a towel, and I could already feel the drop in temperature outside.

I listened for the sound of the sea. It might lull me to sleep, I thought, but the wind was louder.

Then I picked up another sound. At first I thought it might be a loose shutter banging against one of the windows downstairs, before I realized it was not that at all, but a motorcar making its way along the road in front of the house, moving slowly through the ruts and dips that made the surface a washboard.

Eager to see who it was—someone looking for my driver? Even looking for me? Someone I might speak to in the morning and beg a lift back to Swansea?—I got out of bed, ignoring the cold, and hurried to the window.

It *was* a motorcar. I was sure of it. But I couldn't see it at first. Nor its headlamps probing the way.

And then it came into view. To my surprise, the headlamps weren't on, in spite of the condition of the road. The only way I could identify it as a motorcar was by the dark moving shape outlined by Mr. Griffith's whitewashed cottage. I thought perhaps it intended to stop there. That was where the road ended . . .

Looking for Mr. Morgan?

But it went on, continuing quietly past the door and slowly making its way down toward the former coast guard station.

As my bare feet turned to ice, I waited, watching the rear lamp on the motorcar disappear into the darkness as it went on down the road. After a while, the headlamps came on, but it was well beyond the coast guard station's buildings by that time, and closer to the cottage that must belong to Ellen. Then the lights disappeared.

As if the motorcar had arrived at its destination.

The night was silent again except for the wind.

I scurried back to my bed, shoved my feet against the hot water bottle, and pulled the covers tight around me until my teeth stopped chattering and my body stopped shivering.

I couldn't help but think it was a very good thing Ellen hadn't arrived this time on Friday night, to find an unexpected corpse on her doorstep.

Perhaps that explained the hasty burial on Saturday morning?

What mattered, I told myself as I finally got warm enough to drift off to sleep, was that a motorcar had appeared out here on the peninsula. Against all odds. And whether it had tried to slip in unseen or not—or simply wanted not to wake anyone—I could find an excuse to ask Ellen, or whoever it belonged to, to take me back to Swansea. Whenever it left.

The first of the lambs was born in the early morning, and Rachel brought it back with her, to keep it in the warmth of the kitchen until the weather had passed. She and Hugh dragged a box out of the passage to the kitchen door, filled it with rags and old bedding, then put the lamb inside. It bleated, looking for its mother, but Rachel was already heating milk for it.

"The mother is in one of the sheds. It must have been a hard labor, and she seems quite weary. I'll take this little one out to her later on."

"Will it be all right?"

"Yes, I think so. She'd tried to lick it dry, but it was shivering when I got there. When I picked it up to carry it back, she followed me, and I managed with the help of the dogs to get her into the shed. If she doesn't reject it because it has our scent on it now, all will be well."

It was a gangly little thing, and Hugh was rubbing it with another bit of blanket as it found the bottle and began to suck. Its tail was spinning like a top. I'd seen young lambs do the same in fields, and I took that as a good sign.

And then it settled back in its bedding and went sound asleep. The dogs ignored it.

"I can remember a time when my father had ten or eleven lambs in boxes, and fires in all the rooms to keep them warm. That was a very cold winter, and we were afraid we'd lose most of them. My poor, long-suffering mother took care of them, and we kept them all alive until they could return to their mothers. It amazed me, the way each ewe recognized her own lamb. Something in the smell, I expect."

I waited until she had washed her hands and sat down with a cup of tea.

"I roused up in the night," I said, "and thought I heard a motorcar going by. Did you notice?"

"I'm afraid not," Rachel said, curious. "We don't see many motorcars out here. Where did it go?"

"I finally got out of bed to see. But it was beyond the coast guard station by that time."

"Ellen," Hugh said, washing his hands in his turn after draping the bit of blanket over the sleeping lamb. "There's only the one cottage beyond the station."

"Tell me about her."

He shrugged. "I don't know anything to tell. I've never met her. But people speak of her sometimes."

Rachel said, "She's older than I am. I heard she was widowed at the start of the war—her husband was a partner in a shipping line, I think. I remember something about his heart giving out from overwork. We moved in different circles, Ellen and I, and so it was just the occasional gossip that reached my ears. Then in 1915, I believe it was, there were rumors that she'd opened lodgings close by the docks. Her husband's family was not best pleased, but she wanted to do something for the war. Many of those places were barely respectable, and I expect she saw a need. Often the men coming in from the ships or on leave from the Army didn't have time to travel on to their homes, and sometimes the local people took sad advantage of them. I thought it was very brave of her, even though many women felt it wasn't quite proper for a woman of her class. Others applauded her. I sent my mother a cutting from the Cardiff newspapers about her efforts."

"Did you know her, growing up?" I asked.

"She only came here in the summer to visit her grandfather. And I was too young to have much to do with her. I remember once she was talking with Mr. Griffith, and she offered me a toffee when she noticed me standing nearby. But I thought she was rather grand, with her pretty city gowns." She smiled. "I'm sure my mother thought Ellen was rather fast. Certainly she wasn't like the rest of us, but I realize now, having lived in a city, how different we are, out here. Behind the times, slow to change."

"How do the others out here make their living?"

"They run cattle to feed the inland cities, and farm where they can. Sheep are a dying business," she said rather sadly. "When the Army needed blankets and uniforms, we flourished again, but demand has dropped off now that the war is over." She stared wistfully at the window. "I expect we'll all have to leave or find some other way to survive out here."

"Would you go back to Swansea? Or even Cardiff?"

"I don't know," she said slowly, then glanced at Hugh. I thought I knew what she must be silently asking him. If he would stay with her, if there were no chores to do or sheep to run . . . would he let her make a living for both of them, or would his loss of his leg make him bitter and too proud to be beholden.

When he didn't look up or answer, she said quickly, "I worked in Cardiff. Tom wasn't happy about it, but I was always accustomed to staying busy out here. Like you, I wasn't one to sit idle. And our little house didn't need all that much looking after. I took a course, and learned to use a typing machine. It was much easier than I expected, after I got the knack of it and learned the keyboard. I was paid rather well too."

I wondered if that money had helped fund her return to the peninsula. To look after her parents and then to stay on until Tom came back from the war. If so, it must be running out by now.

All the more reason for me to leave, and not be a burden on their meager resources.

"Do you suppose," I asked, following up on that thought, "that Ellen might be willing to let me go with her? As far as Swansea? I'm going to be overdue at the clinic soon, and people will start to wonder what's become of me. My parents will worry, if the clinic contacts them and they've had no word either." And Matron would do just that, for she thought I was with them *now*!

Hugh glanced up then. "I'm not sure you can count on her. She doesn't have much to do with the rest of us. But Rachel can send word to the cottage, and ask."

"Or I could walk down myself, today—tomorrow, if the weather holds," I said, knowing how much Rachel had to do—and who could she send? It was a very long way for Hugh, and he didn't know Ellen.

I don't think either of them quite approved of my going there. But what could they say?

I tried to hold on to my patience, listened all day for the sound of a motorcar leaving. But if Ellen had just arrived, it might make good sense to give her a day to do whatever she had come to do. Then ask my favor. But it was hard to be patient.

We went up to bed early that evening. Rachel had been out a dozen times to look after the sheep, and she would be back at it at first light in the morning. I was restless, and lay there wishing for a book to read. Then around midnight I caught a whiff of cigarette smoke in the night. The wind had veered, for the windows weren't rattling. I got up and went to the window. I could just see someone standing outside the Griffith cottage, and I thought he might be smoking from the way he simply stood there, not moving, for several minutes. And then he turned and went back inside.

The odor lasted a bit longer and then was carried off by the wind. Mr. Griffith, I thought, must lead a very lonely life, there in the cottage by himself, his wife dead, his son lost in France. But he wasn't the most approachable of men, and no doubt that only reinforced his isolation from the other men of the village.

In August 1914, when the war began, everyone had been convinced that it would be over by Christmas. Men had rushed to volunteer, in a hurry to join in the great adventure and come home with stories to tell their children and grandchildren about the Great War. Only it hadn't turned out the way they'd expected. By the new year, it had become a stalemate, and would drag on with no end in sight.

But what if it *had* ended by Christmas? A brief brush with glory, and then all the men would have home. So many lives saved, so many men like Hugh still whole. No gassed lungs, no Spanish influenza, no nightmarish months in the trenches. I thought of all the young men I'd known who hadn't survived. And Mr. Griffith's son and Tom Williams and the two dead soldiers in the village churchyard and Hugh's Welsh companies might have been spared.

It didn't bear thinking of.

Climbing back into bed, stretching my feet out to the hot water bottle, I lay awake, remembering.

On the other side of the wall, I heard the faint sounds of Hugh moving restlessly about his room. I didn't know if he was in pain or just found it difficult to sleep. Many amputees did. We tried not to give them laudanum to help them. It was addictive, and in the end a worse life. In the wards I could sit by a bed and talk to the patient until sleep came. There was nothing I could do for Hugh.

The next day, which dawned clear and bright and brisk, I did what I could in the house, and then after we'd had the midday meal, and Hugh had gone out to a shed to mend a leather strap, I asked Rachel if it would be a good time to go down to the cottage. She hesitated, and then said, "Well, I don't see why not. It isn't as if she's got a houseful of guests. I don't even know why she bothers to come back, except to keep an eye on the cottage. You'd think she might pay Mr. Griffith or myself to look in on it from time to time. Cheaper in the long run."

"A sentimental connection," I suggested.

"I never knew what the story was about Ellen," she said with a frown. "I was far too young for gossip. I don't remember her mother at all. Just her grandfather. I don't think Ellen's mother ever came down here with her. Even though Ellen's mother had grown up here.

Someone from Ellen's father's family would bring her, then come back to fetch her. I often wondered if there had been a falling-out between her mother and her grandfather. But if that was true, why did Ellen visit her grandfather at all? It's not as though he had a grand house and entertained there."

"Who did Ellen's mother marry? I gather it wasn't someone from the village."

"I never knew much about him. Well, I probably never thought to ask. It was just Ellen—her grandfather—and her mother. They were the only ones anyone talked about. I vaguely remember someone saying he was wealthy, someone important in Cardiff. Ellen's mother went to school there. I expect that's how she came to meet him. There was money, obviously. Ellen's pretty clothes, her pretty manners. I did think it was very brave of her to come all the way here." She smiled. "Cardiff might as well have been on the far side of the moon—I had never been there of course, and I could never quite be sure whether it was a place of delights or a den of iniquity." The smile turned sheepish. "It really depended on who was talking. We had a rector by the name of Black. He didn't think much of cities, not in his sermons. Sodom and Gomorrah, in his view. Which only made cities seem all the more attractive to us, the younger ones. Come to think of it, I don't believe many people out here had been to Cardiff either. Well, it was a seaport, you know. And they are notoriously evil places."

We laughed, and then I went up to put on the apron I'd ironed just that morning, brushed my coat, took some polish to my boots, and with my nurse's cap, set out.

It was farther than I'd expected. I'd walked past Mr. Griffith's cottage to the overlook where I could see the sweep of the pretty bay. As I continued down the incline, the wind toyed with my skirts and cap, and I was glad I'd brought my gloves, because it still had a bite to it. I came to the now derelict coast guard buildings. I wondered if they'd kept a boat in the bay or down by The Worm. Or if they were just a watch station, keeping an eye on whatever ships were crossing the sea, reporting any enemy vessels but not giving chase themselves.

I decided they were there simply to keep watch, because I could see no way to get down to the bay from up here.

And the station wasn't all that large. Thirty men? Possibly forty, to maintain twenty-four hours' watch. They would require quarters, barracks, kitchens, dining hall, watch rooms, and equipment. I walked over to the front of the building and peered in the lower windows.

The interior was bare, what I could see of it, with the exception of stacks of iron cots in one large room, and stacks of tables in another. A desk and chairs in what must have been an office. But the windows had been painted over so that I could only look through the scratches in the paint. They *would* have had to be blacked out, or they'd have been seen, lit at night, far out to sea.

For all I knew, the coast guard might have sites all around the end of the headland where they stood watch by turns, keeping an eye on sea traffic. But the question was, how did they alert anyone, if there had been anything of importance to see out there? A submarine charging batteries, enemy war ships, or even troop carriers. These bays and headlands, like areas in southeastern England and even in Cornwall, were ideal places to land spies and saboteurs.

The coast guard must have had radio or telegraph facilities, and I looked, finding where the wires were attached to one end of the buildings. But the wires were gone, and there must not have been high poles, too easy to identify through field glasses, a warning that the Navy had a post somewhere out here. Perhaps they were somewhere inland. Too bad the telegraph hadn't been left for the village to use.

I'd put off my errand long enough and walked on.

In the distance, The Worm was so vividly green in the sun that I could see just how raiders from Ireland or even the Vikings might give it a wide berth. A living thing, waiting for them to come within reach.

I wondered that The Worm hadn't had the opposite effect—with a private dragon like that to protect the people living out here, there must be something worth protecting. That could have made the peninsula appear to be an even more tempting target.

The cottage was still a good forty yards away. How on earth had Ellen's elderly grandfather managed out here with no one to keep an eye on him or see to his needs? How had he managed that incline to attend services at the village church?

Why had he chosen such an isolated bit of land?

Finally I was close enough to see it well. There was a touring car at the door, large enough for several people, and the shutters were hooked back, letting light into the rooms. The cottage was only one story, but it rambled, as if it had been added to over time. I could see smoke coming out of several of the chimneys, and I walked up the overgrown path to the door, knocking on the wood frame.

The cottage was a weathered gray, in need of paint, but since no one lived here, it wasn't surprising that it hadn't been kept up over the years. Still, it seemed sound enough, I thought, built to withstand the storms and stay dry.

No one came, and so I knocked again.

Finally the door opened, and a woman stood there, staring coldly at me. I wondered if this was Ellen.

Or if she'd brought someone with her. How full had the motorcar been, coming down?

A worry, that!

But in a way she fit the description that Rachel had given me. I put her age at thirty-one or -two, perhaps as old as thirty-five. That should be about right. She was fairly tall, slim and dark-haired, with a face that might have been quite pretty once but now had harsh lines around the eyes and the mouth, as if life hadn't been kind to her. She was wearing a very attractive dark green woolen dress cut in a fashionable style, and there was a pretty shawl around her shoulders that reminded me a little of the shawls that Rachel made, although the colors were not as soft and full of light. Still, the effect was one of money and position.

"Ellen Marshall?" I smiled, introduced myself, and asked for a moment of her time.

"Are you collecting for your service?" she asked, frowning.

"No, I'd come to the village to look in on a former patient, and now I need to return to Swansea as soon as possible. My leave is nearly up, and I'm expected at the clinic in Gloucestershire. But I've discovered that there's no way to inform the firm to send my driver back for me." There was no reason to tell her I'd been more or less stranded here. "I was wondering if you might have room in your motorcar to carry me as far as Swansea. Or perhaps you could carry a message to the firm for me?"

I found myself hurrying through my explanation because she was standing there glaring, giving me no indication that she cared a whit about my situation—much less intended to help me.

And I was right. She didn't intend to help.

Instead of inviting me inside or offering a cup of tea, she said curtly, "I have no idea how long I intend to stay. I'm afraid you'll have to find another way to get word out."

I could hear movement in one of the rooms behind her. The scrape of a chair on the floor, quiet footsteps. So she wasn't alone out here.

I really had no hope of pleading my case—she'd made herself clear enough. But she hadn't yet slammed the door in my face, and so I put on Matron's expression of disappointment in something we'd not done properly, and said, "But you do intend to drive back as far as Swansea? I'll wait, of course, on your convenience, but I'm expected at the clinic, and there will be questions if I don't arrive in time to take up my duties."

That got her attention.

"Why are you out here in the first place?" she demanded, looking me up and down. "Did you bring wounded back here?"

I was sure she had heard what I'd told her, but I politely repeated it. "I came with orders to look in on a former patient who has been released."

"Which patient?"

"Captain Williams."

"Who is he? I don't recall that being a local name."

"He's Rachel Williams's brother-in-law. He's staying with her while he recovers."

I realized I had no idea what Rachel's maiden name was.

"Rachel Williams?" she repeated as if she'd never heard of her. And then she seemed to recollect. "Rachel. Wasn't that the name of the child who lived at the top in that large house?"

"Yes, that's right," I agreed, hazarding a guess that she had the right person in mind. She had described the house, not Griffith's cottage or any of those on the far side of the church.

"I didn't know she's married. But of course the last time I saw her was years ago. Well, it doesn't matter. I am not going anywhere anytime soon, and there's nothing I can do to help you."

With that she shut the door in my face. Not slamming it, exactly, but indicating clearly enough that I was not to disturb her by knocking again.

People had more or less been friendly in Wales as I was traveling about searching for Hugh. Helpful and pleasant enough. But out here, the cold wind seemed to have withered any sense of friendliness or kindness.

I stood there for a moment, to see if she might change her mind, then turned and walked back down the short path. As I started the long climb back to Rachel's house, I wondered what I was going to do now.

And my disappearance was going to worry a good many people.

So much for my cleverness in believing I might be able to do something for the men under Captain Williams's command, then possibly spend the last few days of my leave in Somerset.

I should have told someone what I was going to do. But it would have entailed explanations and concern and the suggestion that I take Simon or even my mother with me, venturing into the wilds of Wales.

I had to smile at the thought. It was love that made parents worry, and they'd just been reassured that I was home and safe after the trials and terrors of the war.

The smile faded.

What would they do now, cavalry notwithstanding?

CHAPTER 8

THE LONG WALK back to the house, up that deceptively sloping hill, was unexpectedly tiring, or perhaps it was the surge of guilt I was feeling for what I was about to put my parents through. I paused to look down into the serene bay, little whitecaps just rippling the surface of the smooth water where it met the sand. Nothing at all like the wild waves during the storm that tossed that little boat so viciously.

When I looked back again, I saw that Hugh had come out of the house and was standing there, talking to a very slim man dressed in black, a black hat in his hands.

Hugh must have said something to him, because they both turned toward me, and the other man leaned forward a little as if to take a better look at me. Then he turned back to Hugh.

I kept up my steady pace, and was soon close enough to greet them. Hugh smiled, but it didn't reach his eyes.

"Sister Crawford," he said formally, and I realized that this was someone interested in me. It put me on my guard straightaway, his formal use of my title. As Hugh must have intended it to do.

"Captain," I acknowledged.

"I was telling Rector that you had gone for a walk."

No mention of speaking to Ellen, then. I wondered why.

There was a heavy woolen scarf wound around the rector's throat, and so I hadn't seen his collar. Looking at him, I saw a defeated man who did his duty out of a sense of obligation, but with no joy. I'd seen it before, in the chaplains who had been in the trenches. But I didn't think the rector had been in the war. There was nothing of the soldier about him. Perhaps it was being left out here too long, and losing all hope and most of his dreams. What struck me about him was a sense that nothing was worth the effort any longer. It was in the gloomy way he looked at me, as if I was a problem he didn't have the least idea how to solve.

I recalled Rachel saying that his sermons always ran overlong. As if he was trying to show people how hard he was working, for them and their souls?

"Yes, it's such a lovely afternoon," I said cheerfully. "But I hope I'm in time to help prepare dinner."

That would give Hugh the opportunity to dismiss me—or let the conversation, whatever it was, continue.

"Mr. Wilson has been asking why you didn't come to services on Sunday morning."

I judged the smile I should offer, pleasant but not overly friendly. It didn't seem that sort of question.

"I have been tired from my travels," I said, with a hint of apology. "I'm so sorry."

"Yet you walked a goodly distance just now."

How far away had he seen me? As far as Ellen's? I wondered suddenly if he had been one of the men who had carried the dead soldier down to Ellen's cottage. And if seeing me moving in that direction had brought him out to speak to Hugh. If he *had* been one of them, he wouldn't want me to bring up the latest news of a dead man washing ashore, even if he didn't think I knew about the disposition of the body. It could raise awkward questions, if Ellen cared to ask them.

I had a feeling she wouldn't care enough.

"Yes, it has been good for me."

"Captain Williams says you have come to judge how well his wound is healing."

It must have been galling to admit that. Hugh didn't want to talk about his injuries. He tried to ignore them as much as he could, doing more than was wise in an effort to prove he was still whole and able.

"Such wounds heal differently in different men," I said quietly. "And the adjustment to the changes they bring in their wake can be difficult. These men served England well, and deserve to be given every care. It is their peace too."

"Indeed. How long are you staying with us, Sister Crawford?"

"I don't know. My driver hasn't returned to collect me. I fear there was some miscommunication there."

"We are happy to have you with us, Sister, and if you are still here on Sunday of this week, we hope you'll join us at services."

"That's very kind of you. Thank you."

He hesitated, as if he was about to say something more, then nodded to both of us and walked back toward the church. I thought he looked rather like a skinny crow, his hands behind his back, his head down, as he moved away.

Hugh watched him go, but didn't say anything until Mr. Wilson had turned in just beyond the church.

"Busybody," he said under his breath.

"You don't care for him?" I asked, curious.

"My sister would like him," Hugh replied, and turned toward the house. I matched my stride to his.

There was something on his mind, and I wasn't certain whether it was what I might have learned at Ellen's or the rector's visit.

We were nearly to the door when he stopped and swung around to face me.

"You know as much about my case as the doctors. Am I a good choice for an artificial limb?"

I hadn't expected this question—and I realized that I should have.

"I've never worked with the doctors who make such decisions about replacing a limb. But you've had no recent infection, nothing deep enough to cause problems. You've healed quite well, and I expect you've done your exercises. I should think you ought to inquire. I'll speak to Matron, if you like, and let you know what she says."

Even as I said it, I remembered how difficult it was to get letters to anyone out here. How *would* I let him know?

But his mind was still on the limb. "How well do they work?"

I took a deep breath. "For some men, quite well. There's a noticeable limp, I won't lie to you about that. It's not going to give you back your leg. And the wound has to be carefully monitored for injury from the weight placed on it from walking. To prevent infection. They aren't perfect, Hugh."

"No." He stood there, looking down toward The Worm.

"But in your place, I'd want to explore the possibility," I said, afraid that being honest had discouraged him. "You won't know until you've been seen by the proper doctors."

"In the autumn. There isn't as much to do here then." He finally turned to face me. "Don't mention this to Rachel."

"Of course not." I gave him a moment, then added, "You could go back with me. Start the process, find out what's involved in the fittings and training. Then come back until it was ready."

He shook his head, although I guessed he was impatient to find out about such a limb. "It's almost lambing season. I can't leave now."

"Yes, I do see that," I said. "Well, you know how to find the clinic. When you're ready."

He was silent.

I knew suddenly what was on his mind now. Money. How he was going to *afford* returning to the clinic—or being fitted with a limb? And if he'd sent his officer's pay to his sister, she was probably already receiving his pension. He was too proud to ask Rachel for it, and I wasn't certain she had the money to spare. But I knew her well enough now to believe she would do her best. Whatever the cost.

I decided I would have a word with Matron. The country should help these men. There must be funds available. For travel, for tests, and for the limb and the training. Or if she couldn't help me, I'd turn to the Colonel Sahib. His men had always mattered to him. And by extension, to the British Army.

We walked inside. Rachel was in the shed with the new lamb and its mother, and I put on the kettle while Hugh went to speak to her.

Sitting there waiting for it to boil, I thought back over my conversation with Ellen, and couldn't think of any way of improving on it.

Rachel came in, went to wash her hands, and asked, "Did you see Ellen?"

I had to tell her the truth about what had happened.

"That doesn't sound like her," she said, turning to look at me.

But she was remembering a young woman who was kind to a staring child.

"How long has it been since you've seen her?"

"At a distance of course, several times during the war. But not to speak to. When she's at the cottage, she doesn't visit with anyone out here. Come to think of it, I can't remember if she ever did. I mean, things like popping in for a cup of tea, or being invited to dinner. We weren't—" She looked for the right word. "Her kind of people," she ended. "That makes her sound terribly snobbish, doesn't it? But somehow there was always more money in Ellen's life. Her mother was sent to school in the city, and married well there. And of course Ellen had all the advantages. You could see it in the way she carried herself, how she dressed, her confidence, her ease speaking to people. That comes of money. I didn't realize any of this when I was a child. But living in a town, one soon learns that there are many social levels."

A young married woman who worked as a typist wouldn't have much in common with the Ellens of Swansea or Cardiff. And yet there was that lodging house down by the docks . . .

"Well, perhaps she'll change her mind. She's probably tired from her journey and not ready to think about going back. When she does, she'll come round. Wait and see." With a smile, Rachel took her cup of tea and went into the little weaving room. A few minutes later, I could hear the loom working with a steady beat, and wondered what colors she was using now. But I didn't feel that I could interrupt her.

Hugh came in for his cup and stood there listening for a moment too. Then he finished his tea and went away.

I was left to my own devices.

Feeling more than a little claustrophobic in the house, I fetched my coat and went out to the hedge and the path down to the strand.

I didn't walk down. I just stood there, looking out at the sea. Letting the wind blow my cobwebs away.

And then I heard a step behind me.

Turning, I saw that it was a young girl of perhaps twelve.

"Hallo," I said, smiling. And wondered if she might be the child of the widower who had proposed to Rachel at Christmas.

"You're a nursing Sister."

"Yes, that's right."

"Are you staying with Rachel and the Captain?"

"Yes. I tended his wounds at the clinic. I came to see how he was getting on."

"Are you taking him back with you, for more treatments?"

"No, he's been released from the clinic now. This was—what you might call a last look into his care."

"He falls sometimes, even with the crutches. Not as much now as he did in the beginning. But it's not very level underfoot. My father says he'd be better off in a town. Not out here."

Amputees had been taught at the clinic how to prevent falls, and how to recover from them when they did go down. But it wasn't easy to watch.

"It takes some getting used to, I expect. The roughness of the land out here."

"He's a stranger. Not one of us. My father doesn't much care for him."

I suddenly remembered the gossip about Rachel and the Captain. "Does your father know the Captain well?"

"I don't think so. But he doesn't like him. I can tell."

"Is your house out there on the Down?"

"The one with the small terrace you can see from here. My father put that in for my mother, to give her a sheltered place to sit during the day."

It was on the upper reaches of the Down. A lane snaked past two other houses to get to it and to one other cottage beyond.

"He must love her very much."

"She's dead," the girl told me quietly. "He doesn't like to talk about her. But I want to remember her. I can feel her slipping away. Does that sound strange to you? I don't know any other way to say it. But it's harder to remember her voice. I do have her picture, but it's not as real to me as it once was. It doesn't smile, or talk, or sing to me at night when she would put me to bed."

"That's sad," I agreed. "Perhaps if you told these things to your father, he'd understand and try to help you bring her memory back."

"He says we must move on. That the only way to get over our grief is to move on."

"Rachel had to move on after her husband was killed in the war. I expect that was difficult to deal with too. I have a feeling she loved him as much as you loved your mother."

She shook her head at that. "She couldn't have. She wouldn't have been so willing to let his brother come and fill his shoes."

And with a nod, she took off at a run, leaving me standing there as she set out toward her home.

I'd no doubt now. This was the daughter who needed a new mother. And her father was probably the source of the rumors about Hugh and Rachel. He must have had his heart set on marrying her. It would have been advantageous—he wouldn't have to pay a house-keeper or a charwoman, and he would have gained the house on the hill as well as the property that went with it.

He must have been among the men on the strand, watching the boat. I wondered which one he was.

As I turned away, to walk back to Rachel's house, I glanced up, feeling eyes on me. And Mr. Griffith was at his window again, watching me.

I didn't intend to tell either Hugh or Rachel what I suspected, that the child's father had probably started the rumors about them. I couldn't see that it would be helpful to know, because there wasn't much to be done about it. And it could cause hard feelings because someone was already upset over Hugh's coming into the picture at the wrong time.

Crutches or no crutches, I could very easily see Hugh confronting the man.

And causing more trouble . . .

I was just crossing the road to the house when I saw three people walking toward me. Two women and a boy. Something in the way they were lengthening their strides a little suggested they were hoping to reach me before I'd disappeared into the house. I slowed, smiling, giving them a chance to greet me.

One of the women nodded, and the other called out, "Sister."

I paused, and they came to a halt in front of me.

"I hear you're staying with Rachel," the older of the women said. I realized that she must be the mother of the other woman and grandmother to the boy.

She was comfortably plump, with graying hair and a pleasant face. Her hair had been auburn, but it was losing its color now, although the freckles across her face hadn't faded one whit.

"Well, I had intended to go back to the clinic the very next day, but my driver got his instructions muddled and left without me." I smiled wryly. "I have been hoping that the firm will realize it's made a mistake and come to fetch me."

"I wouldn't count on it," the woman said. "Those people in Swansea are always trying to get the better of us out here. That firm won't want to waste another trip, not knowing whether you're ready to leave or not."

Which was just what I didn't want to hear. Why hadn't they already come back posthaste, to find out what had become of me? Unless, of course, Mr. Morgan had lied to them, and told them that it was my decision, not his.

He hadn't been very forthcoming, a dour man by nature, but I hadn't expected him to treat me so shabbily.

The boy turned to me. I put his age down at fifteen or thereabouts. His voice was just settling into a lower register, making him sound a little hoarse.

"I saw him leave."

"Who?" his mother asked sharply. "You never said."

The boy flushed to the roots of his dark hair. "You never asked."

"What do you mean, you saw him leave?" I asked quickly. "My driver?"

"It was three o'clock in the morning. I got up to stop that shutter from waking you. It woke me," he said to his mother, ignoring me.

"You saw my driver leave at that hour?"

"I did. He went tearing up the road as if all the devils were at his heels. I could see his headlamps bouncing wildly—all over the road. It was a wonder he didn't hit something. The sheep and cattle wander about a lot at night."

I was glad to know Mr. Morgan wasn't dead and buried in the churchyard, but this news was startling.

"Are you sure—" I began, then stopped. It was a stupid question. Everyone must have known within an hour of my arrival who I was, and who my driver was. But why had he abandoned me? And why hadn't the firm said something to him—done something about me? I couldn't begin to understand.

And if Mr. Morgan had been in such a hurry, surely he'd have awakened Mr. Griffith in his haste. But Mr. Griffith claimed he hadn't discovered that his guest was gone until Mr. Morgan didn't come out in the morning. The cottage wasn't so large that one man who was accustomed to living alone wouldn't have heard every sound his guest made! In fact, he might not have been asleep at all. He might have taken in Mr. Morgan for the money, but it must have felt strange to have someone else in the cottage, moving about.

Then why hadn't Mr. Griffith told Hugh *when* Mr. Morgan left, or about the motorcar driving so erratically?

I was about to ask when the younger woman shyly wanted to know something about my nursing, and the subject changed before I could prevent it.

"I've been so grateful to my parents for allowing me to go for my training," I said. "We've saved lives," I added, not bragging but trying to indicate that nursing had its rewards. "It's why we're sent to the forward lines, to bring help as quickly as we can to the wounded."

"Could you hear the guns?" her son interrupted, eager to hear about the fighting.

I'd heard the artillery, I could tell which pieces were being fired, and of course the machine guns, the rifles. I'd watched the aircraft hover overhead, dropping bombs, I'd heard the sound of tank engines. And men crying out in pain and fear.

I smiled, trying to keep my face from betraying what I was thinking. Even now the war was still fresh in my mind, and I couldn't let it go. It was over—finished. But it was as if it couldn't let *me* go. Wouldn't let me go.

"When you're busy with a wounded soldier, you don't notice the noise—" I stopped. He didn't want to hear that part. "Yes, it's very noisy, hard to hear yourself think. And everything is happening at once."

His grandmother didn't want him to be a soldier. I could see that as the friendliness in her face hardened. "His father was killed at Ypres," she told me coldly.

"I'm sorry," I replied, meaning it.

But she put a hand on her grandson's back, and moving him forward, she nodded coolly and walked on.

I looked after them. Was the boy right? That my driver had left in such a hurry? What on earth had possessed him? I couldn't believe that he was frightened by the storm.

If he'd worried about deteriorating conditions, and any danger for me, his passenger, then he'd have come back as soon as the weather passed and rescued me.

And he hadn't. Nor had Mr. Morgan struck me as an easily frightened man. He didn't appear to have the imagination to be. Plain, sturdy, reliable. That was how I'd seen him.

I walked on to Rachel's house, busy wondering if I should instead turn around and knock on Mr. Griffith's door.

The closer I got to her house, the better the idea seemed. Mr. Griffith wasn't a pleasant man, but he was hardly going to attack me.

I wheeled and walked on toward his cottage. The two women and the boy had disappeared, and I saw them again—some distance down the path to the cottages—as I stopped and raised my hand to knock.

He opened the door in my face.

"Sister?" he said coldly.

"Mr. Griffith," I returned, acknowledging him. "I was just talking to those people who were out for a walk. A grandmother, her daughter, and grandson. The boy told me something rather strange. He said that when my driver left, it was in the middle of the night, and he was in a tearing hurry. I wondered if he'd been taken suddenly ill? And why you didn't summon me to help him."

There. He couldn't shut the door in my face. Not with all those questions fired at him.

"I told Williams I didn't hear Morgan leave. With all the storm's racket, it would have been nearly impossible. I've no way of knowing when he left."

"He was staying with you."

"I live on the edge of the cliff. You can see where the cottage stands for yourself. In a storm like that, the wind rattles us something fierce. You'd think it was about to blow right over. So far it never has. But Morgan might not have realized that. He probably left in terror of his life." His eyes were cold as he said that last, but he smiled. "I'm used to the storms. They don't keep me awake anymore. I didn't hear him leave."

"If he thought the storm was so awful, why didn't he come for me, and take me out of harm's way as well?"

"Ask him yourself, when you arrive in Swansea."

He made to close his door, but I said quickly, "If he fled to Swansea out of the storm, why hasn't he or the firm that employs him come back to fetch me?"

He rolled his eyes.

"How do you expect me to know the answer to that?" he demanded, incensed. Or trying to look as if he was angered by the question. "*You* picked the firm, *you* hired the driver. It's at your door if they were both unreliable to start with. Good day, Sister."

This time he got the door shut.

I stood there, swallowing what I wanted to say, that he'd been responsible for my driver that night, and he'd been unreliable, not Morgan.

But there was some truth to his words. *Had* I chosen so poorly?

I'd been tired, I didn't know Wales very well. I might have misjudged . . .

The only answer I could think of was that I'd promised half the fee to set out and half on arrival at my destination. That was when I thought it would be easy to look in on Captain Williams, make certain he was all right and his wound was healing, then return to Swansea the next day. I *hadn't* counted on the Gower. Neither its isolation nor its lack of facilities for a traveler like me.

On the other hand, I'd made it quite clear I was returning with the motorcar in the morning.

Confused, I turned away.

And I thought I heard Mr. Griffith laughing from behind the door.

* * *

Rachel wasn't in, nor was Hugh. I went up to my room, stood by the window, and watched the sun sparkle far out to sea on water that was almost black it was so blue.

And beyond were banked clouds. More weather on its way?

Sighing, I turned back to the little room, and as I did, I heard the outer door open downstairs.

It was Rachel. She smiled as I started down the steps. "The lamb is back with the ewe. They're all right."

"Good news, that," I said, returning the smile. "Would you like a cup of tea?"

"I need to wash up first."

"Before you do—Rachel, most of the cottages appear to have small horse barns. I wonder. Do you think I could borrow—even purchase—a horse that I could ride back to Swansea? I'm worried about the clinic, you see. I should be there tomorrow at the earliest. No later than Thursday."

As I was speaking, she glanced down at my skirts, and I knew what she was thinking. I was a nursing Sister, not a horsewoman. Riding as far as Swansea would be beyond me.

But I'd learned to ride in India almost before I could run. My father had taken me up before him, and then found a pony when I was strong enough to manage it.

Simon had taught me to ride like the wind, control my horse with my knees, as the cavalry had to do, and even use a weapon on horseback. My father had encouraged that, for my safety as well as the exercise. We weren't always in friendly territory, and my mother was already an accomplished horsewoman. A fair shot too.

"I understand you must be worried, Bess. But the only horses we have left out here are trained to the plow. They aren't accustomed to saddles. The Army took every horse we could spare, leaving us anything that was unsuitable for them. Besides, we'll be needing them soon. I share two horses with a widow just up the road. Her stables are a bit larger, and I need mine for any ewes in trouble. Her own plow horse died in the autumn, and I can't let you borrow these, even if you could find someone to bring them back. I don't know that we could replace either of them."

I tried to put the best face on it. "I know, I understand. It was just a thought. I'll just put the kettle on."

I went on into the kitchen. I'd seen the fallow fields, of course. Almost an old-fashioned system, rather than the newer large farms one might find in East Anglia. These were more market garden fields, growing whatever foodstuffs people out here needed.

How long would it take to walk? I wondered as I picked up the kettle to fill it.

And if that bank of distant cloud was coming this way, it could catch me out in the open.

Or, I thought, trying to raise my own spirits, I might walk five miles and find someone willing to lend me a horse or carry me to the next village in a farm cart.

It wasn't much in the way of spirit-raising. I'd seen how desolate it was, coming here.

The door opened and the dogs came charging into the kitchen, tongues lolling, heading for their water bowls. As they lapped loudly, I called to Hugh.

"I've just put the kettle on, if you want to go upstairs first."

There was no answer.

No sound of the crutches making their way either up the stairs or down the passage.

Just—silence.

I listened to it for several seconds, and then went flying toward the door. Something was wrong.

CHAPTER 9

HUGH WAS HUNCHED in the corner where the wall next to the door and the wall next to the front room met. His face was gray with pain, and his eyes were closed. They flew open as he heard me approaching.

"I thought—I hoped no one was here."

"What happened?" I asked, not touching him but looking him over. One shoulder was muddy, with bits of brown grass clinging to it. And one side of his head was muddy as well, his hair every which way.

He'd fallen.

I reached out.

"*No, don't touch me,*" he said quickly, keeping his voice down. "I'll be all right."

"Hugh. You're hurt. And it isn't something that will pass when you catch your breath. *Where?* It's what I do, you know. Take care of wounds."

He put up a good show, straightening his shoulders and squaring himself around to pull the crutches back into place under his arms. But his face went even paler as he winced, and my first thought was *He's bruised his ribs.*

"Rachel is upstairs. You must let me help you into the kitchen, where you can sit down. You don't want her to see you like this."

He resisted, then cast a worried glance at the stairs. Nodding, he let me take his weight on the other side, and between us we made it somehow to the kitchen. I got him into a chair, although it was harder than either of us expected.

Just then the kettle came on the boil, and I had to step across the room to lift it off.

"What happened?" I asked again, finding a cloth and putting it into cold water. "Here, there's mud in your hair."

He used his good arm to try to clean it off, but in the end I took the cloth from him and did what I could. It was then I noticed the darkening bruise along his jawline.

He still hadn't explained what had happened. But I was beginning to piece the bits together.

Rachel hadn't come down. She had had more than enough time to change her clothes.

Had she looked out her window—and seen what was happening out there? And didn't want to come down and embarrass the Captain?

I didn't think Hugh was going to tell me anything.

And so I said, in the face of his reluctance, "You must at least tell me where it hurts, Hugh. I can't help you if I don't know." Then I added, deliberately, "The ground is still cold, it can do some damage if you fall hard."

After a moment he said, "The side of my chest. Just there."

He reached across his body with his right hand to touch the lower part of his rib cage.

It wasn't where I'd have expected damage from a fall. His shoulder was muddy, that was where he'd hit the ground. If that had caused him pain, it would mean the ribs higher up and in the back.

But it was exactly where someone might have hit him with a fist, catching him off guard, bending him over so that the second blow—to the jaw—had sent him flying.

I fought to keep my voice steady, my head down as I helped him unbutton his coat. It was difficult getting it off. I worked slowly, easing him out of it as best I could. But he was gritting his teeth against the pain and the effort he was making.

It was off, finally, and I spread it across the back of a chair. When I reached for the buttons of his shirt, he shoved my hand away.

"It's better now." His voice was cold. I realized he knew I'd see what was there. Another bruise beginning to appear.

A great deal of force had gone behind that blow. Driven by anger and a strong desire to hurt, to punish.

"I think your ribs are bruised. It's going to hurt for a bit. I don't think we need to wrap them."

"No," he agreed.

"Rachel may have something that will help you a little with the discomfort. We can ask."

"Leave her out of this."

"Hugh. Be sensible. You're going to be stiff and sore. There's the bruising on your face. She's bound to notice. The best thing to do is tell her you fell and be done with it."

Anger flared in his eyes, then faded as he saw I was right. Whether he liked it or not, she would have to know something. And that would make it easier for her, if she had seen the attack from her window and knew who it was.

I moved away, going to set the kettle back to make tea.

"There's whisky. In the cupboard up there. Pour a little in my cup."

"Yes, of course."

By the time the tea was ready, and I'd added the whisky to his, I heard Rachel starting toward the stairs.

Hugh tensed, hearing her footsteps too. His eyes met mine, and I held his gaze for a moment before reaching for the jug of milk and pouring a little into each cup. You could smell the warm whisky . . .

Rachel came down the hall, into the kitchen, and said, "Bless you, Bess! I thought I'd never get warm. Sitting on the cold ground beside a ewe is not—" She let herself look at Hugh, and I wondered how much effort it had cost her just to frown and say, "Are you all right? Did you fall?"

"Awkwardly. But no harm done."

She walked over to his coat. "This is still damp. I think it should clean up easily enough."

I handed her another cloth, and she set to work, sipping her tea as she cleaned the coat and found a brush to finish the task. "There." When her back was turned, I refilled Hugh's cup with more tea and a little extra whisky. He glanced at me gratefully before concentrating on drinking it.

But when the teacups were empty, Hugh had to struggle to rise from the table and reach for his crutches.

We both started toward him, but he snapped, "Don't *fuss*."

He managed on his own, and set out toward the front room. "I have some matters to attend to," he said over his shoulder.

"And I need to finish my mending," Rachel said briskly, but her gaze moved from his retreating back to my face.

Shaking her head, telling me not to question her, she fled the kitchen in her turn and went up the stairs again.

I saw the angry tears in her eyes before she turned away.

Rachel *had* seen whatever had happened out there. She knew who had done this.

And angry as she was, I didn't think she knew how to deal with that knowledge.

Was it the girl Anna's father? Mr. Dunhill?

Or was there someone else who had it in for Hugh?

With a sigh I cleared away.

We had just finished our dinner—no one had much of an appetite, and the silence in the kitchen was so deafening as we avoided conversation that I could hear one of the dogs breathing deeply in its sleep—when there was a knock at the door.

Hugh made as if to get up to answer it, but Rachel was closer.

"That must be Mrs. Baker. She promised to bring me a little of her salt in exchange for some sugar."

She rose hastily and went to open the door. We could feel the draft of cold air and hear low voices.

And then Rachel called, "Sister Crawford?"

I was on my feet at once. The alarm in her voice warned me that there was trouble. My first thought was that Barry Dunhill had had the effrontery to come to the house. Even as the thought was forming, I could hear shuffling and someone grunting, as if she might be trying to hold back whoever it was.

Hugh, swearing under his breath, was reaching for his crutches, scrambling to get to his feet.

I came around the table fast, intent on reaching the door from the kitchen to the passage before Hugh was mobile.

But when I got to the door and looked toward Rachel, I didn't see an angry man jostling with her to come inside the house.

Instead, there was a woman wearing a cape, her face hidden as she tried to maneuver a half-conscious man through the door and toward the front room.

I ran to help Rachel and the woman, and we managed to get the man into the front room, down on the rug, flat on his back. We were breathing hard from the effort it had taken.

Rachel fumbled for the matches and lit first one lamp and then the other.

By this time I was kneeling by the man. And Hugh had dragged himself out of the kitchen to the parlor door. I glanced up to see him slumped against the frame, his face drawn from the effort he'd made.

In the lamplight my hands were dark with blood, and there was so much blood on the man's face that I could hardly tell where most of it was coming from.

But I could see—quite clearly—that he'd been badly beaten.

The woman spoke, and I realized for the first time that it was Ellen Marshall.

"He didn't come back—he'd gone for a walk. I went out to see— and I found him like that."

"Did you see who it was that did this?" I asked.

Rachel said, as if waking from a dream, "Clean cloths—warm water," and hurried from the room. Hugh clumsily got out of her way.

I'd got the man's scarf off, unbuttoned his coat, and pulled his collar away from his throat.

He moaned once, but I thought he'd been moving in and out of consciousness for a while. In fact, it was a miracle that Miss Marshall had got him here at all.

"Did you see who did this?" I asked her again.

"No. He was lying in the middle of that wretched lane that runs down to the cottage. Hardly a road, is it? I thought he was dead—he just lay there, not moving, not answering me." She shook her head. "I don't know how I got him into the motorcar. It was all I could think of, getting help for him. There must be some blood in his throat. He was choking on it . . ." She broke off.

His nose was most likely broken, his lip split, bruised cheekbones would turn his eyes black, and a flap of skin hung down into his eyebrow, still bleeding copiously.

I had no idea how many blows to the body there had been.

I opened his coat, got the woolen jumper under that off him, and opened his shirt.

Ellen made a sound as if to stop me when I leaned forward to see more clearly.

His chest was rapidly bruising, and his shoulders as well.

She turned away. "Please God, don't let him die out here."

Hugh was still in the doorway, there was no sign of Rachel, and the woman had hardly moved.

I got up, found the little porcelain jar that held the long matches, and took one of them to light the fire. It was cold in here, and even with the fire burning, I would need pillows, blankets. I didn't think this man was going anywhere tonight.

Returning to his side, I asked Ellen, "What's his name?"

She hesitated.

"I must call him *something*."

"It's Oliver."

Rachel came down the passage just then, a tray in her hands. There were clean rags in a small heap, a basin of warm water, and some sticking plasters.

She brought the tray into the room, flinching a little as she saw the man was half-dressed, and set it down to my hand.

"A pillow—blankets—and Miss Marshall could use a cup of tea. Captain, perhaps you could help with that."

Rachel said, "I'll just go upstairs . . ."

And Hugh turned, walking back to the kitchen.

"You must have some idea why this man was beaten so badly," I said as I began to wipe away as much blood as I could. "What had he done, to incur such anger?"

She had moved away, toward the window and the darkness outside. I could hear the rattle of the glass as a gust of wind came up from the sea.

"I don't know. Nothing—nothing like this has ever happened on my visits."

I remembered the sound of a chair's leg scraping the floor in another room as she kept me standing on the doorstep, while I asked her for a lift back to Swansea.

"He's staying with you? Oliver?"

"He came down. It was to help me with something in the cottage. Something I couldn't do on my own."

I thought, judging by how upset she was, that Oliver was possibly more than just someone who came along to help in the cottage. His clothing was good, not that of a laborer she might have hired. A friend?

I remembered too that she was a widow.

"Has he been here before?"

"No—no, I generally come alone."

"Then he would have no enemies here."

I had got the worst of the blood cleaned off his face, put pressure on the flap of skin to try to stop fresh bleeding, then used plasters to keep it in place. The nose was broken, I was sure of it now, but not displaced, and the bruises on his upper body were the size of fists.

I noticed as I cleaned and closed the flap of skin that there was grit in it, as if Oliver's assailant had struck him with a stone, in the hope of taking the fight out of him, and then administering what was little short of a severe beating while his victim was too dazed to defend himself.

Had the same man who had attacked Hugh also attacked Oliver? But whoever it was, he *couldn't* have mistaken one man for the other. Both attacks must have been deliberate . . .

Rachel was back with an armload of bedding, blankets and sheets for the floor, pillows and pillow slips.

I turned to Ellen. "You might help Mrs. Williams make a pallet for Oliver. And then we can roll him over on it."

Ellen looked surprised, as if she hadn't expected to be asked to work. But she took off her cape, knelt on the floor, and proceeded to help Rachel as I'd asked.

I was worried about my patient having been unconscious for

quite so long. And so I began to speak his name as I worked. I wasn't certain about his ribs, but they had taken a battering, and they could be broken. There was a healed wound in his side, the rough scar running from back to front from his ribs possibly to his hip. It looked like shrapnel. He'd been in the war then, although he was dressed in civilian clothing tonight.

When I examined his hands, I saw bloodied knuckles. Oliver, I thought in some surprise, had put up a fight. Was this why he'd been brutally beaten when he stopped being able to ward off his attacker?

Oliver's eyelids flickered. They were already swelling, but they opened, he jerked wildly, and then he slid into the darkness again. I was sure he thought he was lying in the road and his attacker was still here, waiting for him.

After a moment, his eyes opened again, and he lay quietly, staring up at me. He hadn't seen me at Ellen's cottage door. He'd heard my voice, possibly heard what I was asking. And it was likely that Ellen Marshall had told him after I'd gone what it was I wanted from her.

And so he knew there was a Sister in the village. He hadn't asked if he had been taken to hospital.

That was a good sign. Still, I thought he might well have a concussion. It would bear watching.

I had nothing with me to tend to such wounds. But keeping them clean and keeping the patient warm and in bed would do until he could be driven to Swansea for a more thorough examination.

Thinking about that, I said, "If you wish—I understand there's a doctor in one of the other villages."

"He's better off in your care, Sister," Ellen answered. "I can't get him back into the motorcar tonight. It's beyond my strength."

They'd made the pallet bed, and we pulled it to Oliver's side, and then as I rolled his body onto his side—he cried out at that—we got it under him and then rolled him back on it. I managed to finish the task, and drew the last blanket up over him.

Rachel said, "I'll fetch the tea."

She came back with the tray, two cups, the teapot, milk jug, and a little jar of honey. Pouring one for Ellen, who had gone back to the window, staring out, Rachel took it to her. Ellen thanked her. And then she brought the second cup to me, already containing milk and honey, the way I took it at breakfast and dinner.

I'd washed my hands as best I could in the bloody water in the basin. Taking the cup, I drank a little, and watched Oliver's eyes follow me.

"Not yet," I said gently. "Your lips have only just stopped bleeding." And they were already swollen.

"Did you see who did this?" I asked.

His voice was light when he spoke, higher than Hugh's. I thought possibly he was younger as well, but couldn't be sure.

"It was dark."

"You were set on?" I asked.

But he didn't answer that.

"Have you seen that man before? Could you identify him again, if you saw him?"

"Don't know."

But if Oliver's knuckles were anything to go by, there might well be some bruises that spoke loud enough to identify the face if not the name.

I was still perplexed by two attacks in one evening. I'd thought I guessed who had come after Hugh. But why would he then walk down that wretched road and attack *this* man?

I couldn't believe he'd simply run mad. It didn't make sense.

Getting up, I set my teacup on a table, collected the bloody rags and the basin, and went to the kitchen to dispose of them. Then I washed my hands properly.

Hugh was watching me. I knew what he wanted to ask. But he'd lied about what had happened to him, and he didn't know quite how to get around that.

Keeping my voice low, I said, "He tells me he didn't know his attacker. I don't know whether he did or not. Miss Marshall says he hasn't been down here before. That she usually comes alone. If that's true, then he may also be telling me the truth. But he defended himself. And from the look of it, someone will be bruised tomorrow."

"As a rule, she doesn't bring anyone with her. At least so Rachel has told me." He hesitated. "Is he well enough to go?"

"No. I expect they'll have no choice but to spend the night here." A gust of wind followed by the sound of rain hitting the house seemed to reinforce what I was saying. "I can't see how we can get him back into Miss Marshall's motorcar." I was reminded of something else. "I keep forgetting. She was married. Is it Mrs. Marshall?"

"Out here she's always been Ellen Marshall. I've never heard Rachel call her anything else."

"Well, it doesn't matter. Do you need anything?"

"No."

The bruise on his jaw was dark enough now to be noticeable. I thought that might be why he was staying clear of the parlor. When he was standing in the doorway, it hadn't been visible, and I thought he intended to keep it from Ellen. He didn't want to answer questions.

It occurred to me that Hugh had been about to go into the front room and attend to some matters. Or find a comfortable place to sit? "Hugh. Can you manage the stairs?"

156

"I don't know."

"Then we'll make you a bed in the weaving room. It might be for the best. And it's warm enough in there."

"Don't *fuss.*"

"I'm not," I told him briskly. "I'm facing facts. Unless you want to share the parlor with Miss Marshall and Oliver, you don't have much choice."

He considered that. Finally, he looked up and his gaze met mine. I kept my own as bland as I could. "It might be for the best tonight. Tomorrow I'll be fine."

Tomorrow he was going to be stiff and possibly in pain. But I let it go. "I'll go to your room, collect the bedding, and come back down."

I did as I promised. As I passed the front room I heard voices. Rachel's and Ellen's, in conversation. From the few words I heard, I gathered they were discussing where she was to sleep, for I heard the words *chair* and *pillows.*

I got the blankets and sheets from Hugh's bed, caught up the pillows, and hurried back down the stairs, moving as quickly and quietly as I could.

There was silence from the front room, and I found that Rachel had gone back to the kitchen, bringing the tea things with her.

She looked up as I came in, her face showing her surprise at my burdens, and then she said, "Hugh?"

"This shoulder is a little stiff from my fall," he said quietly. "I thought it best not to try the stairs."

"A good idea. The weaving room?" She turned, opened the door, and went ahead of me to light the lamp. Together we made up another pallet on the floor, this one on the pretty rag rug. Hugh was just there in the kitchen, and we couldn't say anything that wouldn't have been overheard.

As we worked, she asked, "How badly hurt is Miss Marshall's friend?"

"I'm not sure. But he's better off here, where I can keep an eye on him. Do you mind dreadfully?"

She took a deep breath. "Not really."

But I knew she was being polite.

When I went back to the parlor to look in on Oliver, I found Ellen Marshall wearing her cape and preparing to leave.

"If you could spare an umbrella?" she asked. "Although from the sound of it out there, much good will it do me in this wind."

"You're leaving?" I thought I'd heard Rachel trying to persuade her to stay.

"My grandfather's cottage is standing wide open. I must go back."

"Are you sure it's safe?"

"I have the motorcar. It's not as if I must walk. Besides, I'm used to the weather out here."

"We don't know why Oliver was beaten. Whoever it is might be waiting for you in the house. He might not have finished his night's work."

"Nonsense. Besides, there's a revolver in the motorcar. I can defend myself." She looked down at the man on the bedding. "I owed it to him to be sure he was taken care of. He's sleeping a little. I can go with an easy mind." She glanced toward the windows as they rattled again. I could almost read her thoughts. *I've stayed too long as it is.*

There was nothing I could do to persuade her, but I was uneasy with her going alone. If anything happened to her, we wouldn't know until she didn't appear in the morning. By then it might be too late.

"I wish you would reconsider—" I began, but she interrupted me.

"Yes, yes, I understand." Drawing her cape about her, she looked again at the man's bruised face. "He'll be all right. He was in the war, you know." It wasn't so much a question as a statement, as if she was trying to will him to be all right. As if surviving France meant he could survive anything.

I couldn't help but think she might be right. I'd seen the scar on his side.

Turning away, she walked briskly to the door. "Please thank Mrs. Williams for her kindness. May I take this?" She reached for an umbrella in the porcelain Chinese stand, its white background standing out in the shadows by the door. And then she had opened it and stepped out into what appeared to be a gale. With rain blowing into my face, I watched her make her way, splashing through the puddles, to the motorcar.

She had to turn the crank, her cape flapping about her like something alive, tormenting her. And then she was in the motorcar, slamming the door, and as an afterthought, turning on the headlamps. They picked out the driving rain for a moment before turning away toward the road.

I shut the door quickly, before I was drenched.

Rachel was coming down the passage. "Bess?"

"It was Ellen. She just left. She was worried about the house standing open in all this rain."

"But she's coming back? I told her I could make a comfortable enough bed for her there in the parlor."

"I don't think she will." I drew a breath. "She was glad her friend was all right. She asked me to thank you for helping him. I tried to persuade her, but it was no use. She had made up her mind. She borrowed your umbrella."

"But is it safe for her to be out there by herself?" It was the same question I'd asked myself. "That's to say—after what has happened?"

Hugh called, hearing our tense voices, "What is it? Rachel?"

We hurried back to the kitchen. "Ellen felt she had to go back to the cottage. The storm," Ellen told him quietly. "Bess couldn't convince her to stay the night."

He tried to rise. "I should have gone with her—let her close up, then bring her back." But he couldn't drive. And in this wind, he would have found it difficult on crutches.

Instead, Rachel said, "I think she wanted to sleep in her own bed. Just as well. She would have been restless here. Worrying."

"Still."

"We might as well call it a night ourselves," Rachel said. She looked longingly at the weaving room, but she couldn't work there tonight. Then, glancing around the kitchen to be sure all was well—Hugh had cleared away our dinner dishes—she said good night and left us there. It occurred to me that she didn't want to be alone with Hugh. Not yet.

"Is she all right?" Hugh asked, watching her disappear down the shadowy passage.

"I think this has been upsetting for everyone," I replied. "Is there anything I can get for you? Before I look in on Oliver and then go up myself?"

"No. Thank you, Bess."

He fumbled with his crutches, forced himself upright, and crossed the kitchen. "I'll leave the lamp lit here, shall I? In the event you need something?"

"Yes, a very good idea." I wished him good night and went back to the parlor.

Half an hour later, with rain and wind still lashing at the house, I was satisfied that my patient was stable enough to be left alone. I'd given him a little watered whisky earlier, and it seemed to have helped. Most of his wounds had stopped bleeding, although the one on his forehead was still weeping a little. I dealt with that, asked if he was comfortable, and got a mumbled reply.

Taking that as an affirmative, I got to my feet and wished him good night. Seeing that there was an extra pillow, I added it under his head, then stoked the fire to keep it burning.

There was nothing more to be done.

I went up myself.

I got to the top of the stairs and hesitated, wondering if I should tap at Rachel's door. But it was firmly closed, there was no light showing, and I took that to mean she didn't want to talk. I couldn't imagine, given everything that had happened, that she was asleep in that dark room. Still, I had to respect her wishes.

I turned toward my own room, closed the door, and sat down for a moment on the bed.

Taking a deep breath, I tried to make sense of the two attacks.

What had happened out there today—tonight?

What had precipitated the attacks?

Two dead men had washed ashore recently. But I couldn't see how that had any bearing on the beatings. Unless the rumors about Tom Williams being one of them had prompted whatever had occurred with Hugh.

It wouldn't have involved Oliver, surely—he'd come with Ellen, and he was still close by the cottage, not wandering about the village. To attack him would mean walking all that distance. And I hadn't mentioned to anyone that I suspected there was someone in the cottage with Ellen—indeed, I couldn't have said whether it was a man or another woman.

Well. There was nothing more I could do.

And there was no Constable resident in this village.

The question was, would Ellen—who had lived in towns, who was accustomed to the police being there to help in such circumstances—insist on making what happened to Oliver a police matter? Pressing charges?

I could see that tomorrow was going to be interesting.

At the same time, I couldn't help but wonder how my own situation might change. If Ellen decided to go back to Swansea or Cardiff, either to go to the police or to take Oliver to better medical care, she might be more willing now to help me—since I'd helped her friend when he needed it.

Well. That was for tomorrow. I realized I was cold, and I undressed quickly, crawling into bed.

I was just shoving my bare feet down through cold sheets when I remembered that I hadn't thought to fill my hot water bottle.

Neither had Rachel.

We were both going to spend an unpleasant night.

CHAPTER 10

RAIN POUNDED THE headland throughout the night, blowing in the gusts of wind. I heard it off and on, unable to drop into a deeper sleep.

I was grateful the house was sturdy and weatherproof despite its age. But the window rattled with the worst gusts, bringing me up out of sleep just as I drifted off. Several times I put on my dressing gown and went down to look in on Oliver. I'd have asked the night nurse to do just that, if we were in hospital or a clinic. But he was in no danger that I could see. I couldn't be sure of his ribs, but he gave no sign that they were affecting his breathing. Cracks would show up in pain later.

And what of Hugh? He was not spending a very comfortable night. And the bruise on his chin would be all too visible tomorrow. He'd be forced to admit to the embarrassment of a fall, if he intended to say nothing about his own confrontation with trouble.

But when Oliver came, why hadn't he spoken up? Was he so certain there was no connection between his battering and Oliver's? Climbing the stairs in the faint light of the lamp in the front room, I wished I could be as sure.

Still, Rachel had kept what she might have seen to herself as well. More than a little exasperated with both of them, I crawled back into my bed and tried to sleep. In their place, I'd have worried about Ellen going back to the cottage alone and warned her. Revolver or no revolver, she was taking a risk.

My last coherent thought as I drifted into sleep was that these people out here on the tip of the peninsula were a stubborn lot.

When a watery gray dawn broke, barely lighting my little room on the southwestern side, I dressed, went quietly down the stairs, and glanced into the parlor.

Oliver was sleeping restlessly. Not wanting to disturb him this early, I went on to the kitchen.

Hugh was already up, dressed in the clothing he'd worn yesterday. He started when he heard me coming, then nodded.

"Can you fetch my razor? And that small mirror?" He looked down the still-dark passage. "I'd rather not wake him with my crutches."

"Yes, of course." I went back, found what he needed, and brought it down, along with a clean shirt.

"I'll heat shaving water," I said, "and make us a cup of tea. How are you, this morning?"

"I'll do."

Which meant, I thought, that he was hurting more than a little.

"Is your discomfort with those ribs worse? I can't see inside, I can't tell how much they are damaged. Have you noticed any trouble breathing?"

"No worse," he answered tersely. When the kettle had boiled, I gave him water to shave, and he took the mirror to the window for better light. I could see then how stiff he actually was, moving gingerly.

Pretending not to notice, I made the tea, and when it had steeped, poured two cups. He'd finished shaving by then and he drank his tea as if he'd needed it and hadn't had the energy to prepare it himself. Once, out of the corner of my eye, I saw him massaging his thigh where his leg was missing, as if it was throbbing. Phantom pain—or had he hurt it when he fell?

"You've lived here for a little while. Who would have given Oliver such a beating?"

"I don't know. Some of the men aren't very friendly. But I've seen nothing like this since I came. Of course, there's the trouble over that first body. Still, I had a feeling that had begun as a personal matter, not the village as a whole having a say."

"And the rector? Does he help with problems?"

"He's a good man, I'm sure. But this is an out-of-the-way parish, the living is barely enough to get by on, and that house, the rectory, is a leaky old place that the local people claim is haunted. I doubt the church tends to send their best priests here."

I had to agree. The rector had appeared to me to be a defeated man, not one to stand up for anything in this parish. He upheld the moral standard, and that was about all he could hope to do. A leader of men he was not. A changer of lives he was not.

I wanted to ask Hugh who had attacked him—and if he thought it was the same man who had encountered Oliver later. But I couldn't ask. And from his manner, I didn't think he did believe they were the same person. If there was a madman running loose, attacking people on sight, I had the feeling Hugh would be handling this differently.

But was he right?

We had just finished breakfast, and I was preparing a tray for Oliver when there was a knock at the door.

Rachel went to open it, and I heard Ellen's voice, then Rachel responding,

They went into the parlor, and I assumed that the question had been something on the order of how the patient was faring this morning.

When I took the tray in, Rachel was standing by the window and Ellen was there on her knees by the bedding, speaking to Oliver.

"But are you sure? I can drive you to Swansea, there's a hospital there."

"No. I don't want to go to hospital," he said, his words mumbled through bruised lips. And one eye was distinctly dark, giving him an owlish expression.

It was hard to judge, with so much swelling and bruising, what Oliver really looked like. He had dark hair and blue eyes, was fairly young, and possibly even attractive, for all I knew.

It would be some days before his face healed. I'd looked earlier at the chest bruising. I thought he'd been kicked while he lay on the ground, because one place on his ribs was darker, sharper. When I examined the spot, he was uncomfortable but not in dire pain. He'd been lucky then, with his heavy coat and his wool jumper. Just enough padding to prevent a broken rib. But it was going to hurt with every breath, at least for a bit.

He wanted to get up, dress, and go back with Ellen.

I told him I thought it was too soon. But in the end, he got his way, and I helped him dress—with more difficulty than he'd been prepared for—and laced up his boots for him. He was pale and perspiring from the effort it had taken.

There were puddles everywhere, and the wind had a bite to it, as we got him out to the motorcar. Overhead the sky was still heavily overcast, although mercifully the rain had stopped for a bit. The Worm had vanished in a heavier shower out to sea.

He drew his breath in sharply as we helped him into the passenger's seat, and I knew that one particular bruise low on the chest wall was to blame. Leaning his head back, he closed his eyes for a moment.

"Are you sure this is wise?" I asked.

"I'm here in the motorcar. I might as well go," he said.

Ellen was already turning the crank. I closed his door and stepped back, beside Rachel. Hugh had been conspicuous by his absence this morning.

With a nod of thanks, Ellen drove slowly away, trying to avoid the worst of the jarring as the tires found the ruts.

Rachel and I watched her motorcar travel on down the steep track toward the coast guard station.

There had been no mention of summoning the police.

I found that odd. Ellen Marshall hadn't struck me as the sort of person who would have let such a beating go. I would have imagined her incensed at what had happened to a guest under her roof and demanding that the police send someone to find whoever had done this and take him into custody.

Rachel started toward the house. I caught up with her and said, "Rachel. About yesterday—"

She shook her head, hurrying on.

"Rachel, it couldn't have been a fall," I said then.

"I don't want to talk about it."

She went through the door, leaving it open for me to follow, and by the time I'd got to the kitchen, she was in the weaving room with the door shut.

Hugh was trying to pull on his coat, intending to go out to look at the ewes. I had to help him, against my better judgment.

When he left, moving slower than usual, I considered offering to help, but I knew it would be rejected. I closed the door after him and went to clear away the breakfast and see to washing the sheets and pillow slips from Oliver's bed.

I didn't hear Rachel go out. I thought it was when I had taken the extra blankets and pillows back upstairs. But the loom was silent.

Curious, I went to every window on the first floor, wondering if she had decided to confront Hugh outside, away from the house.

But I could see them out there, working in different parts of the property.

And standing by his cottage door, Mr. Griffith was staring at them, as if wondering what had passed here last evening.

Whatever Rachel knew about what had happened to Hugh, she had come to terms with it by the time she came in for the midday meal. The rain had started again, sweeping across the sea and coming over the headland just as Hugh came in, bringing wet dogs with muddy paws at his heels.

Hugh and I dried them, and I wiped up the puddles while Rachel served us a rich barley soup and toasted cheese sandwiches.

"Did you discover Oliver's last name?" Hugh asked as we ate.

"That's the only name Ellen gave us. And he didn't add to it," I said.

"Interesting. I'd have liked to know."

"But what should I call her?" I asked Rachel, now that I had a chance.

"She was always Ellen Marshall out here," she replied, confirming what Hugh had told me last evening. "She married a man by the name of Hobson. Quite a good match, from what I've been told."

"He never came out here?"

"I don't think he did," she said. "That was probably her grandfather's choice. He was reclusive, kept to himself. I don't think he'd have wanted her husband to see where the family came from. There was money—probably inherited, I should think—but he had no desire to move away. Still, he sent his daughter to school in town, and let her marry in town. And his granddaughter as well."

And this visit, Ellen Marshall Hobson had brought someone with her.

For a fleeting moment I wondered if a jealous suitor in Cardiff might have followed them out here and given the interloper a good thrashing. If perhaps that was why Ellen had not pursued the attack by calling in the police. That would make more sense than someone from the village attacking him.

"I don't think it's a good idea for either of you to wander far from the house," Hugh was saying. "Not until we know who did this."

"You think it was someone local?" I asked.

He frowned. "I don't know the people out here very well. That's the problem. In the valley, if there was trouble, we could usually put a name to it. Work in the pits was hard. A few men drank themselves into oblivion when they could, but they weren't likely to cause problems for anyone but themselves and their families. A few hotheads fought from time to time. In the pits you had to depend on each other, and you weren't likely to take matters down with you."

"It's been much the same here," Rachel said, nodding. "We have to depend on each other. There was trouble in the past. I remember my father and mother talking about it, and stopping when Matthew or I came into the room."

"What sort of trouble?"

"Matthew and I never knew." She made a face. "Still, he told me once there had been a murder not far from the village. That was after he'd gone exploring in the prehistoric caves, and he said it would be an easy matter to hide a body in some of them. By the time anyone found it, it would be impossible to tell whether it was ancient or recent. I didn't know whether to believe him or not."

I was reminded of someone in our village in Somerset. Sally Meacham's brother, who ran away to join the gypsies when he was eleven. The gypsies promptly brought him home again, but for several months he was enormously popular with the other village boys because of his daring. It sounded as if Rachel's brother was cut of the same adventurous cloth.

"He must have made a fine soldier," I said. Sally's brother had joined the Colonel Sahib's regiment and was mentioned in dispatches any number of times.

Rachel smiled wistfully. "He was decorated twice for bravery under fire. I wish he'd been a little less brave and survived the war."

My uniform from last evening washed and hung up to dry in the warmth of the kitchen, I went for a walk. Even though Rachel and Hugh were no longer at odds, there still hung over the house an air of uncertainty that I could feel. And the sun had tried to come out, chasing away the last of the storm. The air was fresh, clean.

And so I set out for the path down to the water. Crossing the road in front of the house, I paused to glance down toward Ellen's cottage. Should I look in on my patient? I would have felt more comfortable if she'd taken him to Swansea and hospital.

But she hadn't been welcoming when I came to ask for a lift back to Swansea, and she had taken Oliver away as soon as she thought it was safe to do so. I'd only be intruding. And since she had the motorcar, she could come for me if he took a turn for the worse. Better to leave them in peace . . .

I could feel eyes on me, watching, as I passed Griffith's cottage. But I didn't look that way, continuing along the path at a leisurely pace, watching the gulls wheeling and arguing out at the water's edge or turning to look at the other cottages spread across the Down. Somewhere I heard, carried on the wind, the bellow of a bull, and then a dog barking.

If there was little money out here—from what I could see, cattle and foodstuffs were the only ways of earning pounds and pence—what would the people fight about?

Property? Enough of it to keep food on the table?

I didn't see any signs of a manor house, a squire. But nor did I see signs of the poverty rampant in many towns. There was a distinct difference in the size of houses and the size of the land around them, a difference in how well or poorly outbuildings were kept up. Of course the war had taken a toll there, four years of enforced neglect or not enough men to do what needed to be done. And owning land, either to farm or to raise cattle, meant the need for tenants or laborers. More land meant more of each. And there just wasn't the hunger you might see for amassing an estate, either in the past or the present.

I reached the strand. The tide was out, the gulls picking at it as they hunted for food. I slowed, just enjoying the wind and the sound of water lapping at my feet. I didn't intend to walk very far. But I found it a fine way to blow out the cobwebs and worry about my patients at the clinic or how my mother would view a request from Matron asking when I expected to return.

I walked on, nearly halfway round to the far side, my boots sinking into the wet sand. When I finally turned, I was astonished to see several women watching me from the cottages above me. Standing there like sentinels—like statues of waiting women the world over, watching the sea for the first glimpse of a sail.

But this wasn't a fishing harbor or goods port. Men didn't go out with the tide and fail to return.

What's more, they weren't watching for a sail. They were watching me.

About halfway back to the path leading up to the headland, I paused and turned to look out over the water. Breathtakingly pretty, I thought, here as well as viewed from above.

There was a bit of something lying at my feet, a broken shell. I picked it up and sent it skimming across the water, skipping five times before it finally sank beneath the waves.

I hadn't lost my touch, although I had once seen the Colonel Sahib skip a flat stone eleven times, and Simon nine. All in the wrist, they'd said, grinning. But I was happy with five. I looked down and found another, sent it after the first.

As it sank, someone spoke behind me, and I jumped. I hadn't known anyone was there.

The woman was stout, with a wind-reddened complexion and fair hair pulled back under a kerchief. I put her age at late forties.

We had to shout over the sound of the water.

"What are you doing?"

I thought it was fairly obvious. Skipping stones—well, flat bits of broken shell.

"Amusing myself," I said.

"It's what the *lads* do," she countered, as if I'd lied to her.

"Yes, well, my father had no sons, and so he taught me."

I realized then that she was perfectly serious, and not amused.

"I haven't walked beside the sea like this for a very long time," I told her. "I was tempted to see if I'd lost my touch."

"What did you throw?"

I searched by my boots, found another flat piece, and held it out to her.

When she'd examined it, I sent it flying as I'd done before. But this time, the piece sank like the proverbial stone.

She watched with some satisfaction, then faced me again.

"How long do you intend to stay out here?" she asked now.

"Until I'm ready to leave," I retorted, keeping my voice civil, but refusing to be drawn. Then feeling badly about that, I replied, "When the motorcar comes again to fetch me."

"It's not coming. Surely you know that?"

"Mrs. . . ." I began, hoping she'd tell me her name.

"Florence Tucker," she answered.

"Mrs. Tucker, I mean no one any harm. I came here as a part of my duties at the clinic. Wounds like those the Captain has sometimes don't heal properly. There can be sores, ulcers, draining. Infection."

"No one came to see my father when he lost his foot," she said sharply. "I was left to care for it myself."

"Was he in the war?" I asked gently, thinking of other reasons why a man might lose a foot.

"Of course not. At his age? Don't be daft."

"I'm sorry. I don't know the families out here. Someone should have come."

Did she think I'd been looking for something that might tell me who the dead man was, the one buried in such haste? That I was trying to find anything the storm might have left behind, and making certain that it was sent flying back out to sea?

Surely such bits wouldn't be washing up still?

But of course the storm had churned the water far out to sea, bringing whatever got caught up in the waves crashing up on this shore.

Remembering what she'd told me about the motorcar, I asked, "Why won't the firm send another driver to fetch me? Why isn't one coming?"

She stared at me, tight-lipped, for a moment. Then she said, "Why should it?"

"Because I have duties to return to. At the clinic where I'm posted."

"Are you taking *him* back with you?"

"I don't expect to take him anywhere. I didn't come here for that."

"This is no place for strangers." She cast a glance toward the Down, and the other women watching. "It never was. From the time of The Worm."

"The Captain isn't a stranger. His brother was married to Rachel."

"Well, he's filled his brother's shoes right enough," she said venomously. "Hasn't he?"

"That's a very unkind thing to say. Rachel can't manage without help. And the Captain loved his brother, he'd do what he could for his brother's widow."

"And keep her bed warm as well." She turned on her heel and left me there, staring after her.

"That's gossip," I called after her. "Revolting gossip. I can tell you it isn't true."

She wheeled, looked at me, and said, "You're a fool, if you believe that."

She turned back to the path, and began to climb.

I watched her go, then took my time walking back along the water, refusing to be made to shorten my outing.

But I made a point not to skip any more bits of shell.

I reached the top of the headland, by the hedge, pausing to look back. The women had gone. The Down was bare except for a few men in the distance working at various tasks. I saw one with an armload of hay, another with a wheel sharpening a blade, and a third rubbing down a plow horse.

Why had that woman been so unfriendly?

Why was anything the way it was out here?

I was about to turn away when Mr. Griffith came around the corner of his cottage and spoke to me.

"Good afternoon," I replied, expecting to walk on. But he had come for a chat, as I quickly realized.

"What happened yesterday?" he asked me, tilting his head a little to one side like a magpie looking for something bright.

"Happened?" I answered.

"You know very well what I mean," he said, short with me.

"I don't."

"I saw him knock the Captain down. And later he was being dragged from the motorcar to the house, and taken inside. It was late when Ellen left. But she was back to fetch him this morning, early enough."

He *did* watch what was happening outside his windows. I'd thought as much.

"Are you saying that whoever it was who knocked the Captain down was the man who came to the house with Ellen?"

"Who else could it have been?"

That was confusing. If Oliver had attacked Hugh, who had attacked *him*?

"I saw Rachel setting out down the hill, a shovel in her hand."

"What?"

"Did she stand up for the Captain? Was that it?"

"Mr. Griffith. I don't know what you're talking about."

"They say that when they took that soldier to Ellen's cottage during the storm, the house wasn't what it used to be. Walls pulled down. Floors pulled up."

I blinked at him, I was so astonished.

"I don't know anything about that."

"'Course you do. You went down there. Who sent you? The Captain, I'll be bound. It's not likely to have been Rachel. What's he after? And was that why the man came after him?"

"Mr. Griffith. I never went inside the cottage. And I don't know anything about Captain Williams fighting with anyone. Or Rachel, for that matter."

He just stood there, looking at me. "You're a fool," he said, "but I'm not."

I didn't say anything. I walked away, leaving him standing there.

"You'd best go," he called after me. "If you don't want to hear the truth. She got there before you with that one. Nothing for you here now."

Ignoring him, I went on across the road, up the path to Rachel's house, and opened the door. Without looking back.

What was wrong with these people out here? What was happening?

And why was it happening *now*? What was the catalyst, when had it begun?

Was it the arrival of Captain Williams, the outsider? Or the dead man people wanted to believe was his brother?

Had Tom Williams been a part of something out here, and Hugh's arrival reawakened whatever it was?

Did they think Hugh knew something? Or were they afraid he might learn something?

I shut the door behind me.

The house was silent. I went up the stairs to my room, and as I crossed to the window, I saw Mr. Griffith walking back to his door.

I could hardly tell Rachel about either conversation. Or Hugh for that matter.

But something was wrong out here, and I wasn't sure exactly what it could be. I didn't know these people well enough to judge.

The rest of the day seemed to drag. For in my mind's eye, I could see the long drive up to the door of the clinic, and the orderly at the small desk in Reception. Matron in her own little cubby of an office, and staff moving about on their duties. I ought to be coming up that drive an hour before tea. I was to go on duty at four.

But I wouldn't be there, and Matron would send someone to inquire if I had arrived—and if I had, why I hadn't reported to her. I'd have a new list of patients. Possibly some of those I'd tended before. I'd need to be put into the picture, given what was known about the wounds and the spirits of each man. Any changes in staff would be brought to my attention. And then Matron would ask after my parents and if leave had brought me any peace of mind.

She was an astute woman, she could read us just in the same way she could read patients, alert to a man's depression, to his isolation, even when he smiled and said all was well. It would be there in his eyes, I thought. A difference between the smile on the lips and the shadows in the eyes. And Matron would take steps to deal with the problem.

I sighed as I finished the small chores I'd set myself, and then wandered into the little room where Rachel worked. The loom stood silent witness to the fact that she had used it recently. But it also told me that her mind hadn't been on what she was doing. There was a stiffness in the colors running through the loom now, where before there had been almost a lyric sense of what blended and changed and surprised.

She had worked for the relief it gave her, but that was all she'd done. Something was missing . . .

Closing the door, feeling as if I'd been intruding, I wandered about the house until it was time to begin our dinner.

We'd just sat down to it when there was a knock at the door.

Rachel rose quickly and went to open it. I heard voices, realized that one of them was Ellen Marshall's, sharp with worry. I glanced at Hugh, then got up to hurry down the passage.

Ellen, looking over Rachel's shoulder, greeted me with relief.

"I'm so sorry to disturb your dinner," she said quickly to me. "But Oliver is running a fever. I'm worried about him. What can I do?"

"Would you like me to come down and have a look?" For the motorcar was sitting in the road in front of the house. It wouldn't take long. "I'll just fetch my coat." I could feel the cold air swirling about our ankles and skirts as I came to stand by Rachel.

"No—no!" she said hastily. "It will only worry him more, and I can't have that. But if there is something I might do for his fever—to make him more comfortable?"

I said, "I think it would be best for him to go to hospital. I might be wrong about his ribs. There might be other internal injuries—bleeding—that I couldn't find last evening. I can help you get him into the motorcar, brace him with pillows to make the journey as comfortable as possible."

"You don't understand—I can't leave the house. Not after what happened to Oliver. It wouldn't be—wise."

I thought she had been about to say *safe*, but changed it at the very last moment.

The cottage had been standing empty for years. Surely it was more important to find medical attention for her friend than to worry about it.

But then I'd just been told that she was doing something there, tearing up floors and pulling down walls. Searching for something?

Was that true? Was that what she was afraid to leave?

She was waiting for me to answer her.

Rachel volunteered, "I have some aspirin. Would that help?"

"Yes," I said, nodding. "Just the thing for fever. But there's the issue of internal bleeding, and it wouldn't be a very good idea—"

Ellen interrupted me. "Please. If you could spare them? I would be grateful."

Rachel turned and went up the stairs to her room.

I said to the woman waiting anxiously in the doorway, "Please listen. You could be doing the wrong thing. How long would it take to carry him to hospital? And you could come directly back. I'd even sit in your cottage if you like, until you return. Or let me drive him there, while you keep watch."

"He's got a fever. Nothing more. This will be all I need. Another day or two won't matter, once the fever drops."

I wanted to say, *If you care for him at all, be sensible.*

But I had no authority here. I was a visitor, not a Sister with the backing of the staff and Matron and the doctors on duty. I couldn't order treatment. I could only advise. And it was clear enough that my advice wasn't welcome.

Besides, Rachel was coming down the steps with a few aspirin done up in a twist of paper.

"These should help. I hope Oliver will feel better soon."

"Thank you," Ellen said with the first genuine smile I'd seen. "I'm very grateful. And I won't keep you. Good evening."

She turned and hurried back to the motorcar, and we stood there watching her drive a little too fast to the long slope down to the coast guard station.

That told me she was more worried than she wanted anyone to know.

But about leaving the man—or the cottage—unprotected?

Rachel shut the door and latched it, turning back with me toward the kitchen. "Poor man. He must be in a great deal of pain."

Hugh said as we joined him, "I heard most of that. I think Bess is right, she ought to have taken Oliver to hospital."

Then as I sat down and prepared to serve my plate, Hugh said, "*Would* you have gone back with her, Bess?"

I looked across at him, uncertain what he was asking me. Whether he was hoping I would say yes—or no.

I kept my reply even, but yes. I intended to go.

"If she'd asked me, to help shield him from the worst of the ruts,

I'd have agreed. But I also offered to watch her cottage while she carried him to Swansea. I thought she was worried about that for some reason."

Rachel said, "Do you think so? The cottage has stood empty all these years. I can't imagine why she should suddenly be so concerned about leaving it now."

It was an echo of my own thought earlier.

I waited until we were halfway through our dinner to pose the question uppermost in my mind.

"Rachel. You told me that Ellen's grandfather had sent his daughter to school in Cardiff. Who paid for her fees? It wouldn't have been cheap."

She stared at me. "I have no idea. It never occurred to me to wonder."

"Is it common for people in the village to send their children off to boarding school? I don't recall seeing a school out here."

"There was one before the war. You probably didn't notice it the night you arrived, because it looks very much like just another cottage. Then the schoolmaster enlisted. He wasn't replaced, and Rector stepped in, helped by one of the younger village women. Swansea and Cardiff are Welsh. We've sort of become clannish out here, with our English roots—they do go back hundreds of years, and we're rather proud of them. Still, my father insisted on sending me to Swansea to finish my own schooling. My first year was wretched."

I thought it was a measure of how much her parents loved her, to send her away. All the same, she must have found it just as hard to come home, after living in a town.

She was saying, "I was so taken with Ellen's clothes and manners—what seemed to me as a little girl just the utmost in sophistication. And there I was in school with girls who teased me about *my* clothes and the style of my hair and my accent. I begged to come home again. But I'm glad I stayed and made the best of it. If I'd left, I'd never have met Tom."

I let it go.

But I couldn't help thinking that this house was larger than most out here. There must have been money in this family as well, at one time.

We were just finishing our meal when Hugh asked, "Ellen hasn't told you anything that she'd learned from Oliver, about who'd attacked him?"

I realized that he hadn't wanted to be the one who brought it up. But we hadn't said anything all through dinner, and he'd finally had no choice.

Rachel was silent. I stepped in before it was noticeable. "She was so concerned about the fever. I should have thought to ask if he'd told her anything. I was too busy worrying about what could be wrong. And then she was gone."

Even as I answered him, I wondered why Ellen hadn't told us something. Surely she'd asked Oliver what he'd seen, where the man had come from, what had started the fight. But she hadn't said a word.

Why was everyone out here so secretive?

Why wasn't there a Constable here at the very tip of the peninsula? Or a doctor? Or even a regular post? Why had the residents of this tiny village chosen not to have outsiders in their midst?

What were they hiding? Or hiding from?

CHAPTER 11

WE HAD SEVEN lambs in the shed by the next evening. The ewes were tired but doing their part, cleaning their young and nursing them. It never ceased to amaze me that the lambs, shaky and unsure of their feet, quickly got their legs under them and would soon be gamboling about the fields, steady and playful.

Watching them, Rachel said, "I see this cycle of life every year. That's what keeps me here. It's rather wonderful, isn't it?"

I thought she was regretting the fact that she and Tom had never had children. But many soldiers had made that choice. Leaving a widow behind when they were killed was one thing. Leaving a woman to cope alone with young children and only a small pension was another. And if they weren't killed, it could be worse. An invalid who was a constant drain on his family. So many soldiers had told me they feared that most of all. Death to them was clean and final. A life that was hardly a living terrified the bravest . . .

I shook off my thoughts and watched the lambs with her for another few minutes. Satisfied that they were going to be all right, even the smallest of them—born to an experienced ewe—she turned and led the way out of the shed.

A cloud-ridden moon hung in the sky, giving a hazy light. Instead of going into the house, Rachel crossed the road, and I walked with her to the hedge, where we could look down on the bay. It was almost magical, waves moving the surface with a steady but gentle pace, leaving that lacy foam on the strand as it rolled in and swirled a bit, and then softly withdrew.

I thought she'd brought me here to talk—finally—about what had happened to Hugh. And so I waited for her to begin.

To my surprise, after a moment she said, "Do you think Hugh sees me as his brother's widow?"

"But you are," I replied. "That's your relationship to him."

"You're saying he feels responsible for me. That he must look after me for Tom's sake. Because of Tom."

"Rachel. If you're asking me if Hugh could love you for yourself, I think it's possible. But you must remember that if he does have feelings for you, he's likely not to show them. For fear of overstepping the bounds. After all, you loved Tom, and he knows that. Hugh lives on your charity—no, don't deny it, I am sure that's how he sees it. He's taking care of you—but you are also taking care of him."

"But if I send him away—we have nothing."

"You mustn't send him away. He needs this opportunity to see himself as whole again. Not physically, of course, but mentally. He's useful, he'll do anything you ask of him. Or try his very best to do it. That helps him."

"You're telling me to be patient."

"I expect I am."

She was silent for a time, watching the water.

"I loved Tom. I see a good bit of Tom in Hugh. But Tom is dead, he's been gone long enough that I find it harder every passing day to remember him. I can't bring his face back in the night, or the sound of his voice. He's slipping away from me. And Hugh is—is there in his place. I'm so confused."

"No, you're resilient. You're young, more of your life is ahead of you than behind you. To stop living in the present, clinging to the past, is part of mourning for a while, but you have to make a future for yourself. If not with Hugh, then with someone. Tom would be the first to want you to have a future. He would understand."

"How did you get to be so wise, Bess?"

I shook my head in denial. But I'd listened to dying men for four years. I'd written their last letters and held their hands as they faced what was to come. And I'd heard them talk about sweethearts and even wives. Wanting them to have more than a memory.

What they didn't know, these dying men, was the sheer number of those who had already died—and would go on dying to the end, and even after the end of the war. And there wouldn't be futures for many of those sweethearts and widows, because a generation lay buried in the muddy fields of France and Flanders.

Trying to throw off my own darkening mood, I said, "Rachel. Did you see what happened to Hugh the other evening? Did he really fall?"

To my astonishment, she turned abruptly away and started toward the house ahead of me.

"I don't know what you're talking about, Bess. Hugh fell. He told us so."

I hurried to catch her up. I could see her profile, pale in the moonlight, and set against any further mention of how Hugh had got so badly hurt himself.

I woke up the next morning wondering how long Matron would wait before sending word to Somerset, asking why I hadn't returned from my leave.

It would depend, of course, on how many new patients had been brought in, and how shorthanded the staff might be. But Matron was an efficient and busy woman. She would send to Somerset this morning.

A depressing thought, given the consternation at home when her message arrived.

I took a deep breath. With the best will in the world, I couldn't get word to them or to Matron. But it was still my doing that brought me to this fix. Except of course for Mr. Morgan, who'd abandoned me in the middle of the night. And if I was to be honest with myself, that too lay at my door. I'd hired him.

And where would my mother begin? Would she send word to the Colonel Sahib? But my father might be in France. Or London. And I had no idea what Simon's duties were just now. But I rather thought Mother would turn to him first, rather than worry my father when he might not be able to do more than listen.

She'd travel first to the clinic.

I could imagine that conversation with Matron. Mother being circumspect, trying not to push me deeper into the trouble I was already in. Matron listening with her own concerns in mind, trying to see what was behind my mother's surprising visit.

Mother might even suggest that I'd taken a few days to attend to other matters, and that it was these that were delaying me. A very good tactic. Except that my mother wasn't a polished liar.

I sighed. I'd pitched her into the middle of a problem with nothing to help her.

Would Matron remember my concern for the Welsh patients we'd released to return to their homes in the valley? Would she consider mentioning this to my mother? Or would she simply point out that I'd been on leave, I was traveling to Somerset, and she could think of no reason why I shouldn't have left there in good time to reach the clinic on the appointed hour of the appointed day to resume my duties?

And then it would be left to Mother to draw Matron out.

My mother hadn't been the Colonel's Lady, she hadn't spent all her married life with a regiment of men with dependents and problems of their own, without learning as much in her own way as Matron had experienced in nursing. And her daughter was missing.

I would give much, I thought, to be a speck on the wall and hear this conversation take place. But I wished with all my heart I'd not worried Matron or my mother.

Nothing for it but to start my day. I got up, bathed and dressed in the cold little room, and went downstairs.

Rachel spent the morning in the shed with the lambs, hurrying out there as soon as she'd finished her breakfast, asking if I'd clear away.

Hugh was still sporting a bruised jaw, but he was moving about a little less painfully now. I thought he must have been quietly taking great care to give his chest a chance to heal. Still, it must have been difficult using his crutches. He was taciturn this morning as well.

Whatever had happened to him, I thought, he was brooding over it. And it was clear that any questions from me would not be welcomed.

It would be far better for me to go, leave behind the muddle that was worrying everyone out here, and let them solve their own problems, as they had for centuries. But there was no way out. Except to walk, with the hope of eventually finding someone to carry me the rest of the way.

I was beginning to think I could do it. There were no inns or other places for me to stay, but I'd endured all weathers in France. I didn't even need a map, I could just follow the ruts in that road north. How could I lose my way?

There was my kit. But I'd carried that before. Not so far, not over such terrain, perhaps, but I was used to its weight.

Rachel had taken sandwiches and a flask of tea with her after breakfast, intending to stay with the lambs or work with the other ewes. To avoid me? I was afraid that was the purpose. I was not to ask her more questions.

Hugh came in, ate his meal with only a half dozen words between us, and then went up to his room.

When there was a knock at the outer door, I hurried to answer it, hoping against hope that Ellen had seen reason and was planning to carry Oliver to hospital in Swansea. And I was going to make certain that I was included in that drive. I wasn't sure just how I was going to achieve it, but if need be I'd remind Oliver that he owed me his support.

But when I opened the door, it was the rector standing there, gaunt in his black clothes, bending a little forward as if he was intent on his errand.

"Good afternoon," I greeted him, trying to keep my disappointment out of my face.

"Good afternoon, Sister," he said solemnly. "I thought I might find you at home. May I come in for a little visit?"

Taken aback, I said, "I—yes. Yes, of course."

I opened the door wider, and ushered him into the entry before closing it and leading him to the front room.

There was no fire lit at this time of day, and it was cold. But if I offered him a cup of tea in the warmth of the kitchen, would he take that as an invitation to linger? I couldn't imagine why he'd come to call on me. Except to urge me to attend services, and he'd done that.

I decided to see what he had to say before offering hospitality.

He'd removed his hat and set it on the nearest table by the time I'd lit the lamp, for the room wasn't very bright this afternoon.

I gestured to a chair, then took one across from him.

"Have you enjoyed your visit with Mrs. Williams and the Captain?" he began. An attempt at setting me at my ease?

"I have," I replied, although it was the only answer I could make. "I am happy to see the progress that Captain Williams has made since leaving the clinic."

"Do you think he intends to stay here in the peninsula?"

"I haven't thought to ask him his plans. But I believe the climate has been good for him, and I hope he won't feel the need to leave anytime soon."

Was he here to suggest that Hugh should leave? Seeking my medical opinion to use as persuasion? After all, Hugh was an interloper here, on sufferance to help Rachel with the farm.

If so, then I suspected someone else had put him up to it. Anna's father, for one. Mr. Dunhill would benefit the most from Hugh's departure. I was half convinced that he'd attacked Hugh as well, if he'd said something that Hugh couldn't tolerate. That would explain why Hugh refused to talk about what happened. But that left Oliver's injuries unexplained.

Intrigued, I added, "The clinic where he was treated has seen fit to release the Captain. And he is free to go where he pleases."

"Yes, yes. As for the climate here," he went on hastily, as if eager to shift the subject, "except for the storms, of course, we do have a very agreeable climate. We start planting early, and that has been one of our blessings."

Ah. It wasn't really Hugh that had brought him here or he'd have gone into the subject more thoroughly. I wondered if he was aware that Hugh was in the house, upstairs.

"I've been pleasantly surprised," I offered, "to see how self-sufficient you are out here. How little you need from the rest of Wales."

"This has been a Norman enclave, surrounded by enemies, since the colony was planted here centuries ago. We've had to defend our independence."

I hadn't known that.

The rector smiled. "When I first arrived, I knew the parish wasn't particularly pleased to have an outsider take over the living. Even an English outsider. The late rector was a cousin of one of the families out here, and so he was acceptable, you see. I can tell you I had my work cut out for me in those early years."

"Was it terribly difficult?" I asked, interested in spite of myself.

"It was. I found my flock set in its ways, and not eager to move into a new century. In the end I was the one who had to change."

It was an odd admission to a stranger. I wondered if in some way he was trying to explain to me why he had so little influence out here—not even over who was buried in the churchyard. "Did you consider leaving?"

"Alas, it wasn't possible. I had no sponsor, you see. And my bishop wasn't a man who accepted excuses. He expected me to find my way here, and bring these people to the church as best I could. I tried not to disappoint him."

I was beginning to understand the trials and disappointments that he'd suffered in his service to this village. It also explained to some extent why Hugh wasn't welcomed, even though he'd fought for England. And neither man had had anywhere else to go. For that reason alone, Mr. Wilson ought to have taken Hugh's side against the village. But he couldn't. He never would.

He looked toward the window as he said, "They keep themselves to themselves. It leaves me with the feeling that I've only touched the surface of their lives and know very little about what goes on behind the doors of their houses, or for that matter, behind their faces."

I could see the shadow of a great sadness in him, there for a moment as the pale daylight touched his cheeks and eyes, then disappeared as he turned back to me. I'd sensed it when I first met him, but now I knew why.

I still didn't know why he was here, coming when he thought he might speak to me alone.

"I must admit I find them hard to read as well." I thought at this point I really ought to offer him tea. This was Rachel's house, her hospitality, and I mustn't slight that.

But before I could say anything, he cleared his throat and finally launched into why he had come.

"You will be leaving us soon, I believe? Miss Marshall is here with a motorcar, and I'm sure she'll be kind enough to carry you back to Swansea. I know of course about your driver abandoning you. You must be eager to return to your work at the clinic."

"Then perhaps you might suggest to her that I would be happy to leave when she does. I'm expected to return straightaway, you see."

"Indeed."

So much for depending on him to put in a word for me. But then I hadn't really expected him to.

He looked toward the window again, as if trying to find inspiration, a frown between his eyes.

"There is a bit from the Bible," he began, "about seeing through a glass darkly. Are you familiar with it?"

"I am. Corinthians, I believe."

"Yes, a very powerful chapter, is it not?" He turned back to me. "We don't always see things clearly, do we? We see them through a glass, not as they are, because we don't fully understand what we are seeing. It's vague, uncertain, and often easily mistaken for something else. Something more."

"Indeed," I said, unable to decide where he was going with this.

"It's easy to misunderstand what you've seen out here, in your brief visit here. It would be kind if you could find it in your heart to leave these people—my flock—in peace when you go."

Was he talking about that hasty burial? Or the two attacks? Or what? I couldn't be sure just what it was he wanted me not to talk

about. But I understood one thing. If I wanted to leave here with Ellen Marshall, I needed to assure everyone that anything I'd witnessed
here or uncovered or discovered, it would be better not to raise any
alarms in Swansea.

He looked like such a black crow sitting there, shoulders hunched
as he awaited my answer.

Who put him up to this?

Was it his own idea?

Is he afraid he'll be judged for letting his flock get out of hand?
And recalled as incompetent?

These thoughts flitted swiftly through my head, along with one
more. *He must think I know more than I could possibly do.*

"I have no reason to wish anyone out here any harm, Rector. I
just want to return to my duties as quickly as possible. I'll be leaving
Wales on the next train, as soon as I arrive in Swansea."

And that was true. If I stopped at a police station, I'd be delayed
by questions I had no answers for, a long wait while my accusations
were looked into, and in the end, the police might decide after talking to people out here that I'd misread everything I'd seen. It *was*
possible for me to misread everything.

But I had seen that poor man's body being lowered hastily into
an unmarked grave without any sort of service to give at least a semblance of propriety. With not even the rector in attendance. And it
was disturbing. Still, for all I knew the churchyard was littered with
dead from the sea.

I could see relief and gratitude mixed in his eyes as he nodded.

"Thank you, Sister. They are good people, in their own way. And
I daresay that I have done what I could for them. I would like to go
on trying to help them in my own way."

"I'm not really sure how this conversation began," I said. "What
is it that you want me in particular to overlook?"

His face paled with alarm. "I—I don't believe—that is to say, I don't know what it is you are asking me." Gathering himself with an effort, he went on. "I am merely suggesting that you judge my flock not by the standards of your own English village, but in light of the harder life out here. Nothing more."

"Yes, I do see," I replied contritely. I had no reason to upset him, to judge him. No reason to probe further. In a way I already had my answer.

And to be perfectly honest, I don't think he knew the most pressing problem out here. He'd admitted as much. Then how could I—in a handful of days—possibly know what was best?

He stared hard at me, trying to read my mind, or at least whether I was being truthful. Finally, he said, "You are kind, Sister."

Remembering my duty, I said, "May I offer you a cup of tea?"

"No, no. I've other calls to make. But thank you," he added belatedly. "Mrs. Williams has always been most kind . . ."

He rose, looked around for his hat, and almost gave me a little courtly bow as I rose too, to walk with him toward the door.

"Good day, Sister," he said as he stepped outside and turned toward the path.

"Good day, Rector." I closed the door behind him and stood for a moment with my back to it.

I heard Hugh's door open, and he came to the top of the stairs.

"I thought I heard voices."

"The rector called. I'm not quite sure why."

"No more veiled invitations to appear on Sunday next?" He grinned a little.

"Hugh. What's happening out here? Something he said—the rector—made me wonder whether there were—problems—that were—troublesome in some way."

I'd chosen my words with care.

He shook his head. "I've told you. Rachel must live among these people, and so must I, if I'm to stay and help her. I shut my eyes to what I ought not see, and never question it."

"Yes, but they unceremoniously buried a dead soldier in the churchyard, without any semblance of a service. This man Oliver was severely beaten." I debated adding that he himself was knocked down by someone, intentionally and viciously. Then thought better of it. "And someone told me that Ellen Marshall was tearing her house apart inside, and she's too afraid to leave it vulnerable even to take her friend to hospital in Swansea. Who is she afraid of? Or perhaps I should ask what."

"Bess. Leave it. It doesn't concern you. Or me." The Welsh lilt was suddenly there in his voice, and I thought it was a measure of his worry, to revert to his past.

"I won't mention this to Rachel," I promised. "I wouldn't upset her for the world. She's been terribly kind to put up with me and treat me as a member of the household when it wasn't her fault that Mr. Morgan stranded me. Still, I can't help but see that there's something wrong." I hesitated. "The village has already accused you of murdering Tom."

"I shouldn't have told you."

"You did because you were worried. And you didn't want me to be drawn into it."

"Yes, all right. It was still wrong of me." He took a deep breath. "I can't go back to the valley. There's no place for me there, and in the end, I'll be driven to despair, like the others. Here I have a chance to heal, small as that chance might be. I want to take it. I want to find out what sort of man I still am."

It had cost him a great deal to make that admission, and I wanted to bite my tongue and take back what I'd said that forced him to be so terribly, painfully honest.

"Then I'll respect that, Hugh. We'll say no more about the

village." And then I had to be honest in my turn. "I needed to be sure it was for the best."

"It is. I give you my word." He turned back to his room, closing the door.

I went to the kitchen and made myself a cup of tea. As I waited for it to steep, I wondered how the British Empire could possibly have survived all these years if it hadn't had tea to fall back on in times of great stress.

Rachel came in just in time to begin our dinner. She seemed to have come to terms with whatever was on her mind, because though she was quiet, she was also very much more herself. The dogs, settling into their beds, snuffled and huffed, then curled up and went to sleep.

I told her the rector had come to call on me. I thought it best— but kept my comment light, without overtones.

She smiled. "He has few enough souls to save out here. Poor man. My mother liked him well enough, but my father found him a little tedious. I try to be polite." She added almost as an after-thought, "I've lived in a wider world. I expect that's why I see things a little differently. We had such a lovely rector in Swansea. He called several times after word came about Tom, and I don't know how I'd have managed without him. It was Mr. Timson who told me to come home, and find my way again here. He was very wise. It helped. But then I lost my parents too . . ."

She turned away, as if the pain was still too raw to talk about. After a moment, she said, "I saw Ellen this afternoon. She was stand-ing in the road, staring out to sea. I had the oddest feeling she was crying. That isn't like her at all. I can't imagine her crying."

"I expect she's worried about Oliver."

"Then why doesn't she take him to hospital and be done with it?

She has a motorcar. She could be there and back in a day, the way she drives."

I didn't want to tell her what I'd told Hugh, that Ellen seemed to be more fearful about her house than about her friend.

"Perhaps Oliver doesn't want to appear in Casualty, badly beaten. He might not wish to answer questions about what happened."

She looked at me in surprise. "You're saying it might become a police matter? I hadn't thought about that."

"I don't know. But a doctor might well ask questions and then report the matter. It was rather savage, that beating. Staff would find that hard to ignore."

Rachel, considering that for a moment, said, "I know these people. I can't think why someone would want to attack a stranger."

Perhaps because he *was* a stranger? And not wanted here? But I only replied, "He wouldn't recognize the man again. He says."

"Yes, there's that," she said thoughtfully. She went to open the kitchen door into the yard to put out the peelings from the vegetables she was adding to a stew. Lifting the lid of the bin, she was about to scrape the dish into it when a sound reached us.

I didn't need to be told what it was. A shot.

Rachel listened, then said, "What was that?"

"A shotgun," I said, hurrying to the door. But there was only silence by the time I got there.

"Who could be firing?" Rachel asked.

"Do any of the farmers out here own a shotgun?"

"Several of the farmers have them. My father's is in the closet in Hugh's room."

"Could you tell which direction it came from?" I asked.

She shook her head, still standing there in the doorway, just in front of me. "No, I was too surprised." She looked over her shoulder. "Should I call Hugh?"

"I don't know that he could do anything." The sun had just set. It was already too dark to see much out there. "Besides, it wasn't close by. Someone out to pot a hare?"

"I don't think so."

I moved aside as she stepped back in, closing the door against the cold air.

"How odd," she said. But I could see that the shot had disturbed her.

She mentioned it to Hugh when he came down to dinner.

Looking up from washing his hands, he said, "You should have called me."

"There was only the one shot. We couldn't tell where it was coming from. I didn't want to disturb you over it."

But he *was* disturbed, I could see that.

Covering it up, he dried his hands, then said, "I've finally found the problem with your accounts. You were off by about fifteen pounds."

Suddenly anxious, she said, "In my favor, or—"

He smiled. "Yours."

Relieved, she returned the smile. "Thank you. I could never find it. Where was it?"

"It was the lamp oil. You'd transposed two figures."

"Oh dear. I was never good with numbers," she admitted, and turned to take the stew off the cooker while I poured the tea. "That was my father's gift."

Her back was to us. I caught Hugh's glance as he pointedly stared my way.

It was a warning not to make too much of what we'd heard out there in the dark.

No one came to fetch me, the only person here with any medical training, and so I had to assume that no one had been hurt by the shotgun. But I took that sound upstairs with me and stood at the window, looking out toward the black space that was the sea below our headland. I'd seen gulls and a handful of other seabirds, but no hares out here. Which of course didn't mean that there were none. After all, the land toward The Worm was rather desolate and un-farmed, and anything might roam out there. Rachel's sheep and the other villagers' cattle stayed where the grass was better.

I spared a thought for my mother, who must by now have heard from Matron. Or would that be tomorrow, Matron giving me the benefit of the doubt and waiting to see if I would arrive after all, with a satisfactory explanation for my tardiness?

Impossible to know.

I turned away from the window and undressed for bed.

I dreamed of the war that night. I was at one of the forward aid stations, and we were too close to the lines, because they'd fallen back to regroup after a German assault. Dr. Taylor was worried that the artillery would open up, to give the Germans something to think about while our side used the cover to re-form. There were cases we needed desperately to send back, but there was no chance an ambulance, much less a convoy, could reach us. I was frantically trying to keep one man alive, while Dr. Taylor and Sis-ter Perkins worked with two others. And out of the darkness a line appeared of fresh wounded, making their way toward us. I must have tossed and turned as I worked on men in my dream, torn between duties to the living and the dying, knowing I didn't have a hope of saving them all, none of us did, and in the end, when it was over and the ambulances had come at last and then gone, car-rying the dead back among the living, I'd sat alone in my quarters and cried.

And in the quarters next to mine, I heard the deeper sobs as Dr. Taylor wept, and then swore with such feeling that I put my hands over my ears. Not because of the words he used, but because of the anguish behind them.

I woke with a start, my blankets on the floor, my pillow half off the bed, my hands and feet freezing.

It came again. A quiet tap at my door.

"Bess?" Hugh's voice. "Are you all right?"

"A nightmare," I managed to say. "I'm so sorry. I didn't mean to wake you."

"Good night."

And I heard his crutches quietly cross the floor to his room, the door shutting softly.

I rearranged my bedding, crawled back in, and reached my toes for the now lukewarm hot water bottle.

Lying there, I tried to remember what had brought me out of my dream with such sharpness.

It hadn't been Hugh's tap. I was nearly sure of that.

A cry . . .

Had I really heard it?

Or had it been a part of my dream, the torment in Dr. Taylor's voice?

It was some time before I could fall back to sleep.

CHAPTER 12

I WENT FOR a walk around ten in the morning, moving aimlessly as if just out for the fresh air, although I was sorely tempted to stroll as far as the Marshall cottage. But I could see for myself that the motorcar was still there.

Mr. Griffith, in his own well-placed cottage, seemed to watch everything that was passing his door—or his windows. What did he know about Oliver and the beating he'd endured?

A lonely man with nothing better to occupy his time, I told myself, but it was rather unpleasant to think that he might know what had happened to Oliver and held his tongue. He didn't appear to miss much.

I took my time, watching a bird scrabble under some dead leaves for an insect, then stood for a moment to stare out at The Worm. It was dark green, mysterious, and rather too real in this light, for clouds had rolled in overnight. Sitting there, hunched, waiting through the centuries to frighten off anyone who might want to bring harm to this land. And yet the danger now was inland, not out at sea.

By the time I reached the place where I could look down on the bay, where the wide expanse of water and sand and lacy surf were spread out in all their glory, I was drawn into the scene.

Remembering the photograph of Rachel and her brother playing in the surf, I smiled. It was a place that should have children shouting and laughing, adults walking or sitting there. But except for the women I'd seen there—hardly strolling in summer warmth—as a rule it was bare. These people had little time for leisure, with a livelihood to pursue. And with the war raging, any holiday interest in the peninsula had been shut down. I didn't know if those holidaymakers would ever return to this forgotten place.

I was standing there, lost in my thoughts, when Mr. Griffith spoke.

I jumped at the sound of his voice carrying over the wind. "You are drawn to the water."

"It's beautiful, of course," I agreed. "I don't think I've ever seen anything quite like it, in all my travels."

"Travels? Oh yes? And where have you been?"

He was scoffing.

"India, with my father's regiment. East Africa."

He was surprised, I could see that, when I turned to look at him.

"Where in India?"

"Mostly in the north, of course. But we tried to see a good bit of the country. Delhi, Agra, Madras, Goa, Bombay. Calcutta, when my father was called to a meeting there, but the city had a cholera outbreak soon after we arrived, and my mother and I were sent posthaste back to Delhi to wait for him."

I wasn't sure Mr. Griffith even knew where all these places were, because he was frowning.

"Surely you don't remember much about your travels at that young age?"

"Surprisingly, I do."

He raised dark eyebrows.

"My parents saw to it that I learned about our travels." I didn't add that I'd had a governess who used them for lessons.

"I'll walk you back to the road," he said then, preparing to turn away.

"I'd rather stay for a while," I said, smiling.

"Suit yourself." And he walked off abruptly.

I stood there for another few minutes.

It wasn't until I was turning to go myself that I saw it.

A dark patch at my feet.

I caught myself in time to stop from staring. In the event anyone was watching.

But that dark patch was surely blood.

I hadn't served in the trenches for four years without having seen blood in every possible stage. Fresh, splattered, pooled, black with flies, running across the operating room floor, or dried in a patch that no one had had time to clear up.

I walked away from the spot, as if I hadn't noticed it.

Was that why Mr. Griffith had come to speak to me? Did he know that this was where Oliver was attacked? If so, he was waiting now to see how I reacted. I refused to give him the satisfaction of knowing.

In reality, as I was walking back up the incline I was remembering the sound of that shotgun firing, and a cry in the night. It was more likely that the patch of blood had something to do with that. It was that, not Oliver's beating, that Mr. Griffith had been curious about.

What was happening to this small windswept village in the midst of nowhere?

And no one had come for the Sister, who was the only medical help available.

The violence seemed to be escalating. But what was driving it?

The return of Ellen Marshall?

If so, why attack Hugh?

I should go down to that cottage, I told myself, *and see if everyone is all right. If she herself needs medical help.*

On the other hand, what if the blood here had no connection with Ellen and the beating of the man who was with her?

I kept walking.

I'd just reached the road in front of Rachel's house when someone called, "Sister? Please, Sister?"

I turned. There was a woman coming up from the lane to the Down, struggling for breath as she tried to hurry. She had a bundle in her arms, and for a moment I thought it must be clothing.

I went to meet her, and as I came closer I realized there was a small child in the blankets.

"My baby," the woman said as I reached her. Fighting for breath herself, she said, "She's—oh, Sister, is it *diphtheria*?"

The dread illness that carried off so many children.

We'd seen all manner of things in France, from cholera to measles, and we'd lost men to these diseases.

She all but shoved the child into my arms, and I could feel, through the blankets, that the little girl was burning with fever. My heart turned over with dread. What was I to do, if it *was* diphtheria?

"I can't examine her here in the open," I said gently. "Let's take her home, where it's warm. And you must tell me what you've seen."

Hovering by my side as we walked back the way she'd come, she began haltingly to list the symptoms. A very sore throat, fever, chills. A general malaise.

"Have you seen a rash?"

Shaking her head vigorously, she replied, "No, Sister. But Jenny's only been ill since this morning, and I looked at her throat, and I can't help but think—" Breaking off, she turned from the main path to one leading to the houses along the upper level of the Down.

It was little more than a cottage, but there was a larger barn out in the back along with several sheds. I heard a goat, and then half a dozen chickens were under our feet, expecting to be fed. The woman shooed them away, and as she reached the door, she flung it wide so that I could step in with my burden.

There were two other children there, perhaps seven and nine, and both of them had a bad cough with congestion. They looked frightened as I came in carrying their sister, and I smiled at them.

"Hallo." But they stood back and wouldn't answer. I didn't know if they were children I'd seen on the beach with their mothers or not.

Putting my bundle down on the nearest table, I began to unwind the blankets.

The little girl—I put her age at four—was flushed with fever, but as I worked I saw no rash, and I couldn't feel any swellings. When I got her to open her mouth, I could see how inflamed her throat was. Small wonder the mother was so frightened. But *was* it diphtheria? I asked to see the throats of the little boy and the older girl, and they too had inflammation, which was reassuring.

Please God, the youngest child had just got a worse case of the same infection.

Still, I gave Jenny a gentle but thorough going-over, and she stared at me all the while, her blue eyes too bright in her flushed face. I talked quietly to her as I worked, smiling. But I was worried. She was small and thin, and not very strong. If it was diphtheria, I wasn't certain she would survive it.

Quickly wrapping her again in one of the blankets, I told her mother to put her to bed but to keep an eye on her all evening and into the night, in the event she began to have breathing problems. "Very likely she will have trouble swallowing, and won't want to eat. But a spoon dipped into tea with a little brandy in it can be brushed across her lips as often as possible, to help her throat and give her a little strength. As soon as she can swallow, that should be followed by broths, warm milk thinned with a little water at first, tea with milk.

And after that, a potato broth, with other vegetables in it. Boiled eggs. She'll need to regain lost weight."

The mother stared at me as if she was still waiting for me to tell her the worst, that her daughter might die.

"Mrs. . . ."

She seemed to come back to the present. "Burton."

"Mrs. Burton, your daughter will be all right, but you must be sure she eats." I glanced at the other children, suddenly worried that there might not be any food in the house. But there were chickens, eggs—goat's milk. And the little boy and his older sister were sturdy and healthy enough.

It had been too overwhelming for Mrs. Burton. Her fear for the youngest child, the rush to find help, the knowledge that it might already be too late.

I said gently, "She needs your help. You must be strong for her."

"Yes—yes, I do understand," she said then.

I looked around the room. It was furnished well enough, but the style was that of an older generation, as it was in Rachel's house. On the mantelpiece in pride of place was a silver cup, tarnished now. I could just make out a coat of arms on the side facing the room. It was a rather ornate coat of arms. I didn't think it was that of the Burtons. Some Norman ancestor?

A door opened somewhere in the house and I could hear footsteps coming toward the front room.

Mrs. Burton froze, then seemed to shrink into herself. The children stared at her, and tried to make themselves small.

A man stepped through the doorway and stopped in midstride, glaring at me. He was rather burly, with dark hair and hazel eyes. I thought he might have been one of the men I'd seen moving the body of the dead soldier up from the strand and thence down to Ellen's cottage.

Mrs. Burton said uncertainly, "It's Jenny. Daniel, I thought it was the diphtheria." Her voice was pleading.

"I told you to have nothing to do with the likes of her," he retorted, turning toward his wife.

I said, cutting across her answer, "Mr. Burton. Jenny is quite ill. I don't believe it's what your wife fears, but the next four-and-twenty hours could be critical. I hope that if you need me in the night, you will come for me. Your daughter's life may depend on it." It was Matron's voice, dealing with obstreperous Aussies, and it reached him.

"Then I'll thank you to go now."

"I'll be happy to leave you to care for your family." I turned to Mrs. Burton. "Remember what I said about keeping her strength up. It's the best thing you can do for her now."

And I rebuttoned my coat, taking my time, before nodding to the two adults and walking briskly toward the door.

Honor satisfied. I hadn't been tossed out on my ear, and I had made my point about Jenny's care.

I shut the door firmly behind me, and set out toward the top of the Down where the hedge separated the path from the Griffith house.

Thank God, it hadn't been diphtheria. It could have raced through such an isolated community with impunity, and taken at least some of the children here with it before it was finished. Jenny for one. The village would have had to accept help—there would have to be quarantine, medical care. I'd have gone directly to Ellen and sent her to fetch doctors at once, since her motorcar was the fastest way of reaching Swansea. And I'd have had to stay here until the epidemic was over, since I had examined the patient. My duty would have been clear. And it wouldn't have mattered if Ellen was annoyed or not. Or anyone else out here in Caudle.

I was sure Daniel Burton would have been the first to object. His truculence worried me. His wife was afraid of him, and possibly the children were as well. I saw no indication that he beat them, but I wouldn't have been at all surprised to find that he enjoyed using his fists. He was the sort of man whose anger needed a target. I hadn't wanted to leave them with him, but there had been no choice. Staying would only have angered him more, and they would have paid for it one way or another. I made a promise to myself to look in on them in the morning. There was no Constable here to call on if there was trouble, but I had a feeling Mr. Burton would leave *me* alone. If only to be sure I carried no tales with me.

When I reached the hedge, I stopped and looked back. There were wisps of smoke coming from chimneys, gulls wheeling over the strand, and the sound of the sea and the wind was the backdrop as it always was. It all looked so pastoral, so peaceful. I could frame it with my hands and call it beautiful.

No doctor here, no Constable, a rector who worried about his own soul. What kept these people pinned to an upheaval of limestone cliffs and a Down that ran to the sea? To such a harsh way of life? And yet it seemed inbred in them, part of the fabric of them, to live out here as their medieval ancestors had done. Hardy souls who weren't afraid to leave the soft counties of Devon and perhaps Dorset to try their luck on a storm-drenched headland dominated by The Worm, and somehow make a go of it.

Had these been younger sons, who knew their portion of the family's land wouldn't be enough to live on? Or a collection of ne'er-do-wells only a step ahead of the Constable and the debtors' prison? Or the refuse of larger towns?

For that matter, the Norman lord might have swept up half a hundred people from his own estates and put them on board ships without a by-your-leave. He would have had that right.

It didn't matter. They had survived out here, an English foothold on Welsh shores, and it must have hardened them, made them stronger and more resilient.

They didn't look to me as if they were in any danger of leaving in the beginning of the twentieth century.

In the afternoon, another of those bad storms came up out at sea. The sun set behind a bank of black clouds, and when I stepped outside for a few minutes, I could see flashes of lightning in the darkness moving toward us. It was the time of year for these storms, but they seemed to be increasing in intensity, and Rachel had gone out to be sure the ewes and young lambs were sheltered. Hugh and the dogs helped her bring them in, and by the time I stood there by the door, looking toward the Channel, my skirts were whipping wildly and I had to put a hand to my cap to keep it from flying off my head. I got back inside and shut the door against the wind. It took some doing to latch it.

We ate by lamplight that danced and flung our shadows around the kitchen as the wind rattled the windows and whistled around the corners of the house. It roared down the chimneys, sending gusts of ash across the floor in the front room, and threatened to put out the fire in the cooker. Once it hit the front door with such force that it blew it back against the wall, and Rachel and I had to fling ourselves against it to close it again.

Twice I saw Hugh glance up with worry in his eyes, and I thought he must be concerned about the roof holding. But Rachel assured us that the house had stood these many years and would stand as many more.

But it was as bad a storm as I'd ever lived through, I thought as I climbed the stairs, shielding my candle. Behind me, Hugh was saying, "It will scour out the bay, and send the sea up the strand, if this goes on."

Rachel, bringing up the rear with our hot water bottles, said, "Oh, I don't think so."

I was worried about Jenny with her sore throat. Her mother wouldn't be able to bring her up the road, not in such a gale. But Jenny's father could, he was strong enough. I hoped they would be all right.

Standing at my window, I watched the rain blowing sideways, and I was glad the ewes and lambs were safe. The night was black as pitch, and I couldn't even see a light in Mr. Griffith's house.

I lay awake, listening to the wind howl, and once I heard Rachel coming out of her room and going quietly down the stairs. I thought perhaps she'd put on a show of not worrying for our sakes, and was making sure no rain was getting in. We'd put rags at the foot of the front door to prevent water from coming in, but that was the best we could do.

It was the small hours of the morning when the storm finally began to show signs of slowing down. But it was still raining at six when I got up to look out, and the dawn was gray and very wet. I heard Rachel go out to look at the sheep, taking the dogs with her, and I dressed quickly, thinking I might start breakfast for her.

Hugh had the front door open as I came down the stairs, and over his shoulder I saw people hurrying toward the hedge and the way down to the sea.

"What is it?" I asked quickly, thinking there must be another boat in trouble, caught by the gale and trying to make it into the bay.

"I—it's nothing."

"Hugh—why are they rushing down to the sea?"

"Leave it, Bess."

But there was something about the way the villagers were hurrying that told me it wasn't nothing.

"Is it another boat? Or has something happened to some of the houses out there on the Down?" I wondered suddenly if Jenny's cottage was all right.

He turned to look at me.

"There's nothing you can do. Leave it."

But I'd been trained to help. I couldn't just shut the door and ignore a need.

"Something *is* wrong," I said, still watching the men and women heading toward the hedge. I went quickly back upstairs, caught up my coat and hat. As I was coming down again, Hugh blocked my way.

Hugh said, "Bess. Don't go out there."

"But if I can help—"

He caught my arm as I started past him. "No. You can't."

I broke free. "I have to *try,*" I said. "I can't stand by and do nothing."

Outside, people glanced sideways at me, not wanting to look me in the face, as I joined them on my way to the hedge. But when I got there and looked out across the bay, there wasn't a boat or anything else in the water as it rolled toward the strand.

Jostled by latecomers, I scanned the cottages. There was a scattering of debris, things blown about that hadn't been tied down properly, but the cottages were intact. I didn't see any signs of real damage.

I looked again at the strand as I heard shouting. And in the throng of people along the water's edge a shoving match had started, two women lunging at each other, and then a third joining in, before several men separated them. Others were scrabbling in the surf, running this way and that, as if to find a better place, bumping into each other, too intent on what they were doing to take notice of the cold wind. Farther along, two men nearly got into a fight before dropping to their knees in the same spot and digging with their bare hands in the sand, ignoring the icy water washing over their fingers. A little boy called out, holding something up over his head in his excitement, and a woman came hurrying to take whatever it was from him. So much activity on the usually quiet strand sent the gulls wheeling out to sea. And I stood there watching, unable to believe my own eyes.

It was as if everyone in the village had run mad.

What were they after? Some sort of fish or shellfish that had washed ashore? But they were cramming whatever they'd found into their pockets or their aprons, and the intensity of their need to dig into the surf was beginning to get ugly.

I was alone up here at the hedge, now. And the latecomers were hurrying down the road. I watched one man trip and fall, but no one stopped to help him, and he got to his feet and ran to get ahead of the stragglers.

People found new places to dig at the water's edge, and others came up to try to take whatever it was away.

Hugh spoke just behind me, making me jump.

"Bess. Come back to the house."

"But what is it? What are they doing?"

I could see Mr. Griffith among them, laying about with his own fists.

"Just come with me. Now. I'll explain when you're safely inside. Quickly, now, before someone remembers you were out here."

The insistence in his voice, the look on his face, spoke of fear, and worry.

I turned slowly, hardly able to tear myself away from the spectacle of most of the village coming to blows at the water's edge. And I followed him back to the house.

As we crossed the road, I looked down toward the coast guard station, wondering if Ellen had gone along to the strand with everyone else.

And that's when I saw Mr. Wilson, the rector, standing there by the overlook, not far from where I'd found blood, staring down at his flock, who appeared to have run mad in the aftermath of the storm. His black coat and scarf were blowing in the wind, giving him the appearance of an abandoned scarecrow as he leaned into it.

At that moment, he turned and looked at the two of us, almost at the path up to Rachel's door. He stared for a moment, and then went back to watching the scene below.

I heard Hugh swear under his breath.

But surely we had nothing to fear from the rector?

We came back inside and hung our wet coats on the backs of chairs in the kitchen. Hugh set his crutches to one side and sat down heavily as I went to the cooker and stirred the banked embers to life before filling the kettle. That done, I turned and looked at the Captain.

He stared back at me.

"What is it? What was happening down there? You said you would tell me."

He turned his gaze toward the window. "It's best you don't know."

"They were after something in the surf. Fighting over it. What was it, Hugh? I came back to the house, as you asked. Now you must tell me. Some of those people are going to have serious injuries, the way they were attacking each other. You'd have thought they'd just discovered buried treasure—"

His eyes met mine, and something in his face warned me.

"You aren't serious—Hugh, are you saying there's something down there at the water's edge? Surely not buried treasure?"

"No. Not buried. Well, not precisely. Bess, there was a ship. Back in Charles II's day. It came to grief out there in a storm—I expect very much like the one last night—and they tried everything possible to beach it. But it must have gone hard aground just inside the bay, and it began to break apart. Those on board could see the lights out there on the Down, and they were screaming for help. But there was nothing the local people could do. They didn't have a boat that could reach the ship, and it would have been madness to try. They watched helplessly as it was battered by the storm and finally broke apart. Everyone on board drowned. Their bodies began washing up the next day, along with whatever had been on the ship. The villagers collected everything, clothing, furnishings, bits and pieces of rigging, anything they could salvage, and shared it out. The bodies were brought up to the churchyard and given decent burial. A week later, strangers came, looking to find out what had happened to the ship. It had been sighted off the western coast of Ireland, but then the storm blew up and it had vanished."

"And then?" I said, when he stopped. The kettle had boiled, and I took it off.

He took a deep breath. "Before the strangers arrived, one of the families had found something in the surf. Pieces of silver, lots of them. There were more the next day and the next. Anything that might have identified the ship was hastily burned. The raw graves were erased, older stones set over them to hide who and what they were. And the local people swore they never saw the ship."

"Because of those pieces of silver?"

"Yes. And long after the people searching for the ship had gone, silver continued to wash up. Apparently it was a treasure ship, coming in from India with a queen's dowry."

"It's still washing up *today*?"

"The chests went deep into the sand. That's the theory. And storms bring the contents up. A goodly amount came ashore just after the wreck, and the people here were grateful. You must see that even a few silver coins were a godsend to them. There must have been other incidents over the centuries. Then a large cache was found in 1833. One man left in the middle of the night—he'd been out in the aftermath of a storm, and it was claimed he had a coach full of silver he'd discovered. I doubt it was that much, but the fear was, when he reached Swansea with all that silver, the truth was going to get out at last. The next morning his coach was found wrecked on the road to Swansea, and he was inside it, dead. The silver he'd taken with him was missing. No one knew where it was. Although there were suspicions."

The phantom coach that was heard on stormy nights . . .

"But who had taken it?"

He shrugged. "The fastest horse out here belonged to Ellen's grandfather. And the old coach must have been a lumbering affair out there on the drovers' road. But there was no proof, you see. Her grandfather couldn't have been more than seventeen or eighteen, and he swore he'd been asleep in his bed. The horse was calmly grazing in a pasture and didn't appear to have been ridden hard. What's more, his mother vouched for him. Suspicion lingered, I daresay, but without even a justice of the peace to look into the matter, there was nothing to be done. More importantly, her grandfather never behaved as if he'd suddenly come into a great deal of money. His first wife died in childbirth, and by the time his second wife had given him a daughter—Ellen's mother—and he saw to it that she had everything, it proved nothing."

"And you're telling me that the people out there on the strand right now have discovered more silver washing in, and they're willing to batter each other in their attempt to grab as much as possible."

"Over four centuries, it has been the lifeblood of this village."

I gestured around me. "And this house? Did Rachel's family also share in the silver?"

"I have never asked."

I suddenly remembered the cross I'd seen in her room. Was that one of the treasures from the wrecked ship? And the silver cup in the Burton cottage.

"How much silver was that ship carrying?"

"Chests of it. It was meant for the dowry of Charles II's wife. A Portuguese princess. It was coming from Goa. Over the years there's no telling how much—or how little—of it has actually come ashore. Or how much is still out there. Waiting until the next storm." He hesitated. "There are two very beautiful candlesticks on the altar in the church, and a communion cup and plate."

I reached for the kettle and put it back on the cooker. "And the people out here have spent that money—and no one the wiser?"

"Melted down, silver is silver. I doubt you could trace it. I don't know precisely how it's done, and Rachel tells me that's for the best. But I have a feeling that it's turned into something that can be sold without arousing suspicion. That would make sense."

"I see." Small wonder the village didn't want the police to come prying into their affairs. "How did you come to know about it?"

This time when the kettle came to a boil, I began to make the tea.

He glanced toward the passage, listening for the door. "Tom talked to Rachel's father. And then told me. Apparently that silver made it possible for Rachel to be educated in Cardiff. I don't believe she realized that. But her father wanted Tom to understand that there was almost none left."

The outer door opened, and the dogs came racing down the passage, followed by Rachel. She seemed relieved to find both of us in the kitchen. I saw her face, but Hugh had his back to her.

That's when I knew that Rachel understood more about the silver than Hugh was aware of. She'd been worried that we had been out— had seen the mad scramble to collect as much as possible before the tide turned. Had she been down there? I hadn't noticed her . . .

But she said only, "It's better than I thought, but the sheep are tired. They've found sheltered places to rest. I'll have a cup of that, if there's any left in the pot."

I poured her a cup, and sat down to finish my own before starting our breakfast.

I stayed in the house, away from the front windows, for the rest of the day, washing and then ironing my aprons, but I was worried about Jenny—and worried too about those who had been fighting down by the strand. How many of them had been hurt? But they wouldn't come to me.

It was just before dark—the sun had hardly shown its face, and dusk had been early, with the cloud cover—when there was a knock at the outer door.

Rachel was working in the kitchen and Hugh was upstairs, and so I volunteered to answer it, my thoughts still occupied by Jenny.

But it wasn't her mother at the door, it was Ellen Marshall. She looked tired, drained of that arrogance that seemed to be such a part of her. Behind her, her motorcar was standing in the road, its great headlamps piercing the gloom almost as far as the churchyard.

"Hallo, Sister Crawford. I'm leaving for Swansea. Oliver isn't doing well, and I'm taking your advice about seeing a doctor. If you can be ready quickly enough, I can take you up with me as far as Swansea."

I wasn't sure whether she was making this offer because I could reassure her about her friend, or whether she was actually being kind. Then I realized her face was tight with tension.

"Yes—yes, that would be lovely. I'll only be a moment—would you like to wait in the parlor?"

"I'll stay with the motorcar." She cast a glance over her shoulder. "But hurry. I can't stop here for very long."

There wasn't time to dwell on why she was in such a rush. I could ask her as we drove away. I turned and hurried back to the kitchen, where the aprons I'd ironed were waiting to be carried upstairs.

"Rachel—it's Ellen Marshall at the door. She's returning to Swansea, the motorcar is already out there, waiting for me."

"Oh—oh, I know you're pleased. Go on up and pack your kit, I'll bring these."

She went to take down the aprons while I hurried back down the passage, almost running up the stairs, calling to Hugh as I went.

He came out his door, and I told him that Ellen was here to take me up, and then went into my room, tossing everything into my kit as quickly as I could. Time enough to sort it all out in Swansea.

Rachel was right behind me with the aprons, laying them out on the bed and hastily folding them.

She was talking all the while, telling me how glad she was that I'd come, and how pleased she was that I wouldn't be in too much trouble over my late arrival at the clinic. "For it won't take you long to find a train to Cardiff or even Bristol."

Hugh said, from the doorway, "I'm grateful, Bess. Thank you for caring enough to do what you could for me and my men."

I closed up my kit, smiling at them. "I'm so glad I came. I wouldn't have got to know Rachel if I hadn't. And thank you both for putting me up. Will you keep in touch? I'd like that."

"Yes, of course," Rachel said, and gave me a warm hug before taking up my kit and my coat. Hugh, hesitating, also embraced me.

"I must give you the direction of the clinic—"

"I have it," he said, releasing me, and then swinging around to follow me down the stairs. I went ahead of them, still thanking them for their hospitality, and was halfway to the door.

Rachel exclaimed, "Wait!" and disappeared into her room, catching us up as I reached the hall. "I want you to have this."

It was one of her lovely scarves, and she tucked it under my arm.

"Remember us when you wear it," she said, and I promised as I opened the outer door.

There was a man standing just below the steps now, and beyond him, I saw Ellen's motorcar begin to move, gathering speed, pulling away from what must have been a half-dozen shadowy figures ringing it.

"No—wait! *Ellen*," I cried, starting down the steps, my free hand waving madly toward the motorcar.

Hugh shouted, "Bess, *stop*."

The man standing between me and the road swung around and caught my arm in a grip that was bruising, holding me back. The lovely scarf fell to the ground, and I cried out again as the motorcar inexorably gathered speed.

Ellen never looked back, never hesitated.

And after a moment, there was only the red dot of her rear lamp in the distance, before that too disappeared.

CHAPTER 13

I WAS SUDDENLY so angry I could hardly breathe, and I rounded on the man who was still clutching my arm.

"Take your hands off me," I said in a voice I myself hardly recognized. And he dropped my arm as if it had burned his fingers.

I recognized him then. Jenny's father.

"*How dare you,*" I began, almost shaking in my fury. "After what I'd done for your daughter—"

Hugh was there, between me and the man, and Rachel had come down the steps to take my kit from me and retrieve the lovely scarf.

"Inside, Bess." Hugh put a hand on my shoulder, but I shook it off.

"Bess—please?" Rachel said, pleading.

The other men in the road were watching us. And up the way, nearer the churchyard, almost invisible in his black clothing, Mr. Wilson was shaking his head. I could see his hat moving.

I stood there, my disappointment mixing with my anger. I was breathing hard, as if I'd run after the motorcar. Part of my mind was trying to make sense of what had happened, while the other could only think about Ellen abandoning me.

But I knew, deep down, that she'd been given no choice.

They had let her leave, because she was one of them and could be trusted to keep her mouth shut—which meant that she and her family had benefited somehow from the silver washing ashore.

218

While I, the stranger in their midst, an unknown quantity, couldn't be trusted at all. Especially after this morning. *Someone* had spread the news that I'd watched from the hedge.

But how could they keep me here—and for how long?

I began to realize then that quite a bit of silver must have washed onto the strand during last night's storm. Enough that these people were not going to risk losing it by letting me leave.

Enough silver to make quite a difference in their lives . . .

And by extension, enough to make my own future rather bleak.

They were waiting for me to make a decision—Jenny's father, the watchers in the road, the rector—Rachel and Hugh.

Without another word, I turned and walked straight back into the house, and slammed the door behind me.

It was a moment before Rachel and Hugh got it open again and came in after me.

I hadn't heard a word spoken by any of those men out there. I also couldn't have recognized any of them, except Jenny's father.

Walking on toward the kitchen, pulling out the nearest chair and sitting down in it, I tried to stop shaking. But my fury and my disappointment went too deep. I shut my eyes for a moment, trying to calm down, but to no avail.

I heard Hugh come down the passage and stop in the doorway. And at the same time, I heard Rachel's footsteps going up the stairs. Taking my things back to my room.

And all the while, I was realizing that I was now a prisoner in this house. There would always be someone on watch, to make sure I never left here.

My one hope, the only hope I had now, was that Ellen would send the police back to rescue me.

But she was one of these people. And even as I raised that hope, I knew it was false. She wouldn't betray them. For all I knew, she was carrying silver she herself had found down along the strand.

✻ ✻ ✻

I don't remember much about dinner that night. Rachel and Hugh were kind, they tried their best to make up for what their neighbors had done. Rachel even opened a jar of her spiced plums to finish the meal.

Finally pushing my plate aside, I said, "What am I to do?"

It was Hugh who answered. "Let them think you're not going to fight them. Lull them into believing you've accepted what they've decided. And then I'll help you start walking one night. By the time they realize that you've gone, it will be too late."

He was offering me hope. But I wasn't really certain it would work.

"And what will happen to you and Rachel, when they find out?"

He shrugged. "What can they do?"

But I thought they could do a great deal.

"You're safe here," Rachel said. "That's what matters."

Those men hadn't hurt me. How could they have, with Rachel and Hugh and Mr. Wilson as witnesses? And for all I knew, Mr. Griffith, who watched everything from the windows of his house, had seen what had happened.

But would I have a convenient accident if I wandered too far afield? Or if they decided that watching me was too much of an effort, and that perhaps I ought never to leave?

"People will come looking for me," I said with more assurance than I felt. Even Simon and my parents would be hard-pressed to track me all the way out here. I did know they wouldn't stop looking—but it would be in all the wrong places. "What then?"

Hugh shook his head. "They'll have no choice but to let you go."

Or see to it that I never went at all. Long before rescue arrived. That was beginning to worry me as I calmed down.

What would Rachel and Hugh do, if that happened? They'd be in danger then as well.

But that was beginning to sink in as the reality of my situation. I wasn't overdramatizing it, I was merely looking at what was best for the villagers who were threatened by my presence here. And that would be my disappearance . . .

I'd have to be very careful. And I'd have to be certain that Rachel and Hugh didn't suffer on my account.

In the end, I told myself, the cavalry *would* arrive. Which meant that my task must be to stay alive until it got here.

Rallying myself, I said brightly, "Well. There's nothing more we can do tonight. Let me help with the washing up. I need to stay busy to keep my spirits up."

They tried to hide their relief at the way I'd accepted what had happened. But of course they were worried, it would be strange if they weren't.

And so my first step was to reassure my friends.

Over the next two days I didn't venture out of the house at all. I didn't even stand in the doorway or approach a window. If there were watchers, I was no threat to anyone.

On the third day, gloriously sunny and warm, I helped Rachel in her garden, clearing away the winter's debris and preparing it for the horse to come and turn over the compacted soil.

If anyone was looking, I worked hard, and made no attempt to worry the watchers.

When the horse came, I stayed out of its way. Rachel greeted it like an old friend, giving it an apple from her fruit cellar, scratching the blaze on its forehead. I made no effort to befriend it. I didn't want anyone to think I might consider riding it to Swansea. It was too important to Rachel and the woman who stabled it.

When it had plowed up the kitchen garden, I went inside while Rachel unharnessed it, rubbed it down, and walked it back to its stall.

On the fourth day, I helped her again, this time as the horse plowed orderly rows for the sowing in a long strip of land beyond her sheds. And once more I went indoors before she returned the horse.

The days were lengthening, and before the sun went down, I walked as far as the overlook. The coast guard station was a warm pink as the sun began to set, and down on the strand, the waves moved in with a little hiss. Two young girls walked along the surf, heads together, talking. A line of four or five milk cows made their way toward their barn, and a woman stood in the doorway of her cottage, staring out at the sky as the low-lying clouds turned from gold to pink to lavender far out in the Channel.

No one would have guessed that only a handful of days earlier, that lovely frothy ebb and flow of the tide had brought with it anything more than a few broken shells.

I could feel eyes on me, and I knew it must be Mr. Griffith, watching me from his cottage. I wondered who else had made it his business to keep an eye on me. But no one tried to stop me from enjoying the sunset, although I made a point of walking back to the house before the lavender sky turned to a deep purple and shadows began to fall.

The next morning, after I'd helped Rachel wash and hang the sheets out to dry in the ever-present wind, I went for another walk.

This time I went as far as the coast guard station. For if there was any chance that I might indeed walk toward Swansea, I'd need the stamina and the wind to keep up a fast, steady pace.

In the afternoon, I walked as far as Ellen's cottage.

It was shut up, as I'd expected. Curtains drawn across the windows, and the door latched. I didn't think she was planning on coming back for quite some time. Even before she was encouraged to leave here without me.

Walking up to the path, I saw that the drapes hadn't quite been pulled together in one window.

I went over to it, and cupping my hands around my eyes, I tried to peer inside.

This was the dining room—I could glimpse a long table with chairs and part of a glass-fronted cabinet holding pieces of china.

But what interested me was not the furnishings—the paneling had been pulled from the wall, exposing the latticework of wood and fill behind it.

Had Oliver been brought down here to help her with changes she wanted to make to the cottage? It looked more like searching than renovating.

I made my way around the cottage, looking for another window that wasn't quite covered. The one I found was a bedroom, for I could see a part of the bed, made up with a white comforter, and part of a tall chest that had been pushed aside. Behind it, the wall had been taken down and left to one side.

This wasn't vandalism, and it wasn't repairs. How much of the rest of the house looked like this? And what was she searching for, if these panels had been taken down on purpose?

I remembered what Hugh had said, that it was thought that her grandfather had robbed the coach fleeing to Swansea, and killed the owner.

Had she come down here to search for whatever was left of that missing fortune?

But surely if the cottage had been empty for so many years, others had tried their luck at finding the silver. There had been no compunction when it came to putting the body of the man in the little boat in her house. It meant that others had been there before.

Of course they could hardly tear the house apart. Still I wouldn't put it past any of them to try their luck.

Ellen dressed elegantly. But I remembered too that she'd opened a lodging house down near the docks, for soldiers and seaman looking for a safe place to stay.

Was she perhaps living beyond her means—and hoping to find her grandfather's hoard of silver?

It seemed rather absurd, but I could see the evidence of my own eyes, the sections of paneling pulled down and left. Because Oliver had been beaten too badly to help put the cottage back together? Or hadn't it mattered?

I could hear something moving about in the bushes just beyond the kitchen garden, and I realized that I was well out of sight of the road and anyone watching. Had someone come down to see what I was doing?

Or even seen an opportunity to make me disappear? Had I let my curiosity lead me into danger?

And then a bird flew out of the tangle of limbs and old vines, disturbed by my presence. I took a deep breath.

Still, this was a warning to take to heart, and I quickly retraced my steps to the front of the cottage and walked out to the track that passed for the road this far down. To my left, The Worm hunched at the edge of the sea. In the open once more, I started back the way I'd come.

I was halfway to the abandoned coast guard station when I saw Mr. Griffith at the overlook, but he wasn't staring out at the scene in the bay. He was looking for me.

By the time I'd passed the coast guard station, he'd turned and gone back to his cottage, disappearing inside.

I didn't hurry. Taking my time, stopping at the overlook myself, before climbing the last stretch to the house.

Looking up, I saw Mr. Wilson standing in the churchyard. He turned away as soon as I'd spotted him there, a hand shading his eyes as he scanned the church tower, as if searching for storm damage to the fabric.

I went into the house.

Would they have watchers keeping an eye on this house during the night? In the event I should take it into my head to walk away?

Upstairs there was the sound of singing. I realized that Hugh, thinking he was alone, was singing in Welsh. As soon as I shut the door, it stopped.

That night I stood by the window in the parlor, hidden behind the lace curtains, but it was too dark outside to tell whether there was someone in the churchyard or down by the hedge or even at Mr. Griffith's window, taking his or her turn to watch.

Deciding to test the waters, as it were, I opened the door and stepped out into the night.

Overhead the stars were a brilliant canopy, as they can only be in very dark places. They'd often been hard to see at the Front, with the constant flashes of artillery fire or flares. I made a point to look for a few familiar constellations, and then the North Star. I'd just found it when Hugh came to the door and quietly called my name. I turned.

"I just needed a breath of air," I said, not lowering my voice to match his, as if I didn't care who heard me. "The stars are beautiful tonight. I hadn't realized how close they seem."

As I turned back toward the house, out of the corner of my eye I saw someone in the shadows by the church. Whoever it was had moved a little when Hugh came to the door, and with my eyes accustomed to the night, I'd caught that slight shift in the shadows.

I went back inside, and Hugh said, "Be careful, Bess. Don't test them."

"I just felt—smothered," I said, shutting the door behind me.

"I'm sorry," he replied, and I realized that he felt helpless to protect me. And that it was weighing on him.

"It isn't your fault. Or Rachel's," I told him.

"Your family. Surely they're looking for you."

"I expect they are. But in the wrong places. London, possibly. They'd expect me to go there for a few days, if I didn't choose to spend all my leave in Somerset. By the time they discovered I wasn't in London at all, and I hadn't been, they'll go back to the clinic and start asking questions."

With a smile I didn't feel I added, "But I'm not giving my mother and father or Simon enough credit."

"Who is Simon?" he asked with interest.

"He might as well be a member of my family. Sergeant-Major Simon Brandon, late of my father's old regiment, and once his batman." I smiled. "I can't remember a time when he wasn't there. He was sent out to India with new recruits for the regiment, and it appeared he was either going to be shot for insubordination or court-martialed for not following orders. Headstrong and willful to a fault. He'd also lied about his age, which didn't help matters, but my father couldn't send him back to England. And so he took Simon in hand, and in the end made a soldier of him."

"He was in the war?"

"In a roundabout way. Both he and the Colonel Sahib served at the pleasure of the War Office. My mother and I never knew just what it was they were doing."

"Interesting." He started toward the kitchen, and I followed. Rachel was working on the loom, we could hear the *thump-thump* as it moved.

"Hugh. Why would Ellen Marshall be tearing panels off the wall of her grandfather's cottage? Surely she doesn't think her grandfather hid most of the money there? Or even if he did, once, it probably isn't there now."

"God knows. What I don't understand is why she should be so

desperate for money. There's the motorcar—the way she still dresses. It can't be all for show?"

But in a town like Cardiff there must be a difference between having money and having *enough* money.

I let it go.

Late the next afternoon, Rachel brought in one of the older ewes, worried about her, and penned her in the shed.

"She's carrying twins, and at her age, she might be in trouble. I'll look in on her before I go to bed."

But when she went out to the shed, the ewe had kicked a hole in the partition and got loose.

Rachel came back to the house for a lantern and told us what had happened. "She's a canny beast, she should be all right, but I'd hate to lose her. I'll just have a look around and see if I can find her."

Hugh took a lantern down from the shelf above the pantry door and lit it for her. "Shall I come out with you?"

"No, I think I'll take one of the dogs. He can sniff her out, and she knows me."

She found a scarf and buttoned up her coat, then took the lantern and went out the kitchen door, calling to the older dog.

Hugh stood on the threshold, watching the bobbing lantern as Rachel made her way out to the fields, then closed the door.

She was gone quite a long time, and we were both beginning to worry. Finally Hugh reached for a second lantern and said, "I think I ought to have a look. She could have run into some trouble with the ewe."

He left, and I waited there in the kitchen, standing by the windows. It was nearly a quarter of an hour later when I heard Hugh shouting my name. I went to the door and heard him call, "Fetch your coat. Rachel needs you."

I didn't know what had happened—my first thought was that Rachel might have taken a fall clambering over the walls. My second was that if the ewe had had her lambs, Hugh would be hard-pressed to carry one back to the shed.

I flew up the stairs, caught up my coat and woolen hat, and reached for the last lantern. The wick refused to light. I could see Hugh's out in the field, and so I headed for that, stumbling and tripping over unseen obstacles in the dark. When I caught him up, he said, "This way," and led me farther into the field.

There we found Rachel playing midwife to the ewe. There was one lamb lying by her side, and the ewe was struggling to bring the second lamb into the world.

Rachel said, "Bess—thank goodness. Will you carry this one back to the shed? And rub it down with some straw? I'll stay with the mother."

"Yes, of course." I bent down to pick up the lamb, all legs and bleating for its mother. She turned to nuzzle it, then ignored it as she struggled with its twin.

I got a good grip on the lamb and set off back to the shed, taking my time and making certain to keep my feet. Hugh lit my way until I was on even ground, then went back to stand by Rachel. I knew she was fearful of losing the mother, and I was glad he was with her.

I got my burden to the shed, although it kept struggling to free itself, and put it into the pen its mother had left. Finding some straw, I rubbed it down against the cold, talking to it as I worked, trying to keep it quiet. But it bleated and stumbled around the pen, looking for the ewe. When I'd finished, I blocked it in as best I could, using whatever came to hand, and shut the door. Hugh was still with Rachel. I could just see the two lanterns as I rounded the shed and started toward them.

I'd taken half a dozen steps when something moved behind me.

Before I could whirl and defend myself, a hand was clapped over my mouth and an arm circled my waist, lifting me off the ground.

I kicked out with both feet, connecting with a kneecap even as I tried to bite the hand across my mouth.

Whoever it was swore, and then said in a strained whisper, "Damn it, Bess—*stop*."

I went still. And he put me down, drawing me back into the deeper shadows by the shed wall. On the other side of it I could hear the lamb moving unsteadily.

Simon bent to massage his knee, but before I could speak, he held up a hand, and I waited.

He was listening. All I could hear was the lamb, but Simon had acute hearing, and I said nothing until he nodded. Even then I kept my voice to a whisper.

"What is it?"

"There was someone who came around the house. He was watching the shed. I didn't want him to see me. You had better walk on—to where the lanterns are. I'll keep watch."

"But—" I began.

"Go on. I've camped by one of the caves. If those people come back with you, I'll find you later. Hurry."

I turned and made my way to where Rachel was occupied with the ewe. She had had her other lamb and was busy cleaning it, but I could see she was tired. Rachel was kneeling by her, watching her breathing.

"She's all right. I think. But I don't want to move her just yet."

Rachel's dog was lying quietly in the grass not ten feet away. But its ears were pricked up, and it was staring toward the shed. She noticed that, and said, "He must hear the other lamb. Hugh, take him back to the house. I think I can manage on my own. If Bess can carry the other lamb?"

"Yes, of course."

But Hugh was reluctant to leave us. "I think it's best if I stay."

Rachel looked up at him. "We're all right out here."

"It's late," he pointed out.

The ewe was struggling to her feet, and Rachel moved away to give her room. I knelt to lift the lamb, and the ewe would have none of it. In the end, it was Rachel who carried the lamb, and the ewe followed her, while we brought up the rear with the lanterns. The dog trotted by her side.

Where had Simon gone? I was afraid the dog would start barking as soon as he picked up Simon's scent.

But when he did catch something on the wind, head lifted, nose quivering, he started toward the house, not the shed. He began to bark, and Rachel called him back, telling him to shush, it was late.

He paid no heed, forging ahead of us and rounding the corner of the house. The barking got stronger, and I sent up a silent prayer that he hadn't cornered Simon.

Hugh, his crutches swinging, moved ahead of us to follow the dog, and Rachel called to it again.

She couldn't go after them, not with the lamb in her arms and the ewe prancing impatiently at her side. I moved ahead too, lifting the lantern high to light her way and then pulling open the shed door.

The ewe, responding to the noisy firstborn lamb, trotted forward, and I had just barely got the way to the pen clear for her, holding back the lamb, before she charged into the pen, sniffing it and washing it. By the time Rachel arrived with a squirming bundle and put the second lamb down, the first was already nursing. Bleating, the younger one joined its brother or sister. We hastily re-erected my barricade to hold them in the pen, then went out and shut the door.

Rachel smiled at me in the light from the two lanterns. "I'm glad she's all right. I've grown fond of her over the years."

"You were right to go after her." But my mind was on the dog. It had stopped barking, and I could hear raised voices on the far side of the house.

"Who is Hugh talking to?" Rachel asked, hearing them as well.

She started in that direction, and I followed. When we rounded the corner of the house, I saw that Hugh was talking to the rector. I did my best to disguise my relief.

Mr. Wilson nodded to us. "I saw the lanterns. I thought there might be something I could do to help. But Captain Williams assures me that the ewe and her lambs are safe."

"Yes. With the help of Bess." Rachel hesitated. "Can I offer you a cup of tea, Rector? Against the cold?"

"Thank you, but no. I was just coming back from one of the cottages. They have a child that's ill."

"Not Jenny?" I put in quickly.

"No, it's the Simpson lad. Croup."

"Is there anything I can do?"

"He's better, I think. And able to sleep. Well, then, I shall bid you a good night." Tipping his hat, he turned and walked on toward the road.

"What did he want?" Rachel was asking Hugh in a low voice.

"I don't know," Hugh answered. "It was rather odd to find him lurking here at the side of the house."

"Maybe he thought I'd gone missing," I said, "and you were searching for me. Not the ewe."

Hugh shook his head. "God knows." He turned, and we started back toward the kitchen door. I was busy trying to think of some reason to go back to the shed on my own and look for Simon. But I might easily draw the dog to him.

He'd said he was camping . . .

Why hadn't he come to the door and asked for me?

Late as it was, Rachel put the kettle on, and I couldn't very well excuse myself. And so I sat with them and drank my tea as we talked about the lambs and the ewe. When at last we went up to bed, I lit my lamp and then hurried to my window to look out. There was only darkness, pitch-black as far as I could see toward the end of the peninsula. The shed was out of my line of sight.

Simon had no way of knowing which room was mine. But if he was watching any of the windows, he would recognize the distinctive cap worn by a Sister. And so I moved the little table by my bed so that it faced the window, and I stood in front of it so that I was only a silhouette, apparently looking through my kit.

After a bit, I blew out the lamp and then went back to the window.

A few minutes later I saw it.

At first I wasn't sure I hadn't imagined it, staring into the darkness, wishing for a sign.

But yes, I was right. There was a dim light showing from the direction of the coast guard station—well behind it on the landward side, blocking it from the houses across the road. Or even from Mr. Griffith's cottage, where he watched the world pass by his own windows.

The light was steady for a bit, and then it began to blink in a pattern. Suddenly I recognized it. A code that my father had used on some of his night raids into hostile territory. And a code that couldn't be broken because he had devised it from words only English officers and men would know, then given them new meanings, although they sounded like gibberish when strung together in Morse code. It had worked quite well.

Simon had taught it to me one afternoon, after we'd had an attack on the compound.

As I waited, the sequence was repeated.

Croquet. *I am in position.* Refectory. *To the left.* Lychgate. *Of this place.*

Starlight. *Just after sunrise.* Monastery. *Are you free to move about?* Barbican. *Or under duress?*

What on earth had Simon discovered, that made him ask such questions?

I considered how to answer him. Lighting my lamp again, I moved back and forth across from it to form the *M* of Monastery.

After a moment, a single word came back.

Thunder. *Will be waiting.*

I blew out my lamp, and went to bed.

I didn't know quite how Simon had found me, but I was glad of it. Now I had to find a way to leave that wouldn't put Rachel and Hugh in danger for letting me go.

But that was tomorrow's problem. My toes touched the hot water bottle, and I settled myself to sleep.

It was raining in the morning, a warm drizzle that promised spring. Rachel was up early, looking in on the ewe, making certain she had enough milk for both lambs. I dealt with breakfast, and afterward, she began to sow her seeds in tidy rows in her gardens, mostly the cold-weather vegetables that needed the last touch of winter to germinate. I asked if I could help, but she shook her head. "I know how everything goes in. But thank you for asking."

It was closer to ten than dawn when I finally set out, a borrowed umbrella in my hand, first for the overlook, where I stood for several minutes watching the waves come in. Everyone else had attended services at the church.

And then I strolled down to the coast guard station, peering in the windows and then making my way around the facility to the back. There was a terraced place toward the lower end where I thought the occupants had stood and smoked when off duty, invisible from the sea.

There was no one waiting for me there.

I felt a surge of disappointment.

Just then one of the station doors opened a little, and Simon called quietly, "This way, Bess."

And I stepped into the dry, musty interior, in what appeared to be the kitchen, although everything useful had been taken away. Where the cooker had been there was a large pan lying upside down, with a hole in the bottom, and on the windowsill, a pitcher without a handle. In a corner were what appeared to be mice tracks through something that had spilled.

"I am very happy to see you," I said, greeting Simon with a smile. "I don't know how you found me, but I'm relieved that you're here."

"What the devil have you got yourself into, Bess?" he demanded.

Chapter 14

THERE WAS EXASPERATION in his voice, as well as curiosity.

I shook my head. "It will probably be easier if you tell me first how you found me. Then I can fill in the rest of the story."

From his expression, I expected him to begin with a lecture on disappearing. Instead, he took a deep breath, as if putting that aside for a later conversation.

"When Matron sent word to Somerset, worried that you hadn't returned from your leave and asking if you were ill, your mother was able to reach me in London. She thought you might have gone to Mrs. Hennessey's to visit one of your flatmates. But when I went to the house and spoke to her, it was clear she hadn't seen or heard from you except for that first night you'd spent at the flat. Nor were Diana or Mary in London, and Lady Elspeth was in Scotland. Mrs. Hennessey thought it unlikely that you'd traveled there. I didn't want to alarm your mother, and so I went on my own to the clinic. I avoided Matron and instead talked to the orderlies. One of them told me that you've been concerned about some of the men who'd been released to return to their homes in Wales."

Simon moved across the room and back again. "He wasn't certain where they'd come from, but he thought it was one of the coal valleys. I drove to Cardiff, and after some trouble found the hire firm where you'd taken a motorcar up to the valley. Fortunately, the driver remembered you and told me about the slide and how disappointed you were to have missed one of the patients you'd come to see. Still, he couldn't recall where you'd gone next. Swansea, he thought. But he knew the name of the hotel where he'd dropped you after you got back to Cardiff. There I found a chambermaid who remembered you, and she told me you'd gone by train to Swansea."

"Yes, I'd asked her to press my coat, and she stayed to chat."

"It's a good thing you make friends easily," he said, and I realized then how worried he'd been.

"I sent a telegram to your mother from the station, knowing she'd be on her way to London at the first excuse. I told her all was well, that you were with a patient, and all the while I hoped to God I was right. In Swansea, I found the second hire firm, and the owner brought in the driver who'd taken you out here to the peninsula. He swore you'd told him you'd decided to stay and sent him away. I had a feeling he was lying, and so I followed him home. After a little persuasion he confessed that he'd been frightened out of his wits, and he'd fled to Swansea, abandoning you."

"I can't think what it could have been," I said. "Mr. Griffith is a bit strange, but he was well paid for taking in Mr. Morgan. Why should he scare him away in the middle of the night?"

"Morgan told me something had come at him out of the darkness, terrifying him so much that he barely fought it off. He claimed he had the scars to show for it. I saw them, Bess, his shoulder had been raked with what looked like claws."

He was leaning back against one of the doorframes watching me.

"Yes, well, I think he made all that up. He fled in the middle of the night, that much is true, without even stopping to knock on Rachel's door to see if I wanted to leave with him. I wouldn't put it past Mr. Griffith to tell him tales of Viking raiders and a giant dragon that lay in wait for them. They don't much care for strangers out here. Or Mr. Morgan had a nightmare and frightened himself, then was too ashamed of abandoning me to admit to it. After all, the Welsh themselves have a number of tales about dragons."

"He believed it. I watched his face."

"The problem was, after he'd gone, there was no way to leave here. The only horses are draft animals, no one has a motorcar, and even the post is delivered sporadically. Then a few days ago, Ellen Marshall, as she's known locally, arrived." I told him about Ellen and the attack on Oliver. "But when she was ready to go back to Swansea, on her way to Cardiff, the local people wouldn't let her take me with her. They were afraid I'd talk."

"About what? What have you got yourself into?"

"I'm not sure." I told him about the treasure ship and the silver that sometimes washed ashore after a storm.

Frowning, he said, "The silver would have been in chests. They'd have sunk into the seabed from their own weight, when the ship broke apart. Storms might break them open, or dredge up the silver that spilled out as the chests rotted."

"That makes sense. Still, you'd have thought the local people would have tried to salvage it long ago. Soon after the wreck."

"I'm not sure they could. If it's out that far."

"There's no boat here," I agreed. "And I don't think anyone here would trust someone else to go looking. There's something else." I described the two soldiers who had quietly been buried.

"For heaven's sake, Bess," Simon commented, starting to pace. "Your mother will have a fit if you tell her all this. She was worried enough when Matron sent that telegram. I'm to bring you home as soon as I find you. Her instructions. She said she would deal with Matron."

Knowing the Colonel's Lady, I had no difficulty believing who would come out of that meeting with colors flying.

"Well, yes, I see that. But you must understand. It's going to be difficult for me to go."

"I don't see why. I've got my motorcar by the campsite—well hidden at the moment but easily accessible. If you leave in the night, we can walk there before dawn and be well on our way before your absence is discovered."

"But there are watchers. You saw one of them. It's not as easy as just walking away."

"I'll deal with them. That's not a problem."

I took a deep breath. "The problem is, I can't leave Rachel and Captain Williams to face their neighbors when I'm discovered missing. I don't know what they'll do. And someone has already attacked the Captain. He won't say who. But I suspect it's someone who wanted to marry Rachel, after her husband was killed in the war. He was the Captain's brother, you see, and that's why he's come to help her cope. And that's why she could reject the suitor's proposal."

He shook his head. "You're expected at the clinic, and your mother has already told me she'll be waiting in Bristol to drive the rest of the way with us."

"I know. I know." I changed the subject. "Why did you waylay me at the shed?" I asked, curious.

"What Morgan told me worried me. I decided to reconnoiter before driving up to the door. I didn't know then that you had no way of getting back to Swansea. I was afraid you were in trouble. I'd just come up from exploring as far as the strand when I saw someone watching the house, late as it was. I stepped into the shadows by the shed, and just then the woman—Rachel?—came out and found the ewe missing. That gave me the opportunity to speak to you."

I warned him then about Mr. Griffith. "He sees everything. I don't think he sleeps well at night. I've seen him smoking outside his door."

"All the more reason to get out of here. Bess, can you open your bedroom window?"

"I think so."

"You have only to toss your kit down to me, then leave a note for Mrs. Williams and the Captain. They can't be held accountable, if you slip away in the night. Besides, their neighbors will be too busy searching for you, thinking you've left on foot. And we'll be in Swansea by that time, well out of their reach. They won't be counting on a motorcar."

"It's not as simple as that. Rachel took me in, Simon, and they have been kind to me. I can't leave, not knowing what will happen to them. If something does, I'd feel responsible."

"The villagers can hardly murder them in their beds."

"No, but they could kill Rachel's beloved sheep, or burn down the house—who knows what they're capable of? That silver has been the lifeblood of this peninsula for so long that any threat to it would be taken seriously. And they aren't going to accept any promises of keeping my mouth shut. They're far too suspicious."

"I can't believe the authorities haven't found out about those coins years ago."

"I don't think they knew just where the ship had gone down. And the local people swore they hadn't seen it. There must be dozens of places where it might have got into trouble. Hugh—the Captain— thinks they melt the silver down so that it won't arouse suspicion." I remembered that those men had let Ellen Marshall and Oliver leave. They trusted her. But why would they trust *him*? "The people out here depend on that income, and they are terrified of losing it."

He stopped pacing and went to stand by the window. "You must go back, or someone will start looking for you. And I don't want to be seen. Are you certain your friends are in as much danger as you claim they are?"

"You didn't see Oliver's face. Or what was done to Hugh Williams. He won't talk about it, and Oliver didn't know his attacker—it was the first time he'd been here, but he was helping Ellen take her house apart, looking for where her grandfather had hidden his own hoard. They didn't find it. Her neighbors could have taken it over the years—they felt free to hide the soldier's body in her house. Which reminds me. That might be a safer place to meet. Do you know where it is? Just below here."

"Yes, I found it. I didn't know if it was empty or occupied. Someone has been tearing up the walls."

"Ellen herself, I think. All right, when shall I look for you again?"

"If all is well, another day won't matter. I'll be there tomorrow morning. You won't see me until I'm sure you weren't followed. Be patient. Look for my signal tonight. I'll try to find out if there's a pattern of watchers. It was the rector last night. I followed him home."

"Be careful," I said unnecessarily. Simon always was. But I knew these villagers and he might well discount his danger here.

Then he said, "Bess. If you're in trouble, meanwhile, how will I know?"

"I'll be all right," I replied, putting as much certainty into my voice as I could. "As long as I don't try to leave—or let anyone think I'm about to try."

But he wasn't reassured.

"Please, Simon. I'll be safe enough." But the longer he stayed out here, the more likely one of us would be found out. "Let me talk to Captain Williams and Rachel. Not"—I added hastily—"telling them about you. Not yet. But asking them what they think the risks are if I left."

"All right." But he wasn't happy about it. "Go on, before some-one comes. But be careful. And if you can leave here, the sooner the better."

A reflection of what I myself had been thinking.

He went to a window and scanned the area behind the station. "I think it's safe. But I'll watch from another window, before I leave. To be sure."

"Mind Rachel's dogs, Simon. There are two of them." With a nod to him, I slipped out the door and heard it click shut behind me. I didn't walk back the way I'd come but circled the building until I came out at the other end. Then I made my way to the road and started up it.

As far as I could tell, there was no one about. I didn't turn to look back at the station for fear of giving Simon away. Instead, although my mind was whirling with possibilities, I dawdled on my way, pausing at the overlook for several minutes.

When I turned to walk on, Mr. Griffith was on his way toward me.

"What's so fascinating about yon coast guard station?" he asked.

"I'm not interested in the station," I said shortly. "For one thing I'm bored. For another, I just need to get away for a while, where I'm not watched every minute. It's a relief."

He grinned. But there was no humor in it. "Bothers you to be watched, does it? You don't know the half of it."

And with that he turned on his heel and walked back the way he'd come.

But ten yards from me he stopped and looked straight at me, as if he could read my thoughts. "Don't tell me you've found Ellen's missing hoard? Hiding it at the station, are you? Clever boots, aren't you?"

I was cross with him, and I let it show. "What hoard? Don't any of you people out here think about anything but what your neighbors are up to? Go search the station if you want to. Search the cottage. I don't really care what you do."

"I don't believe you."

"All right then," I said, pointing to the station. "Let's walk back there. Or to the cottage. Go on, you made the accusation. Let's go and see what I was up to. I don't have anything to hide. The question is, do you?"

He glared at me, that last taunt hitting its mark, and I wondered if he'd been busy searching Ellen's cottage on his own, and that was why he was afraid I'd found what he'd missed. Who would have seen him go and come in the middle of the night?

But he didn't answer me at first. Then he said, "To the devil with you, then." And he walked on, shoulders hunched.

I stayed where I was until he'd gone into his cottage and shut the door.

And then I walked the rest of the way back to the house.

For the rest of the day, while Rachel was sowing seeds in her garden and Hugh was keeping an eye on the sheep, with the dogs for his companions, I debated with myself what to say to them about leaving. How to approach it in such a way that they told me the truth and not what they thought I'd want to hear. Because I had a feeling they wouldn't keep me here by bringing up what might happen to them.

When they came in to tea, it was nearly five, and I waited until we had settled to our meal before broaching the subject.

"If I walked away in the middle of the night, would they try to stop me? The men who are watching me?" I asked as casually as I could.

Rachel put down her cup and stared at me. "Are you telling me you intend to try? I don't know that it's wise, Bess. You can't get far on foot."

"Far enough that perhaps I can find someone to take me the rest of the way."

Hugh said, "It's a risk. Rachel is right."

"But what could they possibly do to me? They aren't likely to hurt me, are they? They'd only bring me back here."

Hugh said, "I don't know what they might do."

"And what about you?" I asked. "Would they blame you if I left?"

They exchanged glances. Hugh said, "That's not your worry."

"I think it must be. I can't leave here with that on my conscience."

Rachel said practically, "No one here wants to drive us away. What would be the point?"

There was some truth to that. If I left with Simon—appeared simply to vanish one night—and nothing more came of my departure, no police, no trouble—it might all blow over.

I felt my spirits lift. But was that simply wishful thinking?

When we went up to bed that night, I stood by my window for some time, staring out into the darkness. But Simon didn't appear, didn't send me a message. After a while, I went to bed.

I woke in the night from a dream about being at home in Somerset, helping my mother and our housekeeper, Iris, dry apples for the winter, slicing and setting them out in the sun under thin sheets of cheesecloth, to protect them from insects and birds.

I lay there for a moment before I realized that the birds chirping in the trees just above the trays of apple slices had actually been something else—for that sound came again. A rattling of small pebbles against the shutters outside my window. I got up at once and walked over to it.

There was only blackness out there toward the coast guard station. It occurred to me that I ought to light my lamp, then snuff it out again, to show Simon that I was here and awake.

Doing just that, I took the opportunity to look at my little watch. It was nearly five.

I let the lamp burn for a minute or two, then turned down the wick, plunging my room into darkness that slowly lightened as my eyes adjusted. When I went back to the window, I didn't see anyone below on the grass, or any sign of a light down by the coast guard station. Then it occurred to me that if Simon had come to my window to wake me, it would take him a while to reach that back terrace of the station.

I waited patiently. And then the first flash came.

The word, repeated in case I had missed it the first time, was Treacle. I tried to recall what that meant. *Hold your position.* Then Piccadilly. *Trouble.* Buckingham. *By the river.*

There was no river out here on the peninsula. I frowned. Did he mean by the bay? He must. There had been no sea, no bay in the Northwest Frontier provinces.

I found my shoes and silently made my way down the stairs, keeping to the sides of the treads where they creaked less. I heard the dogs stir restlessly in the kitchen, but when I didn't come that way, they settled again.

But I couldn't see the water from the downstairs windows. And no one was stirring in the village. I crept back up the stairs and into my room. There was nothing more from Simon.

When, soon after the sun broke through on the horizon, its light casting bright rays across the peninsula, I heard Hugh stirring in the room next to mine, I hastily dressed.

By the time I came down, he had filled the kettle and set it on the stove.

"I couldn't sleep," he said, and I could see the dark circles under his eyes. Phantom pain?

I said, "Is there anything I can do?"

He hesitated, then said, "How long can Rachel continue to live out here?"

"I don't know. Does it matter?"

"I have worth out here," he answered after a moment. "In a city, there's not much I can do."

I followed his thinking. If for some reason—my departure, the growing violence out here, anything—Rachel returned to Swansea or Cardiff, she had a skill that would bring her an income. While Hugh also had skills, he was an amputee and might not find work at all. There were barriers for him in the workplace that Rachel wouldn't even notice because she had both limbs.

"I shouldn't worry," I said slowly. "I think Rachel has come to depend on you."

"I have my pride," he said stiffly.

"And rightly so," I replied. "But pride can be stubborn, and get in the way of change."

He smiled. "You put me in my place very easily."

"No," I told him truthfully. "I tried to show you that there are other things that matter besides pride."

He was about to answer when we heard Rachel on the stairs. The dogs bounded down the passage to greet her, and she stopped to pet them.

I said quietly, for his ears only, "Those two will have to face changes as well. She won't leave them behind."

But before Rachel could walk on down the passage, she must have gone into the front room because her voice was muffled as she called, "Hugh? What's happening out there?"

He got up and made his way to where she was standing by the front windows. I was just behind him, feeling a sense of dread. Was this what Simon had prepared me for?

There were half a dozen villagers hurrying toward the hedge and the path down to the bay. Men, their faces grim, and Mr. Wilson among them.

We watched them disappear down the path, and Mr. Griffith came out of his house a moment later to stand by the hedge, looking after them.

Hugh said, "Stay here," and went out to walk over to where Mr. Griffith was standing.

Rachel and I watched as the two men conferred, and then Hugh disappeared down the road. A moment later and he was back again, saying something more to Mr. Griffith.

I moved uneasily. "There isn't another soldier washed ashore? Or a boat in desperate straits?"

"I hope not," she said fervently. "But there may be something else down there."

More silver coins to fight over?

We waited. And then I couldn't stand it any longer. I went up for my coat and then out the back door, ignoring Rachel calling my name, telling me to wait.

I was out of sight of the two men by the hedge. As I rounded the house, I cut across the sheep fields and went on to where the road started down the incline toward the overlook. When I got there, instead of standing in the open where I had the best view, I tried to stay behind some of the scrub trees and grasses that had grown up at the cliff's edge, hoping to be less conspicuous if someone on the strand looked this way.

The water was smooth as silk, the frothy waves breaking gently— the tide hadn't turned yet. Overhead, gulls caught shafts of sunlight, flashing white and calling raucously as they watched whatever was happening at the water's edge. And there was no sign of a boat in trouble.

Peering down through a cluster of bare branches, I wished I'd thought to bring Hugh's field glasses. For there must have been a dozen men gathered on the strand and I was hard-pressed to see what it was they were looking at.

And then they parted, and three of them started up the path.

I saw finally what they had concealed.

There was a body lying on the strand, just above the high-water mark. A man's body, and I needn't go down there to feel for a pulse to know that he was quite dead. It was there in the way his knees were drawn up, arms bent toward his chest, his face down. If he'd been alive, the men would have already carried him up the path, out of the wind and away from the water.

Even at this distance I could see that he wasn't wearing a uniform.

But who was he? And where had he come from?

Poised to hurry back toward the house if they showed any signs of climbing all the way to the top, I watched three of the men—one of them Mr. Wilson—walk up the path. But they turned down one of the lower paths, moving steadily toward a house not far from where little Jenny lived. They made their way to the door, then stood there, as if undecided what to do. And then one of them walked up to the door, raised his hand, and knocked. I thought it must be Mr. Wilson, for even at this distance, he still resembled a crow.

I couldn't hear the knock. But the cry of a woman I couldn't see, for she was inside the house, reached me clearly, high-pitched and in denial as Mr. Wilson told her what they had discovered. After a moment they went inside.

I turned my attention back to the men gathered on the beach. As the gulls swung high above them, their cries echoing over the water, one of the men knelt by the body, as if examining it. As he got to his feet, the others leaned forward for a better look as the first man pulled out a handkerchief and wiped his hands.

After a bit, the men looked up toward the house where Mr. Wilson and his companions had gone inside. There seemed to be some debate over whether to take the dead man there. One man argued with the rest, pointing to the body. And then it seemed that they agreed to wait for Mr. Wilson to return.

I remembered the handkerchief and what must have been blood. What had happened to the dead man?

Increasingly uneasy, I left the overlook and made my way back to Rachel's house, walking to the pasture first and then cutting across to the kitchen door. Rachel was still in the front room, watching Hugh and Mr. Griffith. When I walked in, she looked over her shoulder at me, saying, "You shouldn't have gone out."

"I'm so sorry," I said, "but I had to know. There's a man lying on the strand. He's dead. The rector went to a house on the Down, where he told a woman the bad news. I heard her cry out. It isn't a stranger, there on the strand. It's someone from the village."

"Which house?" she asked, frowning. But when I tried to explain just which one it was, she said, "I'm not sure. It could be the Stephenson house."

"Do you know them well?"

"They're an older couple. They lost their son in the war. Their daughter lives with her husband in one of the villages just north of Bristol. How did he die?"

I hadn't mentioned the blood. "I don't know. It was too far away to see."

"But you're sure he's dead?"

"Yes, sadly."

Looking out the window, she said, "I do wish Hugh would come back." There was worry in her voice.

I was remembering that Simon had warned me about the body at five in the morning. *Trouble by the river.* What had he seen?

We waited in silence a little longer. But Hugh remained out there with Mr. Griffith. I knew he must be chafing at his crutches, for the long descent down the path would mean an arduous climb back to the hedge. Otherwise he would have gone down to see what was happening.

Watching them, I thought that he and Mr. Griffith were the outsiders here. Both men were Welsh in an English enclave, and suspect.

Where was Simon? Safely back to his cave? Or watching as I had done from some safe vantage point? He too was an outsider, and if he was discovered, people might blame him for these attacks . . .

We gave up, finally, on waiting for Hugh, and when he at length came back, Rachel and I had gone on with breakfast preparations, although we had little appetite. Hugh's was in the warming oven, and Rachel got it out while I poured another cup of tea.

"What happened?" she asked. "Could you see?"

He shook his head. "There was a body on the strand. A man's. I think it must have been Edward Stephenson's. Mr. Wilson and two others went to his house. After a while, the other men brought his body there. Mrs. Stephenson was very upset, and a neighbor, Mrs. Tucker, came over to comfort her. That's all I know."

"Was he taken ill?" I asked in my turn.

"There's no word on that. I expect we won't know until someone comes back up."

I wondered if Hugh had seen the man wipe his hands after touching the body. Had I jumped to the conclusion that there had been blood on his hands? Hugh would have had a better viewpoint, after all.

But Simon had warned me away. And he wouldn't have done that if Mr. Stephenson had died of natural causes. If there hadn't been something wrong about the man's death.

The morning seemed to drag. And then as I was helping Rachel carry water from the rain barrel to the new seedbeds, Mr. Wilson came round the corner of the house, startling us when he spoke.

"Mrs. Williams. Sister Crawford."

"Good morning, Rector," Rachel said.

"I see you've sown your garden. I'm behind times this year."

"The weather has held," she replied, looking at the tidy rows.

"I'm afraid I've sad news to give you. Mr. Stephenson died in the night."

"I'm sorry to hear it. Is there anything we can do for Mrs. Stephenson?"

"A neighbor is with her now, but thank you for asking. I've come about another matter. Were you awakened during the night by any noise? A quarrel? Someone shouting?"

Rachel shook her head. "My bedroom is on the back of the house. I seldom hear anything from the direction of the road. Was there a problem? What has happened, Mr. Wilson?"

"Someone gave Mr. Stephenson a savage beating. He was left by the water to die. But no one heard anything unusual on the Down. We wondered if the quarrel, if that's what it was, took place up here, on the cliff."

This was news indeed. What's more, it explained the blood I thought I'd seen on a man's hands.

"But who could have attacked Edward Stephenson? He was always rather quiet," Rachel was saying, unable to keep the shock out of her voice. "I've never known him to be quarrelsome."

The shed door opened, and Hugh came out to join us.

Mr. Wilson turned to me. "Sister Crawford? Did you hear anything unusual last night?"

"I'm afraid I didn't. My bedroom faces the Worm."

"Mr. Griffith tells me your lamp was on in the middle of the night."

"I remember lighting it, yes. I couldn't find my carafe of water. But I hardly think that was in the middle of the night."

"He claims to have seen it around five, when he heard what sounded like voices from the direction of this house."

That was so like Mr. Griffith, causing trouble for someone else to throw suspicion away from himself. But it was also too close to the mark. Had he seen Simon tossing pebbles at my window?

I made myself smile. "I would hardly be wandering about in the dark at that hour of the night," I said. "Whatever Mr. Griffith heard, it wasn't my voice."

"There was no call for your services? I understand young Jenny has suffered from a virulent sore throat."

"Yes, I'd already had a look at it. I was glad she didn't require my services again. A good sign." I added, for effect, "Her father made it quite clear I wasn't to call at the house again."

He raised his eyebrows at that. "Did he, indeed? More's the pity, he doesn't seem to know how to deal with his own stern independence."

It was more likely, I thought wryly, that Jenny's father didn't want me to stumble on any secrets. What else was to be seen besides that cup on the mantel?

"I am more concerned about what happened to Mr. Stephenson. You must know that Ellen Marshall's friend Oliver was also beaten." I was on the point of mentioning Hugh as well when I caught the warning he sent me. "Who could have done either of these attacks?"

"Surely not one of us," Mr. Wilson replied. "I can't believe that one of my flock would be capable of such savagery."

"But who else is there?" I asked.

"An outsider. Someone who has found his way here in his effort to escape the police. A madman, perhaps."

I was suddenly alert. If these people spotted Simon, he would be in very serious trouble.

"A madman? Surely not," I said, putting scorn into my voice. "And as for an escaping felon, he's more likely to disappear into the busy docks at Cardiff than to risk coming out to such an isolated place as this. How could he hide in a village where everyone knows his neighbor?"

He studied me for a moment. "You are wise in the ways of desperate men?"

I could feel myself flushing. "Hardly that. It's simple logic. If I wished to hide, I would choose London, where there were too many people for one person to be noticed."

"This man might not have known the peninsula was so— isolated."

"How could you live in Swansea and not know?" I countered.

"True," he admitted.

I brought the subject back to Mr. Stephenson. "Tell me—what sort of injuries did he have? Were they done by a man's fists or with some sort of weapon?"

"I can't bring myself to discuss such things before two ladies."

"I'm a nurse. I have seen far worse wounds than a beating."

Reluctantly he said, "The death blow must have been the head wound. Although there was severe bruising on the body. Mr. Stephenson put up a good defense but he was no match for his assailant. Which brings us back to the question of a madman."

"If he fought back, you have only to look for someone else with bruises. And bloody knuckles."

"I hadn't thought of that," Mr. Wilson said, rising. "I will make a point to look at every man's hands. Beginning with yours, Captain? To be thorough?"

Hugh held out his hands, turning them up and then down. "And yours?" he asked then.

Mr. Wilson stared at him for a moment, then nodded. "Of

course, you're right. I am not above suspicion." He held out his own, but there was no sign of bruising or cuts to be seen.

"If you will excuse me? I must be about my business."

And with that he was gone, rounding the corner of the house and disappearing.

When Rachel was sure he was out of hearing, she said, "This is worrying." She didn't look Hugh's way. "We've had our differences out here, but there's been nothing like this. I've always felt safe going out at night to look for my sheep. Or before dawn, after a storm."

I remembered that she knew who had attacked Hugh. Was she wondering if it was the same person who had attacked Oliver and now Mr. Stephenson? But she couldn't—or wouldn't—say anything about that. For Hugh's sake.

Hugh was saying, "You don't have anything to fear."

She looked toward the corner of the house again, avoiding his gaze. Then she busied herself cleaning the earth from her hands.

"I wish I'd thought to ask Mr. Wilson why Mr. Stephenson was out so late at night," I said. "Was that why he was a victim? Because he was there—or saw someone—or something."

It occurred to me then that if someone wanted to hunt for those chests of silver, he'd have to do it in the middle of the night, or there would be an uproar from his neighbors. A quiet dive in the dark of the moon—who knew what he might find if he was a strong swimmer? And profit from. Mr. Stephenson might have died because he couldn't sleep, or had decided on a last cigarette before going up to bed.

A last cigarette . . .

"Mr. Griffith is always wandering about in the night," I said thoughtfully. "Did you notice his hands, Hugh? While the two of you were talking?"

"He was wearing gloves."

It hadn't been all that cold, this morning.

Rachel said, "You can't suspect Mr. Griffith. He's quite the one for prying, but he's never been violent."

"People change," I commented.

"Not people you've known all your life," she countered. "His wife was such a lovely person. Very different, warm and friendly. She and my mother would often put up preserves together, sharing the work. I sometimes wondered what it was that drew her to such a gruff man."

But someone in this village was a murderer. And sooner or later, there was going to be a hue and cry, as others came to the same conclusion.

What then?

CHAPTER 15

CHANGING THE SUBJECT, rather than argue the point about Mr. Griffith, I said, "Do you think Mr. Stephenson had enemies? I don't recall ever seeing him."

Unless of course he had been one of the men carrying the dead soldier's body.

"He wasn't the sort of man who got into trouble. More often than not he was there when someone needed him. He came to help my father once when the shed door was blown off in a storm. Without even being asked. And when it was done, he wouldn't let my father pay him. Robbie's death was hard enough, and then Edith married one of the men at the coast guard station, and when he was relieved to serve in the Navy in 1915, she moved to Bristol to live with his parents. She hasn't been back since." She smiled a little. "Tom would call Mr. and Mrs. Stephenson very English, keeping themselves to themselves. It's something all of us are very good at, out here. Minding our own business."

Ignoring that, I replied, "Then I can't see any reason for someone to attack him. It must have something to do with his walking along the strand. Was that a habit of his?"

"I don't know. It isn't as if we can see the strand from here."

I gathered she didn't want to talk about what had happened to

Mr. Stephenson. Hugh, sensing it too, changed the subject, asking her if she needed help in the garden.

Whatever she must know about what happened to Hugh, it could be weighing even more heavily on her in light of this latest attack. Ellen's friend Oliver had survived, and so had Hugh. But it seemed to me that each successive attack had grown in viciousness, and now a man was dead.

I wanted to talk to Simon, to find out what he knew. For he had warned me away, and so he must have seen something, the body if not the attack. But it was broad daylight, and I couldn't go down to Ellen's cottage, to see if he was there. It was best to stay inside and keep my head down. Mr. Wilson had already asked rather pointed questions. I couldn't quite understand why he thought I might have something to do with the death, but I had brought trouble to this village by finding myself stranded here, and inadvertently learning some of the secrets of this place. The hastily buried soldiers. The silver. I wasn't to be trusted not to bring more trouble down upon them by telling other outsiders what I knew.

Which of course I had done, telling Simon.

I glanced up at the sky, wishing the day gone.

We were just finishing lunch when there was a knock at the door.

Hugh went to answer it. He came back almost at once, saying, "There's a woman who wants to speak to you. It's Mrs. Stephenson."

"For me?" I put down the tea towel I'd been using to dry the dishes and walked out to see her.

She was a small woman, plump and graying. Just now her blue eyes were swollen and red from crying. Hugh had left her in the front room, and I walked in, not knowing what to expect.

"Mrs. Stephenson? I am so sorry to hear about your husband."

Instead of thanking me, she said abruptly, "You're a nursing Sister, are you? I hear you came to look in on Jenny, up the way."

"Yes. How can I help you, Mrs. Stephenson?" I expected her to ask me to assist her in laying out her husband's body.

Her request surprised me. "I want you to come and see my husband. I want to know if he suffered, out there in the night alone and dying. The men can't tell me how it was for him. For that matter, they didn't want me to come here. But I want to know what happened. Jenny's mother told me you were kind to Jenny when she had trouble with her breathing. You must have seen dead men. You'll be honest with me."

I'd seen more than my share of the dead.

"Why do you want to know? The answer could be painful," I answered gently.

"Painful or not, Edward was my husband, and I owe him that." There was a fierceness about her, a determination, that belied her appearance. I could well imagine that it was true, she had stood up to the men who wanted her to stay away from me.

"Then let me fetch my coat."

I was back in only a minute but went down the passage first to tell Rachel and Hugh where I was going.

Rachel was alarmed. "I wouldn't if I were you," she said quietly. "I didn't care at all for the way Mr. Wilson was speaking to you. It could be a way of drawing you out of this house. Have you thought of that?"

Hugh said, "I don't think Mrs. Stephenson would be a party to such a trick."

"Yes, but it's odd, don't you think, that she would ask you to tell her how her husband died. It's bizarre. I never wanted to know how Tom died—it was too terrible to think about."

But Tom had died in France. This man had been brought home to his wife, and she had seen what had been done to him.

I said to Hugh, "What do you think?"

"I don't know," he answered, shaking his head. We'd kept our voices low, because Mrs. Stephenson was sitting in the front room. "I must agree with Rachel, but on the other hand, if it's a trick, surely they'd have come up with a much better ruse."

Like Jenny and her putrid sore throat . . .

"I must go," I said, "but it's important for you to know where I am. In case."

"I'm not sure we could do much," Rachel told me.

"There's that. But I'm willing to risk it." Besides, I'd like to see the body for myself.

In the end, I left with Mrs. Stephenson. We walked in silence for a bit, and then she said, "He was a good man. It was what I wanted most, for us to grow old together. But it wasn't to be."

"I'm so sorry for your loss," I said gently. "It's very difficult for you to face alone. Could word be sent to your daughter?"

"How would I manage that? Besides, he'll be in the ground before she could find a way back here. No. I'll write when I feel stronger, and tell her. Perhaps not all the story. She and her husband don't need to know that, do they?"

"No. What could they do?"

She nodded. "Still, something's not right. I've seen men fight each other. It's happened, of course it has. But this—this frightened me. And I look at the faces of my husband's friends, and I can't be sure one of them isn't keeping something from me."

She was far more astute than her neighbors must have bargained for. And I wondered if she had guessed who had done this.

"Who could have done such a thing to your husband?" I asked. "Do you know?"

"I don't. That's what is so worrying, you see. Jenny's father, now, he's fast with his fists. But he's a man who acts first and thinks about it later. His anger blows over. Whoever did this wasn't satisfied until Edward was dead."

"Did you know," I asked, "that the man Ellen Marshall brought down here with her was beaten rather badly?"

"Was he, now? Rector was on about something happening at Ellen's cottage. But none of us knew what it was. Mr. Griffith said he thought her friend had taken ill."

"She took him to hospital," I told Mrs. Stephenson but didn't have the heart to tell her that Oliver would very likely survive.

"All the more reason, then, for you to have a look at Edward."

When we came to the modest cottage where she lived, and where I had seen Mr. Wilson and two other men come to break bad news, I'd expected to see several neighbors keeping her company. But the front room was empty when we stepped through the door.

"I asked them to leave," she said, as if she'd heard the thought. "I needed quiet."

Mrs. Stephenson led the way to the bedroom, where her husband, fully dressed, lay on the bed. There was sand and salt in his hair, and sand thick in his clothing. He was a man of medium height and in his older years added weight that made him seem shorter. His hair, graying, was crusted with blood, and his features were ugly with bruising and swelling, making it impossible for me to tell what he looked like. There was a gash just above his temple, and I thought it must have been made by a stone. There were bits of grit in the wound, and one broken stem of some sort of weed.

Ellen Marshall's friend Oliver had had similar bits of grit in the flap of skin that had fallen over his eyebrow. I started to say something about that, then thought better of it.

It was not the sort of grit one would find along the strand . . .

Most of the other wounds that I could see were made by fists pounding without mercy, with the force of strong shoulders behind them. And they had kept pounding even though Mr. Stephenson must have been beyond any serious resistance by that time. As if driven by a savage need to inflict as much damage as possible, without any regard for the outcome.

If I had been asked under oath, I would have had no qualms about answering that it was very likely that the man who had beaten Oliver had also attacked Mr. Stephenson. Not only was there a similar viciousness in the blows, but there was their placement, punishing the face and the body where it was possible to do the most damage. I could imagine what Mr. Stephenson's chest must look like. And if there was any doubt still in the mind of a barrister, there was the use of a stone to stun the victim.

It was likely now that whoever had attacked Hugh Williams was a different man. Unless the Captain had put up more of a fight than his opponent had expected. A man on crutches should have been a far easier target.

Or was that why the next two victims had been stunned with a stone first?

I reached out to lift Mr. Stephenson's hands. He'd tried to defend himself, there were bruises on his knuckles, but he hadn't had a chance of saving himself. Whoever had done this, he was not satisfied until his prey was dead.

"I opened his shirt," Mrs. Stephenson was saying. "The bruising is so bad I couldn't find any clear skin. And he was kicked when he was on his back. I haven't undressed him all the way. I couldn't bear to do more than I have."

Oliver too had been kicked as he lay on the ground. Hugh as well . . .

She pulled open her husband's coat, and I could see the shirt was unbuttoned. She was right, the bruising was extensive. I thought his spleen must have ruptured.

"Did he lie there, calling for me?" Mrs. Stephenson asked me, gently buttoning the torn and bloody shirt again. "Did he know he was dying?"

I wished I'd seen the body in place, to judge if he'd moved very much at the end. But I did see that he'd been curled up. Dying if not dead.

I said, "I think he was very likely unconscious before the end, and unaware of what was happening. That cut above his temple took the fight out of him. I'm not certain what made it. But I'd guess a stone of some sort."

She turned to me. "Are you telling me the truth?"

"I'm a Sister, not a doctor. But yes, as far as I can judge, he died without coming to his senses."

"That's a blessing, then. And I can curse the man who did this," she added, her face twisting into hate. "I'll find him, trust me. I'll see he pays."

I said again, "Are you sure you don't know who did this?"

"It's hard to think someone we knew could have hurt him so badly," she countered. "I grant you, it's not as if there's a lot of choice in the matter. There's only our neighbors. But I will find which one. However long it takes. I promised Edward that as long as I drew breath, I'd not rest."

"You mustn't take the law into your hands."

"Do you see a Constable coming through that door to do my work for me? Do you see the police questioning my neighbors? Nor do I. It's up to me. And there's the revolver that was Edward's father's. He's used it mostly to put down sick or injured cattle, but I know where it's kept. And how to use it."

I stared at her, and realized that she was telling me the truth. This wasn't just the grief of the moment speaking.

"That will only cause more trouble. You'll be taken up for murder."

"What have I to live for, now my husband is gone?" she demanded. "But I won't hang. There're enough cartridges in the box to see to that." Her eyes were dark with certainty.

Changing the subject before I'd pushed her into having to carry out her vengeance, I said, "Why was your husband out so late? Does he often walk along the water's edge in the middle of the night?"

"Not as a rule, no. One of our cows had a difficult birth. He'd stayed in the barn with her, else I'd have been out looking for him. I don't know why he walked down to the water. I expect he was tired but not ready to sleep. I looked in on the mother and baby this morning, after they'd brought Edward home. They're doing well. I don't think I could have borne it if the calf had died too. Not after Edward trying so hard to save it." With a sigh, she reached out and touched her husband's battered face. "I have something to live for, at least for now. After that, we'll just have to see, won't we?"

And she turned, walking out of the bedroom, ushering me before her, then shutting the door softly behind her, as if she might wake the man on the bed. "Edward is home for now. We'll put him in the ground tomorrow."

She offered me a cup of tea, but I thanked her and told her that I must go. I think she was relieved that I'd refused. She preferred to be alone with her husband, for the little time that was left.

I walked up the path toward the hedge, my thoughts running in circles. I should find Simon and ask him to bring the police here. Before someone else was attacked—or before Mrs. Stephenson discovered who had killed her husband.

Just at the top, I met Mr. Wilson coming toward me, on his way, I thought, to offer comfort to Mrs. Stephenson. He seemed surprised to see me and would have stopped to talk, but I only nodded, and went on my way. He seemed uncertain whether to speak or let me pass, but in the end, he simply touched his hat to me and walked on.

I saw no point in telling him where I'd been, or why.

When Hugh came in later in the day, I made him a sandwich and a cup of tea, then sat down across from him.

"I think it's time to have a discussion about what happened to Oliver, Ellen's friend, and what happened to Mr. Stephenson. Oliver's beating was severe enough, and Mr. Stephenson's was fatal."

He considered me, wariness in his face. "You're going to ask who attacked me."

He said it as if all along he'd known I hadn't believed his account of falling and hurting himself.

"Yes. I think something has to be done. Otherwise, it could happen again, and when it does, there's no Constable present out here to keep people from taking the law into their own hands."

"What happened to me has nothing to do with the other men."

"That's very likely true. After all, I examined both men. But I can't be absolutely sure of that until I know *why* you were attacked."

He moved uneasily. "You can't be sure I wasn't the first. And that the attacks are escalating with each one."

That was a point I hadn't considered.

"Then all the more reason to tell me who it was."

"No. That's not for you to know, Bess. You aren't a policeman. And the *less* you know, the safer you are."

"But don't you see, there is a very strong possibility whoever this man is, he could kill again? *Someone* has to stop him. And there aren't any policemen out here. Do you think Mr. Wilson will be able to stop the witch hunt that will start if there's another death? The village will be looking for someone to blame."

He sighed. "I've thought of that, Bess. But you aren't going to stop a killer, and neither— thanks to the Germans—can I."

I nearly told him then about Simon but decided at the last instant that it wouldn't be wise. Not yet.

"If no one does anything, it's going to become rather nasty."

"If I could, I'd get you and Rachel out of here. But there's no way. Except walking."

"She won't go. There are her sheep. And the loom."

Hugh was suddenly angry. "I know that. It's what makes her—" He broke off. "She loves this house. It was her father's—her grandfather's. The best thing for Rachel is for all of us to stay out of this battle."

So that was why he wouldn't tell me. He was protecting her.

When I didn't say anything, he added, "Leave it, Bess. This is not your war."

"I don't feel as sure of that as you do."

The door to the kitchen opened. We hadn't heard Rachel come in.

"What are you talking about?"

I turned to face her.

"I'm worried about what happened to Oliver—and to Mr. Stephenson. I'm afraid this isn't going to end with Mr. Stephenson's death."

Rachel looked from one to the other of us.

"There's nothing you can do. Nothing I can do. Except to stay out of it. That's what my father always did—that's how he brought up Matt and me. He said it wasn't cowardice, it was wisdom."

"But—" I began, but she interrupted me.

"Don't you see? If you try to interfere, all of us will be at risk. Better to let this matter resolve itself."

I tried to again, but she shook her head. "You're only a nursing Sister, Bess. Not a policeman. You have no right to ask questions. Stay out of it."

With that she turned and walked into the room where her loom stood. And shut the door behind her.

Hugh pulled his crutches closer, got up, and walked out of the kitchen without a word.

I stood there by the table, listening to the loom moving in the next room, listening to the outer door shut behind Hugh.

I'd crossed the boundary of friendship. The question was, had it been in vain? And would it change how they felt about me as a guest?

I could always leave with Simon.

After all, perhaps that was best for everyone.

That night, even though I stayed by my window for a very long time, there was no signal from Simon.

Where was he?

I waited another quarter of an hour, but the darkness in the direction of Ellen's house remained unchanged. I gave up and went to bed.

Dinner had been rather strained, conversation stilted. But I hadn't brought up anything controversial, and by the time I helped Rachel clear away, our old relationship had nearly returned. But I had a feeling it would never again be the same.

The next day Mr. Stephenson was buried. Rachel and Hugh attended the service, and I went with them. It was a somber affair, everyone well aware that Mr. Stephenson's killer was very likely there among them, singing the hymns and repeating the responses. A cold wind had come up while we were in the church, and it whipped around our shoulders as the committal began.

They were all there, Jenny's father, Mr. Griffith, Anna Dunhill and her father. I tried to read his face as he stood beside his daughter, but I thought he made a point of not looking directly at anyone. I could understand why he might have attacked Hugh in a fit of jealousy. I couldn't think of any reason for him to try to kill two other men.

I turned slightly to look across the open grave to where Mrs. Stephenson stared down at the rough coffin that held her husband. Her expression was grim, and during the prayers, instead of bowing her head, she looked around at the people gathered there to support her in this time of grief. I knew she was searching for any sign of guilt, any uneasiness or shifting of feet or clearing of throat that might tell her who had killed her husband.

But it occurred to me, watching her, that this killer wasn't going to be feeling either nerves or remorse. And that would make him even harder to find.

It was almost five when I walked down as far as Ellen Marshall's house. I strolled up the walk and then around to the back, but if Simon was anywhere about, he was staying out of sight.

I wanted to call to him, but that would be unwise.

I couldn't risk staying too long and arousing suspicion, and so I left almost at once, walking slowly back up the long slope.

Simon wouldn't leave me, not after a murder had just occurred. So where was he?

No one was about when I reached the widening of the road just outside Rachel's house. Not even Mr. Griffith, although I was fairly sure he was watching from his windows. A lonely man who had outlived his wife and his son, with only the activities of his neighbors to occupy his days.

Then why had he been wearing gloves the day after Mr. Stephenson's body had been found on the strand?

Much as I found him rather difficult, gloves or no gloves, I didn't see him as a killer. But if not Mr. Griffith, then who among the village men could it be? I was tempted to call on Mr. Wilson, but I knew it would be unwise to speak to him. He was a villager, rector or not, his sympathies and his concerns lay with his neighbors. And I couldn't be sure he would keep any confidences of mine. This village had too many secrets. And most of those who tried hardest to keep them were his flock.

I realized as I stopped by the churchyard, staring across at the raw damp earth that was Mr. Stephenson's resting place, that someone was watching me. He stood by the hedge, half concealed by it, and I didn't recognize him.

He knew who I was, that was abundantly clear, and he gave the impression that he didn't mind my seeing him there, staring at me.

My watcher for today? Or the killer, coming to have a look at me?

I walked on, past the church, past the rectory, and then turned back toward Rachel's house.

He was still there, idly waiting. I went up the path and opened the door, disappearing inside without looking his way.

But once inside, shielded by the curtains, I stood to see how long he would stay.

Ten minutes later he turned and walked back down the path leading to the strand.

We were finishing our dinner when there was a knock at the door. Rachel put down her fork and went to answer it.

She came back with an odd expression on her face. I gathered she didn't care for whoever had interrupted her meal. "It's for you," she said. "Mr. Burton."

"What does he want?" Hugh asked.

"He didn't say."

"I hope it isn't Jenny." I rose and went to the door, saying at once, "Is it your daughter? Is that why you've come?"

"Naught to do with Jenny," he said brusquely. Looking over my shoulder at the open door into the kitchen, he added, "Walk a little way with me."

"The last time I saw you, you threatened me. I'm not sure I wish to walk anywhere with you."

He grimaced. "Only to the middle of the road, then."

I considered that, then nodded. "No farther."

"No."

"Let me fetch my coat."

He waited while I went upstairs, pulled on my coat, reached for my gloves, and came back to the door.

We walked down the path as far as the road, and I stopped in the middle of it. No one could overhear us here, I realized, and I turned, looking up at him, waiting for him to speak.

"I'm told you saw Stephenson's body."

"Yes," I replied warily. "Mrs. Stephenson needed my help."

"She turned down other offers."

"I think she felt I wouldn't gossip about what I saw," I told him bluntly.

"Aye, there's that." He looked down the long slope toward the coast guard station and the Marshall cottage, nearly invisible beyond it. "What did you see?"

"I saw the body of a man who had been beaten so severely he'd died," I retorted. "What else was there to see?" But I was already wondering if he knew something about that head wound, and the stone that had made it.

"I'm not speaking of his wounds," he said. "I saw them for myself." He turned back to me. "Why did Ruth burn the clothes he was wearing?"

Surprised, I said, "Mrs. Stephenson? Did she? I didn't know that."

"Did you help her lay him out? Did you see what was in his pockets?"

"I did not."

I was beginning to realize that he wasn't talking about the wounds, but about something more important to him.

"What is it you really want to know?" I asked, facing him squarely.

He paused, then said reluctantly, "That man with Ellen Marshall.

He was helping her search the house for something belonging to her grandfather. And Stephenson was by the water's edge. He must have found something. Or seen something out there in the water. We've talked, the rest of us, and we're certain that's why he was attacked. We don't think the killer found out what it was."

Just as I'd thought. We were back to the silver.

"If he knew something, he took it to his grave," I said. "But if you suspect that he was killed for what he knew—or had seen," I added, as Mr. Burton was about to interrupt me, "then you must know who did that to him."

"We don't know," he said harshly. "That's the trouble, you see. And Joseph Warren saw strange tracks when he went out to look for strays. He runs his cattle out beyond Mrs. Williams's sheep holding. Down the spine of the peninsula." He turned to point. "It wasn't the Captain, the man had two legs. But none of us had gone out there."

I felt cold. Had someone accidentally stumbled on Simon's tracks? But he would have been very careful there. He'd gone behind German lines and knew the importance of making certain he wasn't discovered.

"How do you know they're strange tracks?"

"Terrence Butterworth's a cobbler. He mends our shoes regularly. And he didn't recognize the sole."

Oh dear. "If I were going to wander about in the dark, I'd make certain no one suspected me," I said briskly. "It would be foolish to wear boots anyone could recognize."

He seemed unconvinced. "Something's going on, and I'm trying to get to the bottom of it. You're sure you didn't see anything in Stephenson's clothes to tell you what he was doing out there by the water's edge?"

"I saw nothing of interest in his clothing except wet sand," I replied. Half of the truth—I needn't tell him what I'd seen in the wound. "But Mrs. Stephenson said he'd sat up with a cow about to calve, and after the birth, he'd gone down to the sea."

Burton shook his head. "That's not like him."

"How do you know what he might or might not do?"

"I'm saying he saw something. It's the only explanation for him being down there."

He was making the facts fit his suspicions. It was clear to me, an outsider, that anxiety and worry had conspired to lead men out on the Down to read too much into the dead man's movements.

And then, as if to prove me right, Mr. Burton said, "We were all right when no one got too greedy. That's the trouble. Someone wants more than his rightful share." With an abrupt nod to me, he turned and walked away.

I watched him turn down the path there by the hedge and disappear from view. When I looked toward the Griffith house, I saw the silhouette of a man's head at the window. He'd witnessed the conversation between Mr. Burton and me—I wondered what he'd made of it.

Had he also shared in the silver washed in by the sea? His wife had been a local girl, and she would surely have had some claim to the treasure.

I realized that he didn't run cattle, and he no longer had the men from the coast guard station coming to his shop. How did he live, if it wasn't by a share in the silver?

I turned away and walked back to the house.

CHAPTER 16

RACHEL AND HUGH were waiting in the front room when I came through the door. I looked up from unbuttoning my coat and said, "He thinks that someone is looking for silver. That Oliver was attacked because he was helping Ellen search for her grandfather's. And that Mr. Stephenson was killed because he was down by the sea and either found something or saw something that someone else didn't want known."

"And had he?" Rachel asked.

"There's no way of answering that. He was dead when he was found. Whatever it was—if indeed it was anything at all—he didn't live to tell anyone. Mr. Burton thought that I might have seen what was in Mr. Stephenson's pockets when I helped his wife undress him. She only wanted to know if he'd suffered and died alone. But Mr. Burton claims she burned what he was wearing. She probably did, because the clothes were soaked with his blood. Not because there were any secrets to be kept."

"We told you it was best not to go with her," Rachel warned.

"I couldn't very well refuse to put her mind at ease," I replied. "What's happening out here? Is the silver beginning to run out? Have people found less and less and are worried that there's no more to be discovered? Is that why someone is willing to kill for more?"

"It's been washing in for centuries," Rachel said, as if she believed it should last forever.

But just how much had the treasure ship been carrying? Most of the silver must surely have been lost in the sea. And what was left, what the tide could capture and bring in, must have been only a part of that original amount. Still—this village's needs were small enough. They had survived, not squandered. A queen's dowry would last out here. But not forever, of course.

Perhaps that was the trouble. Someone believed that there was still a fortune out there. And that sooner or later, someone was going to devise a way of getting to it. Failing that, whatever was left of Ellen Marshall's grandfather's fortune would do very well. Only I thought it was already gone, years ago.

That stirred another line of thought. Folding my coat over my arm, I asked, "Who is money-hungry out here? Who needs it badly enough or wants it badly enough that he's willing to kill for it?"

Rachel and Hugh stared at each other, then she said, "We could all use a windfall. I don't know anyone out here who isn't struggling to survive. The treasure ship has been a godsend. For a long time. It's even more necessary for the foreseeable future. There's no call for cattle now the war's over, and the same is true for wool. There's been talk of taking advantage of the climate out here and growing foodstuffs for Swansea or Cardiff, but how would we get them to market?"

I said, "That's different from being desperate. Or greedy."

She shook her head. "I can't think of anyone willing to kill."

But she knew these people out here, and she couldn't be objective about them, she couldn't see them as murderers.

I tried another tack.

"Who is the strongest man out here?"

Hugh answered. "That would be Heaton's son. Philip. His father died when he was young, and he's been a handful ever since. He's been something of a ne'er-do-well from the time he was twelve. So I've been told."

Philip Heaton.

"What size man is he?"

Hugh said, "If you're asking if he could beat someone to death, he could. He's large for his age, heavy shoulders. Still, I find it hard to believe that he'd do such a thing. A troublemaker, yes, I grant you. Over the years, everyone has had words with him. Including Tom."

Was he defending Philip Heaton because he already knew that he wasn't guilty?

What I found so hard to understand was how much that treasure ship coming ashore had changed this village. It was as if that slow trickle of silver over the centuries had drained away the conscience of those who had benefited from it. They would do anything to protect it, to avoid having the authorities come here and question them and perhaps stumble on a secret that mattered more than human life.

But it was useless to try to change the minds of these people. Even Hugh, who had been here such a short time, had succumbed to their way of seeing things. Although to be honest, I rather thought it was his feelings for Rachel that had changed him. If she believed, so would he . . .

"Where does this man live?" I asked.

"On the road here. Just beyond the rectory."

With a nod, I turned to carry my coat up to my room. I'd only just started up the stairs when I heard Rachel say to Hugh "You shouldn't have told her that. It's dangerous."

I didn't hear the Captain's reply.

It was nearly dusk, and I was helping Rachel water the last of the seedbeds when we saw a flickering light, bright orange, coming from the front of the house and even visible over the rooftop.

Rachel drew in a breath as she saw it. "Fire," she said, staring at it.

It was what everyone feared, for so many cottages and houses all over Britain were built of wood and vulnerable.

She dropped her watering can, lifted her skirts, and ran toward the corner of the house. I followed on her heels, and as we rounded the side, I saw that it wasn't a fire, but a group of men moving silently with flaming torches lighting their way.

I reached out and caught Rachel's arm. "*Stop*," I whispered.

I almost plowed into her as she came to a halt.

"What are they doing?" she asked. "Where are they going?"

"I don't know. Wait and see."

The men's night vision was ruined by the torchlight, but still we pressed ourselves against the side of the house, where we were less likely to be seen.

From the kitchen garden, I heard Hugh calling us, but I stayed where I was.

The parade of men—I counted seventeen—moved up the road past the churchyard, the smoke from the torches spiraling up into the night sky, and the flames sending shadows dancing among the gravestones. And then they were passing the church, and I suddenly guessed where they were heading: Philip Heaton's house.

"Find Hugh," I told Rachel. "He's looking for us. Tell him what's happening."

She was reluctant to go, but I put a hand on her shoulder. "Hurry. Before he's worried enough to go out there, trying to find you."

"All right." She moved past me and was gone in the darkness behind me. I waited until she was out of sight and started after the men.

There was so little cover out here, so few trees, no buildings on this side of the road, and even with my coat on and a wool cap on my head, no way to hide who I was from the marchers. But I stayed back, along the verge of the road, hoping they were too intent on what they were doing to notice me.

They walked past the rectory and the house beyond it, coming to a stop finally at the cottage where Philip Heaton lived.

Somehow these men had come to the same conclusion that Hugh had reached, that Philip Heaton was physically the most likely person to have beaten Edward Stephenson so viciously. Or had someone covered his own tracks by pointing everyone's attention in that direction? For here was a party set on meting out a rough justice of their own.

Now I could hear a voice harshly shouting Philip's name. I moved forward to where I could see his cottage door more clearly.

It didn't open.

"Come out, Heaton. Or we'll set the cottage alight," another voice shouted.

The door opened and a woman stepped out. She was wearing an apron but no coat, as if they'd interrupted her preparing dinner.

"What do you want with my son?" she demanded, wrapping her arms around her for warmth. "State your business with him, or go home," she added when no one answered her.

"Send him out. He has to answer for what he's done."

A figure appeared behind her. He was young, perhaps seventeen or eighteen, but tall and broad for his age. Somehow I'd expected him to be older. He stepped in front of his mother, even though she tried to force him back.

"I'm no coward, hiding behind my mother's skirts," he said. "You have no quarrel with her. Leave her be."

"You're suspected of killing Edward Stephenson," Mr. Burton said. "What do you have to say for yourself?"

"Why should I kill him? Or anyone else?" Philip Heaton retorted.

"You had words with him. Last week."

"That was about money he owed me for helping with his cattle."

This was news—I'd not heard about an earlier quarrel.

"And you threatened him."

"What if I did? It was money owed. I'd earned it. And he kept putting me off."

"And you set upon him down on the strand. What were you doing that hour of the morning, when he saw you there?"

"I was asleep in my own bed. I didn't see him nor he me." There was belligerence in his voice, and I saw his mother reach out to touch his arm. He shook it off. "If anyone says anything to the contrary, he's a liar."

"He was here," his mother put in. "I'd vouch for that."

But it did no good.

"What were you doing down there by the strand at that hour?" Burton's voice repeated. "What were you after?"

"I was after nothing. I wasn't there, I tell you."

"You're the strongest swimmer in the village," another voice called out. "You've bragged about it often enough. What did you find?"

And that, I thought, was the crux of the matter, more important to these men than Edward Stephenson's death.

Philip Heaton, unaware of his danger, tried to brazen it out. "Wouldn't you like to know?" he shouted back at them, a sneer in his voice. "None of you own the sea."

He'd misjudged the mood of the men confronting him. I watched in horror as they surged forward and shoved Mrs. Heaton to one side, grabbing her son's arms and dragging him kicking and struggling from the cottage door.

They carried him bodily out to the road, and there they set him on his feet. His mother came running after them, using her fists to forge through the mob—for that's what it had become now—to reach her son's side.

"Step aside, woman, this has nothing to do with you."

"He's my son, and I won't let you hurt him."

Someone roughly pushed her aside, and Philip fought to protect her, calling the men names and lashing out with fists and feet. Someone behind him hit him over the head with something, and he sagged in the grip of those holding him. His mother cried out, and tried to get to him, but they shoved her away.

Half a dozen men dragged the half-conscious Philip Heaton forward, while others held his mother back, and as they turned to come down the road toward me, I could see their faces. If someone didn't do something, I realized, their victim wasn't likely to survive the night.

I was about to run forward to stop them when someone else appeared out of the shadows. It was the small form of Mrs. Stephenson, and I saw the torchlight reflected on the revolver in her hands.

She shouted something, and as one, the cluster of men around Philip Heaton turned toward her in surprise.

"Are you telling me it was him who killed my husband?" she demanded, pointing a shaking finger at the still half-conscious Heaton. "Are you so certain he's the one did it?"

"As sure as can be," someone called out.

"Then he's mine. By rights. Stand him up and step back."

They were about to ignore her but she raised the revolver and fired a shot into the air. The noise was loud even over the flickering of the torches.

"He's mine," she said again. "Move aside, or I won't vouch for my aim."

The revolver was leveled now, the barrel pointing straight at Heaton's chest.

I could see enough of her face to know that she meant exactly what she was saying, and if no one stopped her, she was going to shoot Philip Heaton.

"Not before we find out what he was doing there on the strand," Mr. Burton responded, standing his ground.

Behind him, Mrs. Heaton was still struggling with the men holding her back.

Her son, shaking his head and trying to clear it, stared blearily at Mrs. Stephenson.

"He owed me money," he tried to say, but it came out as a mumble. Still, she heard it, and she took three steps forward, for a better shot.

I couldn't stand there and let it happen.

I hurried toward her. "Stop this now," I said in my best imitation of Matron's voice, infusing all the authority of the Queen Alexandra's Imperial Military Nursing Service into the words. I heard Hugh call out my name from the darkness behind me. "I saw Mr. Stephenson's body. If you don't want to make a mistake you'll regret for the rest of your lives, you'll hear me out."

I strode into the torchlight until I was close enough to reach for Mrs. Stephenson's gun hand, if I had to, to keep her from firing.

"Stay out of this," Mr. Burton warned in an angry growl.

"I won't stand by and see murder done," I snapped. "Now I am going to approach Philip Heaton and I'm going to examine him. And if you really want to know who killed your husband," I added to Mrs. Stephenson, "you'll lower your weapon."

To my astonishment, after a moment she did. Ignoring the angry faces holding Philip Heaton, I walked through the cluster of men and looked straight at their prisoner.

"Show me your hands," I ordered.

Somehow the words reached him, although he frowned as if he hadn't really understood me. Slowly he raised his hands and held them out in front of him.

I stepped forward and took them in my own, one at a time.

They were calloused and not as clean as they could be. But there was no bruising on the knuckles and no scratches or bloody scrapes on the backs. I looked into his face. There were patches of red that would turn into bruising given time, but these were recent, not several days old.

"See for yourselves," I said, stepping back. "Look at his hands. Some of you saw what had been done to Mr. Stephenson. Tell me that anyone could have delivered such a beating without even so much as a bruised knuckle."

I had already said something about this to Mr. Wilson, but apparently he hadn't thought to pass it on.

"He was wearing gloves," someone called. It was Anna's father—the man who had proposed to Rachel and who—I could think of no one else with a reason—attacked Hugh and knocked him down. "Stands to reason he would."

"As you did, when you hit a man on crutches?" I demanded, and he flushed as his fellow conspirators turned to stare at him.

"I didn't touch him." But his denial lacked conviction.

"Then show me your hands," I said.

He backed off.

Mrs. Stephenson had come up beside me. She reached out and caught Philip Heaton's hands. He started to pull away, then let her examine them. She looked at me.

"On your oath," she said. "He couldn't have done it?"

"Look at him. His face. His hands. You saw your husband's hands. Even with the difference in weight and height and reach, he made an effort to defend himself."

She turned without a word and walked back the way she'd come, the torchlight flickering on her straight, angry back until she had passed on into the shadowy darkness beyond.

The men watched her go, then slowly released Heaton. I thought for a moment he was going to collapse onto the road. But he fought to keep his senses, and he stood up as straight as he could. And then his mother was beside him, offering him the support of her shoulder. She was shaking with the cold and with relief, but her face was red with anger still, and she shoved the men nearest her aside and made a way for her son to stumble after her, back toward their cottage.

"Go home," I said to Mr. Burton as he turned to argue with me. "You've nearly made a dreadful mistake. Remember that."

"Damn it, Sister—"

"No. If you want to find the man who killed Mr. Stephenson, you know now what to look for. And there's something else. If he'd come out of the sea, his hands would have been wet and cold. And therefore, all the more damaged by the ferocity of his attack. Start with the men here, and then keep on looking. You won't need me to tell you when you've found Mr. Stephenson's killer."

And I walked away. When I looked back from the shadows of the Williams's house, I saw each of the men carrying torches being examined one by one. I waited, but in the end they all turned and walked back the way they'd come.

For the first time I let myself relax. Then I jumped when Hugh spoke just behind me.

"Damn it, Bess, that was the height of foolishness."

"Was it?" I replied, my voice colder than I'd meant it to be. "I don't know what they'd have done to that boy, but it wouldn't have been pleasant." I stopped myself from adding that no one else had come forward. I knew why Hugh hadn't, and how it must have galled him that he couldn't walk out there and defend me. "It was best that I did it alone," I went on. "Best that you and Rachel weren't involved. You live here, and she's vulnerable."

I started back toward the kitchen door, and he followed. "Where is Rachel?" I asked.

"She went inside. She couldn't bear to watch."

"I can't blame her. It was going to be nasty."

"Why do you think it was Dunhill who knocked me down?" He was behind me in the darkness, where I couldn't see his face. But there was something in the tone of his voice that made me uneasy.

"He had the best reason. Jealousy. Besides, I think he needs Rachel's money. Be careful, Hugh."

He didn't answer. And he was not behind me when I reached the kitchen door and stepped inside.

Hugh didn't come in for a long while. And Rachel stayed in her little room, working on the loom.

I made myself a sandwich and a cup of tea, taking both upstairs with me, then coming back down only long enough to fill my hot water bottle. I was still cold from being out there, for the night had cooled off quickly.

Taking my plate and my cup to the window, I waited for several hours for some sign from Simon. I heard Rachel come up to bed close to ten, and Hugh shortly thereafter.

When at last there was a brief flash of light from the direction of the coast guard station, I waited for a message, but none came. But the flash was repeated. I thought, catching it a second time, that it was in the road itself, not behind the station, where I was the only one who could see it.

That was taking a risk, which was unlike Simon.

I hadn't undressed for bed, had instead been sitting by the window with a quilt around my shoulders and the hot water bottle at my feet.

I waited again. When the flash was repeated a third time, I knew I had to do something.

I'd turned off my lamp after finishing my dinner, primarily so that Rachel and Hugh would think I was asleep, but also so that I could sit at the window without drawing attention to it.

Collecting my coat and hat, I stepped to my door and listened. There was silence from Rachel's room, but a soft snore from Hugh's.

I slipped out, left my door ajar, and made my way to the stairs. I'd been here long enough to know where the worst of the creaks were, but the house creaked and groaned in the night from wind and age. Halfway down, I decided to go out the kitchen door, and walked quietly down the passage. Stopping at the kitchen, I listened, but no one had stirred. And the dogs, asleep on their beds, raised their heads for a moment, then lay down again. I found the door to the short passage to the kitchen garden door, and let myself out into the night.

It was cold enough that I fumbled in my pocket for my gloves and pulled them on. Then I debated the best direction to take.

I'd been out with Rachel caring for the sheep often enough that I had a good sense of where to go, and I decided to approach the road from inland, where no one would be expecting me to come.

I went past the shed where I'd first encountered Simon, then across to the fields, clambering over the stone walls until I was out of the area where the sheep grazed and down where some of the larger herds of cattle foraged.

Praying that I didn't awaken a bull, I skirted the dark shapes and kept on toward the coast guard station until I was close enough that I could make my way to the road and see who might be there, signaling.

There were no houses out here, and thankfully no strange dogs.

Simon hadn't been in touch since he sent the message about trouble on the strand, and I was very careful now, making certain that each step was quiet.

There was no one in the road.

I'd come all this way for nothing.

And then I saw someone standing in the scrub trees that had grown up along the top of the cliff. If I'd been walking down the road, I'd have come upon him without warning.

I stayed very still for several minutes, and then was rewarded by the figure moving out of the scrub growth to peer up the dark length of the road.

It wasn't Simon. I knew that at once, for I'd have recognized Simon's silhouette anywhere in the world. His height, the way he stood, his military carriage, and something else, indefinable, that I'd grown used to most of my life.

Then who was it? I didn't think it was Mr. Dunhill, nor Mr. Burton. Mr. Griffith? The man moved a little, and I could see most of the shape of his head. It wasn't Mr. Griffith. Who then? Someone who lived out on the Down?

He held up something that had been hidden by his body, and flashed a light up the road. Then he moved back into the shadows of the scrub growth at the edge of the cliff.

I waited, and then I saw him move again, this time down toward Ellen Marshall's cottage.

When he was out of sight, and I was certain he wasn't doubling back, I made my own cautious way back in the direction where I'd passed the sleeping herd of cattle. I remembered only then that someone had found a strange footprint nearby a herd. I wasn't certain which herd, but I didn't linger here. Making certain that my own silhouette wasn't visible on the skyline as I crossed the empty landscape that was their pasture, I soon reached the walled grazing ground of Rachel's sheep. One of them sneezed when she caught my scent on the wind as I scrambled awkwardly over the wall, and I hurried on toward the shadows by the shed. I still had some distance to go, and kept low, but at last I reached the shed and leaned against its rough wood while I caught my breath. It was empty now of new-borns in need of shelter.

It wasn't until I'd come round the corner of the shed that I realized that someone was leaning against the kitchen door, blocking my way.

CHAPTER 17

MY FIRST THOUGHT was that the figure I'd seen on the road had got to the house before me and discovered that I'd left the kitchen door off the latch. I froze for an instant, and then realized that it was Simon waiting there.

I was very glad to see him.

He put up a hand, telling me to stop where I was, and then he walked out to meet me, pulling me beside the shed and out of sight.

"I'm surprised you didn't wake the dogs," I said, covering my relief at seeing him.

"They know me. I've met them several times before."

He'd always had a way with animals. It was what made him such a fine horseman.

"The question is," he said, and I could hear the suppressed worry in his voice, "what are you doing out here at this hour?"

"I saw someone signaling. I was careful that he didn't see me when I got to where he was concealed. On the road just above the coast guard station. Then he went on toward Ellen's cottage."

"That was foolish of you."

"Yes, well, I didn't know if it was you or not. And you've been least in sight of late."

"It wasn't me."

"So I discovered."

"But I've been keeping watch. What in heaven's name possessed you to go out there and face those men?"

"I couldn't very well let Mrs. Stephenson shoot that man. And I had no idea what the others intended to do to him. *Someone* had to come forward."

"I was across the way in the churchyard. Just behind the tower. I was not certain she was going to shoot."

"Yes, well, I was very certain. She's the dead man's widow. You weren't there when she told me that nothing else mattered but revenge."

"At that distance, she was more likely to hit one of the men holding him, not the boy."

"I wasn't going to wait and see."

He turned away, and then back again. "Bess, I refuse to walk into that house in Somerset and tell your parents that you've been hurt. Or worse, killed."

Simon meant every word of that. I swallowed hard.

After a moment, I said, "Do you know what's going on out here?"

"No. But when I saw the man lying there on the strand, I went down to find out if he was still alive. It was too late, he was already dead. I left him there, and coming back, someone began tracking me. I've been leaving a false trail over half of this blood— this god-forsaken peninsula."

"Who is it?"

"I haven't been able to track *him* to wherever he comes from. Not without giving myself away. Not that I'd mind a crack at him, but I don't think you're ready to let the world and its uncle know I'm here."

"I was rather glad I *was* still here tonight. Last night. They're obsessed with the sil—"

He cut me off with a hand over my mouth, pushing me back into the deepest shadows of the shed.

And then he was gone.

It was my turn to hear it. Someone walking up the road. Whoever it was tried to be quiet, but in the silence of the night, I could hear the slither of grit under his feet.

The sound stopped, and I knew he was either standing in front of Rachel's house or already walking down the path beyond the hedge.

After a time, Simon came back. "I couldn't see where he went. I wasn't there in time."

"Do you think it was the man who was signaling?"

"It's likely. Who else would be out at this hour? Go to bed, Bess. Sleep if you can. Next time you see a light signaling, look for your father's code word. If you don't see it, don't respond. And in the name of God, don't go out looking for him. Leave that to me. The only way I'm going to find where he lives is to be free to move without worrying about exposing you."

My father's code word had been Bede. After the Venerable Bede. Short and easy to send.

He was right, I must stay out of his way.

"Before I forget," I said, avoiding giving any promises I couldn't keep, "I am told that tracks were found out there near one of the herds. The shoemaker didn't recognize the sole."

"They aren't mine. I went through the herd to cover my tracks. Whoever this is, he knows the peninsula intimately. Better than I can on such short acquaintance with it. That makes him all the more dangerous."

"I wish I knew who it is. I suggested searching for someone with bruised knuckles. But it's more likely that the man wore gloves."

"Even so, given the beating I saw down there on the strand, I can't see how he could have avoided some bruising."

"They haven't dragged anyone else out to question. Not as far as I can tell. I expect those men are beginning to think again about Philip Heaton, if no one else has turned up."

"They could come for him again," Simon agreed. "But stay out of it this time. I needn't tell you that mobs are not to be trusted, they can turn on someone else in the blink of an eye. You'd best go in. I need to work my way back to the cave. I haven't slept in two nights. It's catching up with me."

"Don't let it make you careless," I warned—unnecessarily, but I was worried.

"I'll stay here until I'm sure you're safely inside."

I slipped away then, walking back to the house and quietly opening the kitchen door once more. When I stepped into the kitchen, the dogs barely stirred. They had already heard me coming.

I made my way around the table and chairs, avoiding the cupboard, and found the door easily enough. The passage was dark, but by this time my eyes were used to whatever light was there.

Turning at the newel post, I started up the stairs, and before I had reached the top I heard Rachel's door open. There was nowhere to go, no time to hurry back down the steps, no hope of reaching my door in time.

I was well and truly caught. And there was no use in claiming I had gone down for a drink of water, not with my coat on. Still, I pulled off my gloves and my hat, shoving them into my pocket out of sight.

She reached the top of the stairs.

"Bess? What were you doing outside? At this hour?"

Oh, dear.

When I didn't immediately answer, she said accusingly, "I saw you coming down the path to the kitchen door."

Had she seen Simon as well? I had to bluff it out, rather than raise any suspicions she might have.

"I couldn't sleep. And so I went for a walk. Not far. I had a look at the sheep, then came back. The fresh air seemed to help."

She stared at me, although all I could see of her face was a pale oval in the blackness at the top of the stairs.

"I don't understand you, Bess. Facing down those men, and Mrs. Stephenson, who was armed. Wandering about in the dark, alone."

"I spent four years in France," I told her truthfully, "in all kinds of weather and every imaginable condition. I've wrestled grown men, wild with delirium, back into their beds, and I've been near enough to the fighting to see the muzzle flashes of guns. It's not that I'm especially brave," I went on, "but I've grown accustomed to facing whatever the war brought my way and dealing with it as best I could." I had a swift flare of memory: of the Germans overrunning our aid station, and a plane strafing our ambulance convoy. Things Rachel Williams had never thought about, much less experienced. She had her own courage, fighting to stay on in the house her grandfather had built. But it was very different from France. I had been forever changed by France. All of us had.

"I expect that's true," she said after a moment. "But it still makes me uneasy. I couldn't watch those men. I was afraid of what they might do to Philip. Hugh told me about Mrs. Stephenson. It troubled him that he couldn't come to your aid."

"Better that he didn't," I told her, and meant it. "No one out here quite knows what to make of me. Or whoever might come out here looking for me. That helps."

"I'd rather you didn't do it again," she said. "For my sake. I have to live here after you've gone, and I don't have your courage. I don't want to have to pretend that I do."

"I understand. But I can't really promise you, Rachel. Even if I wanted to. I don't think matters will get better before I leave, and I have a very strong suspicion that they'll get worse. I don't know what choices I might have to make. But I will promise to remember that you are caught in the middle. Will that do?"

"I don't think so," she told me after a moment's consideration. "I don't like being afraid. Feeling afraid."

"And yet you go out to find a ewe in distress, however dark or stormy it might be, and bring her and her lambs in to safety in the shed until the worst is over. I admire that."

"Don't change the subject."

"I'm not. I'm telling you that you don't fear the dark—but you do fear your neighbors."

"I have to live here," she said again, adding, "I can't change what they are. And I don't want you to bring a killer to us."

I realized then that she was afraid for Hugh.

"I won't," I promised then. "I give you my word."

"You can't be sure of that," she said, then turned and went back to her room, shutting her door before I could reach the top step and cross the landing to my own room.

Breakfast was awkward the next morning. Rachel had little to say, and Hugh was quiet as well. And when Rachel went out to work in her garden, she didn't ask if I'd help her. Hugh left with the dogs, saying he might miss his lunch.

I had begun to rethink my concern for Rachel and for Hugh. Perhaps they would be much better off—and less worried—if I did disappear in the night, and they could honestly claim they knew nothing about my departure.

But would they worry instead about what had become of me? I could write, once I was safely in Swansea, but there was the question of the post, and how long it might take for any letter to reach them. Days? Weeks, even.

By three in the afternoon the storm clouds were gathering again out over the water, blotting out the sun and promising an early dusk. As I was walking down the stairs to make myself a cup of tea I heard the kitchen door open and then close softly.

"Rachel?" I called, but there was no answer. I hurried down the passage and stopped short at the kitchen door, for Simon was standing there in the middle of the room.

"Simon?" I said in surprise.

"Mrs. Williams has gone to see to her sheep. There's a bad storm coming. The Captain is talking to someone by the hedge where the path goes down to the bay. I don't think anyone saw me. Can you come? I need your advice."

"Let me fetch my coat." I hurried up the stairs, caught up my woolen hat and an umbrella, as well, and went back down to the kitchen.

"What's wrong? What is it?" I asked Simon.

"We need to get out of sight, first."

And so I followed him outside. Keeping the shed for the ewes between us and anyone looking our way, we set out across rough grazing land and moved quickly. In the distance I could hear thunder as the storm approached. Keeping pace with Simon I asked again, "What's wrong?"

"Wait."

And so I did. Simon was not one for dramatics, and if he didn't want to talk to me now, there was a very good reason. We walked for some time and the wind was picking up, blowing the scrub growth and whipping my skirts around my ankles.

Simon glanced toward the sky. "This could be a bad storm. We need to hurry."

We picked up our pace, and after a while I could just see the glimmer of the sea ahead. "We've crossed the peninsula," I said. "Is this where you've camped?"

"No. I had to leave that place when I was followed. I was looking for another cave when I found what I want to show you."

At last we came to the water's edge, and the sky behind us was black now.

"There are any number of caves along the coastline," he said then. "Some of them are closer to the waterline, and I was looking for something drier. Be careful, the rocks are treacherous here if they're wet. Give me your hand."

I did, and he led me down a rocky incline that was easy enough to descend if you knew where you were going. I didn't, but I trusted Simon and let him guide me down to an opening—dark now—just above the water's edge.

"Don't worry, it's not difficult."

And he was right, it was amazingly simple to reach the cave mouth and walk down the slight incline to a surprisingly dry space some twenty yards from the entrance.

He'd picked up a torch that he'd left at the mouth, and shone the beam ahead of us to where I could see a bundle of what appeared to be blankets. Simon's bed, on the cold cave floor? I shivered.

Then the bundle of blankets moved, and I couldn't suppress a gasp of surprise.

Simon went ahead of me, knelt by the blankets, and said, "He's asleep—or unconscious. It's hard to be sure. See for yourself."

I reached his side and knelt by him. He pulled the blankets away.

I don't know what I'd expected. Certainly not to see Ellen's friend Oliver, gaunt and bearded, lying there, his face so feverish that I could feel the warmth as I moved closer to him, even before I put a hand to his forehead.

"Oliver?" It was the only name I knew.

He didn't respond, but Simon asked, "You know him, then?"

"Yes, he's Ellen Marshall's friend, the one I told you about."

"I wasn't sure whether it was he, or if he was a new victim of whoever is attacking people."

"But how did he get here?" I asked. "She was taking him to Swansea to find someone to see to these wounds." I looked around me. The cave was dark, chill, and God alone knew if there were bats nesting in here, or any other creature, prehistoric or present day.

"Oliver?" I said his name quietly, trying to rouse him, but he was too deeply unconscious. I didn't like that.

"Did you find him like this?"

"No. He was lying on the bare stone of the cave. I found the blankets airing on a line, and took them. He was shivering, and that worried me."

"He needs medical care," I said. "And soon. Where's your motorcar?"

"Not far from here," he said.

"You must take him to Swansea. There must be a good hospital in the town. He needs a doctor. I'm afraid he'll die if he doesn't get help and soon."

"Yes. That's why it was worth the risk to come to the house. It was important for you to tell me if you knew him before I took him away." A flash of lightning brightened the mouth of the cave. But the thunder was slow in following. "If I'm to reach Swansea before the worst of the storm comes in, I must go now. Come with me, Bess. I don't like the idea of leaving you behind."

"I can't. Not yet. Hurry, bring the motorcar as close as you can. Then I'll help you get him in it."

He put a hand on my shoulder, then rose and walked swiftly to the cave's mouth. He was gone for only a matter of minutes. And between us we managed to get Oliver to his feet. Then we half carried, half dragged him as far as the cave mouth. There, getting him up the incline to ground level was the problem, and in the end, Simon lifted him and carried him to the waiting motorcar.

We got him inside just before the first large drops of rain began to hit the ground around us. Simon gestured to the passenger's seat. "You can't walk back now. It's too far, and you'll be in trouble half-way there. I'll drive toward Swansea, and set you down above the village. Will that do?"

The rain was hitting the motorcar with such intensity that I could hardly hear him. But I nodded, because that was just what I'd hoped he would suggest.

It wasn't an easy journey. We bounced and juddered over the rough ground, and I was worried that Oliver would be hurt. I finally got Simon to stop while I climbed into the rear of the motorcar and braced his head and shoulders as best I could. But we finally reached the drovers' road, and while it felt just as rough, the rain was already softening the ruts. We began to slither where we'd bounced before.

Simon drew to a halt. "If you walk back from here, no one will know where you've been. I'd rather you changed your mind and stayed with me." He gestured toward the storm. "This will be worse before it's better."

I shook my head. Then, hesitating, I looked again at Oliver. I didn't think he could hear me. "Simon. She couldn't have attacked him. Ellen Marshall, I mean. And she couldn't have attacked the others. Still. She's the only person who could have left this poor man in a cave. I can't understand why, not as concerned as she was about his condition. But there's no other explanation, is there? Watch yourself. The police will be asking questions." Reaching for my umbrella, which was in the front seat, I said, "Just hurry back. Please."

"I will. Do you still have your pistol?"

"Yes."

"Don't hesitate to use it if you have to."

I opened the rear door and got down, raising my umbrella as quickly as I could. "Just drive carefully. I don't know the state of his ribs. And he could very well be on the verge of pneumonia."

As deadly in its own way as influenza, it could kill quickly.

"Don't worry. He'll survive. I'll see to that. I want to find out who's behind this."

And I was gone, walking quickly back toward the village—and into the teeth of the storm. I didn't look back as Simon went on his way again. I'd gone no more than a hundred paces when my umbrella blew inside out in spite of all I could do to prevent it. But in another fifty paces, I could see the church and the houses just above it. Simon had taken a grave risk, bringing me this close.

I reached Rachel's door and was more or less blown in by the wind, in a blast of rain. I stood there, dripping. I could smell dinner, and feel the warmth of the cooker.

Rachel and Hugh came hurrying out of the kitchen, calling to me, asking me where on earth I'd been.

Hugh said, worry translating to anger in his voice, "Surely you couldn't have decided to walk to Swansea with this storm coming? Bess, it was madness."

Rachel was taking my umbrella from me and setting it in the porcelain stand by the door, then helping me out of my coat and hat. "You'll take your death," she said, in the voice of a mother chiding a difficult child. "Come to the kitchen."

The dogs had followed Hugh, and they were sniffing my wet skirts and my shoes. I wondered if they could smell Oliver or if it was the scent of a stranger they didn't recognize that interested them. I removed my shoes, and in my stocking feet let them lead me to the kitchen.

The warmth was almost too much, cold as I was, and I knew my hair must be hanging down in wet strands. I tried to brush it back, but Rachel was pouring a cup of tea and handing it to me, and I took it gratefully.

But what was I to tell them?

What excuse could I offer? Without telling them about Simon as well?

"I went for a walk," I said finally. "And came out above the village when I tried to find my way back."

"You *are* looking for a way to leave," Rachel said accusingly. She'd found a towel and handed it to me to dry my hair.

"I was exploring. That's all. I'm used to being busy, tending patients, working with doctors. Hugh can tell you. I need more exercise than I've been getting."

"But surely you saw the storm coming." Hugh was considering me. "And there's blood on your coat."

I turned quickly—more quickly than I should have done—to look to where he was pointing. Oliver's blood on my shoulder, where one of his cuts must have opened. It wasn't much, but it was enough to betray me.

Ignoring the towel, instead wrapping my cold wet fingers around the teacup, I realized I couldn't lie to them any longer.

"There's something I ought to tell you," I said finally as they watched me with uncertainty in their gaze. "A family friend has found me. When I didn't return to the clinic on time, my mother sent him after me. My father is away, and so Simon undertook the search. He tracked me here. Never mind how, but he's ex-Army, and he knows how to find people."

"That's where you went last night," Rachel said, frowning. "You went out to meet him."

"Yes. He'd set up a base camp on the other side of the peninsula while he was trying to find me. For reasons of his own he moved to a different cave after we talked. And there he discovered Ellen Marshall's friend, Oliver. Lying on the floor of the cave and unconscious. If Simon hadn't found him, he'd have died. He's feverish and very ill. His head wound appeared to be infected. That must be the blood you saw on my shoulder."

"But what's he doing in a cave?" Rachel demanded, as if she thought I'd made up the whole story.

Hugh said, "Ellen was on the way to Swansea with him. To take him to hospital."

"So she told me. I don't know what happened. But who else could have put him there? If he was safely in hospital? It doesn't make any sense to me at all. She knew how serious his wounds were."

"Do you think she attacked him?" Hugh was asking. "That would explain why she left him in one of the caves to die. She'd have known about them. And she might have been afraid he'd talk."

I shook my head, and then remembered my wet hair as dripping strands stuck to my face. I picked up the towel and vigorously began to rub it dry. As always when it was wet, it began to curl as it dried. "No, he would have said something after she'd gone home that evening. When she brought him here, she was really afraid for him. Besides, he's bigger than Ellen. He could have stopped her."

"Not if she used something heavy, a board or tool, to knock him down."

I remembered the boards pulled from the walls in the cottage, and up from the floors. "No. It was not Ellen. I'm almost convinced it couldn't have been."

Rachel had been standing across the table from me. She sat down heavily.

"This is awful." And then it dawned on her. What I'd been so careful not to mention. "He's coming back for you, isn't he? This man Simon. And he'll bring the police back with him. They'll want to know who attacked Oliver." The realization horrified her. "Oh, Bess, see what you've done."

"I've done nothing," I told her. "But Simon couldn't have left Oliver there to die. Blame Ellen Marshall, if you like. Or whoever it is who savagely beat him. It's their actions that you must question, not mine."

"But Simon is here because of you."

"And if he hadn't come here for me, Oliver would have died in that cave, and someone would have found his bones and wondered who he was. And you'd have been none the wiser." It was harsh, but I had to make her see the truth. In the end, she might have blamed Hugh as well, for being the reason I'd come here in the first place.

She had the grace to flush. "No, of course, not—I didn't mean that."

But she had, in a way.

Hugh said, "That's rather severe, Bess."

"Yet it's true. Everyone here has turned a blind eye to men washed up by the sea, to others being beaten to death, to the use of silver that was never theirs to begin with. Even you've come round to believing it was best to stay out of it." I could speak my mind because Simon would be returning. I would be leaving with him. And yet I owed it to both Rachel and Hugh to point out their own complicity in what was happening out here. The complicity of silence. Because if the police came, they too would be drawn into the questioning, and secrets would come out, like it or not. I didn't want to see them suffer.

"They will say that it's your friend Simon who has been attacking people. That he was looking for you and didn't care how many other people he hurt as long as he found you." Rachel's voice was cold. These were her people, in spite of everything. And she'd benefited from the silver, just like everyone else.

I answered gently. "He didn't bury those two men who washed ashore. He didn't spend silver that should have gone to the Crown. And he had no reason to attack anyone. He knew where I was. Mr. Morgan told him."

She toyed with the congealing food on her plate. "I'm sorry, Bess. It's just that it's my world that will be turned upside down. Not yours."

"That's true, and I'm sorry. But even if I'd never set foot out here in this peninsula, sooner or later it would all come out. Mrs. Stephenson is very angry. She nearly shot someone just the other night. She might even decide to call in the police to find her husband's killer. And it's only a matter of time before there's a next victim."

But Rachel, for all her time spent in Swansea and Cardiff, was not convinced. Rising, she took a plate from the dresser and began to fill it with my dinner. They had more questions, of course. I tried to answer them as truthfully as I could.

"Ellen Marshall was married to a wealthy merchant," Rachel pointed out. "I don't understand why she should leave her friend in a cave to die. Not unless she'd caused his injuries and was afraid he'd tell the police."

Why had she come to this village and torn her grandfather's house apart—almost literally—if she was wealthy? But I kept that to myself. She dressed expensively, she owned a large motorcar. Perhaps his money had run out and she had hoped to find her grandfather's silver from the coach he'd stopped years before.

That reminded me that he was also suspected of murdering the coach's owner. Did murder-for-silver run in that family?

I was very tired and excused myself to finish dealing with my wet clothes. Rachel helped me spread out my coat over a chair close by the cooker, where it would dry more easily, and then I went up to my room and tried to do something about my rebellious hair. Looking in the mirror, I wondered where the Sister with her prim cap and hair twisted into a tidy knot had gone.

When I came down to fetch my hot water bottle, I could hear the loom before I stepped into the kitchen. The dogs were asleep, undisturbed by the wind pushing sheets of rain against the house and howling down the chimneys. Hugh was still there, his head in his hands. He looked up at me as I entered, his face drawn.

"You did the right thing, Bess," he said. "You couldn't have left Oliver, or whatever his name actually is, to die in that cave. But I'm afraid the repercussions will destroy all of us."

I knew what he was thinking. That if Rachel had to leave this house until the furor died down—after all, she'd taken me in, she would very likely be blamed for that—where would he go? He'd found sanctuary here, and it had helped him heal. But I knew he was afraid that there would be no work for him, despite his training. And he would have to go back to the valley. He couldn't live with Rachel when there was nothing for him to do to earn his keep, though I didn't think she would let him go. I knew she cared too much. But he might let his pride stand in the way, and refuse to be dependent on her.

I said, "We mustn't borrow trouble that hasn't arrived. This village has survived for over five hundred years. It will survive a hundred more, surely. Your lifetime and mine."

Hugh's expression was bleak. "God knows." He rose and pulled his crutches to him. "I think I'll go up too."

"Then I'll fill your bottle as well," I told him, and carried it up the stairs for him.

He paused on the landing, his expression thoughtful. "You're an amazing woman, Bess. I understand why your mother sent someone to find you. I've never had anyone care that much for me, except perhaps Tom, and so I envy that. I'm glad you'll be going back to your own world. You changed mine. And I am grateful. Whatever happens here."

"I think Rachel has had more to do with your world than anything I've done."

"She's my brother's widow. I won't step into his shoes." His expression was wry.

I opened his door and set the hot water bottle on his bed. "Is she to live the rest of her life alone, grieving for the past? I hardly think your brother would wish that for her."

"Tom had both his legs."

"And you are any less for having lost one? I think not." I crossed the room to where he was standing just outside his door. Rising on tiptoe, I kissed him lightly on the cheek. Matron, I thought in a distant part of my mind, would have an apoplexy if she'd seen me. But she was not here. Hugh was. And from what I'd seen of his sister, I could guess she would never give him the confidence he so desperately needed. Smiling, I said, "The woman who marries you will be very lucky. But you must give her a chance."

Then I walked away, into my own room, and shut the door before he could recover and answer me.

There was no word from Simon all the next day. That was worrying. Either the severity of Oliver's condition was keeping him in Swansea, or the police were. I tried to tell myself it was the weather and the state of the road that held him up, because the storm didn't abate until after nine that morning.

Careful as I was, someone—my first guess would have been

Mr. Griffith—had seen me walking back through the village in the rain last night, and remarks were made to Rachel when she went to check on the ewes and their lambs just after ten. Apparently she gave whoever it was short shrift, for the rector came calling just after noon.

He was uncomfortable in his role as chief warder. I was in the house alone at the time, and he followed me into the front room but declined my invitation to sit down.

"We were worried about you last evening," he began. "It won't do if you bring pneumonia upon yourself. Mrs. Williams has so little time for nursing the ill."

"I find I'm in need of exercise. Being shut up here in the house has been very uncomfortable."

"You are free to walk down to the strand whenever you care to."

"Am I?" I countered. "I expect I made enemies the other night, and I feel it's unwise to show myself there."

"The odd thing is," he said, coming to the point, "no one saw you leave for this . . . bit of exercise."

So that was it. I smiled. "I don't care to be watched either."

"My dear, it's for your own good. Walking to Swansea is not wise. For one thing it's a distance, and for another, the state of the road is unpredictable. You could twist an ankle and have nowhere to turn."

"I've decided that I shan't be trying to walk to Swansea or anywhere else," I told him then. "But one day there will be someone who isn't afraid of taking me up in his—or her—motorcar. My father is a high-ranking officer in the Army. A man who has the ear of important people in London. He's probably searching for me now, and I would not wish to be in the shoes of anyone who stood in his way."

There. I'd done what I could to pave the way for Simon's return.

Mr. Wilson's eyebrows rose. I could imagine him wondering how much of this warning to take back to whoever had sent him.

"I don't think anyone would wish to stand in his way," he said then. "But of course he must find you first."

That was a warning meant for me. I thought of Oliver being left in that cave to die. But surely that must have been Ellen's work, however odd that seemed. Oliver had left here in her motorcar, and he'd been in no state to come back on his own. Nor was there any way that a villager out here could have reached him in hospital. If Ellen had actually delivered him there.

"Someone will tell my father where to find me," I said with a smile, "if only to prevent the Army from descending on this village and conducting a thoroughly unpleasant search. Who knows what they might turn up?"

He stared at me. "I'm only trying to protect you," he said finally. "It's my duty to try to prevent trouble."

"Thank you, Rector. I appreciate your concern." I rose, ending the interview. He turned and walked to the door. I followed.

For the first time he made a comment that I was sure hadn't come from Mr. Griffith or Mr. Burton or even Mr. Dunhill. "You don't understand. You threaten the livelihood of too many people," he said on the threshold. "That's not wise."

"I didn't choose to stay here. Perhaps if Mr. Griffith had dealt with Mr. Morgan's nightmare instead of trying to frighten him, I'd have returned to Swansea the next morning as arranged, and you wouldn't have been troubled by my presence here."

"As I understand it, Mr. Morgan was a little too curious about a family heirloom on the mantelpiece. Mr. Griffith was worried he might take it."

I remembered the ornate cross in Rachel's bedroom. Someone in her family must have saved that too from the wrecked ship—or from the bodies of the drowned.

I wanted to ask how many such "heirlooms" were scattered about the village, but I knew it was unwise.

When I didn't reply, he nodded, put his hat on his head, and walked down the path to the road.

I watched him go before shutting the door after him.

CHAPTER 18

WHEN THE SUN came out in late afternoon, I walked as far as the overlook, and stood there for a time, watching the tide ebb and flow down on the strand. My coat had dried, although I'd had to give it a thorough brushing. It had been rather stiff with rainwater and I had no way of cleaning it.

As I watched, Mrs. Stephenson came out of her door, far below me. She stood there staring down toward the strand. There was something in the way she held herself that suggested she was still uncertain whether she could have saved her husband. It would haunt her, I thought, for as long as she lived.

My pistol in my pocket, I decided to walk down and speak to her. Passing the hedge by Mr. Griffith's house, I was reminded of that heirloom. As I looked toward his cottage I saw him at his window, watching as he always did.

By the time I reached Mrs. Stephenson's cottage, she had gone inside. I knocked at the door, and after several minutes she answered the summons. Her expression wasn't friendly.

"Why are you here?" she demanded. "After what you did the other night?"

"I'm sorry. I was afraid a terrible mistake was about to be made."

"I'm a patient woman. I can wait." Her voice was cold.

Until I was gone? Or until there was more proof?

"I came to see how you are. You've suffered a very great shock, losing your husband. I can't blame you for wanting to find out who killed him. But taking out your anger on the wrong man won't make you feel any better. Or bring your husband back to you. Let me help you find the right person."

"Step in."

Surprised, I did, and she offered me a chair.

There was an awkward moment, and then she said, "I can't get used to the silence. He was always around. I'd hear him even if I didn't see him. If I didn't, I knew it wouldn't be very long before he'd be back." Tears filled her eyes, but I quickly realized that they were angry tears. "Someone took him before his time. I can't forgive that, no matter what Rector says."

"Who held a grudge against your husband? Who could have done such a thing?"

"There's no grudge. It's the silver. It's turned all of us into greedy monsters, wanting more and more. Needing it to get by."

"But your husband wasn't looking for silver, was he?"

"We all look for silver, there on the strand. It's in our blood and bones, to look."

But Oliver hadn't been looking for silver when he was attacked—nor was he on the strand.

As she talked, it was clear that she'd listened to others discuss Philip Heaton and the money he was owed by her husband. I heard more than she realized. For one thing, no one liked Philip very much. For another, most of the men in the village were as uncertain about who had killed Edward Stephenson as she was.

She made tea after a time, and I sat with her, letting her talk. She told me about her husband, showed me a photograph of her son and daughter when they were young. "They escaped the peninsula.

I don't know that it did our boy much good. But Edith is happy enough." There was a world of loneliness in her voice. "Now her father is buried, I expect she won't come."

When I rose to leave, there was an abrupt change in her. The loneliness and grief that had begun with the tea, that had seemed to be helping her face her loss, vanished as if they had never been.

"It was good of you to come," she said, as if she actually meant it. And then, "Next time—when I find who did this to him and to me—don't stand in my way. I'll have my revenge, and neither you nor anyone else will stop me."

And the door closed in my face.

As I turned away, I saw how late it was. In the cottage, with the curtains drawn in mourning, I hadn't noticed. Sunset was just beginning to fade. There was still a faint afterglow as I reached the hedge by Mr. Griffith's cottage and walked on to the road in front of Rachel's house. I was just starting across it, my mind still on Mrs. Stephenson, when I glanced toward The Worm, only a black silhouette in the distance. It had been the guardian spirit of the peninsula for generations, but silver coins had been the village's curse.

A flicker of light halfway to The Worm caught my attention, and I froze.

Had someone just lit a lamp in Ellen's cottage? I was sure it hadn't been there when first I'd looked that way. But there was a brightness just showing in one of the windows now.

Had Ellen come back while I was calling on Mrs. Stephenson?

I couldn't believe it. But Simon wouldn't have let a light show where anyone could see it.

I started down toward the cottage. Was she still driven to search for her grandfather's silver? After what she must have done to Oliver?

The farther I went, the clearer the lamp light became. And then it went out.

Even more uncertain, I kept going. I'd nearly reached the cottage when I glimpsed Ellen's motorcar, well hidden at the side of the house. Only the gleam of the chrome radiator gave it away. And now I could see there was another lamp burning somewhere inside, its faint light showing through the curtains as I came to the path to her door.

How many people had seen her arrive? Mr. Griffith, for one, I was sure of that. It was close to the dinner hour, which meant most of the villagers would be in their kitchens at the rear of their cottages.

It was completely dark now. I hesitated. No one knew where I was. On the other hand, Ellen might have come back only to collect something, and she might be gone before morning.

I went up to the door and knocked.

I was almost certain she wouldn't answer. And I could hear Simon's voice in my head telling me I ought to turn and go. But I had my little pistol in my pocket. That was comforting.

I was just about to walk away when she came to the door, and I was shocked at the change in her. She was haggard, with dark circles under her eyes as if she hadn't slept in some time.

"What do you want?" she demanded.

"To see if you were all right. And to ask after your friend Oliver. How is he? Did you reach the hospital in time?"

"Yes. Yes, he's doing well," she said brightly. "I called in to see how he was, just before I left Swansea."

She was lying about looking in on him. And she wasn't very good at it.

But I said only, "I'm glad. You look unwell. Is everything all right?"

"Oh, yes. I haven't had much rest, worrying about my friend. I intend to go to bed shortly."

"I won't keep you, then. I saw your light, and I was concerned. I'm glad he's better."

She shut the door as quickly as she could, almost before I'd said good night and turned away.

I started up the slope, wishing I'd brought a torch, but then I hadn't expected to be walking back in the dark.

Ahead of me was Mr. Griffith, coming my way.

I sighed. He'd want to know where I'd been and why.

I had just reached the coast guard station when he cried out a warning. I registered the sound of running footsteps behind me, and I ducked to make myself a smaller target. Something came down hard on my shoulder striking a nerve and sending a searing flash of pain down my arm into my hand. I was barely aware of Mr. Griffith shouting again as he broke into a run toward me. I was trying to draw my pistol out of my coat pocket but my fingers wouldn't work. Before I could turn and confront my attacker, whoever it was grunted and hit me again between my shoulder blades, knocking the wind out of me and sending me to my knees.

Then Mr. Griffith was there, and whoever had struck me was running away. I tried to turn, desperate to see who it was, but moving made the world spin, and I stopped.

I managed to say, "Did you see? Who was it?"

He was helping me to my feet. "It was dark. A woman—Ellen. It must have been."

The dizziness was passing, my breathing returning to normal. I turned in his grip, but I couldn't see anyone in that shadowy stretch between here and the coast guard station. And the running had stopped. Whoever it was must still be nearby.

"I need to search—help me."

He was shaking his head. "She'll reach her cottage before us. And you'll need your wits about you when you face her."

He was right, I couldn't get to the cottage ahead of her. Not now.

Then I remembered the force of the blows. I looked down, scanning the ground around my feet. And there it was, among the loose chippings. A good-size stone. I freed myself from Mr. Griffith's hold, and bent down to pick it up. I almost dropped it, the fingers on my right hand still numb. I caught it with my left.

"Here," he said uneasily, "what do you want with that? She's gone, I tell you. You don't need to be afraid."

The stone fit my hand well as I tested it. I could grip it and still use it to strike someone. I remembered the prehistoric ruins out here. A stone-age man would have found this to be a handy weapon.

There was no way to prove it had been used to hit me. Still, I held on to it.

Mr. Griffith was asking, "Sister Crawford. Where are you hurt?"

"My shoulder," I said, still feeling the tingling in my fingers." I thought it best not to mention the blow to my back. Mr. Griffith being solicitous made me wary.

"Here, I'll help you to walk back. You need to sit down as soon as possible."

At first I thought he meant his cottage, but realized a moment later he must mean Rachel's. It was not that much farther, but my arm was aching, and between my shoulder blades there was what surely must be a gaping hole in my back. But of course there was no such thing, just my spine throbbing.

Mr. Griffith was scolding me as we started up the incline. "You weren't wise to be walking out after dark."

"I didn't expect—they were men. The other victims." I shook my head a little to clear it. "Are you sure it was Ellen Marshall?"

"It was a woman. Who else could it have been? And coming

from the direction of her cottage? I saw her motorcar pass by not an hour ago."

But I had just spoken with her, and she could have invited me in and hit me over the head there in the house. I *had* asked her about Oliver. Was that what had set her off? If she had fled here to avoid the police asking her questions about that cave, she might have been afraid I knew too much . . .

We had almost reached Rachel's house. Ahead, a man came out of the church and started in our direction.

"Damn," Mr. Griffith said under his breath, "Davis. The worst gossip in the village."

I looked up, and thought I recognized Mr. Davis as one of the men who'd helped carry the blanket and the dead soldier in it.

He hesitated as he saw us, then picked up his pace to meet us just at the path to Rachel's door. Looking closely at both of us, he said, "What's wrong?"

I said quickly, "I tripped walking. Mr. Griffith saw me home."

But Mr. Griffith spoke over me. "Sister Crawford was attacked— like the others. It was Ellen. Good thing I was there or she might have finished what she started."

Mr. Davis looked from Mr. Griffith to me, peering at me in the dark. "I don't see any signs of a beating."

"Her shoulder. Look, there's the stone Ellen struck her with. I saw it happen."

I stepped away from Mr. Griffith. "We can't be certain," I began. "I picked this up as a precaution. That's all."

But Mr. Davis's eyes had narrowed. "Are you sure?" he asked Mr. Griffith, ignoring me now. "She left. Ellen did."

"She's back. Not an hour ago," Mr. Griffith informed him.

"It was dark," I interjected. "And Mr. Griffith was some distance away."

"It was a woman," Mr. Griffith repeated. "Who else could it have been but Ellen?"

I was angry with him. He seemed to be relishing the story. But then he'd always been a troublemaker. Why shouldn't he spread rumors now?

"Let it go. I'm not hurt, and there's no proof. I've told you, I only picked this up for protection." But Mr. Davis wasn't listening.

"Why should Ellen Marshall attack the Sister?" he asked. "Or Stephenson for that matter? She brought that other man down here herself. I can't see that she'd attack *him*."

"God knows. Why is she ripping the cottage apart? Stripping the walls? And she took that man away with her. Who's to say she didn't murder him before ever they reached Swansea?"

It was far too close to the truth. I stared at him. But he wouldn't look at me.

Mr. Davis was saying, "I'd best be going. Susan will be expecting me." And with the briefest tip of his hat to me, he walked on toward the hedge and vanished down the path.

"Why did you tell him that?" I said, turning on Mr. Griffith. I caught him off guard and saw a look of satisfaction on his face before he could change it. "You said he was the town gossip. He'll spread your accusations to anyone willing to listen. And that will only cause trouble."

But Mr. Griffith replied solicitously, "You're home now. Ask Rachel to have a look at that shoulder." And he turned his back on me, walking away

"Mr. Griffith—" I began. But he paid no heed.

I wasn't up to running after him. After a moment I went up the path to the house and opened the door.

Rachel was just coming down the stairs. "Has your friend returned? I heard you speaking to someone just now."

"Ellen Marshall has come back. I went down to the cottage. I wanted to know how her friend Oliver was recovering."

"But you said—"

"I know. I wanted to see how she would answer me. And she lied."

I didn't want to answer any more questions. I went on down the passage to the warmth of the kitchen. My shoulder was troubling me now, and my back as well. But I smiled at Hugh as I came in, and asked if there was more tea in the pot. For he was just finishing a cup.

"You're late," he said, an echo of Rachel's words. "That isn't wise, Bess."

"She went to call on Ellen Marshall. She's at the cottage," Rachel said from behind me.

"I heard the motorcar. I thought it must be her when it continued down the road. Bess? You've told us she's all but a murderer. Was it a good idea to go there alone?"

"I don't know," I said, struggling to manage the teapot. "I wasn't even sure she was there—I didn't see or hear the motorcar. But there was a light showing in the window. And I was surprised." I set the pot down again to keep from dropping it.

Hugh reminded me of Simon as he said, "You shouldn't be so fearless, Bess. It will get you into serious trouble one of these days."

But I thought he was feeling he should have been able to go with me down there, to protect me. And it bothered him that he couldn't.

I smiled. "No harm done."

Rachel stepped forward and held out the stone I'd quietly laid on the umbrella stand in the hall, hoping she wouldn't notice. "What's this?"

"Oh." I couldn't think what to say.

Hugh was already reaching for it, hefting it in his hand. Then he looked up, his gaze meeting mine. "What happened, Bess? Tell me."

"I'm not really sure," I said slowly. It wouldn't do to lie—Mr. Griffith had seen to it that word was already spreading through the village.

"*Tell me.*" He was already reaching for his crutches.

"Walking back from Ellen's, I heard someone behind me, and before I could turn, whoever it was hit me on the shoulder. Hard. Mr. Griffith was coming toward me, and whoever it was ran off. He swore it must be Ellen. He claims he saw her. Somehow I find that hard to believe."

"Why?" Hugh was standing now.

"Because if she had been the person who attacked Oliver, he would have told us so—he'd have refused to let her take him back to the cottage. He'd have been afraid of her. And he wasn't. What's more, she wasn't here when Mr. Stephenson was killed."

"Yet you believe she left Oliver in that cave to die."

"Yes, everything points to that. I know. But somehow—for some reason—that's different." I looked at the disbelief in his face, and added, "I know. I don't quite believe that myself. But there's bound to be some explanation."

Rachel said, "She could have been here when poor Mr. Stephenson was killed. And we didn't know it."

"No," I said, remembering. "Simon was here then. He watched the cottage."

"Then who was it who struck you?" Hugh asked.

"I don't know. But I'm convinced that whoever attacked Oliver and Mr. Stephenson hit them with a stone just like that, half stunning them, and then beat them viciously when they were in no condition to offer much resistance."

"That's a coward's work," Hugh said tersely.

"I know." I looked him straight in the eye. "Who attacked you, that same day?" I demanded. "You must tell me. It could matter. It could tell us who is out there hurting other people."

But he stood there, his mouth in a tight line.

Rachel said, "It was Anna's father. I saw it happen. And he didn't use a stone. Only his fists." Hugh swung around to look at her.

I asked into the strained silence, "Why would he go on to attack Oliver—and Mr. Stephenson? Or me?"

"I don't believe he did," Hugh said abruptly. "It was—personal." He was still looking at Rachel.

"Who else could it be?" Rachel said finally. "And if it isn't Ellen, why is Mr. Griffith spreading the story that it was her?"

"Let's go and ask her. Now," Hugh said.

"No." Rachel shook her head. "Enough has happened tonight."

"We must warn her," I said, suddenly realizing the danger she was in, once half the village had heard Mr. Griffith's tale.

"Tomorrow will be soon enough. In the daylight," Hugh said. "Promise me you won't try to go there tonight."

I tried to argue with him, but he wouldn't listen. "Yes. All right," I agreed at last. The truth was, my back was in no state to walk that far. I knew he couldn't, and it would be dangerous to ask Rachel to go alone. "But first thing. Early."

Rachel came forward and poured my tea for me. When I'd finished it, I picked up the stone and for the first time looked at it in the light of the kitchen lamp. Turning it this way and that, I saw a speck of blue wool from my uniform coat, from where I'd brushed it, caught on a rough spot on the stone.

I told myself that it could have got there from carrying it home.

Taking it with me, I went upstairs to put up my coat and hat. Then, drawing the window curtains, I opened the top of my uniform and pulled it aside to look at my shoulder. There was already a bruise forming, and it was going to be black by morning. The tingling was wearing off, and I thought no serious damage had been done. But that blow would have stunned me if I hadn't ducked aside.

There was no way to see my back in the mirror, but I could

almost guess what that bruise must look like. And I didn't want to ask Rachel to look for me.

In the night, finding it difficult to sleep, I got up and went to the window. The peninsula was pitch-black. Overhead the stars were bright pinpoints of light, and I watched them swing across the sky for a bit. I was cold and about to go back to my warm blankets when I saw the glow of a cigarette down below my window.

The shadows were deep there, and I couldn't see who it was, just the tip of the cigarette burning brightly as he inhaled. Simon didn't smoke, and I'd been at Ellen's door, I didn't think she smoked either, although some women had taken up the habit.

Whoever it was, he must now be directly beneath my window. The smell of burning tobacco was that strong.

I dressed as quietly as I could, opened my door softly, and set off down the stairs with my coat in my arms. Along the passage, into the kitchen, and out the kitchen door. Moving easily on the soft ground, I reached the corner of the house and sniffed the air. Yes, cigarette smoke. I peered around it. But there was no one beneath my window now. Only a shadowy figure just crossing the road and disappearing near the hedge.

I followed, but whoever it was had vanished into the night—or the nearest cottages on the Down.

Tomorrow I would ask Rachel who lived in them.

When I stepped back into the kitchen, someone moved, and I stopped stock still, ready to retreat as fast as I could. It wasn't possible that whoever I'd followed could have doubled back and come into this house by the path door. The dogs would have set up such a racket, everyone would have heard them.

Then Hugh spoke. "I'm here. I heard you go down. Has your friend come back? Or did you break your promise and visit Ellen?"

"Neither. There was someone smoking just below my window. Staring up at it. I didn't like it, and I went out to see."

A match flared, blindingly bright, and then Hugh lit the lamp. Keeping his voice low so as not to disturb Rachel, whose room was just above us, he said, "That was foolish."

I took the little pistol from my pocket. "I wasn't afraid."

"Good God," he said, staring at it. "Do you know how to use that thing?"

"Of course I do," I answered him, affronted. "That's why I was given it."

He grinned suddenly. "Of course you do. Why should I have doubted it?" Then the grin faded. "You should have roused me."

"Two of us going down the stairs would surely have awakened Rachel."

"Yes. Where did this figure go?"

"I could see him as far as the hedge. Not where he went after that. Who lives in the nearest two cottages beyond the hedge?"

"The Richardsons and the Greenes."

"Does Mr. Richardson or Mr. Greene smoke?"

"I have no idea. But you must realize that whoever it was could have ducked into the shadows by the Griffith cottage and waited until you'd gone? There's no telling where he might be now."

It was true. I hadn't considered that. "There's nothing more to be done tonight. Besides, he knows someone was on to him. He'll be careful now." I pulled off my hat and shook out my hair. "I'm so sorry to have awakened you, Hugh. I promise, I won't go back out. Shall I put the kettle on? Would you like something warm to drink?"

He shook his head. "Go on to bed. I'll turn out the light when you've reached the stairs."

But I stopped at the top of the stairs, listening, afraid Hugh was going out to look around too. He came down the passage, opened the door to the road, and stood there for some time before shutting it. I made it to my room before he turned to the stairs.

It was not quite sunrise when I woke up to angry voices. It took me several seconds to realize they were outside, not in the house. Just a sound like angry bees, without definition. I got up to look out my window. When I couldn't see anything from there, I dressed as quickly as I could with a bad shoulder and bruised back, caught up my coat and hat, then went down to the front room.

Hugh was already there.

"Trouble," he said, glancing over his shoulder as I came in. Then he turned back to the window. "Mrs. Stephenson is standing in the churchyard, arguing with Mr. Wilson. I don't care for the look of it."

Joining him at the window, I said, "Nor do I." I peered at the two people standing among the gravestones. "That's her husband's grave, isn't it? It should be just about there. Possibly she couldn't sleep and came there to mourn him." The church door was open, as if Mr. Wilson had just come out—or had been about to go in when he saw her.

The rector was bending forward, speaking vehemently. I couldn't hear the words, but he appeared to be pleading. Mrs. Stephenson was shaking her head, wanting none of it. Finally she turned away from him and started toward the road. Her back was ramrod straight with determination. "She's heard about Ellen," I said and pulled on my coat. "This is madness. Didn't she learn her lesson the last time?"

"You can't be sure what she's going to do."

But Mrs. Stephenson wasn't a grieving wife returning to her cottage. She was marching down the road with the determination of Joan of Arc striding toward the massed English Army. Only she was marching toward an unsuspecting woman who might be a murderer but who didn't deserve to die this way.

This was Mr. Griffith's doing. A troublemaker and a meddler. Why he'd told the village gossip about Ellen was beyond my imagination, but he'd been pleased with himself afterward.

Hugh said, "Bess. Don't."

"I have to do something," I told him, and walked to the door.

Rachel was just coming down the stairs. "What's all that shouting?"

"Mrs. Stephenson is going after Ellen Marshall." I didn't stop to talk, I just opened the door and stepped out, ignoring Hugh shouting at me as he crossed the front room.

I ran down the path, calling to Mrs. Stephenson. She had just reached the Griffith cottage—and she hadn't turned toward the hedge. She was carrying on straight.

"Please wait! There's been a mistake."

She turned, frowning. "I heard you'd been attacked." She said the word as if she'd expected me to be lying at death's door.

"I was—but it was only my shoulder that was hurt. And I'm not convinced that Ellen Marshall was behind it. I didn't see who it was."

"Griffith did, he said it was her."

"He's lying. I don't know why."

She had started to move on, but she paused, looking me straight in the eye. "Why should he lie about Ellen Marshall? They were friends once."

Just beyond her, I could glimpse Mr. Griffith standing by his door, watching us. The gray light washed out his face, giving it a ghostly appearance.

"I don't know. But I believe he's wrong. Why don't we ask him?"

She considered me. I thought I'd convinced her to listen to reason. But she said, "You should be thanking me for what I'm about to do. If Mr. Griffith hadn't come along when he did, you'd be dead as well."

The sun's first rays broke the horizon, casting long shadows.

She walked on. We were just passing the Griffith cottage now. As we did, he withdrew into the shadows by his door.

I hurried after her. Was she armed? I couldn't tell, given the heavy coat she was wearing, but I had to assume she was. She'd had a revolver before. Why had she gone to the church first? To make her peace with God? Or tell her husband what she was about to do for his sake? Mr. Wilson had tried to persuade her, judging from what little I'd seen of their confrontation, not to do anything foolish. But he hadn't stopped her. I didn't think he had the nerve to try.

I glanced back, hoping Mr. Wilson might have found his courage and followed us. He was nowhere in sight. But Hugh was coming after us. And Mr. Griffith was keeping to the shadows by his door, watching all of us. I was angry with both of them—Hugh for attempting that long walk down to the cottage, putting himself at risk, and Mr. Griffith for telling lies to Mr. Davis.

I caught up with Mrs. Stephenson. There was no expression on her face. Neither anger nor hatred. Just—emptiness.

I looked back again, hoping that Hugh would have stopped. But he was still making his way down that dangerously rutted road. And Mr. Griffith was still watching us. Whatever his reasons for throwing Ellen to the proverbial wolves, he wasn't likely to care now. Or he'd have come out and called to Mrs. Stephenson when he saw where she was heading.

I almost missed my step and tripped, looking over my shoulder. Hugh had halted. He was calling to Mr. Griffith.

It was then I saw Mr. Griffith watching from the rear window of the cottage.

But how could he be? He'd been right there by his door, and even now Hugh was saying something to him. That meant he hadn't moved.

I stopped. But the figure I had seen in the window was no longer there.

Something Simon had told me came charging back into the fore-front of my mind. That Mr. Morgan had claimed he'd been attacked in the night . . . and had the scars to prove it.

I hadn't been mistaken. Someone else was there, in the cottage.

But who was it?

I stood there for a moment, torn. Should I follow Mrs. Stephen-son—or find out what Mr. Griffith was hiding? There wasn't time. She was already passing the coast guard station, marching steadily toward Ellen's cottage.

I ran then, catching her up just beyond the station.

"Listen to me. I know now why Mr. Griffith lied."

"It doesn't matter. We're almost there. Let her speak for herself. If she can."

I tried everything I could think of, but nothing I could say made any difference in her determination.

And now it was too late. Here we were at Ellen's cottage. Mrs. Stephenson was striding up to the door. She didn't hesitate. She banged on it with her fist.

Ellen didn't come to the door, and I was just drawing a breath of relief, when it opened after all, and she stood there, framed by the shadows in the dark rooms behind her. She was dressed, but her clothes were rumpled, and I wondered if she had slept in them.

"What do you want? If you're here for my grandfather's silver, it's all gone. Gone, I tell you. I should know. I've been looking for it." There was anguish in her voice.

"Be damned to your grandfather," Mrs. Stephenson said. "It's my husband I've come about."

"Well, he's not here," Ellen snapped.

I thought Mrs. Stephenson was going to explode into anger. But she held her temper on a short rein and said through clenched teeth. "He's in the churchyard. Where you put him."

"I haven't put anyone anywhere," Ellen said. But she found it hard to be convincing. Was Oliver still on her conscience? It could explain sleepless nights.

So could the knowledge that all the silver was gone.

Ellen was about to shut the door, but Mrs. Stephenson reached into her pocket and pulled out the revolver I'd seen before.

"No, wait!" I said quickly.

But she went on inexorably. "I want to know why you killed my husband. And you're going to tell me. Or lose a foot."

Ellen opened her mouth to say something but I cut in.

"You can't do this." I remembered someone had said her name was Ruth. "It makes you no better than the person who killed your husband. Ruth, please put the revolver away, and we'll talk civilly. Please."

"Stay out of this," Mrs. Stephenson told me sharply, the revolver wavering in my direction.

Ellen tried to use the distraction to shut her door, but Mrs. Stephenson pulled the trigger, and the shot, almost deafening in our ears, went wild, striking the door's frame. Ellen cried out and vanished into the house. I thought flying splinters had struck her face, and I turned on Mrs. Stephenson. "*Stop!*"

She waved the revolver at me. "You may have forgiven her, Sister, but I haven't. Stay out of my way."

I heard the sound of the revolver cocking, but I didn't think she had realized what she was doing, as upset as she was. The revolver went off, and I heard the shot pass all too close to my ear before it broke the window glass beyond me.

I could hear a motorcar coming fast down the road, but I had no time to think about that. The cottage door was standing wide. A shotgun roared, and it was only because Mrs. Stephenson was bearing down on me that she was out of range of the blast.

Flinching, she said, "Is that the behavior of an innocent woman? I ask you."

The motorcar had come to a screeching halt, scattering the chippings everywhere. The door opened, and I turned quickly to see Simon stepping out and walking fast toward us.

I didn't know who Mrs. Stephenson thought he was, but she shouted, "Another of her soldiers, are you?" And she fired at him. "Clear off!"

I saw him jerk to one side, and knew that she had hit him.

CHAPTER 19

"*No!*" I SHOUTED at her, and before she could fire again, I had reached her and slapped her hard. While she was still shocked, staring at me, I grasped her wrist and twisted it. Her fingers opened and the revolver fell to the ground. My reflexes were faster, and I had scooped it up before she could move.

Mrs. Stephenson reached for it, tears running down her face. "No, you don't understand . . ."

I kept it well out of her grasp as I called to Ellen, "It's over, I have her weapon."

I was answered by the shotgun, firing at us again. Missing both of us.

Ignoring the women now, I raced to Simon.

He was standing by the motorcar's wing, out of range, grinning, his good hand holding his upper arm. The grin turned into a grimace. "You had the situation well in hand," he said, but I was prying open his fingers and watching blood soaking into the sleeve of his tunic. "It's all right," he added curtly. "I've had worse."

"I didn't expect you," I was saying. "Not this soon."

"Captain Williams was at the top of the hill. He told me what was happening."

Men were running down the incline toward us, alarmed by the sound of gunfire.

I said quickly, "Simon, can you drive Mrs. Stephenson back up to Rachel's house? I hope she's come to her senses, but I don't trust her. She shouldn't be left alone."

"I'm not leaving without you."

"But there's Ellen—" I began.

"She won't be leaving. Go on, fetch Mrs. Stephenson."

Simon was reversing the motorcar, careful to stay out of shotgun range, as I tried to persuade Mrs. Stephenson to come with me.

She was alternately shouting at Ellen over her shoulder and ordering me to give her the revolver. Then she saw the villagers hurrying toward us, and that renewed her energy, as if she thought they would stand with her.

I said, "No. You'll get one of them killed. Is that what you want? Ellen is armed. And you aren't."

She stood there, staring toward the villagers. Then she nodded reluctantly.

"This isn't finished," she said, and went toward the motorcar on her own. But once she was inside, I noticed that tears were running down her cheeks as she huddled in a far corner of the rear seat. "Now give me back the revolver," she shouted, but I ignored her.

"Shall I drive?" I asked Simon, opening his door.

"I haven't bled to death yet," he retorted and started up the hill as I closed my own door.

As we reached the straggle of villagers, Simon called, "Go home. It was all a mistake."

They had no idea who he was. He hadn't been wearing his uniform when he was moving around in the dark, but he had it on today.

I saw one man silently mouth the word *Army* and stop in his tracks, staring at us.

"Oliver?" I asked quietly, when we were near the top of the incline.

"He's very ill—but he's going to live. His name is Oliver Martin, and he'd just been released from the Army when he and Ellen came out here. He'd been in hospital before that, a wound that had tried to go septic. That might explain why he couldn't defend himself properly."

"Could he tell you anything about the cave?"

"That was Ellen's doing. I'll explain later." He glanced toward the woman in the rear seat.

"I need to know. Who gave him such a vicious beating?"

"He didn't know. A man. It could have been anyone in the village, he said. It was dark, he never saw the face clearly. He did say he was stunned by the first blow."

"Simon. Do you recall what Mr. Morgan told you? About being attacked in the night? There was someone in Mr. Griffith's house today. A man. I think Mr. Griffith must be protecting the killer."

I didn't think Mrs. Stephenson was listening, lost as she was in her own wretchedness. But she spoke now from the rear seat. "There's no one else in his house."

"But I saw him. Just a little while ago. I'm sure of it."

She leaned forward. "His wife is dead. His son died in the war."

"Then someone from the village."

Simon turned to me. "It's possible. Escaped prisoners. Men on the run. It could be anyone with the money to pay Griffith for sanctuary. If people have accepted that he's the only one living in the cottage, who would know?"

"Then how did he find Mr. Griffith? He smokes," I added, still putting all the pieces together. "Whoever he is."

"I've never seen Mr. Griffith with a cigarette," Mrs. Stephenson objected.

We'd reached Rachel's house. Hugh was standing by the path.

"What's happened?" Hugh asked at once. "We heard gunfire."

"It's all right," I said, hurrying to get out of the motorcar before Mrs. Stephenson.

"Then why is the Sergeant-Major bleeding?" Hugh asked dryly.

Once out of the motorcar, Mrs. Stephenson had stopped and was staring thoughtfully at the Griffith cottage. "Are you sure someone else was in there?" She shook my hand off her arm and started across the road, toward the cottage. "I intend to find out."

I caught her arm again. "You've shot one person, and nearly got yourself killed. That's enough."

But she broke free. "As soon as our back's turned, he'll be away. Whoever he is."

Simon was there, blocking her. "What will you do if he comes to the door? Sister Crawford still has your revolver."

That stopped her. She stood there, uncertain.

Simon's arm was bleeding too freely. The patch of red was spreading.

"I must do something about this man's wound," I told her, this time not mincing my words. "It's your fault, and I don't want to hear any more nonsense from you. Do you understand?"

"He's Ellen's friend. I don't much care," Mrs. Stephenson said stubbornly.

"No, he's mine," I said, angry with her. "My parents sent him to find me. And they'll soon have the police here, taking you up for shooting him."

Mention of the police nearly started her off again. "I don't want the police. I'll do what has to be done."

"You'll get precious little revenge from a cell in Swansea," Hugh told her.

Alarmed now, she stared at him, then turned around.

Once inside, Hugh stayed with her in the front room while I led

Simon into the kitchen to dress his arm. Rachel was there, her eyes anxious.

"We heard shots fired," she began, then broke off as she saw Simon and the blood on his arm.

I introduced her to Simon, then said, "He arrived when Mrs. Stephenson was a little confused." As I spoke, Simon was unbuttoning his tunic. "It's best to hide that," I went on, leaning forward to set the revolver on the table. "Fortunately her aim wasn't very good. I've brought her here. I don't think she should be left alone. Hugh is keeping an eye on her."

Rachel nodded, though I could see she wanted to ask more questions. Then she picked up the revolver very carefully and put it in a drawer of the dresser before taking Simon's tunic from him.

"I'll just try to sponge away some of this blood. I'm glad you're here, Sergeant-Major. I'm sure Bess is as well." But her voice was strained, and her gaze flicked to me.

Simon was rolling up his bloody shirtsleeve, and I began to work on the wound. He winced as I cleaned it. "It will do," I said quietly. "I can't see any serious damage. But Mrs. Stephenson doesn't need to know that. Still, there's always the possibility of infection. Be careful."

Rachel set aside the tunic long enough to find clean cloths for bandaging, then asked as she picked up the tunic again, "Any news of that poor man left in the cave—"

She broke off as Mrs. Stephenson came hurrying into the kitchen. She looked at the bloody water in the basin and the bandages. "Dear God. I didn't bargain for this."

Turning, Simon asked, "Why were you so certain that woman had killed your husband?"

"Because Mr. Griffith saw her as plain as day when she attacked Sister Crawford."

Before I could answer, Simon demanded sharply, "What's this?"

"I'm all right," I assured him, although my back and shoulder were protesting.

But Mrs. Stephenson hadn't finished. "It's that and the men," she said earnestly. "I thought you were another of them."

"What men?" Hugh had come to stand in the kitchen doorway.

"Nobody knew. *We* never told. It was when my daughter was ill after she had her little girl. Edward went to see her in that Bristol hospital, to be sure she was all right. He was looking for a tea shop and there was Ellen Marshall just coming out of a church on the arm of a Welsh Corporal." Mrs. Stephenson nodded to us. "Now you see why I knew she'd killed Edward. Once I heard that Mr. Griffith had seen her attacking Sister Crawford."

"I don't quite understand—" I said.

"She was *marrying* him. With a white veil and a bouquet. And her poor husband not a fortnight in his grave. She kept her late husband's name all the while. Only it was that man, the one in Bristol, who washed up here in the bay. My husband recognized him, you see. But he never said a word to anyone about it."

"Washed up—?" I repeated. "Are you saying—he was one of the two men who are buried there in the churchyard? The one in the boat?"

"That's right. We didn't know his name, but my husband didn't doubt it was the Bristol man. And he said he wouldn't be at all surprised if the first one who washed up was another of her men. When the war was finished, and they started to come home, what else was she to do? She couldn't have all those men who thought they'd married her finding out about each other."

"Ellen *killed* them? And then put their bodies into the sea?" I asked her. Was that why Ellen was so worried about Oliver? If he'd died in her cottage, she could hardly drag his body down to the strand . . .

"What else was she to do with all those husbands of hers? All she had to do is drive down the other side of the Gower in that big motorcar of hers, take the body out to The Worm, and put it into the water," Mrs. Stephenson said. "Who was to know?"

"Oliver Martin—" I began, but it was Simon who broke in.

"He had just been demobbed. He was to help her find her grandfather's hoard. They were married in 1917."

"Then she *did* attack him," Rachel said.

"No, that wasn't Ellen. But she got rid of him all the same. Or she believes she has," Simon replied. "Oliver was still breathing, and so she left him in the cave, probably intending to come back when he was dead."

"She used a rotted boat for the second body," Hugh commented.

"But why did she come out here tonight? Wasn't that rather foolish of her?" I asked.

"Another soldier turned up at her lodging house this morning. Looking for her. I met him when I went there myself. Before I went to the police."

"The police?" Rachel asked. "Surely you haven't—are they on their way?"

"I'm afraid so. They want to talk to her about Martin. Neither he nor I knew about the others."

"Look what you've done!" Rachel exclaimed, turning to me.

"Was *he* another husband?" I wanted to know. "The ex-soldier who turned up at her lodging house today? Simon, how many does that make?"

"God knows. But he didn't say anything about looking for his wife. And I didn't know then to ask. He was sitting on the steps to the door, waiting for her to come home. A neighbor told us Ellen had got his telegram yesterday and early this morning she'd gone out to do her marketing. Only she hadn't returned. I suspected she had gone to earth out here. I came looking for her. And just as well I got here when I did."

Hugh said, "She must have been collecting their Army pay. That's the only explanation."

"But her husband—late husband—was rich. Everyone knew that," Rachel objected.

"He was. But there was only a pittance for her in his will. Everything went to the children of his first marriage." Simon looked at me. "So that same neighbor claimed. Ellen opened the house by the port and took in lodgers, to embarrass the children—they're grown, they have a social position to protect."

"And her grandfather's share of the silver is gone too," I said. "That's why she was tearing the cottage apart."

Mrs. Stephenson, as alarmed as Rachel had been about the imminent arrival of the Swansea police, broke in. "We don't want the police here. They never came when we needed them. They've never protected us," she said now. "I won't have it. And I haven't finished with Ellen Marshall. If Edward saw her outside that Bristol church, she must have seen him. I'd have got my answers, but for you," she added accusingly to me. "You and that nonsense about Mr. Griffith. It would have been *finished* by now."

There was no reasoning with her. "Not with that shotgun," I reminded Mrs. Stephenson. "You couldn't get close enough to use your revolver."

"She can't stay awake all night. I can be patient." She started for the door, but Hugh blocked her.

"We've got enough trouble already. Go home. Let the police come and take her into custody. They'll leave then. She's the only one they're after. Unless you and the rest of the village give them cause to stay."

"He's right," Rachel told her, setting Simon's tunic over a chair and coming forward. "Let her go. You'll put all of us at risk if you don't stop this mad insistence on settling up with Ellen."

"She won't hang for what she did to that man Oliver," the woman said stubbornly. "And it's only Edward's word about the man in the boat. Edward's dead."

Rachel shook her head. "She'll go to prison for a very long time. Please, let that be enough."

But it was too late. There was a thundering knock at the door, and I knew even before Hugh swung around to answer the summons that the police had come. I saw Simon reach for his tunic, putting it on before the police could see his bloody sleeve.

And Mrs. Stephenson sat down at the kitchen table and began to cry.

The Sergeant on the doorstep had been told he'd find Ellen Marshall Hobson at the last house on the left.

He'd mistaken Rachel's house for the cottage, for that was nearly invisible from where he'd stopped.

It took us a few very anxious minutes to convince him that he'd come to the wrong house. What's more, he wasn't one of the policemen who had interviewed Oliver Martin as soon as he regained consciousness, and so he hadn't met Simon. In the end, I'm certain it was my uniform as a nursing Sister that persuaded Sergeant Barnes that we were telling the truth, because he kept referring to me for confirmation as Rachel and Hugh tried to explain the matter.

Simon had remained just behind us, offering what support he could, but the rather noticeable stain on his sleeve so far hadn't caught the eye of Sergeant Barnes, who would soon be seeing evidence of gunfire at the cottage.

Mrs. Stephenson was sitting in a corner of the kitchen, taking no part in the conversation with the Sergeant.

Finally satisfied that we were telling him the truth, Sergeant Barnes went back to the motorcar driven by a young Constable, and set off down the road toward the Marshall cottage.

I looked up just in time to see Mr. Griffith standing in his doorway, watching the proceedings with interest. He disappeared inside when he saw me staring.

By this time I'd become more or less persuaded that either I'd been wrong when I thought I'd seen someone else in the Griffith cottage—or someone from the village had come up to call. Jenny's father, very likely. Mr. Burton, worrying about what Mrs. Stephenson was about? He was ill-tempered enough to have beaten anyone, and it was a coward's way to use a stone to knock a man down, then batter him while he was half-conscious. In many ways he and Mr. Griffith deserved each other.

By common consent, we hadn't shut Rachel's door, and it wasn't long before we heard the shotgun fired again.

Sergeant Barnes and the Constable didn't come back up the road, indicating that no one had been hurt, and so we finally shut the door and went back to the kitchen.

Mrs. Stephenson rose as we came in. "I'll just be going off home," she said. Her face was tired, drawn.

"Shall I go with you?" I asked, concerned for her. "Or perhaps you'd prefer Mr. Wilson. It won't take me more than a few minutes to bring him here. He can walk with you."

She shook her head. "No. Thank you, Sister." She reached for her coat. "She's getting away with murder. You know that as well as I do. Good night."

To be certain she was going home, I walked as far as the hedge with Mrs. Stephenson, and stood there watching her until she disappeared inside her own cottage. Poor woman, I thought, turning away.

As I started back to Rachel's house, I saw Simon standing in the doorway, watching, to be certain I was all right. I made a face. He wasn't wearing the sling I'd fashioned for him. He shrugged.

I realized as I crossed the empty street that no one in this village had come out to see what had brought the police here. All the doors I could see from here were firmly shut. There were no children playing in back gardens, no one working with the grazing cattle. It was almost eerily silent in Caudle. I could hear the waves coming in, above the wind.

Looking down toward the cottage, I could just see the rear of the motorcar that the police had arrived in.

In some fashion I could feel sorry for Ellen Marshall. Her grandfather had tried to give her the best of everything, and she had married rather well. But her life hadn't quite turned out as the fairy tale it was meant to be. Her husband hadn't loved her enough to provide for her after his death, and she must have been too proud to beg his children to give her an allowance that suited her station as his widow. What had happened then was on her own head. The girl that young Rachel had admired and even envied had become a stranger.

Hadn't someone said that her grandfather had been suspected of murder?

And that reminded me about the two bodies I knew about in the churchyard.

No one in the village was going to bring police attention to them. And if Mrs. Stephenson was right, that Ellen might have killed at least one of them, *she* most certainly wouldn't mention them.

Should I? They deserved justice too . . .

I walked into the house and Rachel called, "I've just made tea. I think we need it."

I joined the three of them in the kitchen, glancing at Simon for any signs of feverishness from his wound, for I hadn't had an antiseptic to clean it. But he gazed blandly back at me, and I said nothing. He'd made friends with the dogs, who had a head on each knee.

I didn't remember having any breakfast, and Rachel must have read my mind, because she went into the pantry for eggs and bread. Returning, she said, "I expect you'll want to leave today?"

Simon spoke for me. "Tomorrow early. Once the police have finished here."

She looked at him warily. "Surely they'll take Ellen back to Swansea today. There's nothing else to keep them here. It will all be over."

But he was petting the dogs and didn't lift his head.

I said, "Rachel. There's the question of who attacked Oliver Martin and killed Mr. Stephenson. Not to mention those two dead soldiers in the churchyard. If the police look closely into Ellen's affairs, it's likely they'll find more than you've bargained for."

"Why would they even consider looking for those men here? Even if they discover she had married them?"

Hugh said, "Rachel."

She shook her head. "No, Bess is going to make all our lives wretched—she's so sure she's in the right, so certain she knows what's best. I can't bear it." She dropped the loaf of bread on the table.

"I'm not going to tell the police anything. But Ellen has brought them here—and I'm afraid this is just the beginning. You and Hugh must be prepared."

"I won't listen to any more of this."

She ran into the small room off the kitchen, and in the silence that followed we heard the loom starting.

Hugh said grimly, "This has been a shock for her. She'll come round. But you're right, Bess. Before this is over, we'll all be questioned. They'll want to know why the deaths weren't reported. Why all of us conspired to keep them secret. That's how the police will see it. That will be bad enough. If they learn about the silver, then there's no turning back."

I went over to the cooker and began to slice the bread for toasting before starting the eggs. "Perhaps you and Rachel might consider visiting my mother in Somerset. For a little while."

"There are the sheep. She won't leave them." There was resignation in his voice.

There was nothing more we could say, Hugh and I.

We were not destined to finish that already delayed breakfast. While we were still eating, there was a knock on the door. Hugh went to answer it.

I could hear Sergeant Barnes's voice. And Hugh's in reply. But not the words.

After a moment, Hugh came back down the passage. He was clearly shaken.

"Sergeant Barnes wants you to come. Ellen killed herself. He wants you to pronounce her dead, since there's no doctor. Before he removes the body."

"I'll go. It's best." Simon rose and started toward the door.

"I'm sorry. More sorry than I can say. But they want Sister Crawford."

Simon went with me, over the objections of the Sergeant. I was glad he had. Ellen had turned the shotgun on herself when the police came to her door. There was no doubt she was dead.

There was blood everywhere, and the smell of it was overpowering in the small bedroom. I went through the formalities, then nodded to the Sergeant. As I turned to go, I was careful not to step in the pools.

I paused in the bedroom doorway while the Sergeant asked about the destruction he could see throughout the cottage. I replied that rumors had always held that Ellen Marshall's grandfather had hidden a fortune somewhere. "I don't live in the village, as you know. I can only pass on what I've heard in the short time I've been here." Avoiding Simon's gaze I looked down. And there on the threshold was a gray smear.

I could almost have said it was the ash from a cigarette, but the two policemen had been in and out of the room, and there wasn't enough left to be sure.

I almost missed the Sergeant's reply.

"A fortune? Out here? Well, it appears she never found anything. Else the destruction would have stopped soon enough."

"I expect that was a great disappointment to her," I agreed. We moved on, into the passage by the bedrooms. "I'll be leaving in the morning," I told Sergeant Barnes then. "I'm due to return to the clinic where I'm posted. I had come here to look in on Captain Williams. I'm happy to say he's no longer in need of medical care. The Sergeant-Major here was sent by my parents to escort me. Do you need a statement from either of us?"

"No, Sister. But I'd like to know who the deceased was firing at, before we got here. We couldn't help but see the scars."

"At shadows," I said firmly, and went out to Simon's motorcar, getting in without looking back.

He was reversing to drive back to the house when a thought occurred to me.

I put down the window and called to the Sergeant, who was already disappearing into the cottage.

He turned and came back to the door. "Sister?" He was polite but slightly impatient.

"Did you see her kill herself?"

"We didn't need to. We knocked at the door, called to her to identify ourselves. She didn't answer, and so I told her that if she didn't step to the door, unarmed, her hands up, we'd be coming in after her. That's when we heard the shot. We didn't realize what it meant. We thought it was a warning. And so we took our time going in." He nodded to me, and started back inside.

"Are you sure it was suicide?" I called after him.

"You saw the body, Sister."

I had.

Simon said quietly, "Let it go, Bess."

I leaned back against my seat. "He's not going to listen, is he? Inquiry closed. I told the police the absolute truth. Just not all of it."

He started up the incline. "Who killed her, if she didn't kill herself?"

"Whoever attacked me—Oliver Martin—Mr. Stephenson?"

"If you think that's possible, then you should speak to the Inspector in charge, in Swansea."

"Yes. I expect you're right. But the villagers won't like that, will they? I wish I knew what to do."

CHAPTER 20

WHEN WE RETURNED to Rachel's house, she and Hugh were waiting in the front room.

She had been crying. "Is it true? She took her own life?" When I nodded, she added, "How sad. I thought her so—so wonderful. She was everything I thought I wanted to be. What will they do with her . . . her body?"

"Take it back to Swansea. There will be an inquest. Afterward, the body will be released to the family for burial."

"She doesn't have any family."

I said, "Mr. Wilson might ask that she be brought home to be buried with her parents and her grandfather."

"I'll ask him. Will you take the letter to Swansea with you? I know she tried to kill that man. Mrs. Stephenson might well be right about the others there in the churchyard. Still—" Rachel broke off.

"I'll take the letter. And see that it is put in the right hands."

She excused herself to go and speak to Mr. Wilson.

Hugh said, "I expect it's best this way. For everyone, including Ellen Marshall."

Simon, standing by the door, shook his head slightly.

"Yes," I said. Simon was right, this was neither the time nor the place to say more.

That afternoon I put my clothes and personal belongings into my kit, save for what I needed that night and to dress in the morning. I tried to stay out of Rachel's way and took longer than I really needed to. Downstairs, Simon and Hugh were talking together in the front room, and I was glad they had taken a liking to each other. Occasionally I caught a word. The troubles out here had long since been replaced by discussions of the war. The fact that Hugh was an officer mattered not at all. But then Simon was accustomed to speaking to my father as an equal—with deference, but as an equal. Hugh hadn't had much in common with these villagers of English descent. He must have missed another man he felt free to talk to. His crutches and his missing leg were forgotten as they refought battle after battle.

The police had gone, Hugh told us at dinner. I hadn't heard the motorcar leave.

After dinner, we made the best of the situation. None of us was in a merry frame of mind. Hugh was rather quiet, and Rachel was still sad, although she'd persuaded the rector to write that letter. It was already tucked into my kit, ready for our departure in the morning.

Simon was a little restless, and I changed the bandage on his arm, expecting to find early signs of infection, but the wound was still clean. After that we called it a night. He was to sleep in the front room, and I thought about the pallet we'd made for Oliver Martin. He'd come close twice to dying. I was glad he'd responded to care and would be all right.

Rachel went out for a last look at the ewes, and I heard her come up half an hour later.

The house seemed to creak and groan as the wind came up around midnight and the temperature dropped. I found it hard to sleep, tossing and turning, seeing Ellen's body over and over again in the dark room. I'd faced worse sights in France, but I was uneasy about her death. Just as well, I thought, that I was leaving. Rachel and Hugh could get on with their lives, and I could return to my own. Whatever was happening, whatever *had* happened, would have to sort itself out. But there was still a killer out here. And that kept me awake. It was close to two o'clock when I finally fell asleep.

I woke with a start as my bed moved under the weight of someone sitting down on the edge of it, but before I could cry out, Simon put his hand over my mouth and spoke softly. "Be quiet. I want you to come with me. Get dressed quick as you can, and I'll meet you by the kitchen door. No apron or cap."

I nodded, and he was gone.

I dressed, took my time going down the stairs, thanking the wind for covering any sounds I might make, and reached the kitchen door without rousing Hugh or Rachel.

Simon was waiting in the dark just outside. He took my hand and led me out toward the pasture where Rachel's sheep were huddled in the lee of the low walls.

I started to speak, thinking we were far enough from the house, but he squeezed my hand, a signal to be quiet.

I could see the white bulk of the coast guard station now. We were passing on the inland side of it, some distance from it and the road.

The night was overcast, I could hardly see my hand before my face, and the ground underfoot was uneven and hummocky. But Simon seemed to have no difficulty finding his way. And then I realized that the shape looming to our right must be Ellen's cottage. Simon stopped.

After what seemed like several minutes, there was a flickering light in one of the windows—someone flashing a torch around a room. It moved on to the next room, then vanished, as if whoever it was had gone into a passage.

"Who?" I whispered.

"I don't know."

We went closer, taking care with every step. I nearly stumbled over a stone, but Simon's hand steadied me. By the time we'd reached the cottage and stood near one of the windows, we couldn't see the torch at all.

"Gone?" I breathed.

Simon shook his head. And after a time, the torch appeared in the room nearest us. Edging closer to the wall, we raised our heads ever so slowly, only to eye level with the room. But I couldn't tell anything about the person holding the torch—the light was too bright for my night vision.

I heard Simon swear under his breath, and I knew he'd had the same problem.

He ducked, and I did the same, then he led me around the house to the front door. It was standing wide.

Simon pressed himself against the wall a few feet from the door, and I moved beside him. After a while, which seemed like hours to me, we could hear footsteps coming toward us from inside the cottage. Simon dropped my hand and tensed.

A figure, darker than the darkness around us, came through the doorway, and Simon leaped.

They went down rolling, and I heard Simon grunt as his opponent landed a blow on his wounded arm.

The fight didn't last long. Simon was taller and stronger, and more accustomed to using physical force. But it was as vicious as it was short.

I was feeling around for the man's torch, my fingers moving lightly over the ground until they touched it. I picked it up, and flicked it on. The beam caught two faces staring at me. Simon and someone I hadn't seen before.

He was of middle height, slim, and quite pale. I realized after staring at him that it wasn't just paleness but that odd milky whiteness of someone who seldom went out into the sun. Or, I revised that quickly, someone who hadn't been in the sun for some time.

Simon was asking, "Who are you? And what were you doing here?"

The man said, "I could ask you the same thing. Looking for the bloody silver too, are you?"

"It's gone," I said, lowering the beam away from their faces. "Ellen learned that before she died."

"You're wrong. The old man had hidden it well. She just didn't know where to look. She was tearing out the walls and flooring. He wouldn't have been so stupid."

"Bess?" Simon spoke out of the darkness.

"I'll just have a look." I turned and went into the house, ignoring the bloodstains where Ellen had been lying only that morning, as I went from room to room. But there was no sign of a cache of silver anywhere.

I came back to the door. "There's nothing I can see."

"You're wrong," the man said again, his voice strained. "It *has* to be there. I'll share it with you. If you let me go on looking. I need it. I'll find it, if you give me a chance."

"There's no silver here."

"I tell you you're *wrong*. I can find it." He was agitated, beginning to strain against Simon's grip. "He was rich. He had to be. He'd robbed that coach. Everyone said so. *I need that money.* I can't stay here any longer."

I could just see Simon's grim expression.

"Take him to the house," I said. "Maybe Rachel can tell us who he is. He's wearing only a light coat. He can't have come far."

"No. I tell you, *no*."

He was struggling now in Simon's grip.

"Find some rope if you can," he told me.

I hurried back into the house and swept the torch beam around each room except the bedroom with its bloodstains. In the kitchen there was a hemp rope that appeared to be half rotted. I picked it up and it fell apart in my hands. In the short passage leading to the back garden door, there was a shorter length of rope in a bucket. That was sound enough, and I carried it to Simon.

The man fought him, but Simon succeeded in binding his hands behind him.

"What's your name?" Simon asked, in the voice that raw recruits quickly got to know.

"Tom. Tommy," he said defiantly. "Let me *go*."

I stared at the man.

Oh dear God, not Hugh's brother—! And I remembered what one of the Welsh miners had said to me. *Much of the year we never see the sun. We're down in the pits before ever it comes up, and we walk home after it's set.*

"No. Not to Rachel's house," I said quickly. "To the rectory."

It was a long cold walk back up the incline. Simon's arm must be hurting like the very devil, I thought, as he dealt with the man's efforts to break free. When we reached the rectory, Mr. Wilson thrust open a window and called out, "Who needs me?"

"Come down. There's trouble," Simon answered, and the window shut. After several minutes, Mr. Wilson came to the rectory door and peered out into the darkness.

"Sister Crawford?" he asked, surprised. He stepped out of sight, into the entry, and we heard a match strike before a lamp bloomed into brightness. He came back with it in his hand and looked from me to Simon and then to Simon's prisoner, who had turned his head away.

"Tom?" he said in a shaken voice. "Is that you? I thought you were dead—we all thought—the memorial service—the brass plate on the south wall—" He turned back to me. "I don't understand."

"We found him in Ellen's cottage. Searching for her grandfather's silver," I told him.

"She's dead. What does it matter to her if I take it?" Tom demanded then. "I'm tired of hiding. I'm tired of living in the dark. The war is over. I want to go away."

"Did you kill her?" I asked him. "Did you kill Ellen Marshall? Before the police could come in and question her?"

But he turned to glare at me, refusing to answer.

"Did you attack Oliver Martin? Or Mr. Stephenson?"

No answer.

I stood there, torn. How was I to tell Hugh that his brother was alive? And a murderer? And my next thought was, did Rachel *know*?

Oh dear God . . .

She'd been right. I should have stayed out of this. I should have left the village that first night, before dinner, before Mr. Morgan had been frightened in the night and fled. As soon as Hugh told me that it wasn't safe here . . .

It would have been better for everyone if I had.

Mr. Wilson was saying, "What are we to do? If the police find out, they'll turn him over to the Army. He's a deserter, he'll be shot." He was shivering in the cold wind. And wishing himself back in his warm bed. I could see it in his face as the lamp flame danced and flickered.

Simon spoke. "I don't have any choice in the matter. I must report him."

"You can't," I began, thinking of Hugh. And Rachel.

"I can't let him go," Simon told me. "What's more, there are questions to be answered. If he's behind these assaults, he's dangerous. Something has to be done."

And if he'd killed Ellen, he had to be held to account. She hadn't deserved to die at his hands.

But better than the hangman.

I made a decision. "Go and get your motorcar." I took my little pistol out of my coat pocket. "I'll keep him here. We'll drive straight to Swansea, and let the police deal with him. It's for the best, Simon."

A voice spoke in the darkness beyond the lamp's pale circle of light. It was low, rough, and I couldn't identify it straightaway. A Welsh accent. Mr. Griffith—or Hugh, in time of great stress?

"I've a shotgun says he's not going anywhere."

Mr. Wilson backed away, his eyes terrified, taking his lamp with him, and shut the rectory door. The lamp went out in the same moment, not even a glimmer through the glass of the door to help us.

I whirled, turning on the torch in my hands. The battery was fading, but it swept across the face of the man holding the shotgun, and with a surge of relief, I recognized Mr. Griffith.

"You gave him sanctuary, didn't you?" I accused him.

"Of course I did. That's my son."

"But—he's dead—" I felt almost dizzy, the wash of relief was so great.

"I saw to it that everyone thought so. Even closed the shop. Cost more than I liked to put that brass plaque up on the church wall, but it was convincing, wasn't it? Tom, come here. There's the motorcar standing by Rachel's house. Take it and get as far from here as you can. In my pocket you'll find enough money for now."

"I can't. He's got my hands tied."

The shotgun swung toward Simon. "Cut him loose."

"No. If you shoot me, you'll hit your son too."

The shotgun swung toward me. "Doesn't matter to me who dies."

Grimacing, Simon released Tom Griffith.

"That's better. Come on, lad, take the money and go."

"What will you do with them?"

"Leave that to me."

"I want to be sure. I don't want to hang. That man's Army, he'll send the Foot Police after me."

"Damn it, get out of here before someone raises the alarm."

"There's the rector," Tom pointed out. "He saw me too."

"I told you. I'll deal with them."

Reluctantly, Tom approached his father, reaching into his pocket and pulling out a handful of pounds, shoving them into his own pocket. And then before anyone had an inkling of what he was about to do, he caught the shotgun's barrel and wrenched it out of his father's hands.

"Tom—*no*! There's been enough killing," Mr. Griffith shouted, trying to pull the shotgun away. But his son had a tight grip on it, and used the barrel to clip his father across the ear. The older man collapsed at his feet.

"Now then," Tom said, and pointed the barrel toward Simon. "You first, so that I can reload. Then her."

I dropped the torch, and as it tumbled on the hard winter ground, the light flashing skyward and then across our feet, I had my pistol in my hand and I fired.

Tom Griffith cried out in pain, and the gun went off.

Neither Simon nor I were in the line of fire, but the side of the rectory took the full force.

Simon had already dashed forward as I scooped up the torch again, tearing the shotgun out of Tom's hands.

Tom lay there on the ground next to his father, and the shoulder of his light coat was turning black with blood in the pale torchlight.

I could hear people coming on the run, shouting. Men from the nearest houses, in their nightclothes. They came to an abrupt halt as they saw Simon holding the weapon. I was already bending over Tom Griffith. His father, groaning, was trying to sit up.

"Summon Captain Williams," I said. Mr. Griffith, crying and calling his son's name, was trying to crawl to him. "It's a shoulder wound," I said to the father. "But he needs medical care. The bone is splintered, I think."

The door of the rectory opened and Mr. Wilson stood there on the threshold. Simon had broken open the shotgun and put it well out of reach.

"What's happened?" one of the men asked while another man hurried across the road toward Rachel's house.

"Mr. Griffith's son tried to kill us. I've got to take him to hospital as quickly as we can."

And just then the torch winked twice, and died.

I could hear Simon running toward the motorcar, and I guessed what he was doing. Someone was pounding on Rachel's door.

"No, you mustn't take him away," Mr. Griffith cried, trying to shield his son's body with his own.

"If your son doesn't go to hospital and quickly, he could die," I told him coldly.

"I'd rather him die here than hang," he said.

Without warning the motorcar's large bright headlamps turned on, and the vehicle swung toward us, lighting the scene garishly.

Hugh's voice called, "What's going on? Simon, is that you in the motorcar? Where is Bess?"

"Ask Rachel to bring out our kits. There's been trouble. We need to get a man to hospital in Swansea as soon as possible. He's been shot. Hurry."

Hugh had been an officer, and a good one. He didn't waste time asking more questions. I could hear him shouting up the stairs.

I said to the other men, "I need blankets. Quickly. Then we must get him to the motorcar."

A woman came running with an armful of blankets. I thanked her, and she pushed Mr. Griffith aside, helping me to wrap the wounded man in them. And then she realized who it was. "That's Tom *Griffith*. But he's dead."

"Very much alive. And I want him to stay that way."

Another woman brought me clean rags for the wound as I worked to staunch the bleeding.

Behind us Mr. Wilson was telling people what had happened. But he hadn't seen me fire. He thought it was Simon. "He saved us. The man's run mad. Tom. Tom Griffith."

"He was such a quiet boy," the woman helping me said softly. "He should never have enlisted. He wouldn't have made a soldier."

But Mr. Griffith was scrambling to his feet, shouting, "He's not mad. He never was. I kept him safe all these years, ever since he left his training."

Tom was mumbling something, and I bent closer to hear. "I couldn't bear being locked away any longer. But people saw me. I had to stop them from telling my father. Or the Army." He began clawing at my hands, trying to tear them away from his wound. "I don't want to hang, I tell you."

It was all I could do to stop him. And then, mercifully, he fainted from the effort and the pain.

Rachel was there a little later. "Bess, I finished your packing. And Simon's too. It's all in the boot." She reached across awkwardly and hugged me. "I'm so sorry. About everything."

And then she was ordering several of the men to help me lift my patient. Simon brought the motorcar alongside us, and after arranging the blankets across the rear seat, we got Tom in and covered him again. He was shivering with shock now. His father pushed his way to the door and said, "I'm going with him."

But Simon pulled him away. "And throttle him while we're driving? I think not."

Hugh was there. He put a hand on my shoulder. "Thank you, Bess Crawford. I owe you more than I can ever repay." And then he leaned forward and kissed me on the cheek. Stepping back, he said to Simon, "Travel safely."

Simon nodded and got behind the wheel. I got in the other side, and we set out for Swansea. Behind us, Mr. Griffith was swearing at us, accusing us of killing his son.

Tom Griffith lived to be tried for the murder of Mr. Stephenson and the attack on Oliver Martin, who had glimpsed him in the dark. I thought it best not to report my own encounter with him, but I understood why Mr. Griffith had pointed a finger at Ellen Marshall, to protect his son.

There was no proof that Tom killed her, but I learned later that she had helped spirit Tom out of Swansea after he'd deserted, and she'd taken him to one of the caves on the other side of the peninsula. From there Tom had managed to make his way across to the village, to beg for his father's protection.

Had he shot Ellen because she'd helped him escape—and knew where he was hiding? Or for the silver he was so certain was still hidden in her grandfather's cottage? But that wasn't brought up in Tom Griffith's trial.

Despite his father's pleas, Tom was sentenced to life in prison. Mrs. Stephenson was furious, but the jury had found that there was not sufficient evidence to warrant a hanging.

Hugh and Rachel were married in the spring. I was given leave from my duties to attend the wedding. It was a quiet one, in the Swansea church where Rachel's parents had been married. The only other guests were my mother, the Colonel Sahib, and Simon. But Rachel didn't mind. There was no one else she cared to invite.

The dead men in the churchyard and the silver from the treasure ship never came up at the trial either. Ellen was dead, there was nothing—and no one—left to connect her to either of them. Tom, even to escape the hangman, never offered to tell what had become of the ship's treasure in exchange for his life. It was the village's secret, not his. His father moved to be nearer the prison where Tom was serving his sentence. Or so Hugh told me just before the wedding when he and I had a few minutes alone.

He also told me that only three days before, in the latest spring storm, a handful of coins had washed up again.

Authors' Note

THE GOWER PENINSULA in South Wales is isolated, quite beautiful, and protected so that it will stay that way. The bay is unbelievably lovely. The people there, of Norman descent rather than Welsh, are warm and friendly, and our coast guard station is a National Trust shop with a tempting selection of goodies. The Worm and the caves are places for the adventurous to explore. We enjoyed our time there immensely, and never intended to do more than take pictures after a very good lunch in what in our story is Mr. Griffith's cottage, but in fact is a small but excellent little café attached to a variety of shops. The fuchsia hedge just outside was in full bloom when we were there, scarlet ballerinas dancing in the wind. The sheep and cattle are gone, but storms still roll in wild as ever.

Then someone mentioned the *Henrietta,* a treasure ship carrying silver from Goa in India, and meant as part of the dowry of the Portuguese princess who was marrying Charles II. Catherine of Braganza, that was.

How can a mystery writer, much less two of them, walk away from an account of a wrecked treasure ship? And what happened to all that silver? A clue: there's a story about a nineteenth-century coach and horses racing up from the bay in Ellen Marshall's grandfather's day, laden with a fortune in silver that had washed ashore in

Authors' Note

a recent storm. But that silver had vanished by the time the coach was found—abandoned. They say it still haunts that road on stormy nights, the rattle of the wheels, the hoofbeats of the horses, the jangle of harness carrying above the sounds of wind and rain.

How had all that silver changed the lives of those who lived out on the tip of the peninsula, isolated, far from Authority, nearly a law unto themselves? What were their feelings as they watched the *Henrietta* come to grief in their bay—then realized what she was carrying? What happens when all that unexpected largesse begins to dwindle over the centuries, only to pop up again in 1813, giving local people fresh hope? Just the place for Bess to travel to in 1919, to carry out her sense of duty and responsibility for those the war has left behind, only to find herself caught up in the complicated problems of Rachel and her neighbors.

Still, we sincerely apologize to the residents of the peninsula if we've offended them in any way by creating our own account of a village by the name of Caudle overlooking a bay just like theirs. And we urge our readers to visit Gower for themselves and see *why* it is such a fascinating place.

Our thanks, meanwhile, to Nicky, tour leader extraordinaire, who planned our excursion into South Wales. We'd follow her anywhere—and often do!

And we might add we hope Captain Hugh Williams and his men exemplify soldiers of every war who came home badly wounded and lost their way for a time—then found they were still men and the bravest of the brave. As we finish writing this on the eve of Veterans Day—once Armistice Day, commemorating the end of the Great War—it's fitting to remember the men and women who serve.

CHARLES TODD is the author of the Bess Crawford mysteries, the Inspector Ian Rutledge mysteries, and two stand-alone novels. A mother-and-son writing team, they live on the East Coast.